46 481 294 9

D0831153

ONLY A MOTHER KNOWS

In the midst of The Blitz, four young women have witnessed the heartache and pain that Hitler's bombs have inflicted on ordinary Londoners. Tilly is desperate to wed her beau, Drew. Terrified that something will happen to prevent them from being together, her fears seem to be coming true when he is called back to America. For her concerned mother, Olive, this only adds to her worries for Tilly. For Dulcie, the war has brought an old flame, David, back in her life. But his terrible injuries have changed his life forever. And Agnes is about to find something that will change her life, too.

ONLY A MOTHER KNOWS

ONLY A MOTHER KNOWS

by

Annie Groves

Magna Large Print Books
Long Preston, North Yorkshire,
BD23 4ND, England.

British Library Cataloguing in Publication Data.

Groves, Annie
    Only a mother knows.

    A catalogue record of this book is
    available from the British Library

    ISBN   978-0-7505-3848-0

First published in Great Britain by HarperCollins*Publishers* 2013

Copyright © Annie Groves 2013

Cover illustration © Colin Thomas

Annie Groves asserts the moral right to be identified as the author of this work

Published in Large Print 2014 by arrangement with
HarperCollins Publishers

All Rights reserved. No part of this publication may be reproduced, stored in a retrieval system, or transmitted in any form or by any means, electronic, mechanical, photocopying, recording or otherwise without the prior permission of the Copyright owner.

Magna Large Print is an imprint of Library Magna Books Ltd.

Printed and bound in Great Britain by
T.J. (International) Ltd., Cornwall, PL28 8RW

This novel is entirely a work of fiction.
The names, characters and incidents portrayed
in it are the work of the author's imagination.
Any resemblance to actual persons, living or
dead, events or localities is entirely coincidental.

In memory of Penny Halsall

24 November 1946 – 31 December 2011

FOREWORD

The news of Penny Halsall's illness came as a great shock. I had been her editor for a number of years at HarperCollins and she was one of my favourite authors. I'd worked with Penny both on the books that she wrote as Annie Groves and on some of the ones that she had written as Penny Jordan – she really was a joy and was much loved by everyone here. Her books were special, they were full of heart and it was impossible not to fall in love with the characters she created. It felt like a great honour to be working on her novels; her books had sold millions and millions of copies all around the globe and she was a legend. It was such a thrill when a new, complete manuscript landed in my inbox and I was eagerly anticipating the next book that she was due to send to me in a few months' time.

Penny had been working on the Annie Groves Article Row novels, all of which are set in and around the Holborn area of London and all featuring the hopes and heartaches of Tilly, Dulcie, Sally, Olive and Agnes. We had just published *My Sweet Valentine*, the third in a planned series of five books, it had been a bestseller and there was lots of excitement about the future. Penny and I had recently had a long and fruitful conversation about what she was planning next for the girls of Article Row and I couldn't wait to read the next instalment. Penny was completely rooted in her characters and had very definite ideas about where they were all going. She spent an awful lot of time researching all of her books and one of my abiding memories of Penny is watching her head off determinedly on a research mission to Holborn after a business lunch in town. Penny constantly thought about her characters and was always playing around with ideas about what the war would hold in store for them all. I was full of anticipation.

When her sister, Prue, broke the news about Penny's advanced illness, it came completely out of the blue. Penny was such a consummate professional and had never given any indication that that she was ill, despite living with cancer for some time. There was little chance to digest this information properly when the devastating news came shortly after that she had died over the Christmas holidays in late December 2011.

At Penny's funeral, the church was completely packed, not just with family but also with fellow writers, friends, fans and publishing colleagues. But despite the sadness there was laughter too. Penny loved a party and when her favourite song was played – The Mavericks', *I Just Want to Dance the Night Away* – we were reminded of what a wonderfully happy and positive person she was.

Once back at my desk in London, my mind turned to the difficult issue of what would happen now. *My Sweet Valentine* was in the middle of the series and Annie Groves' fans would be desperate to know what was going to happen to those much-loved characters. I had a many long talks with Penny's brilliant agent, Teresa Chris, and both of us agreed that Penny would have wanted nothing more than to have the series completed – she really had put her heart and soul into every page and it would have meant so much to her. Teresa approached Penny's wonderful sister, Prue, and to our delight, she was a keen supporter of getting the series completed. She allowed me the great privilege of access to Penny's files, so early one spring morning in 2012, I made the trip up to Prue's house in Cheshire to see what I could find. We already had some idea of what Penny had in mind, but it wasn't a complete picture and I knew there were some big gaps. Penny couldn't have left things in better shape – not only was there a large chunk of manuscript in her files but there were also detailed notes and plot outlines that would help us to complete the puzzle. Penny was such a trooper!

The last piece to be put in place was to find somebody who would be able to marry all of the pieces together and to turn all of this into a narrative that was worthy of Penny. We were almost running out of ideas when Teresa discovered the writer Sheila Riley. Not only did Sheila have something of Penny's style, but she also hailed from Penny's beloved Merseyside – without her, this book could never have existed – thank you, Sheila. We were also lucky enough to have the services of Susan Opie, copy editor extraordinaire, and someone who knows the Annie Groves books inside out.

So, some months later and after quite a lot of

effort from many marvellous people, I'm sitting here writing this and explaining how this book, and the one to follow it, have come about.

Penny was an amazing person for so many reasons. There was an old-fashioned dignity and modesty about her, and one of the reasons she was so successful was that she knew, instinctively, that although life can sometimes deal you a rotten hand, with guts, determination and plenty of love and kindness, everyone has the power to change their fate. Only a Mother Knows and A Christmas Promise (publishing autumn 2013) really deliver the authentic Annie Groves experience, and I know that you, Reader, won't be disappointed.

HarperCollins would like to extend their heartfelt thanks to Sheila Riley, Teresa Chris, Susan Opie and especially to Prue Burke and the Halsall estate for their tremendous help in finishing the Article Row series. They have all done Penny proud.

Kate Bradley
Editor

ONE

June 1942

'...So you let her swan off with her young man on her own ... without as much as a by-your-leave? Well! I must say.'

'I'm very well aware of what you must say, Nancy,' Olive sighed with thinning patience, honed from years of living next door to the local busybody, wondering how much more carping she could take from her next-door neighbour, whose watchful eyes and razor-sharp tongue made her a woman the rest of the street avoided at all costs.

Olive had noticed lately how her other neighbours dipped back behind their front doors when Nancy was at large. However, she didn't feel the need to worry about what they all thought or did; Olive was far too busy minding her own business and getting on with her war-work, collecting and sending parcels out to the troops from the Red Cross shop as well as her fire-watching duties and driving the WVS van to unfortunate beleaguered bombed-out victims who were so traumatised half the time they didn't even know their own name. And even though the war had worn her saintly patience a little thin it didn't give her the right to take it out on Nancy. Olive knew that she might have become a bit quick tempered of late, but with the war – no, that was no excuse, she realised. Too

15

many people were blaming their shortcomings on the war and she didn't want to be one of them.

With a weary sigh Olive, who didn't have the luxury of standing around all day indulging in idle gossip, made to move but the other woman seemed to be bursting with things to say. Given that every time she left the house Nancy was out in a flash, Olive wondered if her neighbour kept a permanent lookout from behind her front-room curtains but she didn't voice her thoughts. Live and let live, that was her rule in life – and it usually stood her in good stead where her next-door neighbour was concerned.

She had to silently congratulate the woman on her tenacity; she would have been a boon behind enemy lines as she missed nothing. Olive smiled to herself. Nancy must have that new radar they were talking about on the wireless this morning, the Radio Detection and Ranging system that had been brought out last year and was, according to the Home Service, the country's best chance of winning the war in the Pacific. Olive, her mind wandering a little, was surprised that it had been made public as so much was hidden from them.

Nancy must have the system installed on her wall, because Olive could not make a move towards her own sandstone scrubbed step without the woman being out waiting for a chat. No matter how much the posters told them to 'Keep Mum and Save Dad' her loose-lipped neighbour still got her twopenny-worth in. But this time she was not there just to pass on some gossip, she was trying to make a point, and Olive wanted no part of it.

Bridling now, something she hadn't experienced

much before the war, Olive suspected Nancy wanted to talk about her daughter, Tilly, who had been getting away from the bombing raids in the city and having a few quiet days in the countryside with her young man, Drew, whom they had feared had been badly injured – or worse – in the last raid. Olive had decided it was just the tonic Tilly needed after such a shock. She had assumed the worst, well, they all had. It was only being so busy looking after baby Alice, the new addition to the family, that had kept Olive's mind from conjuring up what could have befallen Drew that night, and that really didn't bear thinking about. Tilly adored him so much she would have been devastated if even a hair on his head had been damaged.

No, thought Olive defiantly, this time her domestic arrangements were her own concern and not up for debate whatsoever with Nancy Black.

'...So I said to Mrs Denver, you know the woman who lost her husband when he was on fire watch in the Blitz ...'

'Yes, of course I know Mrs Denver.' Olive, growing impatient, cut off Nancy's diatribe in mid-sentence knowing she would only repeat the awfully tragic story of Mr Denver being blown to smithereens on the roof of a dockside warehouse and whose remains were never found, even though they had all been with Mrs Denver when she received the terrible news.

'...So I said to her ... I said...' It was obvious Nancy was not going to be silenced, but Olive didn't have the time to stand around on her spotless step that had been scrubbed only that morning, and she didn't want to hear Nancy's views on how Tilly should or shouldn't behave.

'...I said to Mrs Denver, "the way these young girls carry on these days, running around, fast and loose"...'

'I hope you are not insinuating that my Tilly...'

'... No, of course not,' Nancy patted Olive's arm, 'certainly not your Tilly; she's a good girl, she is.' Nancy shook her head, making the steel dinky curlers under her turbaned scarf rattle. If Olive had been mean-minded she might have wondered how Nancy managed to keep the curlers from going for scrap, along with every other superfluous household item, to be used in the war effort to make aircraft for the RAF, but she wasn't that way inclined and the irrepressible Nancy had started again.

'...I was just saying to Mrs Denver, it's not right. It's not the way we behaved when our chaps were at the Front in the Great War...'

'Great War!' Olive spluttered. 'What was so "great" about it?' She almost spat the words, she was so angry now. 'No war is "great", Nancy, young men dying is not great, losing loved ones is not great, yet you seem to wear the war like your own personal badge of honour.' Olive took a deep breath, knowing she was in danger of saying things she would later regret, but the milk of human kindness would sour in Nancy Black's breast, she was sure, and she didn't know how she stopped herself from saying so.

However, taking a deep sigh, she was immediately sorry for the outburst she had kept locked inside for so long. Nancy would try the patience of a saint, everybody knew that. 'My Tilly knows how to behave,' she said determinedly.

It was not her place to go taking it out on Nancy just because she was upset at not seeing Tilly much lately. When the girl told her of her plans to spend a few days with Drew Olive had been shocked, initially, that her unmarried daughter would contemplate going away for a few days with her young man, alone. Yet she knew Drew was a level-headed young man and he would keep Tilly as safe as was humanly possible. Olive was convinced that nothing untoward would take place, unlike her narrow-minded neighbour who only saw the wrong in people, it seemed.

Olive had consented to Tilly and Drew having a short holiday because she didn't want any more of Tilly's strained silences. She didn't like it when she and her only child were at loggerheads, she wasn't used to it. Also, Olive had to think of the effect it had on the newest member of the household; Sally's baby half-sister depended upon them all so much now after her parents had been killed in an air raid in Liverpool and she'd had to be brought to London by Callum, who had been Sally's sweetheart before his sister married Sally's father. It was complicated, Olive knew, but luckily the child was now blissfully unaware of the circumstances behind her move to Article Row.

Thankfully Alice was the least of Olive's worries at the moment. It was becoming more and more difficult to satisfy her pristine requirements around the house, with cleaning utensils being rationed and requisitioned for the war effort, and with dust and smoke everywhere it was a job and a half to keep things as clean as she would like.

With all these things vying for attention, in the end, it just seemed easier to let Tilly have her few days with Drew – and now she wondered what she ever worried about.

Tilly had looked so happy when Olive said yes. Starry-eyed, she promised they would have separate rooms and a landlady who would give Hitler a run for his money. Everything would be proper and above board, there would be no hanky-panky. Olive gave an involuntary, indignant shiver at the thought, and ... if she was honest, she had a sneaking regard for her daughter who was being open about her devoted feelings for the man she loved. To say nothing of the decent way she had been brought up; her daughter was a credit to any mother.

Her only nagging concern was that Drew would still love and respect Tilly when she came home. But why shouldn't he? she thought, knowing her daughter was head-in-the-clouds happy with adoration. Although Olive realised it was possible that Tilly's judgement could be clouded, she also understood that wartime had a way of clarifying one's heartfelt emotions. Life was precious and, above all, love was precious too. It must be nurtured and protected at all costs, Olive sighed.

'Well, let's see if she does know how to behave when she's away from home,' Nancy Black said, her eyebrow cocked, 'away from the confines of a protective mother's watchful eye.' Straightening her back Nancy clasped her hands under her voluminous bust, her mouth scrunched like a wrinkled prune.

'Time will tell, Nancy,' Olive said suddenly, not

really caring what her neighbour thought any more.

'Well I never!' Nancy exclaimed, blowing a long stream of outraged air from ballooning cheeks.

'Oh go on, you must have done!' Olive, feeling reckless now, bit her lips together to stop herself from saying anything else she might repent later, and for once Nancy seemed dumbstruck, lost for words. If it were any other time Olive would have been thrilled. But all too soon Nancy recovered her equilibrium and sallied forth regardless.

'Well,' she gasped, 'I must say!'

'Yes, Nancy, I know you must and everybody else knows it too.' Olive could not stop herself now, her words, like water through a ruptured dam, bursting uncontrollably forth. 'And let me tell you something, you are an interfering busybody whom everybody tries to avoid, and if it's all the same to you I'll bid you good day!' At that Olive pulled on her gloves and, with her head high, she slammed her front gate firmly behind her and marched straight-backed up the street. Nobody, but nobody, was going to cast aspersions on her daughter.

Olive had just reached the top of the street when she literally bumped into Sergeant Archie Dawson, who was ambling around the corner. She was heartily glad that Nancy had retreated into her own house as he caught her deftly around the waist to stop her stumbling into the road and into the path of a horse and cart. Olive could imagine only too well what her vindictive neighbour would insinuate about her innocent friendship with the upstanding policeman. Feeling the warmth of colour rising to her cheeks, she chided herself for being so gauche. She wasn't a girl any more, with a head full of starry dreams; she was a grown woman with a grown-up daughter ... who was having starry dreams of her own right now.

'Oh, hello, Archie, I'm so sorry, I wasn't looking where I was going.' Olive could feel her heartbeat quicken and reprimanded herself for being foolish. However, she didn't want to dwell on what Archie, a married man and serving police sergeant, would think. Instead she concentrated on a couple of children stretching a length of rope across the street and wondered where they came about such a good length, as everything was needed for the war effort.

'Hello, Olive,' Archie Dawson said with that usual warmth in his kind, mellow voice as he held her securely until the cart had passed. 'You look a little flushed, is everything okay?' He used the latest expression that seemed to be doing the rounds due to the huge influx of American soldiers, who the young ones referred to as GIs on account of the initials on the padded shoulders of their very smart uniforms which stood for Government Issue.

Olive smiled. She never would have imagined someone as upright and respectable as Sergeant Dawson using American slang, but it showed that he was keeping up with the times and that he wasn't as buttoned-up as the impression he gave to the rest of the community. And if she was honest, she thought it sounded quite good coming from him.

'Oh, I've just had a bit of a run-in with Nancy

Black,' Olive explained. 'That woman would try the patience of angels.'

'Oh, you don't have to say any more, the old witch gave me chapter and verse about...' He stopped abruptly and Olive could see he was trying to be tactful when he continued '...about Tilly and Drew carrying a suitcase and going off in a taxi cab. But we'll talk no more about it,' Archie Dawson said gallantly, taking his hand from her waist and giving a low rumbling laugh that seemed to soothe Olive's bubbling indignation. 'Suffice it to say, Olive, you are right, she would try the serenity of a saint.'

'Oh, Archie.' Olive smiled for the first time that day and in doing so felt all her tension slip away.

'Not that I'm saying you are not a saint, Olive, you are a very good woman, hardworking, a pillar of the community...'

'Oh, Archie, you flatter me, I'm nothing of the sort,' she laughed in that carefree way he always provoked in her. 'You will have my head swelling.' Olive could feel little sparks of delight shoot through her. However, they were quickly followed by a heaviness that reminded her she was a busy widow and he was a respectably married man with a young, impressionable foster son who needed the close eye of a decent man to keep him on the straight and narrow. Suddenly, her attention was drawn to Nancy, who was now hurrying up the street resplendent in her carpet slippers.

'Some of us haven't got time to stand around indulging in idle chit-chat,' Nancy said as she hurried by. 'There is a queue forming outside the butcher's shop; Mrs Finlay just told me he's got

23

oxtails on the go.' In seconds she had passed them and was halfway up the street before turning and saying in a loud voice, 'Oh, Sergeant! Was that your wife I heard calling just now?'

Olive and Archie watched in stunned silence as Nancy scurried past them in the direction of the butcher's shop. As she disappeared their gaze remained fixed on the corner of the street. Then, slowly, they turned to each other and, just for a moment, there was a shared intimacy as their eyes locked. But then the spell was broken when Archie's attention was caught by a passing pigeon swooping down and landing on the road. It was an insignificant thing, but effective in reminding Olive she had things to do.

The lingering connection between herself and Archie ... Sergeant Dawson ... all at once consumed her with an overwhelming feeling of guilt. However, if she was truly honest, only to herself, even the feeling of guilt was deliciously pleasurable. Turning away quickly now, afraid her thoughts would be plain for Archie to see, Olive took a deep breath, hoping it would calm her obvious raging flush of colour.

They had never done a thing wrong. Nothing improper had ever occurred between them. But Olive had been a married woman. She knew the delights of a man's strong arms holding her securely through the night. She knew the intimacy of an unexpected stolen kiss. And if she was honest she was finding it increasingly difficult these days to disguise the longing she felt whenever Archie was anywhere near her.

But disguise her feelings she must as Archie was

a married man and pillar of the community as well as a serving police sergeant who must uphold all that was decent in these tragic times, in a world gone mad through the ferocious needs of a madman. What would happen if they all gave in to their desires? Everything would fall apart in no time.

Olive drew her fervent thoughts to a close. There never would be anything between them, she knew. There couldn't be. He had a foster son who looked up to him and needed a stable home life in these uncertain times and she had the girls to look after.

'Well,' Olive said, uncomfortable now, 'I'd better be off before those oxtails have all gone. Good day, Sergeant Dawson.'

'Good day, Olive,' Archie said, and she could feel rather than see his lingering look as she hurried up the street.

TWO

'Will you be able to manage at home on your own?' Dulcie asked in a rare moment of empathy, taking hold of David's hand. His head was bent and she couldn't quite see his expression as the sun was in her eyes. Slowly, she tilted her face to one side to try to take a peek.

'Under Mr McIndoe's instructions,' he said, 'the hospital has put into place a system whereby I can manage at home with the help of a daily nurse.'

Dulcie noticed he looked rather pleased with

25

the news. However, she wondered if it was too soon and couldn't keep the erratic feelings of alarm from her voice. 'I should think you need more time, David.' It seemed to her that he hadn't long been sitting out of his hospital bed and now they were throwing him onto the street.

'Hardly,' David smiled. 'Anyway, I can't wait to get back amongst my own things and wallow in my own bathtub without having a nurse wash me. A man has to have some privacy, you know.' He gave a guarded smile and Dulcie watched him quietly for a while, as if seeing him for the first time. He was the bravest person she had ever met, though more reserved now, unlike Wilder, the brash, dare-devil fighter pilot who paid her little attention since they discovered her sister, Edith, hadn't been killed after all and who made a bee-line for Wilder every chance she got. Whereas David always listened patiently whilst she poured her heart out. Now why couldn't Wilder be like that, she wondered.

'Seen something you like?' David said, offering a beaming smile.

'Sorry, I was miles away.' Dulcie laughed, knowing she'd always had a short attention span, especially when other people were talking about themselves, it was so boring. 'You were saying?'

'It doesn't matter.' David, sitting regulation upright, smiled and slowly shook his head.

With one arm of his striped pyjamas pinned against his proud shoulder, so it didn't flap around getting in his way, and a plaid woollen rug across his knees, he looked just like any other patient and that was how Dulcie treated him; nobody would

26

have known they were socially and economically worlds apart. David, being landed gentry, was distinctly upper class whereas she came from a terraced house in the backstreets of the East End. But that didn't bother David or Dulcie; they were just good friends and she knew he would always be there to listen to her grumbles.

'Did I tell you that Wilder is acting very oddly at the moment, David? He never listens to a word I say.' She gave a half-smile of confusion when David took a deep, long-suffering breath of air.

'What?' Dulcie asked when she saw him smile. However, saying nothing, he indicated with a nod of his head that she should continue, which Dulcie was only too happy to do.

'It's not fair, really it isn't,' she resumed and then, seeing David's quizzical expression, she explained. 'It's that blousy cat, Edith.'

'Your sister?' asked David, his face the picture of easy-going amusement.

'The same,' said Dulcie, eager to get on with the character-slaying. 'She's got no right carrying on the way she does with my boyfriend and her being my sister makes it even worse. Oh, I can't stand her at times, she's always been Mum's favourite and doesn't she know it.' Dulcie gave an emphatic nod of her perfectly styled curls and carried on. 'Edith's been getting away with all sorts from the minute she was born, Mum can't see any wrong in her – well, she should look at her through my eyes, that's all I can say!'

Dulcie was forced to stop talking in order to breathe as they sat together in the beautiful sunshine, David in his wheelchair and she on the wooden seat next to him in the gardens of the hospital where he was staying whilst he recovered from his injuries and subsequent amputation of his lower legs which had been badly damaged when the aircraft he had been piloting had been shot down.

He viewed her with grateful amusement. Dulcie, his little cockney sparrow – if sparrow could ever be used to describe a girl as stunningly beautiful as blonde-haired, brown-eyed Dulcie, with her luscious curves combined with a manner that told a man that he'd be very lucky indeed if he ever got close to actually touching those curves. She always cheered him up and took his mind off his own problems when she made him laugh. There were no such things as molehills in Dulcie's life; all upsets were mountains.

They had known each other since the beginning of the war, when he had been a good-looking young barrister with the world at his feet and a wife-to-be with an eye on his future title. Dulcie had been a shop girl working on the perfume counter at Selfridges and very ready, he knew, to flirt with the fiancé of her upper-class colleague to whom, she later admitted, she had taken a distinct dislike.

Now his wife was, like his lower legs, feet, and most of one arm, destroyed by the cruelties of war. But they weren't his only injuries; Dulcie was also privy to the information that the damage to his groin would, as far as anyone knew at this stage, prevent him from fathering a child. Such a shame, she thought, as David was one of the most devastatingly handsome men she had ever set eyes on.

Lydia, his wife, lay in her grave, having been caught up in the bombing raid on the Café de Paris where she had been dancing with her current lover, whilst he had lost his legs in the gun battle between his Spitfire and a German Messerschmitt.

Now he was a patient at the famous Queen Victoria Hospital in East Grinstead under the care of the pioneering plastic surgeon Mr Archibald McIndoe, whilst Dulcie worked in a munitions factory and lodged at number 13, Article Row in Holborn, where she lived with the owner of the house, Mrs Olive Robbins, a widow, and her daughter, Tilly, who worked in the Lady Almoner's office at St Bartholomew's Hospital. Two other girls also rented rooms: Sally, a Liverpudlian nurse who worked at Bart's, and Agnes, a mouse of a girl who worked in the ticket office at Chancery Lane underground.

In the way that things were now happening during wartime David knew that those girls and the house on Article Row had become Dulcie's mainstay and he also knew that communities, friendships and relationships destroyed by the war were reformed by its survivors. He also knew Article Row well, as it was very close to the Inns of Court where he had lived and worked before the war and where he intended to return once he left hospital.

'And as for Wilder...' Dulcie, aggrieved, was still talking and David realised he had to pay attention. 'Well, I had a thing or two to say to him, I can tell you, especially after he asked Edith to come dancing with us next week.'

'London is full of newly arrived Americans from what I've heard, Dulcie, why don't you find yourself one who will treat you better than this Wilder chap?' David suggested. He knew that she had been dating the American pilot, who had originally come over to England to join the Eagles unit of Americans attached to the RAF, for quite some time. He had never met him, of course, but from the way Dulcie talked about him and his wandering eye, David doubted he would like him very much if he did, and he certainly didn't approve of the casual, not to say occasionally openly unkind, way in which he treated Dulcie.

'What?' Dulcie looked outraged. 'Give him up and let Edith think she's won and that Wilder prefers her to me? Never.' Her response was determined. 'Edith only wants him because she wants to get one up on me. I said as much to our brother, Rick, when he came home on leave from the desert and he insisted on taking me and Edith to see Mum and Dad.'

'So your mother has been reunited with Edith, then?' David said as the hot sun beat down on his face whilst Dulcie dabbed her cheeks with powder.

'Oh yes,' Dulcie said, pausing momentarily and looking over her gold compact. 'Mum was all over her, carrying on as you'd expect. I was completely ignored for the whole afternoon; nobody would have known that it was thanks to me that they'd been reunited. I have the feeling that Edith would have been just as happy to leave her own family in the dark.'

'What makes you say that?' David asked, always

interested in Dulcie's chaotic lifestyle.

'Well, it stands to reason, never once did Mum or Dad ask Edith why she hadn't made a bit of an effort to find out where they lived after they left London at the beginning of the Blitz.'

'Well, Edith knew where you lived, surely she could have contacted you?'

'Exactly,' said Dulcie with an emphatic nod of her head. 'That's precisely what I said, but no, it was all "how wonderful" to see her and Mum called it "a miracle" but did I get one word of gratitude? Not likely! And to think if I hadn't seen her in the chorus line review they'd still be thinking she was a goner now.'

David's heart went out to Dulcie knowing, first-hand, what her younger sister was like. He'd met her briefly when she came down to East Grinstead when Dulcie was on one of her regular visits. If he remembered correctly, Edith was a hard-faced, shallow little madam if ever there was one, he thought, concerned only with herself, and from what he could see nowhere near as pretty as Dulcie. He recalled that Edith had soon lost interest in him and the other men on the ward when she realised how badly injured they were.

'As for letting another American serviceman take me out – and don't think I haven't been asked because I have. Many a time I've been invited out by some of those that have finally decided to join us in the war.' Dulcie gave a small, proud toss of her head, seemingly satisfied that she had been stopped in the middle of the street by the new influx of Americans who had been arriving since last January and had become Briton's active allies since the December bombing of Pearl Harbor.

'If I was to see anybody else in uniform I think it would have to be one of them Poles, not another American.' David watched her for a moment. Dulcie talked in a matter-of-fact way about everything, even her love life, which, he thought, was probably more exciting in her own mind than it ever was in real life – not that she didn't have a wonderful time when she dressed to the nines and went out on the town dancing, but somehow there seemed a vulnerability in Dulcie that he was sure nobody else could see.

'You're too good for Wilder, Dulcie, let your sister have him and good riddance to the pair of them.' David hadn't intended speaking the words out loud but when he saw the surprised expression on Dulcie's expertly made-up face he realised that he had done just that.

'What! Let her have him? She'd crow till the cows came home and no mistake. She'd be on his arm before it had a chance to get cold, that one.'

'Would that be so awful?' David felt really sorry for her now. She didn't deserve this treatment after all she had done for her sister, reuniting her with her family.

'You bet your sweet potato it would,' Dulcie said in an outraged tone. 'She would make it her business to tell everybody she knows that Wilder dropped me for her and that ain't gonna happen. You'd hear the crowing halfway over London.'

'Well, you know best, Dulcie,' David said with a hint of resignation, as he didn't like to see her so upset like this.

'And you'll never guess what she did last week.

She only sent Wilder a free ticket for her new show. Just, the one ticket, mind, and Wilder is so trusting he probably thought she'd forgotten to send me one. I said to him, when I saw it fall out of his pocket, that she was trying to get her claws into him and he wanted to beware of her tricks to get him alone.'

'Good for you,' said David, realising how naïve Dulcie really was, now he'd been privileged enough to see beneath her brittle exterior. 'What did you do after that?' Just listening to Dulcie somehow eased the nagging, ever-present pain in his phantom lower legs. Other people might accuse her of being self-obsessed and even sometimes uncaring but David welcomed the fact that she didn't make any emotional allowances for him, or treat him as though a part of his brain had been damaged along with his legs.

'I ripped the ticket into a hundred pieces, that's what I did.' Her expression was one of relish, he noted, and then suddenly it changed to a frown when she looked up into the pale blue sky and announced, 'That sun's going to be in my eyes any minute now, here, let me turn you round so I can see you properly.' Dulcie got up from the wooden bench and flipped David's break with her foot so she could get a better view of him.

'Has that mother of yours been in to see you recently?'

David gave a little half-laugh. Nobody else would ask something as directly as Dulcie did, nor with such candour. 'No, I told her not to come. What's the point? We can't agree on anything. She can't forgive me for not giving her a grandson and heir when it was still within my power to do so.'

'She can't hold it against you now, David.' Dulcie was horrified.

'You don't know my mother,' he said grimly. 'Furthermore, I cannot forgive her for caring more about the title than she does about her own flesh and blood.'

'Your mother sounds every bit as stuck-up as your wife Lydia was, if you don't mind me saying. Serves them both right that neither of them got what they wanted in the end.'

David knew that Dulcie didn't mean to sound unkind. She was just upset on his behalf, and as she turned his wheelchair around he could hear the regret in her voice. At least she was honest in her emotions, he thought, unlike his mother and his late wife.

As the summer sun rose in the sky and cast its scorching rays at the hottest time of the day, Dulcie asked David if he would prefer to go inside and he agreed. He didn't want to add sunstroke to his list of ailments, he laughed. It didn't take Dulcie long to settle him into the chair at the side of his bed; she prided herself at getting quite good at the exercise and was pleased that David had every faith in her ability to move him from his wheelchair to the chair or bed. Nobody had ever trusted her that much before.

Once he was settled she poured him a glass of water and unconsciously examined her perfect oval talons for any sign of breakage, her eyes widening when she said suddenly, continuing their earlier conversation as if she'd never had an interruption, 'I told her straight, I said, "Edith, you lay one paw on my Wilder and there will be trouble," and she got the gist.'

'And will she?' David looked thoroughly amused. 'Lay her paws on him, I mean.'

'She wouldn't dare, I'd scratch her eyes out.' Dulcie let his obvious cynicism sail over her perfectly curled blonde head.

'I think you would, too.' David could hold in his mirth no longer and laughed aloud. 'Only someone as beautiful as you could say a thing like that and make it sound inevitable, Dulcie. You are such a tonic.'

'Why thank you, kind sir, I do agree.' She, too, laughed now. 'Oh, you are such a good friend, David,' she said eventually, 'but you've delighted me long enough and I must be off.' She gathered her bag and gloves from the bed. 'I'll see you soon, don't go home without letting me know what day, I don't want to waste my time coming all the way down here to see just anybody.'

'Heaven forfend, Dulcie.' David's remark was laced with a tinge of irony but it was lost on her as she bent and gave him a friendly kiss on the cheek.

'What would I do without you to pour my heart out to, David? Now, have you got Olive's address?'

'You gave it to me earlier,' David smiled, nodding to the piece of paper as Dulcie fussed around the bed, uncharacteristically straightening the cover where she had been sitting – he knew she wouldn't want people to think she was a slut and couldn't tidy up after herself.

David nodded, but before he could say anything Dulcie, with swaying hips and the clip-clip heels of her ankle-band peep-toed shoes, moved

35

towards the door at the end of the Nightingale ward. When she reached it she turned and blew him a kiss and waved.

'Toodle-oo for now,' she mouthed, not waiting to see David raise his one good arm and wave back.

THREE

In the woods beyond the hospital, one of Dulcie's fellow lodgers, Sally, was walking with her fiancé, New Zealander George Laidlaw. Sally's two-year-old half-sister, Alice, was between them as, securely, they each held one of her hands.

Sally and George had originally met when she had left Liverpool to work as a nurse at Bart's hospital in London where George had been training as a registrar. George was now working in East Grinstead under Archibald McIndoe. When the war was finally over they planned to marry and live in New Zealand close to George's parents.

'Have you had no word yet from Callum about us adopting Alice when we get married?' asked George over the child's head.

'Not yet,' Sally answered. 'I'm not sure where his ship is and it may be difficult to get post to him. But I don't think he'll object, he wants what's best for her, that he brought her straight to me when her parents were killed goes to prove it.' A small shadow crossed Sally's face. She had been adamant she would have nothing to do with her orphaned half-sister when Callum brought her late that night. After all, it was Callum's sister, Morag, who had been her best friend before betraying her in the worst possible way by marrying Sally's father within months of his wife's death and had then become pregnant with Alice.

It had come as a great shock and Sally, usually so caring, was determined that Alice should be handed over to the authorities and put into a children's home. Olive, her wonderful landlady, had taken over in that gentle way she had and before she knew what had happened for sure, Sally discovered the little girl had found a place in her heart.

Now she couldn't envisage a life without her any more than she could imagine one without her darling, steady and caring George, whom she loved so very much. It seemed laughable that she had once had a youthful crush on Callum, who'd been a school teacher before joining the Royal Navy, imagining herself in love with him.

'Swing!' Alice commanded firmly, bringing Sally out of her reverie and causing the two adults to exchange understanding looks before obliging the toddler and lifting her off her feet in a swinging motion that had her laughing with innocent delight before demanding, 'More, Georgie, more...'

Georgie was her own special name for George and it never failed to touch Sally's heart to see how much the little girl adored him and how very much she was adored in return.

'Every day she reminds me more of Morag,' Sally told him as they strolled through the leafy wood and was quite surprised when he said, 'She has your mannerisms.' She had never imagined the child had watched her so closely as to pick up her ways and those of the other girls back in Article Row, where she also loved trotting around in Olive's heels 'helping her' around the house. Sally knew that one day she would tell Alice the story of her parents and her loving home. She was determined now that the child would know the security and happiness of that kind of secure home life.

In Hyde Park another member of the household at number 13 was also enjoying the July sunshine. Tilly, Olive's eighteen-year-old daughter, was sitting on the grass with her head in her American boyfriend Drew's lap, whilst she read the newspaper article that carried his by-line.

'Oh, Drew, it's sooo good,' she exclaimed when she had finished. 'I do wish you'd let me read your book though.'

'It's our book,' he told her, 'but I don't want you to read it until it's finished. You know that,' Drew reminded her, as he had done every time she begged him to let her read the book he'd started writing shortly after his arrival in London after the beginning of the war. But he softened his refusal with a tender smile and Tilly smiled back.

'I can't wait for you to finish and for it to be published. I think it should be published now.'

'It won't be finished until the war is over,' said Drew, 'and besides, there isn't any paper to publish new books at the moment.'

'That's so true,' Tilly said with a tinge of regret. 'Like so much else,' she mused as the country prepared to enter its fourth year of the war in September. 'You could get it published if you took it

38

back home to America. Your father owns a news-paper and publishing group after all.'

Immediately Drew sighed and then took hold of both Tilly's hands, gently pulling her upright so they could face each other.

'You know I can't do that, Tilly,' he said firmly. 'My father wants only one thing from me and that is to step into his shoes and take over the business – to live the life he wants me to live and not the life I want to live.' With you, he thought silently.

'There's nothing I want more than for you to be here with me, you know that, Drew, but I can't help feeling guilty sometimes. Your family, es-pecially your mother, must miss you so much.'

Drew sighed again. He knew that he'd never be able to make Tilly understand how different his family values were to those of her own. Tilly might be an only child, but Olive had given her far more love and a happier, more secure childhood than he'd had from his parents and his sisters too. There was a coldness that came ultimately from his father and it affected everything he grasped in his icy, domineeringly cruel embrace in the same way as the warmth that came from Olive's love for her daughter reached out to all around her.

'They might miss the person they want me to be, a figment of my father's imagination,' said Drew, 'but that person isn't me, Tilly.' He looked away for a moment and then turned to her again, his eyes red-rimmed as if he was stemming un-shed tears. 'Please believe me when I tell you, honey, that I have spent the happiest days of my life here with you and your family.'

39

Tilly gave him a look of adoring love, although as her mother had brought her up to be considerate to others she felt compelled to say, 'America is your home though, Drew, and seeing so many of your fellow countrymen over here since America joined the war must make you feel so homesick. I know it would make me feel unsettled.'

It was true, Drew thought as he paused for thought, seeing so many young Americans filling London's streets had caused him some sharp pangs of patriotism and pride in his country and his fellow man, and as he and Tilly had vowed to always be honest with one another he knew that it would be an insult to Tilly's intelligence to deny ever missing America.

'Yes, it does,' he admitted, 'and yes, there are any number of things that I love and miss about my homeland, but nowhere near as many as I love and would miss about you if we were to be parted. England is your home and I hope it will one day be mine too. You are my home. You are my life and you always will be. Always.'

'Oh, Drew,' was all Tilly could say before he took her in his arms.

It wasn't the done thing to kiss publicly in the street, but right now it seemed the most natural thing in the world, and for every disapproving look they received there were many more indulgent smiles from passers-by. It was wartime after all and who could blame a young couple who were so obviously in love for wanting to share every kiss they could?

A while later Drew told her softly, 'I don't feel I am making a sacrifice or that I would secretly prefer it if we made our home in the States. The truth is...' He looked into the distance, across the park and sighed. 'The truth is that by being here with you I feel like I've escaped from something and someone I was afraid I might have become. I'm a writer. I knew that deep down before I knew what it really meant. Nobody back home understands that.'

Again, that sense of fairness instilled into Tilly by her mother had her playing devil's advocate in support of Drew's absent family. 'But surely once they see how important it is to you?'

'No, Tilly. That will never happen. My family are different to you, they live by a different code of ethics than the ones you know. Money, and the power it brings, is what means the most to them. My father thinks he can buy anything or anybody and he usually does.'

Hearing the sadness, even despair, in Drew's voice, Tilly was reluctant to press him any further. They had talked before on many occasions of his family situation, and the wishes of his father with regard to Drew's own future.

'London is where my book is set,' Drew said as if she didn't already know. 'It is peopled by Londoners I have met and talked to all through the war... It's where you are.' He pulled her close to him, his heart thumping heavily, and he saw the way she looked at him, her love for him so openly and honestly on display. He knew that Tilly wasn't the kind of girl to play games with a man she loved, and if that made her feel vulnerable it also made him more protective of her, he acknowledged as he cupped her face to kiss her.

Tilly didn't object to his public show of love. Why should she? She loved being kissed by Drew and fervently wished they did more than just kiss, but Drew was insistent that they did not cross the line her mother had drawn. And they weren't the only couple taking advantage of the warm sunny afternoon after the disappointment of the Whitsun Bank Holiday earlier in the year and Hyde Park was full of people out to enjoy themselves despite the war.

'I can't think straight when you kiss me like that,' Tilly giggled when he finally released her, 'and you know it. I just wish...' All the longing in her passionate nature was there in her voice as well as the look she was giving him whilst Drew's heart slammed in his ribs.

'It is tempting and would be so easy for us to go back to my lodgings right now... And then I could truly make you mine forever.' He wasn't going to do that though and not just because her mother wouldn't approve. He had his own sense of honour and he had his love for Tilly. Their wedding wasn't going to be a rushed event with the eyes of the guests wondering if their first child would be born 'early'. 'I know what you wish, but our love for each other is something we will have all our lives, Tilly. I, too, want us to be together as husband and wife and we shall be. Your mom just wants to protect you and make sure I don't take advantage, that's all.'

'I know that,' Tilly was forced to concede, loving him even more if that was possible.

'It won't be long until you're twenty-one and your mom will have no say in the matter then.'

'She did say we could be married in the June before my twenty-first birthday. It feels like a lifetime away,' Tilly groaned. 'Do you think we will still be at war then, Drew?'

As she stepped off the train at Blackfriars and crossed the busy road, ominous dark clouds were low in the sky. Dulcie raised the collar of her belted herringbone coat and fixed her black felt sailor-style hat with a rhinestone pin, securing it through the upturned brim in such a way as to show off her beauty to its best advantage. She patted the higher left side of the hat to a jaunty angle over her shiny blonde curls. With the black leather clutch bag firmly under her arm she raised her chin and made her way to the bus stop where she would catch her bus to Holborn.

If she was lucky she would be in time to join Tilly and Olive, who were going to the pictures to see the Three Stooges. After a full week in the munitions factory she felt she deserved a good laugh; the film was on at the Rimini and she had been dying to see it. Although Olive would probably want to go and see the new Greer Garson film, *Mrs Miniver*. However, Dulcie had to admit that even though Walter Pidgeon was easy on the eye, she'd seen enough of bomb-damaged London streets to last her a lifetime.

Wilder, as was usual lately, was on flying duty this evening and she had nothing better to do. She was walking along Queen Victoria Street still in view of Blackfriars railway station when a flash of someone familiar caught her eye. But just as quickly she was gone again. For a moment,

43

Dulcie thought she had caught sight of her sister, Edith, heading towards the train station carrying a suitcase.

How ridiculous.

Smiling to herself, Dulcie realised that she might be tired after all. Fancy imagining a thing like that, she thought, straining to catch another glimpse through the crowds, especially when she knew well enough that their Edith had just landed the part of leading lady in the West End show *Lucky Girl*. It was the kind of show Edith had dreamed of playing a starring role in all her life. A once-in-a-lifetime opportunity to go from understudy to star as the original leading lady had gone down with chicken pox. So Dulcie couldn't see her sister hopping on a train with her suitcase packed and miss the best role of her career so far.

Yet as Dulcie zigzagged between the horse-drawn carts and slow-moving rush-hour traffic she saw the girl again. In astonishment Dulcie stopped dead in the middle of the road and was almost run down by a trolley bus.

The dipping sun caught the glint of her sister's unmistakeable titian curls as the familiar beaver-lamb box jacket swung around Edith's inimitable snake-slim hips. She was carrying the dark brown cardboard suitcase that had once belonged to their father and was hurrying towards Blackfriars station. Dulcie lost sight of her momentarily as the crowd surged forth. But as it dispersed there were only two people left on the pavement, their lips glued together in a passionate kiss, and she was right – one of them definitely was Edith.

Hurrying to cross the road towards her younger

sister, Dulcie wanted to know what Edith was playing at, seeing as her name was all over the front of the theatre with 'sold out' plastered right across it. Why was she carrying a suitcase? She had a show to do that evening. And that was when Dulcie saw who Edith was kissing.

For a long, painful moment her heart seemed to ricochet against her ribcage. She recognised the leather flying jacket with the American wings on the sleeve and she knew for certain that the man kissing Edith so passionately and so blatantly in the middle of the street was none other than Wilder.

Dulcie's mouth dried and her heart sank to her shoes. Edith had done some unpleasant things in her time but even Dulcie wouldn't have suspected her sister of something as callous as this betrayal. How could she be so cruel as to steal her man? But as Dulcie's temper rose she was able to grasp that if her sister could be so heartless as to allow their parents to believe she was dead, she was capable of anything. Dulcie's teeth clamped so tightly together it made her head ache and she knew that if she could possibly get her hands on the hennaed head of her deceitful sister right now there was no telling what she might do.

However, she was spared the chance as the couple moved towards the entrance of the railway station. Edith and Wilder seemed blind to those around them. If Dulcie hadn't seen it with her own eyes she doubted she would have believed her sister could act so wantonly in the middle of the street. She had been all but eating Wilder alive and he was doing nothing to stop her. Although,

45

Dulcie realised with a sickening lurch, him being a red-blooded male he wouldn't resist, would he? In fact from what she could see, he was actively encouraging Edith's scandalous intimacy and taking part with as much enthusiasm! But she didn't have time to confront them before they suddenly parted and hurried inside the train station.

Angry beyond reason, Dulcie only just stopped herself from pursuing them, understanding her pride wouldn't allow such a thing, and turning now, she hurried so quickly down the road that her ankle strap snapped.

What did she expect, she fumed, her face ablaze with indignation as she scraped her shoe along the pavement, nothing was any good these days. Shoddy shoes. Shoddy boyfriends and even shoddier sisters!

The brazen hussy could never keep her hands to herself, Dulcie silently raged, trying to ignore the curious stares of passers-by, knowing Edith always wanted what she had and thought nothing of taking whatever she fancied without asking. In fact, thought Dulcie as the acid bile rose to her throat, the more she liked something – or someone – the more Edith wanted it. It was like an obsession. But Dulcie also knew that when Edith had taken her fill she would discard Wilder like one of her pretty blouses. Well, she thought grimly, when he came scuttling back with his tail between his legs she would damn well chop it off!

FOUR

Angry, salty tears coursed down Dulcie's cheeks making her mascara run and blurring her vision. She knew she couldn't possibly get on a bus looking such a sight, and then a thunderclap broke the clouds and the pewter sky released great splashes of rain onto her ashen face, soaking her beautifully styled hair. At any other time she would have been mortified at being seen in such a chaotic state. But what did it matter now? How could her sister be so brazen, she thought as she hurried to the shelter of the bus stop to gather her thoughts and retreat from this deluge. How could Wilder be so callous?

'Excuse me, ma'am, would you like to share my umbrella to cover your golden curls?'

Dulcie only just stopped herself from telling the owner of the polite American accent where he could put his umbrella. She'd had enough of Americans and wasn't in the habit of being picked up in the street.

If he was really interested in her, he could catch her in a West-End dancehall every fourth week-end, when she had time off from the munitions factory and her *golden curls* were temporarily released from the turbaned headscarf they were forced to wear to protect their hair from being caught in the powerful machines.

Lifting her eyes to tell him in no uncertain

terms where he could go, Dulcie was amazed to see the most gorgeous silver-blue eyes she had seen for a long time. Quickly re-thinking the angry retort she gave a trembling half-smile and wondered if her mascara had run all the way down her cheeks.

'Are you okay, ma'am? You look upset.'

'Thank you for asking,' Dulcie answered, noticing the wings on his immaculate uniform and realising he was an airman, and reminding herself that moments earlier she had sworn she would have no more to do with them. But nobody else knew of her self-imposed promise so her volte-face could not be held against her. Anyway, she thought, he didn't seem like the loud, brash Wilder. This one seemed kind and, by the sound of his softly spoken enquiry, she couldn't even begin to compare the two men and, Dulcie thought, giving him her most demure smile, she shouldn't throw all the eggs out because one had gone off. Maybe she shouldn't be in too much of a hurry to give him the cold shoulder after all.

He was being kind and thoughtful offering her the shelter of his umbrella in this torrential downpour as the bus stop was full, and a girl shouldn't refuse herself a little male attention, especially when she had been so badly deceived by someone she thought she loved – even more so when she had been betrayed by her sister and her boyfriend, she thought, her heart now full of retaliation. A little harmless flirtation with a handsome man did wonders for a girl's ego.

'Can I get you anything? I see you've snapped your shoe.' His striking eyes looked so caring and she realised she hadn't been exactly hospitable to this young man who was a long way from home. She rummaged in her bag under the protection of his umbrella, as much to collect her thoughts as to retrieve the gold compact she had treated herself to when she left Selfridges to work in the higher-paid munitions factory.

'I tripped on a broken pavement,' Dulcie simpered. 'I've just had a terrible shock.'

'I am so sorry. Ma'am, is there anything I can do?'

'How good of you, I think I just need to sit down for a while,' Dulcie said as she popped the concealed button on the side of her compact. She gasped when she saw the black rivulets of mascara that had run down her once perfectly made-up face.

'You look beautiful to me, ma'am,' said the young airman. 'In fact I don't think I've seen a better-looking woman since I got over here a month ago.'

'Flatterer.' Dulcie could feel the delicious warmth only a really good compliment could bring, and wondered how he could say such a thing when she now had panda eyes, and long white tracks where her tears had smudged her pan-stick foundation. 'I looked perfect until...' She paused. She had only just met this man, she wasn't going to pour her heart out on the street, and without any hint of self-consciousness or false modesty she dabbed at the dark track lines.

The amused airman, standing so close, still holding the umbrella over her head, smiled as she expertly applied a slick of vermilion lipstick to her bee-stung lips. After pressing them together, revelling in his complete attention, Dulcie turned to the airman and pouted in the same way she used to do when she worked the busiest beauty counter in Selfridges. Without warning the airman took her actions as an open invitation, and he kissed her full on her ruby-red lips. When he let her go Dulcie gasped, completely taken aback.

'How dare you!' she exclaimed, secretly delighted.

'I'm sorry, ma'am, but you are so irresistible, I couldn't help myself.' He then went red to the tips of his ears and gave her a bashful smile. Dulcie knew she couldn't be angry with him.

'You had no right to steal a kiss from me like that,' she smiled coquettishly. 'You saucy devil ... just you wait to be invited next time.'

'I am so sorry, ma'am; I don't know what came over me.' Then they both laughed, and for a moment Dulcie forgot that her sister had just run off with her man.

'Would you like to go for a drink?' asked the airman. 'You look like you could do with one.'

'It's that obvious,' Dulcie said, remembering again. And then, perhaps as a gesture of retaliation for what Edith had done, she decided that two could play at that game. 'I'd be delighted,' she said as she took the arm he offered, helping her across the road to the little pub opposite the train station. Once inside, much to her embarrassment, he removed her shoe and then the offending strap leaving just a sling-back and the front peep toe.

'It looks great,' said Dulcie, 'but what about the other – they are now odd.'

'May I?' he asked as he removed her other shoe and as Dulcie nodded her consent he took a penknife from his trouser pocket and sliced off the other ankle strap. 'There,' he said, satisfied with his wonderful handiwork. 'They're both the same again now.'

'Thank you,' Dulcie said, slipping the straps into her clutch bag. 'I suppose Olive will soon find a use for these.'

The airman laughed as he went to the bar and got them both a drink. A young Tommie sitting in the corner with his pals gave Dulcie a withering look as if to ask if Englishmen weren't good enough for the likes of her.

Dulcie turned her attention to the posters on the wall advertising Dobie's Four Square cigarettes and the smily face in the froth of a glass of milk stout; she didn't want any trouble and she knew that some British men were very touchy about 'their' girls fraternising with American servicemen and had all sorts of unattractive names for them. But she wasn't one of them. She was just upset and being helped by a kindly airman. After her drink she was going straight back home.

After finishing her third port and lemon Dulcie realised she wasn't so angry now and she certainly didn't want to scream any more. Feeling very mellow indeed, she told the airman all about her sister and her boyfriend. She hadn't meant to tell him – she didn't want to tell anybody, sensing that in some way it might have been her fault for keeping Wilder at arm's length, but the alcohol had loosened her tongue somewhat.

However, her new beau reassured her that

Wilder's infidelity couldn't possibly be her fault, she couldn't be blamed for picking the bad apple in the barrel, and assured her that all American servicemen were not all like that at all.

'Another drink?' the airman asked and Dulcie nodded, feeling cordially tipsy, so much so that when the piano player struck up a popular tune she joined in with all the enthusiasm of a practised entertainer. She would show them that her voice was as good as their Edith's.

The bar was crowded and the airman had been gone a while. Long enough for Dulcie to gather her thoughts.

Edith, it was true, had a better voice and was more popular, it had to be said – no wonder she had taken her sweetheart, Dulcie thought, knowing he was the gift that she was never going to get any enjoyment from. And, whereas Edith never felt she had to wait her turn or be grateful for cast-offs, Dulcie was used to being second-best. And it was the insecurity of seeing her younger sister being fussed and preened over from the moment she was born that made her what she was today, Dulcie was sure.

'You were dreaming with your eyes half-closed there, honey,' the airman said as he brought more drinks to the table. Dulcie wondered if she'd had enough but he soon managed to persuade her that she'd had a shock, and drinking port and lemon was good for shocks, he laughed.

The last drink seemed to disappear much quicker than the others, Dulcie noticed, and dragging her thoughts from the doldrums she once more joined in with the rousing chorus of songs.

'Bless 'em all, bless 'em all, the long and the short and the tall...' Dulcie swayed along with everybody else and very soon the room began to swim.

'Are you all right, ma'am?' said the airman, whose name she hadn't yet asked for. Dulcie nodded and scrambled to the door for fresh air.

'I'll be fine in a minute,' she said, holding up her hand to keep him at bay in case she deposited the alcoholic contents of her empty stomach onto the pavement. After a few huge gulps of balmy summer air she was able to nod to let him know she was better now.

'Do you want to go back inside?' he asked and Dulcie gently shook her head. Instead, she allowed herself to be escorted with his protective arm around her tiny waist towards Article Row.

'Isn't it a beautiful night?' he asked, supporting her as she leaned a very sleepy head on his shoulder. It was lovely, Dulcie thought, taking in the sweet scent of parkland grass.

'*C'est la vie*,' she said lazily, having read the phrase in a magazine. She had been dying to try it out even if it didn't fit the occasion, as she slipped her hand around his slim hips to huddle close. If Wilder didn't appreciate her then there were plenty of men who did.

They were halfway down Keynes Road, sauntering alongside each other without a care in the world, when the warning banshee wail of the air raid began. Dulcie giggled, she knew her way around the area, and she knew there was an air-raid shelter in the park.

'Here,' she said, her voice slurred, 'let's cut

through here.' She took his hand and pulled him towards the low coil of barbed wire, realising that under ordinary circumstances she would never have dared do this with a stranger. But these weren't ordinary circumstances and he wasn't a stranger now.

'I know where the shelter is,' she quipped, noticing all the railings had been taken away to help build war planes and the park was quite open except for the low roll of spiked wire. Then to her complete surprise and obvious delight she felt his strong hands lift her up with ease, and the handsome airman whose name she hadn't even asked carried her over it.

'That was close, ma'am,' he said, taking off his jacket and laying it on the grimy wooden bench that went along the wall of the empty air-raid shelter. Dulcie was about to protest when she remembered that she was wearing her best skirt and didn't fancy ruining it on a grimy seat so instead she smiled and decided to make herself comfy for the duration of the raid.

'Can we have less of the "ma'am" please, Soldier.' Dulcie giggled again. 'You make me sound like Methuselah's mother.' She paused and gave a thoughtful pout. 'Well, his sister at least.' Then she laughed, really laughed as if she had heard something so delightful. He made her feel good, this handsome GI, and ever so glad she'd met him.

'I don't know who this Methuselah guy is, Ma'am, but...'

'Dulcie,' she sighed. 'My name is Dulcie.' She gave another throaty laugh and she rocked a little as he enfolded her in his arms whilst she tried to focus on his handsome features. He was so close now she could smell the clean fresh tang of his cologne.

'Well, Dulcie, that's some raunchy laugh you got there if you don't mind my saying...'

'Not at all,' Dulcie all but whispered. 'And you are?' She noticed a delicious, unexpected warmth rise to certain parts of her body, making her feel decadent. She had never felt this way before. Not even with Wilder. He was closer now. The nearer he got the more her desire soared. And the more she craved his lips on hers. Maybe this was what they meant when they talked about their finest hour. Another giggle was only a whisper away and she watched him from under her lashes.

'Well, Dulcie.' His voice was low, intimate, with a little catch to it, and he never took his eyes from her. 'My name's Reece Redgrave the third...'

'The third?' Dulcie drawled and he told her yes in his deep Southern accent and Dulcie's heart melted right there. He felt so powerful holding her like that, tanned and muscled in all the right places, and he was so polite: soothing her nerves, making her feel so special, unlike Wilder... Dulcie didn't want to think of Wilder's treachery now.

She wanted to forget the death and destruction going on around them and, if she was honest, even forget poor, injured, incapacitated David who flashed through her thoughts momentarily. What kind of a life would he have now? Who would have thought it? Fit and agile one minute... Then... But those thoughts were for another time. Now she needed strong arms around her to feel safe and above all she wanted, no needed, to be desired.

Wilder never paid her the compliments that Reece was doing now. He never made her feel like a red-blooded woman the way Reece did. And if she was perfectly honest she wanted Reece to... Well, she couldn't put into words what she wanted him to do, not even to herself.

Her heart, beating faster now, caused her breath to come in small, shallow pants as she pushed the fallen fringe from her eyes with both hands and crossed her legs, allowing her shoe to dangle from her red-painted toes, enjoying his lingering, open appreciation of her body.

'So, Reece Redgrave the third.' Dulcie's voice came in short, whispering gasps. 'Why don't you sit here next to me.' She tapped the wooden bench with her long red fingernails after making herself comfortable on Reece's uniform jacket and in no time at all he was sitting so close to her she could feel every muscled curve of his body.

When he nuzzled her ear Dulcie giggled as the delicious ripples of pleasure woke up parts of her body she didn't know existed before and as Reece trailed feathery butterfly kisses on her neck and décolletage, causing her to throw her head back in delicious abandonment, ignoring the swimming sensation in her head, Dulcie knew what was going to happen next and she savoured the anticipation as his lips sought hers.

Live for today, she thought lazily. Live for the moment. Tomorrow may never come. Suddenly Reece Redgrave was kissing her with an urgency and passion that made her head spin. Dulcie was caught up in a haze of desire so enjoyable she never wanted it to stop.

The clean, fresh tang of his cologne had her wanting more ... much more... A small, involuntary groan escaped her lips as his kisses rained across her neck, her eyes, and her lips. They were breathing in shallow, panting unison now, and she did nothing to stop Reece as ricochets of delight exploded through her body.

Feeling reckless and wildly excited Dulcie could not get enough of Reece Redgrave the third. Tonight was the night she was going to lose her virginity! The alcohol she had consumed gave her an air of indestructibility. Nothing mattered now. She didn't care one iota. They were alone in the shelter; obviously the earlier deluge had kept people away. It was so right.

'Kiss me... Kiss me...' Her voice came in small guttural bursts and she found it hard to breathe. Arching her back Dulcie accepted his exploring hands as they roamed every inch of her yielding body. She knew she had never let Wilder go so far ... never let any man ... go this far...

'You sure are beautiful, Dulcie...' Reece was panting now, his hands feverishly pushing up the tight, pencil-slim skirt and gently pushing his fingers beneath the rim of her silk cami-knickers, pulling at her suspenders and stroking the warm silken flesh that peeped over her stocking tops.

'I never ... thought ... it would be ... this easy.' His words were coming in short sharp gasps now and it took a moment for their meaning to sink into the fog.

Easy?

All yearning disappeared suddenly, as the word sank into the craving miasma... The realisation hit Dulcie like a slap in the face.

Easy?

He was intimating that she was no better than the 'Piccadilly commandos' who plied their trade in Soho! How could he? He had been so polite. So charming and so, so convincing.

Dulcie opened her eyes and saw him, lost in the grip of passion, oblivious to anything around him. The glazed expression of his once-beautiful eyes told her that he wasn't seeing her at all. She could have been anybody.

Lifting her head, feeling suddenly soiled, Dulcie looked at Reece, lost in the same trance of ecstasy she had been consumed by just moments before. This isn't what she wanted any more. They hadn't even stopped to ... to... Oh no, she thought frantically. How could she have been so stupid?

'Get off me!' Dulcie cried, pushing him away, but he was too strong for her. All desire was gone now and tears ran down her face. It was futile to try and get him off her. He was too far gone to stop now.

The loud-mouthed, uncouth girls back at the munitions factory who boasted about their nocturnal exploits with American servicemen flashed through her mind. She had scorned them as common, unladylike. But here she was, doing exactly the same thing. Worse, in fact. She'd never heard any of the girls say they had been seduced in an air-raid shelter by a man they had met only minutes before!

'Get off me!' She had gone too far, she'd behaved like an alley cat. She hadn't meant to lead him on.

It wasn't her fault! 'Leave me alone, leave me...' But it was too late, she could tell. And, as inexperienced as she was, Dulcie knew he was spent, as every muscle relaxed on top of her.

The deed, she refused to call it lovemaking, was over in mere moments. It would have taken longer to make a cup of tea, she realised as he got up and fixed his pants and tucked in his shirt without looking at her. It would have taken longer to smoke the cigarette he was now offering her. Then, to her absolute horror, she saw Reece Redgrave slide to his knees and with his head buried in her lap he sobbed like a baby. She didn't know what to do. She had never seen a man behave like this before. He was saying something, his words barely coherent.

'I am so sorry, Dulcie, please forgive me, there was nothing I could do ... please believe me, Dulcie. I am so, so sorry, I beg of you...'

Dulcie, stunned, dazed, almost without thinking, reached out and stroked his thick black hair before lifting his head to see tears rolling freely down his face. She was surprised when he took her hands, and cupping them in his he kissed them and she could see the pain of shame in his eyes.

'I couldn't help myself,' he said, his eyes looking almost dead now. 'I just couldn't stop... I didn't realise until it was too late that you were a ... that it was your first time, too.'

Dulcie looked at him and sighed. How could she face anybody now? Wilder didn't matter any more, he had shown his true colours and she wasn't going there again. David... Poor, fractured David ... he would be so disgusted if he knew what she had done. She would never be able to look anybody, not even Olive, in the face again.

Quickly, covering herself, trying to tidy herself up, she knew that when Sally and George went away it was plainly obvious what had taken place; the sun had shone from their eyes. Their love oozed from every pore. But this wasn't love. This was madness. And she had encouraged it. If the truth be known, she had longed for him to make love to her... But for all the wrong reasons.

'I can't say sorry enough, I didn't mean to ... to force myself on you. It wasn't like that, honest it wasn't.' For a long, difficult moment Dulcie looked into the face of an inexperienced, frightened young man who, like herself, had been a virgin.

No doubt he was scared of what she would do now, Dulcie thought, and wondering if she would report him to the authorities. But she couldn't do that knowing she was as much to blame as he was. More so if the truth was known, because she could have stopped him going too far any time, until...

He was a long way from home, she knew. And, given his show of utter remorse now, she doubted there was anybody he would tell. Reece looked at her and said, his voice gruff, hesitant, 'Back at the base they said English girls were...' He couldn't finish telling her of the lies he had been fed from his buddies back at camp, but Dulcie knew what he meant, she had heard the girls in the munitions factory, and for a moment she wanted to she wanted to... Oh, God, she wanted to tell him it was all right.

But it wasn't all right. He had been tricked into

thinking that English girls were easy. And by the way she had seen some girls acting she could see how some of their American allies would think that, too. It still wasn't right though, she thought.

Hurriedly she stood and fixed her clothes, smoothed down the creased skirt that had been so immaculately pressed and roughly pushed her damp, tangled hair from her face before moving towards the shelter's exit. But Reece pulled her back.

'You can't go out there yet!' His eyes were a mixture of distress and apology. 'The all-clear hasn't yet sounded. I promise I won't do anything, please don't go,' he pleaded. 'It's not safe.'

Dulcie edged back into the shelter without saying a word. What a way to remember something that should be forever in your mind as the beautiful first time. Slowly she edged towards the wooden bench and resigned herself to the fact that whether she liked it or not she and Reece were stranded together for the duration. And as she listened to the crump and boom of the battle beyond the air-raid shelter Dulcie likened it to the conflict going on inside her now, and she knew that as soon as the air raid was over she would be out of here so fast, he would never see her again.

FIVE

'You're very quiet today, Drew, is there something wrong?' Tilly asked.

Drew shook his head and smiled but Tilly wasn't convinced; they were so in love, with an almost uncanny perception of each other's moods, that she couldn't help noticing when something was bothering him, even when he didn't appear to be outwardly worrying. But try as she might she couldn't get him to tell her what was wrong. She decided to leave it for now and change the subject, as she didn't want Drew to feel she was pressurising him into telling her something he wished to keep to himself. No matter how much she longed to know.

'It isn't looking good for our boys in the desert, is it, Drew?'

'No, Tilly, it isn't,' he replied, watching her make little knots in the long grass she had plucked from the lawn on which they were spending their last evening together. Even though Tilly didn't yet know this. His heart ached with love for her. But he couldn't voice the news that his mother was critically ill, which his father had told him this morning when he telephoned to say he had booked Drew on the next flight to Chicago – later this evening.

Drew's capricious, even half-baked inner fear that Tilly might find someone else if he wasn't around gnawed at his insides, but he knew he had to remain calm, even relaxed. He knew she loved him with every beat of her heart – whilst he was around.

But loving her as much as he did now was making him feel suddenly insecure. Would she wait for him to come back? He was sure she would. But there were plenty of red-blooded servicemen roaming around London who would jump at the chance of a date with Tilly. He would never voice his fears to her, *of course not*. She'd be so messed-up. He had to act normally, behave like nothing was wrong. Although he knew Tilly already guessed something.

'Is Dulcie's brother still in the desert?' Drew searched Tilly's eyes for any flicker of emotion at the mention of her former sweetheart. She nodded slightly and continued to concentrate on the blade of grass she was curling between her short neat fingernails. She didn't say anything, perhaps heeding the advice that anybody, no matter how innocent-looking, could be eavesdropping and share the information. Drew was well aware that Dulcie's brother Rick was stationed at Tobruk in Libya, which had fallen to the Germans in June. It had cast a pall of anxiety and dismay over the whole country and he secretly wondered if Tilly was worried about her former flame. It was swell of her to worry; it showed her caring nature. But it didn't stop him feeling an unfamiliar emotional insecurity.

'Do you think the enemy will take Cairo as well?' Tilly whispered, her eyes observing the people around them in the park, and Drew shook his head in answer to her grim question.

'I don't know,' he said, his hand resting gently on her shoulder. He felt Tilly shiver beneath the short-sleeved, thin woollen cardigan, even though the day was still very warm.

'Sally told us one of the nurses back at Bart's said that she has a sister who is also a nurse, working out in Cairo.' Tilly repositioned her head so that it lay comfortably on his lap as she plaited the long grass and tickled his chin with it, then sighing in that beautiful way she had she continued, 'Sally's friend was thinking of going out to join her sister, because her letters were full of the fun she was having, and all the parties she'd been invited to,' Tilly sighed again, 'but now she's not so sure. After what's happened in North Africa she says that nothing would entice her to go over there.'

'The world is going mad,' said Drew and then seeing Tilly's eyes open wide he reassuringly squeezed her hand.

'Dulcie says that there's been talk of her sister Edith's dance troupe being sent out to entertain the troops on one of the ENSA tours. But what if the Germans do take Cairo...?'

'They haven't taken it yet,' Drew said, trying to calm her fears, 'and knowing what I do about the brave British bulldog spirit I'm sure the Allies will fight to the last man to stop that from happening.' He was quiet for a moment. Then he said in a hesitant, almost non-committal voice, 'Has Dulcie heard anything from Rick?' He watched as Tilly shook her head and looked a little uncomfortable, then Drew smiled and gave her hand another squeeze; he'd put her in a real uncomfortable position and hated himself for being so selfish, thinking only of his own feelings.

'You mustn't feel that you can't mention Rick's name around me, Tilly.' He wanted so much for Tilly to understand he was a modern man. He recognised that other men would be just as smitten by her beauty as he was. 'Just because he used to be sweet on you doesn't mean you can't talk about him.' Drew bent and gently stroked the tip of Tilly's nose, making her smile. 'I know I can trust in your love for me – and Rick's a decent guy.'

'Oh, Drew, I would never do anything to make you think badly of me, especially...'

'Nothing could make me feel that way, honey. I like Rick, he's a nice guy, and you knew him before you knew me, right.' Drew had almost convinced himself that he wouldn't be in the least bit anxious if Rick was on his way home whilst he was back in America. 'I know you love me and I know I can trust in that love. You're my girl and I'm your man, right?'

'I could never look at another man who isn't you, my darling.' There was a delicious giggle in Tilly's voice that made Drew feel weak with love for her. How was he going to survive without seeing her every day? But he tried not to dwell on that now.

'Rick's fighting for his country and it stands to reason that you'd worry,' he said, trying to keep his mind focused on the here and now with Tilly – not what would happen tomorrow without her. 'You wouldn't be the caring kinda gal I know you are, if you weren't anxious.'

'Oh, you are understanding, Drew, it must be

terrifying for Dulcie.' Tilly was overcome with relief that he understood and there were tears in her eyes as she fervently responded, 'Is it any wonder that I love you.'

She turned, balancing on her elbow, blew him a kiss and said, 'Everything you say and do proves what a wonderful, special person you are. I am concerned about Rick, and I know Dulcie is too although she tries hard not to show it.' Tilly wiped away her tears with her hand and Drew bent to try and kiss her fears away once more.

'I know Rick was laughing off the fighting he would have to do when he was home last,' he said, his little finger gently outlining her beautiful features.

'That's Rick; all jokes and good spirits,' said Tilly, her voice relaxed as if seeing the scene in her mind's eye, then her tone changed, revealing her carefully hidden distress. 'I noticed when he thought nobody was looking he stopped smiling. He looked thinner, too, and...'

'Battle-hardened,' Drew suggested, wondering what Tilly would say if he told her how much he envied men like Rick who were doing their bit, and how he felt he was having it easy whilst they were risking their lives.

'Yes, that's it,' Tilly agreed, sombre now, knowing the first time she had met Rick she was bowled over by his good looks and easy charm.

In fact she had more than a bit of a crush on him. But that was before she met her darling Drew. Now there was nobody and nothing in her heart except him, even though her love didn't prevent her having a very natural concern for Rick.

She looked up and shielded her eyes from the golden dipping rays of sunshine to see that Drew had commenced writing in his journal, probably recording their time together.

'How lucky I am to have a man who is so clever as to write such a wonderful book,' she said, trying to inject a little light into their dark conversation.

'My greatest achievement is finding you, my darling Tilly.' Drew smiled and stroked her hair. 'You fill my life with sunshine every day, no matter what the weather.' He reached out and touched the ring Tilly wore on a chain around her neck. The one he'd given her the first Christmas they had known one another.

'Remember what we said to each other about this?' he asked her, his eyes tender. Tilly nodded; how could she ever forget? They would only break up for good if she sent him his ring back, or if he ever asked her for it.

'I will never ask you for this ring back,' Drew said, his words thick, his eyes solemn.

'And I will never offer it to you,' Tilly said, her brow puckered in a confused crease. They gazed into each other's eyes for a long time, neither one wanting to break this idyllic moment. This precious time they had together was sacrosanct, when nothing and nobody could come between them. Then, all too soon, the keeper was patrolling the park, and one of the only sets of gates that had not yet been requisitioned for the war effort was about to be locked.

'C'mon. We'll have to get back.' Drew's voice was laced with regret before he bent to kiss her gently on her ever-accepting lips.

'I know, we're on fire-watch duty tonight,' Tilly offered. 'Not that there are likely to be any bombs tonight, thank goodness, the enemies are too busy fighting overseas.' She looked pensive. 'But we mustn't become complacent; there is talk that Hitler could start bombing again but probably only when he's finished attacking Russia when winter sets in over there.'

'You're right,' said Drew. 'No attacking army has been victorious against the Russian winter – as Napoleon Bonaparte learned to his cost.'

'You are so clever to know that,' Tilly said, adoration in her eyes.

'I know, I can't help it,' Drew laughed. 'But come on, we'd better make tracks.'

He was talking about anything he could think of to try to prevent him feeling like the heel he most certainly was, afraid that if there was a moment's silence between them then he would blurt out the very thing he had been keeping from Tilly all day.

He knew she deserved to be told that he was leaving as soon as he dropped her off home. It was her right to know. But he wasn't the courageous hero Tilly thought he was. In fact he felt like a spineless rat and not the desert kind like Rick either. Drew was too damned scared to tell the woman he loved that he was going away. And had no idea when he was coming back.

'Oh, hello, Dulcie, you're home late,' Olive said as Dulcie popped her head around the front-room door. 'I'm glad you're back safe and sound though, did you manage to get to a shelter?'

Dulcie nodded, unable to say much, and kept the door half-closed, covering herself so as not to alert Olive to her dishevelled clothing and hoping her humiliation didn't show on her face. She had a splitting headache and all she wanted to do was crawl into bed and forget tonight had ever happened, and she certainly didn't want to go into the front room where questions might be asked.

'I was hoping to be able to take a bath, is there any hot water?'

'Enough for five inches I would say,' Olive answered, her brows meeting in a troubled frown. 'Is everything all right, Dulcie?'

'Fine. Just a bit of a headache,' Dulcie lied with uncharacteristic calmness. She had a lot to think about and she needed privacy to do it. Thankfully, Olive had the company of Mrs Black from next door and Tilly, who had just come in from fire-watching.

'I'll make you a hot cocoa and see if we have something for your headache,' Olive said, rising from the chair.

'Maybe later,' Dulcie said, not wanting any fuss. 'The bath might do the trick. I won't be long,' she managed to add as she closed the door, tears just a blink away as Olive's kindness touched her heart and made her feel tawdry, whilst Nancy Black's strident opinion echoed after her.

'I don't know as I like that common voice on the wireless,' Nancy said, sitting on Olive's settee, wrinkling her flared nostrils like there was a bad smell floating about the room, much to Olive's chagrin.

'It's Wilfred Pickles!' Olive exclaimed, retriev-

69

ing the newspaper, which Nancy had borrowed and brought back two days late. This was becoming a regular occurrence, and even though Olive didn't mind lending her the newspaper, she did object to not getting it back when the news was still fresh, instead of being fit for nothing except tomorrow's chip wrapper; especially when Nancy took half of it to polish her windows and Olive had to remind her who it actually belonged to.

'It comes to something when the news has to be read in a Yorkshire accent,' Nancy continued. 'Have all the true Englishmen gone to fight? That's what I want to know.'

'I quite like a Yorkshire accent, myself,' Olive replied, 'and of course he is a true Englishman.' She folded the paper to give her hands something to do to stave off the nervous energy Nancy always seemed to encourage in her and, then, putting the paper on the arm of the chair she continued, 'I told you, he's a very fine actor, is Wilfred Pickles. I think he's got a lovely soothing voice and he's very handsome.' She gave an emphatic nod of her head and just stopped short of telling Nancy that she was being absurd.

'It's not right,' Nancy began, but she was cut off mid-sentence.

'Oh, I dunno.' Tilly imitated the common slang, knowing it irked Nancy, cautiously splaying her fingers down the inside leg of her last pair of nylons that Drew had given her to examine it for ladders. 'Mum's right, his voice is very gentle on the old nerves, I must say.' Olive smiled at her daughter whilst Nancy sniffed her disregard, her mouth set in a straight line.

'Is she sickening for something?' Nancy asked Olive and it took all of Tilly's resolve to stop herself from bursting into hysterical laughter. 'It just doesn't seem right somehow,' Nancy continued, 'unpatriotic.'

'Maybe if the BBC has a word on your behalf, as you're such an avid listener.' Tilly couldn't look at her neighbour in case she gave the game away. Her mother gave her a raised eyebrow, but Tilly could see she too was amused and even more so when she actually joined in.

'They could get Mr Churchill to do the honours and read the nine o'clock edition if he's got nothing better to do,' Olive suggested. Tilly's lips formed a silent moue of surprise.

'Well,' Nancy exclaimed, obviously peeved at their impudence, 'I've got better things I must be getting on with. I haven't got time to sit around here gossiping all night with you pair of giddy kippers.' Shrugging her discontent Nancy shuffled out of the room.

'Don't let me keep you, Nancy, I'm sure you must be very busy,' Olive managed to say, only just subduing her laughter until they heard the front door slam.

'Oh, Mum, you are a one,' Tillie laughed, hugging her sides as she rolled on the arm of the chair. Olive was glad to see that Tilly was in good spirits; the war seemed to have made her a little too serious than was good for her and she was pleased that Tilly had suggested she might go to the pictures with Dulcie on Saturday night.

'Well, serves her right, frosty-faced perisher, she...' Olive stopped herself just in time when the back door opened and Sally came into the room. Then, in a more sober tone, she said, 'I don't know what's got into me lately, I would never have said boo to a goose before the war.' She was laughing softly as Sally was followed by Dulcie, clad now in her dressing gown as she entered the front room. Tilly was laughing still, glad to see her mother carefree for a change.

'Are you going to share the joke?' Dulcie asked, so glad to be home. Her 'episode' in the air-raid shelter with Reece Redgrave had been played over and over again in her mind even though she tried to force herself not to think of it; a trick she'd learned years ago when her mother ignored her in favour of Edith, it was her safety mechanism and it worked well usually, but not tonight. The air-raid tryst was something she was going to try her very best to forget. But she had the feeling it was going to be difficult, very difficult indeed.

'Alice is awake if you want to see her before you eat your supper, Sally,' Olive said. 'I put her down for the night but she's a bit fretful since the air-raid siren went off.'

I know how she feels, Dulcie thought, then remembering the envelope she said to Tilly, 'This was on the mat in the hall.' She handed over the letter.

'It is Drew's handwriting,' Tilly said, surprised and pleased all at the same time.

'He adores you so much he even sends you love letters a couple of hours after he's seen you,' Sally chuckled. But their happy chatter faded when there was a volley of impatient-sounding raps on the front door.

72

'I'll go,' Tilly said but was stopped by her mother who looked a little concerned and hurried to the hall. 'Wait there, I'll see to it,' Olive called over her shoulder.

'One day Mum will see I'm not a little girl any more and quite able to answer the front door in the blackout,' Tilly laughed but her amusement was short-lived when she saw Drew standing behind her mother.

'You'd better go into the corridor,' Olive told Tilly, her eyes troubled. 'Drew has something he wants to say to you.' Tilly felt her heart slump in her chest; this didn't look good. It didn't look good at all.

'Drew?' was all she could manage before she noticed his suitcase. No! Her mind refused to believe what she could see with her own eyes.

She didn't like this. Not one bit. Drew hadn't dressed in his best suit to go fire-watching. Her instincts were bristling now, telling her that no matter what he was about to say, there was nothing she could do about it.

'I have to go. Forthwith.' Drew made an attempt at humour but it didn't work.

'Forthwith?' Tilly asked, bemused, but his answer came all too swiftly, and a chill sliced right through her.

'It means I have to go away tonight.' Drew's voice dropped to a whisper as he gazed into her tearful blue eyes. 'Now. Immediately. I have to catch the flight my father has arranged tonight...' His smile slipped a little and she could see tears brimming in his eyes.

'You mean you can get a flight to the States at

73

such short notice, even though you're not in the Forces?'

'If there are seats available you can be sure my father will wangle one,' Drew said.

'Why do you have to go, Drew?' Tilly's voice was barely a whisper as she asked the question. His mother was ill, he was telling her. He'd be back some time soon. *Some* time, soon? She couldn't bear the thought of not seeing him every day.

'I knew I would have to go back someday, you knew that, tell me you did, Tilly.' Drew searched her face as if imprinting her beauty on his memory forever. 'I tried to leave you with the letter but I couldn't. I had to see you one more time...' He tried to keep the obvious misery from his voice but eventually he accepted defeat as his shoulders slumped and all his jovial bravado disappeared. 'Tilly, I gotta say...' There was a strange look in his eyes, like he was trying to read her, 'today was swell, I never wanted it to end...'

'I'll never see you again!' Tilly gasped the words that suddenly struck her, forcing them from her lips. She wanted to get away from this, be anywhere except listening to her one true love tell her he was going tonight. This isn't right, she thought frantically, first she lost her father then her grandparents – now Drew was leaving her, too. She'd never get over it, she wouldn't! Tilly could see his beautiful lips moving and forced herself to concentrate.

'I won't be gone forever, Tilly, you know that, don't you?' Drew gently took her in his strong arms. But Tilly didn't know any such thing. His plane could be shot down in the middle of the

Atlantic. His father might not allow him to come back. Anything could happen.

'You're too beautiful to stay away from, my darling, you make my every day complete...'

'I don't know what I'll do without you.' Tilly blinked her tears away but more came.

'My mother is very ill.' He looked down at her for a long time as if trying to choose the right words. But there were none. Drew took a long, deep breath, whilst Tilly tried to swallow the restriction in her throat that had suddenly threatened to choke her.

'Do you remember when I told you that I may have to go back to the States someday?' Tilly nodded like a child who needed to be reassured and he continued, 'I prayed every night that they could find a cure for Mom, and for a while that seemed to be the case.' Tears were running freely down his handsome face now. 'I longed to stay with you in this wonderful, devastated place where there is so much love, and a kind of freedom I never had before...'

'Oh, Drew,' Tilly whispered, unable to say any more when he gently placed the tip of his finger on her lips.

'I dreamed we would set up home together. I planned to build us a house when this war is over ... our children go to decent schools, be happy and free. I dreamed that one day we would have the perfect life, oh, honey, please don't cry any more, I can't bear it...' Drew gently outlined her face, his touch almost imperceptible, before kissing her tears away. 'I will come back to you as soon as I can, I promise.'

Tilly had to believe his words or how else could she let him go? They had both known he would have to go home someday. But it would always be too soon.

'I will come for you, believe me.' The forced smile on his lips did not reach his eyes and Tilly could not control her agony any longer. Her body gave way to deep, shuddering, convulsive sobs and he held her for a long time, until she was exhausted.

'Oh, Drew,' Tilly said eventually, calmer now, remembering the unopened letter still in her hands. 'Were you really going to leave me without saying goodbye?'

'I couldn't – I know that now.' His words, low, threaded through her hair.

'You promised that you would take care of me,' Tilly said, her head on his chest, longing to behave with dignity, since she didn't want him to remember her with red, swollen eyes and a blotchy face, but it was useless, she couldn't control this desperate emotion that was seizing her and in the end she didn't care that she was making a fool of herself.

Drew held her for a long time, silently stroking her hair. Then gently he held her at arm's length and said in a calm, quiet voice, 'My darling Tilly...' Tears filled his own eyes. 'Please don't send our ring back to me.' His voice ebbed and, unable to speak now, Drew bent and tenderly kissed her wet cheek.

Tilly gazed up at him, her arms circling his neck, and through a mist of tears she too was unable to voice her loving, if selfish, thoughts, knowing he had to go. He had no choice. She had a powerful,

76

unbreakable bond with her mother and Tilly knew how devastated she would feel if anything should ever happen to her. How could she deny the man she loved his need to see his own mother, perhaps for the last time? She must let Drew go with the knowledge she would be here waiting for him when he got back. Because, for her to get through this, she had to believe he was coming back. He would come back. She knew he would.

'I love you, Tilly Robbins.' Drew's voice was gravelled with emotion. 'I will write to you every day. You know that, don't you?' He had a desperate need to be reassured. With scalding tears streaming down her cheeks Tilly nodded, her voice refusing to articulate this love she would feel until her dying day.

'I'll leave you with a kiss to build a dream on until we can be together again,' he said before kissing her with a fevered power that took Tilly's breath away. Then, reluctantly, he walked away. His back was stiff, his head held high as he made his way to the waiting cab.

Tilly watched as its door clunked shut and she waited, desperate for him to turn and wave out of the back window. He didn't. She waited, and waited, until long after the reverberations of the taxi's engine could no longer be heard and the chill of the night air caught at her throat. She felt weak with grief, and the eerie silence that had wrapped itself around her was broken now only by her devastated sobs as the vibrant colour of her world disappeared, making everything grey, drab and miserable.

Her mother's protective arm around her

quaking shoulders was just too much right now and she shrugged it away. She didn't want to be cajoled or coaxed into being calm. She wanted to scream, she wanted to throw herself on the floor, to kick, and beat her fists. She couldn't bear it! She would die!

'Come on, my darling.' Her mother's voice came from somewhere a long way off. 'Let's get you inside.'

'Oh, Mum,' Tilly sobbed; her head buried in the crook of her elbow. 'I don't know what to do.' The crumpled letter she had received from her darling Drew was crushed in her shaking hands. He'd sworn to her in church that he would love her forever and she so wanted to believe that as her trembling fingers turned the ring that was now obviously on the third finger of her left hand, the one that she had proudly showed off when she and Drew arrived home from holiday. Tilly had ignored the pained expression on her mother's face, willing her to be as happy as she was. Drew's promise to love her and be with her forever more was still deeply etched on her memory.

'Oh, Mum, how will I be able to carry on without him?'

'You will find a way, my darling, we women always do.' Olive rose from where she had been sitting on the corner of Tilly's bed and went to her daughter's side, cocooning her in a loving embrace. Hadn't she, too, had to endure the departure of the man she loved at an early age? 'I know you are hurting,' Olive said, rocking Tilly back and forth, 'but you must be strong. Drew will come back, I'm sure.' But even to her own ears the words didn't sound convincing.

'I don't think I will ever see him again, Mum,' Tilly cried, and it's not just the war. As soon as he gets home he will be back in his father's clutches again.' Her voice wavered as the fragrance of summer grass, still clinging to her clothes, reminded her that only a few short hours ago she and Drew were the happiest couple in Hyde Park – or so she had thought. When he'd gently outlined her face with his fingertip and lovingly stroked her hair, was he trying to find the words to tell her he was going away? Or was he counting the minutes knowing his flight would be leaving soon?

'Shh, my darling, don't cry,' Olive whispered, worrying now if Tilly had the strength and maturity to carry on alone, without him. She hoped so, otherwise the girl was lost.

All Olive could do was be there for her heart-broken daughter, and see her through this painful episode as best she could. As a mother she knew she would do everything in her power to prevent the pain and suffering Tilly was going through now.

SIX

'Dulcie,' Olive called up the stairs, 'you have a letter here.'

Dulcie pulled the blanket high up to her chin, wondering if she had truly heard Olive calling her, or if she was still asleep; that luxurious pastime seemed to be in short supply since her work at the munitions factory took up most of her waking hours of late. She wasn't sure if it was the repetitive drilling of holes and riveting metal or the long, laborious shifts that robbed her of her stamina. But whatever it was she intended to finish her sleep today.

'Dulcie!' There was no mistaking Olive's voice this time. Dulcie opened one blurred eye and tried to focus on the little alarm clock she had managed to save from the salvage people, who took everything they deemed necessary to go towards the building of airplanes and ammunition.

What time was it, she wondered as the muzzy wakefulness began to irritate her. Or, more importantly – what day was it? She had been sent home from the factory yesterday because of a stomach upset, in case she passed it on to every other worker. Thankfully Olive let her rest when she said that she felt so ghastly and also telephoned the munitions factory from the call box at the end of Article Row to say she wouldn't be in today either.

'Dulcie, did you hear me?' Olive called again. 'There is someone here to see you.'

'Ohhh, go away,' Dulcie groaned, feeling nauseous now. If she moved quickly she was sure she was going to disgrace herself and throw up all over Olive's clean linoleum. She must have eaten something that didn't agree with her from the newly installed canteen, or maybe it was the whelks her mother had plied her with when she went to see her on Sunday for church. Whatever it was she doubted she could hang on to it much longer.

Olive had chanced a little tap on the door earlier, giving Dulcie an old-fashioned look when she made no effort to get up, then she put a sanitary towel, a Beecham's pill and a glass of water on the bedside table, and told her she would be back later. Dulcie had said she just needed a long sleep; she didn't need any pads or powders today, thank you very much.

Thoughts were lazily drifting through her rising consciousness, and as she became more alert questions formed. When was the last time she had been in need of a sanitary pad? Sitting up quickly in bed, she realised it must have been about seven weeks ago! She put her lateness down to the upset caused by Wilder running off with her sister, Edith.

She knew she wasn't the world's most regular girl so it didn't bother her too much that she hadn't seen her 'visitors', as she always called her monthly period; after all, nothing had happened between her and Wilder. She'd made sure of that, and now she was glad the cheating airman hadn't been able to chalk her up as another willing English girl eager to catch herself a handsome, love-'em-and-leave-'em American. And she was sure that Reece Redgrave didn't count.

Dulcie had put her air-raid shelter tryst with the young airman down to nothing more than an accidental misunderstanding. It had only been the once and everybody knew that girls could not get caught the first time – and anyway, it had only lasted for moments, not even minutes. Nobody got caught that fast. Dulcie's heartbeat raced, and beads of perspiration broke out on her top lip and her forehead. You couldn't get caught that easily, surely?

'Dulcie, did you hear me? There is someone here with a letter for you.' It was only when she heard Olive's obvious impatience that she realised the urgency. Her mind automatically darted to her brother, Rick, whose regiment had been deployed to the desert; she knew because she had actually seen him on the Pathé newsreel at the pictures. His regiment was in Tobruk and had been taken by surprise and captured by the Axis forces. They had got word that he had been taken as a prisoner of war.

Dulcie's mind was racing as she pulled back the sheets and blankets. She knew that the authorities would send a telegram to her parents if anything had happened to Rick – but they had moved from the East End! Scrambling from the bed her foot got caught in the bedclothes making her stumble. What if he had been involved in an accident? Surely his platoon sergeant would come to her in person. No! They would go to Edith now. Her parents! What if something had happened to them? Oh lord, she thought, there was a war on, people were dying and she was laid up with a stomach bug! She had to do her bit, no matter what. Keep calm and carry on, that's what the posters said. What if something had happened to her family? The niggling voice persisted. All self-pitying thoughts suddenly went out of her head now as she scrambled into her pink dressing gown she'd bought second-hand from a stall in Portobello market.

Berating herself for her unkempt appearance as

she lurched from the room, Dulcie felt her stomach heave again. She hadn't felt this bad since... In her haste to be downstairs she realised she had never felt this bad. Tying the belt of her dressing gown around her so tightly she could hardly breathe, she saw Olive at the bottom of the stairs.

'There's a young American airman in the front room and he wants to see you.' Olive looked calm and motherly now as Dulcie almost fell on the final step.

'Who is he?' Dulcie asked as her heart began to race. Olive knew Wilder so it couldn't be him. She watched as her landlady shrugged her shoulders. 'What does he look like?' She surmised Reece Redgrave had come to visit. Well, she thought, if he had she would give him a piece of her mind. Coming here unannounced and uninvited! How dare he!

Turning, she checked her appearance in the oval oak-encased mirror on the wall opposite the stairs, then, grabbing the comb that was kept on the little occasional table, she ran it quickly through her hair and grimaced, wondering if she looked sufficiently ill to garner a tremendous amount of sympathy. Taking a deep breath and smoothing down the pink imitation-silk dressing gown she strode, head high, shoulders back, towards the front room like a leading lady about to make her Broadway debut.

Sweeping through the door she was dismayed to see that it wasn't Reece Redgrave who was sitting on Olive's best settee. As soon as she entered the room the airman stood up and offered his hand to

83

Dulcie, whilst in the other he had an envelope.

'Hello, ma'am, my name is Joe; I'm a friend of Reece Redgrave...'

'Oh, he's sent you to do his dirty work, has he?' Dulcie said, angry now that he wasn't who she thought he would be.

'I don't know about that, ma'am,' said the surprised American, 'but he's been moping around the barracks, he didn't go out nor nothin'. This letter is for you, it has your name and address on it so I thought I would deliver it...' The rest of his words were left unsaid as Dulcie seized the letter he was holding out.

'I suppose it's a grovelling apology. Well, if he thinks he can get around me by sending his messenger he's got another think coming because I'm not won over that easily.' She was so annoyed that Reece had sent one of his buddies to give her the letter. 'Some English girls have more pride than to fall at the feet of the next American airman who winks his eye and snaps his fingers, and another thing,' she began as she roughly tore open the envelope and pulled out the letter.

'I'm afraid he's dead, ma'am,' the airman said simply.

Dulcie heard a gasp and she realised that Olive was standing behind her.

'This was in his locker; it was sealed and addressed to you so we thought it only right that it should be delivered. I am so sorry to be the bearer of bad news, ma'am. He was shot down off the coast of Northern Ireland.'

Dulcie's hands shook so badly she almost dropped the letter, and after hurrying up the stairs she slammed the bedroom door and cried bitter tears until she was physically sick. She was still sobbing when Olive knocked a couple of minutes later.

'Can I come in?'

Dulcie barely choked her consent and she couldn't even utter the words screaming inside her head. Reece was dead. It was a nightmare. She'd met him fleetingly. She'd forgotten that she told him where she lived because she was so proud of her address. She hadn't expected him to remember it so vividly, but, she recalled, he had no family, but he must have somebody – anybody. Surely she wasn't the only girl he had been friendly with?

Dulcie cried as she tried to make out his neat, copperplate handwriting that told her he was sorry he had mistaken her friendliness for something else and that he really did like her a lot. He went on to say that although he had never been loved like that before he would always treasure the memory and he hoped that she would too. He really liked her and thought she was a great gal, and if he could summon up the courage to ever send this letter he would love to ask her out and start all over again...

Dulcie quickly wiped away her tears with the pad of her hand. He must have written the letter just after... She couldn't bring herself to think about the time in the air-raid shelter. She had been so wanton, so decadently immoral and ... drunk! But not drunk enough to forget.

Dulcie could not ignore the fact that she gave Reece his first and probably his last thrill of a woman's body. And now he was dead.

'Here, drink this,' Olive said as she sat on the

bed and handed her the glass of water. Dulcie looked into Olive's kind, motherly eyes and without any need of proof, she knew for certain now that she was carrying Reece's baby.

'Oh, Olive,' Dulcie cried, 'is Sally home?'

'No, Dulcie, she isn't,' Olive said, 'but judging by the look of you I think I'd better call Dr Shaw.'

All morning Sally carried out her duties with a smile on her face, a spring in her step and a song in her heart. The sun was shining through the sash windows of the Nightingale ward where injured servicemen were recovering in regimented rows of iron beds whilst a few of them had actually commented on her sunny personality.

'You look like the cat what's got the cream, Nurse,' said one Geordie wag before she briskly popped a thermometer in his mouth and plumped his pillows.

'You can't beat a lovely sunny morning,' Sally smiled, giving nothing away. Everything could have been so different if George had accepted back his engagement ring and they had actually broken up, when they'd had their big discussion earlier in the year. She had been so sure he wouldn't want a ready-made family, and she couldn't have rejected baby Alice after all she had been through. It wasn't the child's fault, after all, that she had been born into such a treacherous family.

However, George had proved he had a heart of gold when Sally returned home to Article Row to find him playing in the back garden with baby Alice and reassuring Sally that nothing could diminish the love he felt for her.

'There's a dark cloud coming over that horizon though,' said a patient on the other side of the men's surgical ward, 'so I'd enjoy it whilst it lasts if I were you, Nurse.'

'Don't be such a pessimist, soldier,' Sally laughed, knowing nothing could dampen her spirits today. When her morning shift was over, George was meeting her for lunch, as he had come to Bart's to see her, having a couple of days off from the Queen Victoria, and she couldn't wait to see him. They were going to the National Gallery, as Olive was taking Alice out for the afternoon, and she was so looking forward to their time together.

But an hour later as she and George left Bart's, the soldier's forecast became reality when the clouds burst and a powerful downpour came so quickly and so forcefully it bounced off the pavement and had them running for the nearest shelter.

'Let's get something to eat before we go to the gallery,' George said, pulling up the collar of his Crombie overcoat and lowering the brim of his herringbone-patterned trilby against the deluge, whilst Sally wrestled with her umbrella against an unseasonal sudden gust of wind. George took the umbrella and opened it with ease before Sally linked her arm through his. His long, rapid strides caused her to almost run to keep up with him.

'Hey, what's the rush? You must be hungry.' Sally gave a small, nervous laugh. George seemed preoccupied, his thoughts elsewhere and he certainly was not talkative.

'Is something the matter, George?' Sally looked up at him and, with his head bent and him being slightly ahead of her, she couldn't read his expression beneath the rim of his hat. Being a quiet, thoughtful man by nature it wasn't unusual for the two of them to walk in a companionable silence, each lost in their own idyllic thoughts of the future, content in the security of their love for each other.

But that was before she told George about Alice. He still wanted to stand by his promise to spend the rest of his life with her, he had assured her, but since then his whole manner had become so different from the way he had been before that Sally worried George was having second thoughts. With her arm outstretched in an effort to keep hold of his coat sleeve she wasn't sure he wanted to be with her at all today.

'Let's go in here,' George said, steering her into a nearby British Restaurant, almost causing her to trip. Then, steadying her without a word, his eyes seemed to say it all. Their usually warm glow was replaced with a sad reproach. She had never seen him like this, and momentarily it unnerved her as she could feel her heart sinking.

'George?' Sally wanted the truth, and she wanted it now. 'Have I said something wrong?'

'No, darling,' George said quickly – too quickly, 'of course you haven't.' He took her hand and wrapped his capable, talented fingers around hers as he edged her into the window seat they were lucky enough to bag even though the place was busy with lunchtime workers and shoppers.

After placing her umbrella in the stand near the

door George went to find a waitress and Sally watched him. He looked tired, suddenly. She hadn't noticed that before, and she wondered if he was getting enough sleep. There hadn't been an air raid for a few weeks now, so his shift patterns were more stable than they had been during the worst of the Blitz. But Sally still worried that he did too much, knowing he thought nothing of jumping into another shift if the hospital was busy, or if another doctor needed help he would be the first to offer.

Feeling slightly uneasy sitting in full view of people passing the window, with its criss-cross tape adorning the large plate glass, Sally turned her engagement ring around her finger, mesmerised by the glint from the weak rays of sunshine now popping through the clouds as the rain eased, and was glad when George returned to the table.

'They said the menu is on the wall,' he informed Sally. 'Anything you fancy?'

'Just soup for me,' she answered after quickly studying what was on offer today and not really wanting anything to eat for some reason. She had been so happy and full of hope this morning. For the first time in weeks she felt she could tell George anything. But now she wasn't so sure.

'I know it must have come as a shock when I told you about Alice,' Sally ventured as they waited for their order, all the time watching him closely, worrying what impact her words were having. 'I was concerned that, being such a kind and gentle man, you would feel duty bound to take the two of us on after saying you would and then regret it but be too kind to say so?'

'It isn't like that, Sally.' George gave her hand a gentle squeeze. 'That's not the case at all. I think Alice is a lovely child and I would be proud to bring her up as my own. I am so glad you told me about her, because I want to get to know and love her as much as you do.'

'Then what's wrong George?' Sally asked, knowing George had been acting strangely for a while now and she still didn't have a clue why. He seemed even more reserved and distracted than usual. And given that he wouldn't look her in the eye, as he usually did, she wondered if he really had gone off her and was trying to gently let her down. 'Is it me, George?' She had to know.

'No, never!' She saw the look of alarm flash across his face. 'Never, never would I stop loving you, Sally, I couldn't.'

'Be that as it may,' Sally answered, acknowledging he sounded sincere enough, and in his heart he probably meant every word. But what about his family? What would they think of their talented son taking up with a girl who had a child to bring up? George might have every intention in the world of bringing up Alice, but his mother could well have other ideas, and it was this thought that worried her now.

Sally didn't have time to answer as the waitress brought them each a bowl of vegetable soup and some bread. There was an uneasy silence between them now broken only by the low buzz of conversation from fellow diners and the distant singing voices of Flanagan and Allen urging the rabbit to run, run, run.

And Sally knew exactly how it felt, as they com-

90

pleted the rest of their meal in a strained silence. If it hadn't been for the fact that it would be a criminal waste of good food she would have left it, as her appetite had all but disappeared, and she was having a difficult job of swallowing the soup even though it really was delicious. Slowly they managed to clear their bowls, each lost in their thoughts.

'Have you had enough to eat?' George asked and Sally nodded with an air of inevitability; the meal had been a disaster, and after George threw half a crown onto the little plate for the two threepenny soups, he helped her into her coat. They walked out of the restaurant without waiting for the two shillings change and Sally knew the smiling waitress was going to have a happy day today with such a good tip to spend.

'Sally, I...' He was finding it hard to say what needed to be said, so she helped him.

'George, do you mind if we don't go to the gallery? I am so tired, I didn't sleep well last night, Alice was fractious and...'

'No my dear, certainly not.' His words came out in a relieved rush. 'I have a mountain of paperwork, and reports coming up to my knees.' He gave a small stab at humour but neither of them was in the mood for frivolity. 'I will walk you back to Article Row and...'

'I don't mind walking alone if you have to take the train back to the hospital,' Sally lied. She did mind. She minded terribly, but there was nothing she could do about it as the sinking sensation of disappointment threatened to overwhelm her. However, quietly, she refused to let George see her disappointment.

'I wouldn't dream of letting you walk home on your own. Anyway, I'm staying in Drew's room just for a couple of nights, now that he's gone back to America,' George said kindly, taking her hand as if there was nothing wrong. 'Makes me feel quite nostalgic for when everyone used to lodge there. You must have a rest, you look tired.'

'Alice will soon put paid to that idea,' Sally laughed with forced brightness, 'but Olive will welcome the break from looking after her, I should imagine.'

'I'm sure she won't,' George said, unconsciously tucking her hand into his pocket, something he had done since they spent their weekend away together. 'From what I've seen, Alice is smothered with love from every direction; she's a very lucky little girl to have such an adoring female family.'

Sally looked up at him and for the first time that day he smiled, really smiled, as if the thought actually brought him pleasure and for a fleeting moment Sally wanted to beg him to spend the rest of the day with her, but she didn't. Her pride wouldn't let her.

Back at number 13, Article Row, George politely refused Olive's offer of a cup of tea, explaining he had a lot of work to finish before the next morning. And after walking with him down the long hallway, Sally was more than a little surprised when she received a chaste kiss on her cheek. Placing his trilby hat on his head at a jaunty angle, George turned without another word and walked out of the front door.

Olive recounted to Sally that she'd had to call

the doctor for Dulcie who had received a terrible shock: a friend of Wilder's, whom she had known too, had been shot down and killed the night before.

'I'll check on her later,' Sally said a little distractedly, looking out of the window.

'Is something the matter, Sally?' Olive asked, her voice full of concern when she came into the kitchen after checking on Dulcie and putting baby Alice down for her afternoon nap. 'You look a bit pale, I hope you're not coming down with this bug as well.' She didn't like to see the young woman so down.

'I think George has gone off me now he knows about Alice,' Sally said abruptly.

'No!' Olive's eyes widened: she'd worried this might happen after their weekend away together. And even though they were a very mature, responsible couple, George had savoured the fruit of Sally's love, and now it looked like he was losing his appetite. Olive sighed; she didn't have George down as a love-'em-and-leave-'em type of chap but who knew what was going on in a man's mind these days?

'Oh, don't mind me,' Sally countered. 'I'm being silly, I'm sure everything will be fine,' she added over-brightly, not sure at all.

'Of course it will,' Olive said. 'George is very busy; his mind must be full of worries.' 'Worries' being the war and the added casualties, she thought, pulling her chair from under the table, knowing everybody was under a huge amount of added pressure. However she couldn't bear to see 'her girls' upset, and even if she was overstepping the mark she wouldn't let any of them suffer alone and in silence; one never knew what the next few hours could bring.

'I did think he looked a little pre-occupied, if you don't mind me saying...'

'Oh, you're right, Olive, he's been ever so busy at the hospital,' Sally said quickly, 'and in his spare time he has to deal with writing up all those reports and...' It was no use, her throat constricted and her chin trembled and she couldn't continue. Without any more warning Sally suddenly burst into floods of tears. In a flash Olive was at her side, cooing and shushing her like her mother used to do, cocooning her convulsive shoulders.

'Never mind, my dear,' Olive cooed, 'you just let it all out.' After a few moments Sally's tears receded and Olive offered her hot tea after putting in an extra half spoon of sugar and put down the cup, which thanks to the shortages was resting on a mismatched saucer. 'Drink this whilst it's hot, it'll do you the world of good.'

'Tea solves all ills.' Sally didn't intend her voice to sound so abrupt. 'I didn't mean to sound ungrateful...'

'Don't you give it another thought, my dear,' Olive said, stalling Sally's apologies. 'You don't have to say anything if you don't want to, but I'm here if you need me.' She resumed her seat on the other side of the table and her warm, caring eyes viewed Sally's sadness with maternal compassion. 'You know where I am if you ever need a shoulder to cry on, or an ear to listen.'

'Thank you, Olive, I'll remember that.' Sally gave

the other woman a watery smile before blowing
her nose and shrugging a little. She couldn't possibly tell Olive that there was also the question of
what would happen to Alice if she and George
didn't marry now; someone had to look after the
child – and she had to work. How else would they
be able to afford to live in Article Row if she wasn't
earning? Olive was a wonderful woman, everybody
knew that, but she couldn't conjure up food and
heating out of thin air.

'Why don't you go over to him?' Olive asked
Sally after draining her cup. 'You will feel much
better if you know one way or the other.'

'Know what?' Sally asked weakly, not feeling
strong enough for this.

'Know how much work he has to do, maybe you
could help.' Sally looked at Olive and wondered if
she should? She knew she wouldn't rest until she
and George had cleared the air and she found out
what his problem was, because it was obvious
there was one, no matter how much he tried to
persuade her everything was fine. Also, Sally knew
she couldn't risk another night without sleep.

'Go on,' Olive said, 'take as much time as you
like, Alice is fine here with us.'

Sally jumped up before her courage could fail
her again and she gave Olive a huge hug. 'Thank
you, thank you so much.'

'Get away with you.' Olive smiled and rolled
her eyes. 'And don't come back here until you've
got everything sorted out once and for all.' She
knew her girls seemed wrapped up in their own
personal conflicts now. She had to be strong for
all of them.

In Hyde Park on their last day together, Tilly thought, Drew had let her waffle on, talking about the war and how it must feel to lose somebody they loved, and all the time he was aware that he, too, could lose the woman who had brought him into the world and gave him life. Drew, kind, loving Drew, who had let her talk of how things could be, when all along his heart was breaking.

A dry sob shook her body as Tilly realised yet again how special he really was, how considerate of the feelings of others who were suffering even when his own emotions were being put to the test.

Unable to hold it all together any longer, the dam of Tilly's sorrow burst forth and scalding tears coursed down her cheeks. Alone in her room she dared not let her mother see her until her tears had subsided and she didn't think that would be for a good while yet.

However, she realised when she could think more clearly, lying still and calmer now, it wasn't Drew's mother she had cried for – she didn't know the woman – but she did know that Drew would be deeply shocked and saddened. And it was he who was deserving of her commiserations now. Tilly knew he felt things more keenly than most people. He cared deeply for those he didn't even know, so she could only imagine how his mother's passing would devastate him. He would be suffering so much and she was heartbroken that she could not be by his side to comfort and console him. And this grieved her more than words could say.

Feeling a little reckless and with Olive's encouragement still ringing in her ears Sally knew she wasn't going to let George go as easily as she first imagined she would. Slipping the key he had given her earlier into the Yale lock, Sally vowed she would coax him with her own method of loving, which would persuade him that she and Alice were the only family he would ever need. And as Drew had gone back to America she knew they wouldn't be interrupted.

Silently opening the sitting-room door Sally wasn't surprised that the only sound in the house was the heartbeat tick of the clock on the mantelpiece, and knowing George would be concentrating on his files in the study she crept in so as not to disturb him. However, as she stepped into the room another unexpected sound could be heard.

The clink of a bottle hitting the rim of a crystal glass was followed by the gentle glug of liquid being poured, and Sally wondered, all of a sudden, if she was intruding. Maybe George had company? Her heart beat accelerated.

'Hello, George,' Sally managed to say quietly when she saw him at the sideboard and realised he was alone. George had been oblivious to her presence it seemed, going by his astonished expression when he wheeled around and spilled some of his drink. 'I'm sorry, I didn't mean to startle you.' But it wasn't his look of amazement that gave Sally cause for concern – it was the realisation that he was absolutely stumbling drunk.

'Shally.' George slurred her name and raised his glass, giving her a lopsided half-smile. 'Come and have a little drinky with me.'

'I think you've had enough, George.' She had left him not more than an hour ago. How could he possibly have got himself into this state in such a short space of time? He must have drunk the alcohol like water.

'C'mon, let's have a little drinky and then...' His eyes had a glassy gleam she had never seen before, and she wasn't sure she liked it. He flapped the brandy bottle in the air and invited her, with a come-hither wave of his other hand, to join him. Sally wasn't even sure he could see her properly, he was so drunk. However, he wasn't so drunk he didn't notice her hesitation. Slowly, with great concentration, he placed the bottle on the sideboard, then, taking a deep breath, he said in slow, measured tones, 'Shally ... let me exshplain ... hic...' His intoxicated state had led to an outbreak of hiccups, which he found quite amusing – even though Sally did not when she recognised he was so sloshed he couldn't make it back to the sofa unaided.

'Here, let me help you before you fall over.' Sally wrinkled her nose as he tried to give her a big wet slobbery kiss on the cheek and succeeded in landing in a dishevelled heap on the sofa, scattering cushions and laughing inanely at nothing in particular. She knew George wasn't a heavy drinker; in fact neither of them cared much for alcohol. Instead they much preferred going to the pictures or the theatre, but most of all they liked to keep a clear head. So for George to get into this state Sally knew he must have something very disturbing on his mind.

'I'll get you a cup of black coffee, George, it

might sober you up a little,' Sally said in her most professional, no-nonsense voice which she used to settle unruly squaddies who tried it on. She turned to leave the room, but felt herself being held back by her wrist, and as she quickly turned she found herself being pulled towards George, and landed on top of him with a thump. For as much as she loved him and would usually welcome such an intimate embrace, Sally wasn't too keen on the strong brandy smell that seemed to emanate from his every pore, nor the one-eyed stare as he tried to focus.

'Let me get you that coffee, darling,' Sally said in her most soothing tones as she scrambled to her feet. There was absolutely nothing George could do to stop her as he couldn't get to his own feet in such an inebriated condition, and in fact he was so far gone he couldn't keep his other eye open either.

When Sally returned moments later with two cups of black coffee, George's head was hanging over the side of the settee, his tongue lolling from the side of his mouth and he was snoring like an overstuffed pig. Sally noticed the brandy glass, balanced precariously between his fingers, was spilling its contents onto the carpet. George, she noted with concern, was dead to the world and experiencing no pain, but Sally couldn't guarantee he would feel that way when he woke up later; in fact she would lay money on him feeling very sorry for himself.

Looking at him now, even in this drunken state, she knew she would forgive him, eventually. However, she worried it would be too dangerous to leave him alone.

'What if you vomited in your sleep?' Sally asked the unconscious George. 'You could choke to death. What if you tried to climb the stairs? You could fall down and break your neck!' No, she thought, there was nothing for it but to stay until he was safely awake. 'And when you wake up later with a screaming hangover there will be words, George, and most of them will be coming from me.'

It was late and growing dark when George began to stir, and Sally could tell just by the putty-coloured tinge around his gills that he was suffering an explosive hangover.

'Feeling queasy, George?' Sally asked, secretly satisfied he wasn't feeling up to answering her back. 'You have slept like a dead man for hours, I daren't leave you.' She hoped that Olive wouldn't be too cross about looking after Alice all this time, but it was imperative she made sure George was safe. 'I've taken advantage of Olive's good nature for too long already, George,' she said, watching as he leaned forward and buried his head in his two hands. 'I can't expect her to look after Alice indefinitely.'

'Sally, darling, can you just be quiet for one moment.' George had never so much as disagreed with her before now, and she was shocked to the core to hear him telling her to shut up now. She opened her mouth to say something in retaliation and then, thinking better of it, she closed it again. How could he speak to her like this? Was this the proof she needed that he had gone off her after all and decided to drink himself into oblivion before he could break the bad news? 'I've joined up,' he said simply, looking defeated. Momentarily, not one single thought passed through Sally's dumbfounded brain. Then the realisation began to creep in. Joined up? Joined up!

'But George, you have a job here!'

'A safe job, you mean!' George looked so angry when he said that and then he told her he had enlisted in the Royal Navy that very morning as a ship's surgeon and no matter how many times he tried to get it into her head that he was doing the honourable thing Sally would not listen.

She was so angry she left him standing in the middle of the room looking dishevelled and smelling like a brewery whilst she went to make him some black coffee. Once she had gathered her thoughts together she would decide on what to do next.

'Don't you understand, Sally, I need to do this.' George followed her to the kitchen 'I cannot let my fellow countrymen down and hide behind the privilege of a consultancy – oh, did I tell you I got the consultant's job?– Today, would you believe.' He gave a hard, almost bitter laugh; Sally knew he'd waited so long for the position.

'But, George, you are needed here!' Her words, so strangled, were barely audible.

'Tell me, Sally, who needs me more than those poor brave men torpedoed out of the water?'

'I do, George,' Sally answered, all her fight depleted now.

SEVEN

Drew knew there were two ways to go to the mall. There was the lower east side, which was the shortest route and the one everybody usually took. That meant passing where all his old buddies hung out, who would no doubt want to know about England or ask about his mother's funeral yesterday and he didn't want to talk about it. Then there was the longer way round, which of course took longer.

Although, he silently reasoned, if he took the short route he wouldn't need to take the car his father had bought him as a bribe to keep him in the States. However, the guys would stop him for catch-ups on every corner and he didn't need that today. His mind made up, he decided to take the Chevrolet Sedan to the mall.

Feeling unusually unsociable because he was missing Tilly so much, Drew knew Al's Diner was the only place he could get a burger on rye and a fresh cup of coffee without being badgered for information about his trip overseas. As the car glided to a halt outside the diner, he wanted to think about the wonderful girl he'd left in London.

Sitting on the high stool at the counter waiting for his order he settled, once more, into the familiar smell of hot percolated coffee and fresh doughnuts that had been absent in England. But it was Tilly, so keenly missed, that he wanted right now.

He wondered how long it would take for her mail to reach here, knowing he couldn't go much longer without hearing from her. His mind was in turmoil. What if she got hurt – or worse? A pony-tailed girl in bobby socks, carrying school text books, sat next to him and smiled. Drew, not having the heart to ignore her, smiled back, but heck, he wasn't in the mood for talking right now.

'Say, didn't you used to live in England?' she asked and Drew nodded. 'My brother's over there,' she continued in a forthright way, 'he's in Liverpool – have you heard of it?'

'Yeah, I've heard of it.' Drew said, shrugging his shoulders. He was glad when her girlfriends came into the diner drooling over the latest Frank Sinatra photo in a magazine. Drew sighed with relief.

His father had used every trick in the book, Drew knew, short of actually having him arrested to keep him here. But he was determined when he'd finished the latest harebrained assignment his father set for him he was going back to Tilly. His wonderful mother was gone now, so what did he have to stay here for?

His thoughts drifted back to London and girls no older than the ones in the booth across the shiny blue-and-yellow tiled floor sharing a soda, who would be working in munitions factories or driving buses. They would be on fire-watch duty like his Tilly, or manning ack-ack guns like the girls in the Forces, dressing the open, livid wounds of their brave countrymen like Sally or keeping essential services going like Agnes, brave women one and all...

Distracted, he took a peek at the newspaper his father published. It was being read by a large truck driver sitting next to him who didn't lift his head when he called to the waitress for eggs over easy, whilst the young girl across the floor dropped a dime in the juke box. Everything was so normal here, a million miles away from the devastation in London. He listened to the haunting melody of Glenn Miller's 'At Last' fade to be replaced by the whirr and click of another record dropping on the Wurlitzer juke box, with its flashing lights and glass-domed top.

Drew managed to sit at the diner counter only long enough for the beautifully melodious tones of Vera Lynn's voice to tell him there'd be blue birds over the white cliffs of Dover, which caused a restriction so tight in his throat he could hardly swallow. The last time he'd heard that song he and Tilly were dancing together, making plans for their future. It was all too much and he couldn't take any more.

'Skip the order,' Drew managed to say to the waitress behind the counter who didn't bat an eyelash at his request as they would have done in England, he noticed, for the simple reason that rationing hadn't hit here. Maybe it never would, he thought, who knew?

All he did know was that there was no shortage of food and drink at his mother's funeral, which had been like a who's who of his father's shallow supporters. All of them in the business of lightening his load if he wished to avail himself of their services, all of them his 'yes' men.

Listen to yourself. Drew angrily crossed the sidewalk to the Sedan. *You're already beginning to sound like one of Dad's people, who use ten words where two will do.*

'Oh, Tilly, I gotta get outta here!' Drew said aloud, ignoring the suspicious stares of people passing by. 'Oh, honey, why do we have to live so far apart?' He was so deep in thought he didn't even see the truck coming, nor hear the screams of the women who tried to grab his arm to stop him walking into the road. He didn't feel a thing.

'Get outta my way!' The doctor dressed from head to toe in theatre whites didn't care if he ran people down as he rushed the stretcher towards the operating theatre after another seizure had gripped Drew Coleman's body, stopping only momentarily to tell his father he would do everything he could.

'You'd better do more than that!' Andrew Coleman had growled over a chewed-up twelve-inch cigar hanging from the corner of his mouth. But as doctors later gathered around Drew's bed in the large, pristine Chicago hospital, they shook their heads in concern. Drew had been unconscious since he came in – he was someplace else, somewhere they couldn't reach. The best medics in the country had fought to save his life after he was hit by an oncoming truck getting into his automobile two blocks from his own home.

The daily letters from London, England, were dispatched to the huge safe in his father's office and remained there. Unopened.

Surely, thought Tilly, Drew would at least have written telling her he wanted his Harvard ring back if he'd decided their love was over? But what else was she to make of the complete lack of letters from him? Her fingers caressed the gold band she wore around her neck. They had made a pact that he would not ask for it unless he wanted nothing more to do with her, and she vowed she would not part with it unless she found somebody else. And that would never happen. Nobody could replace her wonderful, kind-hearted sweetheart. Nobody.

Tilly took comfort from the fact that Drew hadn't asked for the ring back and until he did she had no intentions of returning it. In her heart a small flicker of hope still burned.

Every night before she went to sleep she took out the band of gold that had initially been a sign of their good friendship. Then later inside the small country church cocooned within the moon's silver rays this ring had come to symbolise something that had become a deep abiding love between both of them, she was sure. She didn't know how she knew but she was certain that when Drew was ready he would come back for her one day. And when that day came she would be waiting for him, knowing he could only have been so earnest if he truly loved her, and when he said that he would love her until the days beyond forever she believed him. Drew had also been so steadfast that Tilly had no choice but to believe him. Surely he would have had to be an actor of great magnitude to be able to convince her he was true to his word if he really didn't love her? How could his love have been a sham?

It was impossible. Drew loved her and she loved him. They had a special bond that couldn't be broken no matter what anybody said. Drew was her one true love. Her soul mate. If they died tonight they would meet again in another life. He was the other part of her. Without him she was incomplete.

EIGHT

'Aren't you going out tonight, Agnes?' Olive had just finished listening to Valentine Dyall, owner of the deep sepulchral voice known to avid wireless listeners across the country as 'The Man in Black', who brought dark stories to his plucky audience. Agnes shook her head.

'I've just been listening to *Appointment with Fear*.' She paused for a moment and then a thought struck her. 'Oh. Agnes, is that why you spent so long in your room?' Agnes nodded her head and gave a little smile as she took her seat on the other side of the fireplace.

'I would have changed the station if I'd known you were staying in.' Olive thought it unusual for Agnes to be home on her night off, but knew she would never listen to ghost stories. The girl was frightened of her own shadow half the time.

'I don't mind, Olive, honestly. I was polishing my shoes for work tomorrow.'

Usually when Agnes and her chap, Ted, had a night off they went to the café with their own seat

107

near the window, and spent hours over one cup of tea each or they went for a walk along the Embankment; anything that was cheap – or even better, free – suited Ted. But she shouldn't think unkind thoughts. Olive gave herself a silent reprimand. He had a family to support, a mother who needed almost all of his money from what Olive could gather from her own observations; not that Agnes ever said anything, she thought the sun shone out of Ted – the only problem was, so did his clingy mother and she had the upper hand right now by the looks of it.

'I thought you and Ted would go out, seeing as there haven't been many night raids of late.'

'Nancy from next door,' Agnes said conversationally, 'told me the Allies were having a hard time of it at Tobruk, where Rick is serving.' She picked up the evening paper.

'I know, it's terrible. I really feel sorry for Dulcie now, especially since her American friend was killed; she has been very quiet since she got the news.' Olive shook her head, knowing she had initially been quite wrong about Dulcie; the girl wasn't flighty at all. Yes, she liked to give the impression that she had been everywhere and done everything and had men falling at her feet to take her to the Saturday night dances, but if the truth be known, Dulcie was just like any other girl trying to get by in these strange times. She had settled into the dangerous work at the munitions factory without carping, which surprised Olive no end.

She'd never thought she'd see the day Dulcie would parade up and down the hall in the style of a Paris catwalk model in a pair of navy-blue bib-and-brace overalls and wearing a turban over her immaculate curls. She recalled the impeccable if somewhat gaudy clothes the young woman wore when she first came to stay in Article Row. She sighed. War was changing all of them in one way or another.

'Ted tries to keep me away from the wireless,' Agnes was saying in her meek, almost inaudible voice, 'but I like to keep up with what's going on. He said it makes me fretful and suggests we go for long walks instead.'

'Does he now?' Olive suspected it was also to keep Agnes out of his hostile mother's way, but she didn't say anything else on the subject knowing Agnes was a simple soul who took people as she found them; she didn't go looking for people's faults and believed there was good in everybody. Olive had a hard time understanding the good in Ted's mother, there seemed so little of it.

'You don't want to listen to everything Nancy has to say either, Agnes, she sometimes gets things wrong.' Nancy, had her own version of events, and none of them were optimistic. 'Is Ted coming to pick you up?' she ventured again.

'He's taking his mother and two sisters to the pictures,' Agnes said from behind the newspaper.

'Did you not fancy going, then?' Olive persisted, getting her knitting from under the cushion. She didn't like to see the girl at a loose end, whilst Agnes gave a distracted nod.

She didn't mind staying in of a night sometimes; Olive had a lovely way about her that made everyone feel quite contented, and always made the

cocoa around nine thirty, which Agnes loved –
even when they were in the middle of an air raid,
the routine made her feel safe, somehow. She
loved living here since the beginning of the war. It
was the only place she had ever known apart from
the orphanage, which she dare not talk about in
front of Ted's mother, who lived in the flats
provided by the Guinness Trust and was very
respectable. Agnes felt that Mrs Jackson didn't like
her very much.

Her mind was racing now. Mrs Jackson was of
the opinion – and she said so, loudly – that foundlings, which was what Agnes was, were no better
than they ought to be, and also said she knew that
a baby left on the step of an institution had been
put there for one reason only, and that was because the child was a bastard, been abandoned by
her father because he wouldn't marry her slut of a
mother.

Agnes wriggled as if her seat was hot. Those were
the woman's very words, and Mrs Jackson had
said them when Ted went to fetch his two sisters
from school leaving her and his mother to get
acquainted. Mrs Jackson wrinkled her nose like
there was a bad smell under it. Agnes remembered
she had felt very uncomfortable after that meeting
and tried to stay out of Mrs Jackson's way as much
as possible from then on and wasn't keen on going
to Ted's home.

Not that Ted invited her to his home very often;
it was too cramped, he said. And Agnes was quite
satisfied with the explanation as, the last time she
went to visit, Mrs Jackson stayed in the little kitchenette all the time she was there. Ted wasn't best

pleased but he tried to hide it from his mother. And Agnes didn't tell Olive about it either, she would only get upset. She was a good sort, was Olive, would do anything for anybody – even for Nancy Black from next door – and, Agnes thought, Nancy would try the patience of a saint.

'I was wondering,' Olive said, interrupting her thoughts, 'would you be a love and take that apple pie down to Mr Whittaker for me, he's been...' Olive lowered her voice '...bad on his legs, poor soul.' Then her voice rose again. 'I promised Sergeant Dawson I'd pass it in later when he told me Mr Whittaker had been ailing.'

'Yes, I'll take it,' Agnes said brightly. 'It's still light and there are people in the Row so there's nothing to worry about.' Her voice sounded relieved, thought Olive, recalling Agnes was sure that number 49, next door to Mr Whittaker, was haunted. She had been fed the lies by those Farley boys who ought to know better, and no matter what anybody said they couldn't convince Agnes that there was no such thing as ghosts. Her Ted, being the protective type, made sure Agnes didn't go anywhere alone either. Olive wasn't sure this was at all good for the girl but she didn't say anything, it wasn't her place to interfere in their lives.

'I'll take the pie down now,' Agnes said, going into the kitchen to retrieve it from the top of the stove. In minutes she was knocking on Mr Whittaker's door. It seemed a long time before she heard the old man's tiny, painfully slow footsteps coming down the hallway to the front door.

Agnes shivered and had an overwhelming feeling that somebody was watching her. She looked around but could see no one apart from the people who were going about their own business. Giving a little shudder she told herself not to be so silly. She was less than a hundred yards from her own front door and, it being double summertime, it was broad daylight.

Turning quickly she heard a small rumble from number 49. It sounded like something heavy was being moved around but there was no sign of anyone. The house had been empty for a long while now – the landlord had given up trying to mend houses that the Germans later flew over in their bombers and tried to flatten, so it had been boarded up and, by the looks of it, forgotten about.

Nancy Black had been livid; she said it lowered the tone of the whole row. Agnes, if she thought about it, would say Hitler was more to blame for making the place look untidy. She looked up at the window of number 49. Maybe it was haunted, or maybe a German had got in and was spying on the whole street. She wondered if she should mention it to Olive – she'd be the best judge of whether Sergeant Dawson should be told or not.

'You took your time,' Mr Whittaker said almost, frightening the life out of Agnes. 'I thought Olive had forgotten about me.'

'She would never do that, Mr Whittaker,' Agnes said in her most friendly voice, glad to have someone to talk to and stop those stupid thoughts running through her head. But there it was again! There was a definite bump next door.

'Did you hear that, Mr Whittaker?' Agnes asked, still holding the plate containing the pie.

'It'll be the cat, she's always getting into places she shouldn't,' Mr Whittaker said, nonplussed, taking the valuable pie and shuffling down the hall, obviously looking forward to eating it. He stopped when he got to the kitchen door. 'No custard?' he asked.

'No sugar, I'm afraid, sir,' Agnes answered with a polite sigh, following the old man.

'Sugar? Sugar? They didn't have sugar in my day, neither, but we still had custard.'

'I'll let Olive know.' Agnes took the pie and slid it onto one of Mr Whittaker's own dishes. 'I'll have to return the plate to Olive, Mr Whittaker, I'll see you tomorrow.' She closed the front door gently behind her, leaving Mr Whittaker to eat his pie in peace. Custard? Agnes smiled as she hurried past number 49. Where did he think he was? The Ritz? Then she caught sight of Sergeant Dawson coming down the street on his bicycle and as he passed her she decided to summon all her courage to tell him about the strange noises she'd heard. He assured her he would have a little scoot around the place later.

She'd reached the gate of number 13 when she saw Tilly rounding the corner. Agnes waved and Tilly waved back, quickening her step a little.

Tilly saw Agnes waiting at the gate and wondered if she dare confess what she had done. She knew she had to tell someone and Agnes was a decent sort of girl who would not only keep a confidence, but would probably offer some tentative although nonetheless valuable advice, which Tilly was in need of.

Tilly couldn't explain, even to herself, what had come over her, but in a rush of excitement she had written to the labour exchange and put her name on the list of girls who were enlisting in one of the services.

Initially, she had toyed with the idea of joining the Queen Alexandra's Royal Army Nursing Corps, or the QAs as they were more commonly known, having some wildly romantic if misguided notion of tending wounded soldiers who would then fall at her feet and declare undying love for bringing them back to A1 fitness – until the woman in the recruitment centre pointed out in rather cynical tones that, as well as saving mankind from utter destruction, Tilly would have to do some very unheroic chores like emptying bed pans and providing succour and support to blind, maimed and harrowingly disfigured men as part of her duties. So that idea went right out of the window.

Instead, the glamorous conscription posters of the Auxiliary Territorial Service finally persuaded Tilly that it might be fun to join the army. And she liked the idea of being treated in the same way as those in the regular army and would wear a smart khaki uniform, although she was relieved to hear that she would wear black shoes instead of army boots – she couldn't see herself clodhopping around in big boots all day. And she was rather pleased to discover that, although they would be trained to use guns, they would never have to fire them; she didn't think she could actually *kill* someone.

'No Ted tonight, Agnes?' Tilly asked as she ap-

114

proached the gate.

'He's taking his mum and his sisters to the pictures tonight, my turn next week.'

'You make sure it is your turn too,' Tilly said a little too sharply. 'He took his mum and sisters last week.' It was a shame the way Ted took Agnes for granted and always favoured his family over her. Not only that, but poor Agnes just seemed grateful for what little attention he did give her. It wasn't a bit fair.

'Ted's mum wanted to see *Mrs Miniver* with Greer Garson and Walter Pidgeon.'

'And what did you want to see?' Tilly asked, not unkindly, feeling very sorry for Agnes now. If Ted's mother said jump he asked 'how high' and it didn't matter what Agnes, in her own placid way, thought of the change of plan because Ted's mother got her own way no matter what Agnes felt. Tilly wished that family would desist from playing on Agnes's obviously trusting and very kind nature.

'Oh, I don't mind either way,' Agnes replied. 'I'll watch anything as long as I'm with Ted.'

'You are too soft-hearted, Agnes,' Tilly gently admonished her friend, 'that's your trouble.'

'Is everything okay, Tilly?' Agnes was a little taken aback at the other girl's forthright manner.

'No, everything is not okay,' Tilly said as she fished inside the letter box for the key that her mother tied to a piece of string so they could get in at any time of the day or night. 'I don't think you deserve to be fobbed off, Agnes, and the way Ted's mother looks down her nose at you is tantamount to snootiness. Who does she think she is?'

'Don't let it worry you, Tilly, I know Ted loves me. He tells me all the time.'

'That's as maybe,' Tilly interjected, 'but actions speak louder than words, Agnes. He needs to put his foot down and tell that mother of his to stop taking the mick.'

It was plain to Agnes that anything she said now would only inflame Tilly's annoyance, so she kept quiet, knowing Tilly must have something troubling her to speak with such undisguised exasperation.

After a few moments Tilly seemed calmer and said in a low, barely audible voice: 'Agnes, I can trust you to keep something to yourself, can't I?'

'Of course you can, Tilly, I would never betray anything you told me,' Agnes said benignly, feeling privileged to be taken into Tilly's confidence like this.

'I've put my name down for the ATS.' There was another moment's silence to let this important piece of information sink into Agnes's head. And as the ramifications dawned on her, her eyes widened and her mouth opened of its own accord. 'The ATS?' she gasped, when she found her voice.

'Yes, the Auxiliary Territorial Service.' Tilly's eyes shone. 'The advertisement said "non-combatant duties with military units", you get a uniform and everything. They teach you to drive motors, ambulances, and all the other things that require the energy and initiative that I've obviously got, they said.' Tilly proudly straightened her back and looked very pleased indeed.

'So you haven't heard from Drew, then?'

'I don't want to talk about Drew,' Tilly said in a

low, hurt voice whilst her fingers sought the ring that was hanging from the gold chain around her neck. She knew she had to be brave. Life was too short to linger over thoughts of what might have been. Now was the time to grow up and show everybody, including her lovely mum, that she was mature enough to make her own decisions and carry on. After all, lots of worse things were happening all over the world and, she now realised, she must knuckle down and stop feeling sorry for herself.

'Oh, Tilly, you mustn't think that way, you'll see Drew again one day, I'm sure you will.'

'You have a romantic heart and it could be your undoing, Agnes,' said Tilly with a sad smile, 'and it may be too late if Drew comes back. Because I know one thing, I can't sit around moping, I have to do something.'

'Your mum will go mad,' was all that Agnes could think of to say, deflating Tilly with five short words.

'I know.' Tilly bit her lip. 'Will you stay with me whilst I tell her?'

'Shall I put the milk on for the cocoa, Mum?' Tilly asked quickly, maybe too quickly as she took her coat off and threw it over the back of the chair. She had to remain calm. She had to explain in composed, unruffled terms that she was grown-up enough to be of service to her country at this awful time, and not expect everybody else – her mother especially – to protect her forever.

Tilly could feel her pulse quicken and at one point she even forgot to breathe. It was only when

Olive gave her one of her puzzled frowns that Tilly realised she needed to say something, do something ... anything to stop her imagining the agonising distress her mother would go through when she told her what she'd done.

Taking the cocoa tin from the shelf, Tilly knew she had to focus. Girls were being called up all over the country. What made her so different? Why couldn't she go and do her bit?

'Oh, lovely,' said Olive as she went to the cupboard. 'Agnes, let's get the cups ready.'

Tilly took a deep breath when she and Agnes exchanged puzzled expressions. As she took the milk from the marble slab in the cool pantry, she listened to the gentle chatter of her mother and her best friend exchanging news of their day. She would miss this most of all when she went away, Tilly thought, pouring milk into a small pan and watching as it slowly came to the boil, like her courage.

'Mum...?' Tilly said hesitantly. 'You've always brought me up to think of others and not just myself, isn't that right?'

'Of course, darling.' Olive's voice came from behind her and Tilly could tell she was now sitting at the table with Agnes. She didn't dare turn around; she couldn't bear to see the pain in her mother's eyes.

'Well, as I am not a child any more and I have been more or less molly-coddled – no, that is the wrong word,' Tilly said hastily, 'as you have taken the very best care of me all my life I felt that I should give something back and make you proud of me.' But you don't have to prove anything to

118

me, Tilly, I've always been proud of you,' Olive replied, making her daughter feel even more apprehensive.

'I know you have, Mum,' she said quickly. She had to try to get her thoughts in some sort of order, as she was close to making a real hash of the job now. 'Mum, I've joined the army!' She could have kicked herself, she hadn't meant to blurt it out like that and now her mother was going to be so angry or upset or...

'Oh, Tilly, I am so proud of you!' Olive cried as she scraped back her chair and, arms wide open, came over and threw her arms around her daughter in a huge hug. 'You are so very brave and after your training I'm sure you will see some wonderful places, there will be new people to meet, not counting the many adventures you will have ... although not too many adventures!' Olive gave her a look of mock severity and then she burst out laughing.

'Oh, Mum, I am so relieved.' Tilly let out the lungful of air she had been holding since she blurted the whole thing out.

'Oh, away with you,' Olive said, giving Tilly another hug before handing her daughter and Agnes their cup of cocoa. 'Now off you go, you and Agnes will have a lot to talk about. I'll see you both in the morning.'

The two girls left the kitchen chattering and laughing, and Olive could hear the obvious relief in her daughter's voice as she took her cocoa upstairs.

Sitting alone at the table now, Olive's fears had come to fruition. She knew she would miss Tilly more than life itself and worried what the big bad world had in store for her little girl who had suddenly become a woman who made decisions of her own now. And Olive did not think she could bear it as she put her face in her hands and quietly sobbed whilst her heart shattered into a million pieces. Everything was changing and there was nothing she could do about it.

Long into the night Olive sat at the kitchen table knowing that even the most basic of necessities were rationed now; coal and soap and food were the stuff of life, yet, along with her daughter, they were things she had to do without – and not only that, but do it with a smile on her face to lift morale. Olive wondered if she could keep up the charade, alone, for the rest of this awful, awful war.

NINE

Sally stifled a yawn as she headed down Article Row and longed for the comfort of her own bed. Last night had been exceptionally busy as incendiaries had set fire to a warehouse on the docks. When the roof collapsed a number of people were trapped inside, but it wasn't them that had caused the staff to be almost run off their feet, it was the explosion of tar barrels that had spread and injured workers in the next warehouse too. There had been complete mayhem right up until first light; even some of the fire crew were coming in for burns treatment. Then there was George, quiet, unassuming George who had volunteered to serve in the Royal Navy and had left yesterday stating that he would consider himself a failure if he didn't do his bit.

A failure? George? Sally had been so shocked by his sudden outburst that she could only re-assure him that he wasn't a failure, far from it; he was the kindest, most talented doctor she had ever met, to which he had said with a hint of un-characteristic cynicism that she would think that, wouldn't she? And no matter how much she tried to coax or even bully him into staying here with her, George could not be persuaded – he had to do it, she knew.

In one way Sally was extremely proud of his sacrifice and in another she wanted to shake some sense into him. However, she had come to realise that she couldn't stop him doing what he felt was right. That would be beyond selfish, and she couldn't live with herself if he felt a failure because of what she had said. But it didn't make their parting yesterday any easier.

'You do understand, don't you, darling Sally?' George had asked before he boarded the train to Devonport in Plymouth to join his ship. She wanted to answer no, she didn't understand, but he kept talking, not letting her tell him how much she would miss him until the very last minute. He was a good man, a caring doctor who was doing an excellent job. He would be an asset to the navy, she knew.

As her scrambled, weary thoughts flickered and waned in the half-light of dusk she saw something, or someone, dart into the vicar's garden. Sally knew it was strange at this hour for the vicar to be gardening, as he was no longer in the first flush of youth and much preferred to do such work when it was light enough to see properly. And also, she could tell that the person was too small to be an adult.

She stopped and watched for a moment, unsure if whoever it was had seen her and was hiding behind the privet hedge. She waited, not moving, for a while longer and then to her complete surprise she saw young Barney creeping out of the vicar's garden and, crouching, looking the other way.

'What are you up to, young Barney?' Sally demanded, making her voice as stern as possible, although she felt sorry for the kid, who hadn't had it easy before he was taken in by Sergeant Dawson and his wife.

However, she was worried that Barney was going back to his old ways after seeing him loitering around the underground a few days earlier. It used to be a favourite hangout of his rather dubious older acquaintances and she had to have a little chat with Sergeant Dawson, who told her that Barney was still settling in and he was sure that the boy wasn't up to anything untoward. Be that as it may, thought Sally, but what child wanders around the neighbourhood this late in the evening? One who was up to no good, that's who.

'I wasn't doing nothing, honest.' Barney looked the picture of guilt.

'You weren't doing "anything", you mean.'

'That's what I said, miss. I was just looking for shrapnel...' His words dissipated into the evening air as Sally drew alongside him.

'Does your father know where you are?'

'I ain't got no father, miss, he's lost in the war.' His grubby face and crumpled pyjamas were a far cry from Mrs Dawson's usual tidiness, thought Sally.

'I meant Sergeant Dawson,' she said patiently. Sally had seen many young lads just like Barney who'd had their childhood stolen from them by the war; they had to grow up fast and take responsibility. Luckily for Barney, the sergeant and his wife had taken pity on him and given him a good home and plenty of care and attention. And this was how he repaid them?

'I ain't done nuffin', miss, you can search me if yer like, I ain't got nuffin' I shouldn't.'

'I should hope so too, Barney,' Sally said, giving him the benefit of the doubt, 'but why are you out at this hour of night in your pyjamas? You should be tucked up in your bed.'

'I can't get in, miss,' Barney said in simple matter-of-fact tones. 'I ain't got no key an' Aunty won't let me in.'

Sally's forehead puckered in doubt, as she knew that Mrs Dawson doted on young Barney; he was like a substitute son after the tragic death of her own young boy years earlier.

'She dragged me out of bed and would you Adam an' Eve it, she told me I was trespassin'. Frightened the life outta me, she did!' Barney's eyes widened and Sally instinctively knew he was telling the truth.

'Mmm,' she said, confused. 'Let's get you home and see what can be done.' Barney seemed reluctant at first but Sally persuaded him that he was not in trouble. 'Your aunt doesn't sound too well,' she said, putting her arm around his shoulder, guiding him up the street. It was on the third knock that Mrs Dawson came to the door. Sally could hear her shuffling down the hall like an old lady, but assumed she must only be in her late thirties, much the same age as Olive, she guessed.

'Ahh, Nurse, you're here at last,' Mrs Dawson said, her dull eyes brightening. Then she caught sight of Barney and shooed him off the step. 'Be off with you, boy, you have no business here. Now go away before I call my husband; he's a policeman, you know.'

Sally's eyes took in the woman's appearance. She was dressed in every stitch of clothing she owned by the looks of it, and it didn't need Sally's professional assessment to see that the woman was, perhaps temporarily, not her usual self as she took on a condescending manner in dealing with Barney.

Mrs Dawson looked twice her usual size as dresses and cardigans were piled on top of each other and her dark coat was dragged over the clothing in such a way that she could hardly move her arms. Sally turned to Barney who was sniggering behind her and quickly shushed him with a stern glance.

'Here, take my key and let yourself into number 13,' she told him in a low voice. 'Tell Olive to go to the police station and fetch Sergeant Dawson, he needs to come home urgently. I will explain everything as soon as I can. Now hurry and don't dawdle around the street, you don't want Nancy Black seeing you when she's putting her milk bottles out and complaining again.'

Barney took the key and sped down the street as Sally ushered Mrs Dawson into her front room. When she went to turn on the light the other woman stopped her with a strength that had gone previously undetected.

'Don't turn the light on or open those curtains!' Mrs Dawson's voice was shrill, making Sally turn towards her. 'I don't want them looking in the window.' She didn't elaborate on who 'them' were. Sally realised that the woman could be very volatile if not handled correctly as Mrs Dawson grabbed her hand and said, 'They took my baby, you know.' She was shaking all over, Sally could see. 'They took my boy! Don't you see? I've got to get away from here! I've got to find him quickly!'

'Who took your boy, Mrs Dawson?' Sally's gentle tones brought a little calm and, still in her uniform, her medical expertise came to the fore. By the looks of it, Sally thought, Mrs Dawson was able to recognise that she was here to help her.

'The Germans. They came in the middle of the night and they stole my boy – and they took my husband too. You've got to help me. It's not safe here any more.'

Sally could see, even in the very dim light of the room, that Mrs Dawson's eyes were wild and she tried to calm her whilst she still had the other woman's attention, because any minute now Mrs Dawson might not recognise Sally as someone who was here to comfort her.

'I knew something like this would happen, I said to my husband that I wanted to move but he wasn't having any of it – he's in league with them, you know, he has a uniform and everything. And he keeps a gun. Did you know he keeps a gun? The vicar would be scandalised!' Sally listened to Mrs Dawson's rambling with the serenity honed from years of nursing.

'Shall I make us a nice cup of tea, Mrs Dawson?' she asked, when Mrs Dawson grew calmer.

'Who is Mrs Dawson? My name is Miss Teasdale.' Mrs Dawson looked suspicious. 'I think you may have me mixed up with somebody else my dear,' she continued, seeming very lucid. If a stranger was to come in here now, Sally thought, they would possibly believe that Mrs Dawson was Miss Teasdale, such was her conviction. It was all very worrying.

'I do apologise, maybe you would like a cup instead then, Miss Teasdale?'

'How very kind of you, I'm sure, but I shall wait until my guests arrive and then you may serve tea.'

Sally noted that Mrs Dawson, wearing a mountain of clothing with her arms outstretched, was talking like the lady of the manor – which Sally supposed was half-true as she had done a very good job keeping the house going, even though she was giving the impression of belonging to a more refined Victorian establishment. Sally knew that something had clearly snapped in Mrs Dawson's vision of reality; she had seen this type of dislocation from the real world since the beginning of the war. Women who had been getting on with their daily routine without a word of rebuke or fuss suddenly could take no more – and it was usually, like now, when things had settled down a bit after the earlier blitz, that they could no longer cope.

'How is she?' Sergeant Dawson asked, hurrying into the front room, looking highly embarrassed that his neighbours were witnessing his poor deluded wife behaving like this. 'She's been ill for some time,' Archie said in a low voice to Sally, and to Olive who had come with him after taking the news to the police station. Archie put his arm around his wife, who appeared not to even know him.

'I think...' Sally looked doubtful but carried on. 'In my professional opinion, Mrs Dawson needs more expert care than I could give her.' Much to her relief a short while later their general practitioner came to give his assessment too.

'I telephoned him from the station,' said Archie, shocked to hear that his wife would have to be admitted to hospital for complete rest and recuperation.

'Don't worry about Barney,' said Olive, taking the matter out of Archie's hands. 'I'll make sure he's well looked after whilst you are busy with other matters.'

'Thank you, Olive, I won't forget your kindness,' Archie said whilst Olive dismissed his grateful thanks with a wave of her hand.

A short while later, after a cup of cocoa and a round of toast, Barney was shown to Dulcie's bed, as she was on nights at the munitions factory. Olive was sure she wouldn't mind – especially if nobody told her. And anyway, she silently reasoned, the boy would be up by the time Dulcie got home from work tomorrow.

When she went into the kitchen she was a little surprised to see Sally sitting at the table where she had left her nursing a cocoa cup, her eyes red-rimmed as if she'd been crying.

'Is something the matter, Sally?' Olive asked in her gentle tones as she sat at the table.

Sally took a huge breath and said in a short faltering voice, 'George joined his ship last night.' She couldn't continue for a while, and then she said, 'I'm being silly, I know. Girls are saying good-bye to their chaps every day, I've got to be strong.'

Olive listened to Sally and once more cursed this ugly war as she took her handkerchief from the sleeve of her cardigan and gave her nose a jolly good blow whilst attempting a quivering smile.

'Oh, Olive, I'm sorry. I didn't mean to upset you too.'

'You didn't, Sally.' Olive's chin wobbled as she spoke. 'I'm being silly. It's the soap shortage and the grey bread and the rise in income tax ... and Tilly's joined the ATS.'

'Oh, Olive,' Sally cried, coming to her side and giving her a hug, 'when will it all end? That's what I want to know.'

'You and I, both.' Olive gave a huge sigh and got up from the table.

'When will she go?' Sally asked, knowing George had had to be given special permission to leave the hospital.

'Three weeks,' Olive said, her voice wavering, 'and please don't be nice to me, that would finish me off altogether.'

TEN

Tilly's eyes were still closed as she listened to the hubbub of activity downstairs, to the chatter and sporadic laughter of her mother and Agnes who were probably getting everything ready for this afternoon's little get-together with the neighbours before she left for her new life in the army. Dulcie was in the next room after her night shift at the munitions factory and Sally was on duty at the hospital, but she would be here at five o'clock this afternoon to see her off, she was sure.

Even though her eyes were still closed Tilly could not stop the build-up of tears behind her lids and she knew that this time tomorrow she would be rising from a different bed surrounded by strangers, and the thought momentarily frightened the life out of her. Apart from the booklet she had been given telling her what she had to bring, and where she had to be at a specific time, she knew nothing of the Auxiliary Training Service except that she liked the look of their glamorous uniform. Tilly wondered if that was enough to change her life forever. She wouldn't stir to the sound of her mother's voice gently rousing her from sleep with a welcome cup of tea and her usual breakfast of hot porridge and freshly made toast either.

However Tilly knew that wasn't the reason her heart was near to breaking, far from it, if the truth be told. She was looking forward to branching out on her own, away from her mother's ever-watchful eyes, and the more difficult the process was to become a useful member of the Forces the better she would like it. Because then, hopefully, it would take her mind off Drew and his treacherous betrayal. She hadn't heard a word from him and now, more than ever, she was certain his father had persuaded him not to come back to England or her.

Turning to face the wall before slowly opening her tear-soaked eyes Tilly realised she had done the right thing joining the ATS; it felt good to be doing her bit for the country even if it was for all the wrong reasons. Her mother was capable, stoic and honest and Tilly wanted her mum to be proud of her and not have to witness her daughter dissolving into a gibbering wreck because of a man who freely made false promises.

Tilly knew her thoughts were all over the place, but recognised that the one thing in she was afraid of, especially now, was saying goodbye – she had never been good with it. She couldn't cope like others seemed able to do, hold her head high and get on with life. No, she clung with magnetic tenacity to the things she held dear, refusing to let go of people who mattered.

But it was futile to even try to rid herself of this painful longing for Drew whilst she still lived at home in the comfort of her friends and family. Every day she hurried to the hallway at the sound of the letter box and fall of envelopes, hoping that one of them was from her beloved Drew. And every day her heart fractured a little more as she found it more difficult to cope here in London.

Tilly knew she had to fill her days with something other than hopes and dreams of her future with Drew. The only thing she could think of was to serve her country. And any moment now her mother would call her to go down for breakfast, and she would pretend everything was fine, like it was just another day, and she would move automatically with practised ease through the day. Tomorrow her new independence would begin.

Tilly watched her mother busying herself, going back and forth with plates of sandwiches covered in damp tea towels from the kitchen to the front room, and imagined she felt the same gnawing pain.

It would be just as difficult for Mum, Tilly realised. They had been so close, much closer than many mothers and daughters; for a long time their lives had revolved around, and depended upon, each other and now that was going to change. And it was all her fault. Mum was trying to put a brave face on it as usual; Tilly knew she would never wear her heart on her sleeve. That just wasn't Olive's style.

Tilly admired her mother's generation of women who'd had to be strong, like women of her own time whose men had been called to war; they kept their fragile feelings to themselves and didn't fall apart or run away. How things had changed since the beginning of the war, Tilly thought as she folded the clean washing she had just brought in from the garden, and how many more challenges would women like her mother fight to overcome, before the war was over and done with?

All morning Olive had been on the go, whilst knowing Tilly wanted to sit down and talk to her. But it was her way of coping. She had to keep busy to stop her mind dwelling on the thought of her daughter leaving home and... Her mind couldn't even contemplate the thought that Tilly might not come back. It really couldn't.

The day of Tilly's departure for ATS training in the Surrey countryside had come all too quickly for Olive's liking. But then again, she quietly admitted to herself, even if her only daughter had not been called up for another five years, it would still have been too soon.

Olive had decided to hold a small farewell get-together for Tilly, with Dulcie, Sally and Agnes, Sergeant Dawson and not forgetting poor, young Barney, Nancy and her family, a few other selected neighbours – anyone who could take her mind off her daughter's imminent departure and keep the tears at bay. Nancy's ten-year-old grandson, Freddy, who was staying for a couple of weeks as Nancy's daughter was in hospital having her new baby, would also be in attendance.

Mrs Dawson was now recuperating in a country hospital where it was peaceful, away from the bustle of the city, and Olive had suggested to Archie that she would pop in whilst he was at work to make sure everything was as it should be until Mrs Dawson came home. Her mind whirled, then she smiled momentarily as she looked out of the back window, watching the two boys playing war games out in the garden, and realised that Archie had done a wonderful job keeping young Barney in hand lately. Even though his wife had been taken poorly, there weren't nearly as many complaints about the young lad's rough-and-ready behaviour of late as there had been when he first came to Article Row – well, not from most people anyway. Nancy was another matter altogether; Olive was certain that the woman would find fault in angels.

True to form, this was the first thing that Nancy mentioned. 'I hope that Barney boy isn't too much for my Freddy, he's not used to any rough-and-tumble and prefers a nice game of chess or a jigsaw puzzle, having been brought up properly.'

'Yes, Nancy, you have told me,' Olive sighed patiently, 'and from what I can see you are right; your daughter has done a marvellous job all on her own. Especially since her husband joined the other millions of men who had the audacity to leave their wives to bring up their children, whilst they went off enjoying themselves saving the country from the hands of dictators!' Olive took a deep breath whilst Nancy stood open-mouthed and speechless. 'But playing in the back garden with Barney won't do Freddy any harm.'

Olive wanted today to be perfect for Tilly and she didn't want Nancy to spoil it with her carping. She left her neighbour looking out of the window and, picking up her tray, went to collect empty tea cups.

Dulcie seemed quiet today and was deep in thought in the chair near the door, Olive noted, knowing her lodger's subdued behaviour was most uncharacteristic; she would normally revel in a good old get-together. Perhaps she would start one of her usual sing-songs around the piano in the front room later on, but right now it didn't seem as if she had any such inclination.

As Olive walked towards the kitchen door she noticed Archie further down the hallway. 'Excuse me, Nancy, I think I hear the kettle boiling,' she said as her neighbour, with obvious rage written all over her face, made a beeline for her.

'He's definitely got his eye on you, Olive, it's as plain as the nose on your face,' Nancy began.

But Olive was in no mood to hear the woman's comments; she was far too busy making sure her other guests were properly looked after. Also, she didn't want Nancy to see Archie being his usual amiable self towards her. She would only jump to the wrong conclusion – again.

As Archie drew near, Olive suddenly felt a glow of guilt suffuse her neck and face; she'd thought of him a lot since Nancy had insinuated he might have feelings that were more than neighbourly, much more than was proper for a widow to think of a married man. She ought to be ashamed of herself. And she was, especially since his wife was in hospital.

'I must go and see to this tea,' Olive said hastily, heading for the kitchen.

'Something I said?'

Olive heard the amusement in Sergeant Dawson's deep voice that could do one of two things: either put the fear of God into the most hardened felon or fill the heart of the most frightened child with hope and security. And for this, at least, Olive felt a tremendous respect for the man who had looked after his ailing wife with tender loving care, as well as helping to bring up the wayward child of a serving soldier.

In the kitchen she smiled to herself, relieved that everybody, apart from Nancy, seemed to be having a good time, especially Tilly, who was now laughing at something somebody had said. Olive was glad she hadn't made a song and dance about her going into the Forces. In reality she had no choice, all the young ones were being called up to do their bit and it now happened to be Tilly's turn. However, knowing she had to go didn't make the parting any easier.

Olive had decided to have a little tea party on the Sunday afternoon because Tilly was leaving by train later that day and it was much easier to have everybody around her than mope around, walking on eggshells in case she set Tilly off crying or vice versa. No, it was much better to do it this way, she thought, putting the washed cups on the draining board. Having saved her points and coupons Olive had purchased a few luxuries especially for today, including a tin of red salmon – pink was almost impossible to get hold of even if she did have the money and the coupons – which she used to make sandwiches. Agnes had brought in the last of the home-grown lettuce, radish and spring onions from the little garden and Olive managed to make a nice salad with a few ounces of ham she had gleaned from the butcher on the high, street yesterday.

The ham was a bit dry around the edges where it had been lying in the sunny window but she managed to shave that off and it was as good as new now. What with all that and the Victoria sponge she made with her dried-egg ration, Olive was quite happy with the way things turned out, especially when Nancy brought a jelly she had made along with some condensed milk. She wasn't all bad, Olive thought with a smile.

Taking the clean, damp tea towels off the food, Olive made sure everything was perfect before putting it on the table in the front room and, was so engrossed in her task she didn't hear Archie coming into the kitchen with his empty cup. His little cough of introduction startled her and she wheeled around, her eyes wide as she gave an involuntary gasp of surprise.

'I hope you're not eating all the goodies.' Archie gave a low rumble of laughter.

'You gave me such a start,' she said, turning back to the tray as much to hide her self-conscious flaming expression as to pour half an inch of milk into each clean cup.

'I'm sorry, Olive,' Archie said in his usual friendly way. 'I didn't mean to startle you, is there anything I can do to help?'

Olive, conscious of the nearness of this man whose wife was going through such a difficult time, shook her head, knowing he was doing his best to put a brave face on his domestic difficulties.

'Shall I take the tray?' Archie asked.

'Thank you, Archie.' Olive's voice sounded quite stiff even to her own ears and she knew she would have to put Nancy's sometimes spiteful insinuations to the back of her mind otherwise she would be no use to Archie or Barney or Mrs Dawson come to that. Taking a deep breath now she wondered how she could have been so gullible as to let Nancy Black get to her like that.

'Here, let me,' said Archie, reaching for the tray. Olive found the room suddenly hot.

'No, thank you. I'm fine.' Olive's voice was brusquer than she'd intended as she picked up the tray of cups and she immediately regretted her impatient remark at a simple act of goodwill from a helpful neighbour. However Archie, being the thorough gentleman he so obviously was, seemed not to notice as he opened the door for her to take the tray through.

'You and Archie were in the kitchen a long while,' Nancy said with an 'I-know-what-you've-been-up-to' expression on her face.

'Not that it's any of your business, Nancy,' Olive said, straightening her good white damask tablecloth to keep her trembling hands busy, 'but he was just offering to help me out.'

'Oh, I bet he was,' Nancy smirked. 'I've heard he's very good like that.'

'Like what?' Olive turned sharply and delivered the question straight to Nancy's face. She could feel her own cheeks burning now, only too aware that Nancy could be so infuriating when she jumped to the wrong conclusions.

'Well, with you having no man about the place, it must get quite difficult when little jobs need doing, you know what I mean?'

'No, I don't know what you mean, and if any "little jobs" need doing around here I'm sure I can manage them by myself, I've always had to do so in the past.' Olive moved the tray with such force the cups rattled on the saucers.

'Pardon me, I'm sure,' Nancy said, put out at being spoken to like that. Olive took a deep breath watching her neighbour flounce out of the front room and wondering if she really should have given the woman the sharp edge of her tongue.

'At it again is she?' Sally laughed as she brought another plate of food and put it on the table and breaking into Olive's thoughts.

'Oh, you know Nancy,' said Olive, 'she'll never change, always got her nose in someone's business.'

She was still standing with her hands gripping the back of the chair when Agnes came into the front room and said, 'I have to be in work in half an hour.' Olive noted she looked almost shy as she handed her a little package. 'Would you give Tilly this for me? It's not much, just a little lucky charm I've had since I was a child, it'll keep her safe.'

'Wouldn't you like to give it to her yourself, Agnes?' Olive watched the young woman vigorously shake her head. 'I'd rather not say goodbye.'

Before she could say anything else, Agnes, with a little tear in her eye, turned and hurried from the room to leave for her shift at the Chancery Lane. Olive sighed, taking a little rabbit's foot from the crumpled tissue paper that had obviously seen better days. 'I'll make sure she gets it, Agnes,' Olive said to the closing door.

'How d'ya fancy a game of togger?' Barney asked young Freddy as they sat in Olive's back garden, pulling at short blades of grass. They had finished their food now and were bored. Barney looked up at the back window and could see the adults talking in little groups and wondered what they found to yak about for so long.

'Togger?' asked Freddy, three years younger than Barney but almost the same size.

'Yeah, togger, soccer... Football! Now don't tell me you've never heard of football.'

'Of course I've heard of football, me and Dad used to play it before he...' The young lad's lip wobbled and then he burst into tears. Barney shrugged his once-skinny shoulders that were beginning to fill out a bit now he was being well looked after, worrying that he would be scolded for upsetting Freddy.

'Oh lordy, doncha go an' start squawking, you'll 'ave your granny out playing merry 'ell.'

'What is merry 'ell?' asked Freddy, bemused now, his tears suddenly subsiding.

'That fing your granny plays every time she sets eyes on me,' said Barney with a world-weary sigh, 'so d'ya wanna play or doncha?'

'All right,' said Freddy, jumping to his feet. 'I'll just go and tell Grandma.'

'Best leave it, we'll only be outside Olive's front door,' said Barney, doubting Nancy would allow her precious grandson to play something as un-civilised as a game of football in the road. 'We'd best go further daan the street, that way we can't get into any bother.'

'Righto,' said Freddy in a trusting voice. Then he stopped and pointed towards number 49. 'What do you suppose those two men are doing?'

Barney followed the direction of the younger boy's fingertip, and felt his heart sink when he recognised one of the dockside boys, now dressed in a sharp suit and sporting a pencil-thin moustache that had not been there the last time they saw each other.

'Let's scarper,' he suggested, not wanting to get involved. 'We don't want to see this.'

'They've got a gramophone ... and is that a wireless? They must be moving in,' Freddy said, watching closely and forgetting the football game. But Barney could feel his spirits sink when he saw the older of the boys come towards them.

'That's torn it,' he said, knowing it was too late to make a run for it now.

'Wotcha, Barney, long time no see, me old china,' said the moustachioed one, pushing back a pork-pie hat, his exaggerated swagger making him look as if he'd just got off a ship in turbulent waters.

'Hello, are you moving in today?'

Barney gave Freddy a little dig in the arm with his elbow to stop him asking any more daft questions; he knew these people and they were not to be messed with. It would be better for both of them if they didn't ask what was going on in number 49. From what Barney could see this was a 'need to know' operation and he didn't need to know a thing.

'What's it got to do wiv you, shrimp?' said the taller of the two menacing boys as Barney began to tug Freddy's sleeve.

'C'mon, it don't matter what they're doin',' Barney hissed in a low voice. 'Let's get outta here. When I say "now" you run like the wind, right?'

Freddy looked a little bewildered but when Barney gave the signal they both ran as fast as their legs could carry them up Article Row. Barney didn't want to know about or be involved in anything these lads were doing any more, especially now he was living with Sergeant Dawson and his wife who had been good to him since his mother and grandmother were killed in an air raid during the Blitz. Also, he worried that once you knew the secrets of these hoodlums you were sort of bound to them, part of the gang. It was very hard to get away from them once they had something on you, and Barney knew he'd done more than collect shrapnel with them. They wouldn't forget the time they saved him from being put in a home for receiving stolen goods.

'They're a tough lot an' no mistake,' said Barney as he and Freddy crouched behind a low wall out of sight. 'If they get their 'ands on us there's no saying what could 'appen.'

'Do you think they will hit us?' Freddy looked terrified. If this weren't so serious, thought Barney, he would have laughed out loud at the young lad's innocence – but now was not the time.

'Sure as eggs is eggs,' Barney said, keeping a look-out, then he spotted one of the boys. 'Quick, let's scarper, they're comin'!'

'Has anybody seen my Freddy?' Nancy's shrill voice was only a couple of decibels below a screech as everybody broke off from their conversations and turned in her direction.

'He won't be far, Nancy,' Archie said. 'He's only playing with Barney in the garden.'

'But he's not in the garden now and neither is

your young upstart of a foster son!' Nancy's face was a livid red and everybody was shocked at how forthright she was to Sergeant Dawson when he was plainly trying to calm her fears.

'Nancy, Archie was only trying to help you.' Olive jumped to the sergeant's defence but it was lost on her next-door neighbour who was running around like a headless chicken, opening the cupboard door under the stairs to see if her grandson was hiding inside.

'I'm sure he isn't in there,' Olive said, obviously put out that her home was being all but ransacked.

'I've got to find him! His mother doesn't let him out of her sight, she won't even let him play in the street she is so scared something might happen to him!'

'Listen,' Olive said, taking Nancy by the shoulders, 'you have to calm down, hysterics are not helping.' Olive was worried she might even have to slap Nancy's face and, much as she had sometimes longed to in the past, she didn't believe she could actually bring herself to do it. 'We will all go and search around, he's probably up a tree laughing at us all being worried.'

'No, not my Freddy, he's not that kind of boy.'

Olive sighed. 'I'll go upstairs and check.' But when she came down a little later she shrugged. There was no sign of Freddy upstairs and, more worrying, there was no sign of Barney either.

'I'll check the street, he might be playing a game of football,' Archie said, noting his neighbour's look of disgust and disapproval, knowing something as harmless as a game of football was anathema to Nancy.

142

After an hour's search in the surrounding area there was still no sign of the two boys and the adults were beginning to grow concerned because, much as it was commonplace for children to play in the street when the bombs weren't falling, Nancy's obvious anxiety told them that it was not a usual occurrence for her grandson. In fact, thought Olive, the boy was probably enjoying his new-found freedom so much he had completely forgotten the time.

'We'll go and search up by the park. He's bound to be there with Barney,' Archie said, inviting Mr Black, Nancy's husband, to follow him so they could search in different places whilst the women went back into Olive's house to wait and see if they came back.

'They will walk in, bold as brass, when their stomachs are empty and ask if there's anything to eat, I should imagine.' Olive tried her best to allay Nancy's fears but her neighbour was having none of it.

'His mother will faint clean away when she finds out I've lost her beloved son – she will go doolally... I will never be able to look after him ever again!'

'I'm sure that won't be the case, Nancy,' Olive said in soothing tones. She looked at the clock and hoped that the men would come back with good news, as Tilly had to leave for the station soon.

'You mean you've never played football in the street ... ever!' Barney could hardly believe his ears. Freddy had just told him that his mother never usually let him outside the house on his own. 'Blimey.' Barney shook his head in wonderment, temporarily forgetting they were being pursued by the two dockside bullies who now wanted an explanation of why Barney never came to visit any more and also some kind of reassurance that he would keep his trap shut, especially now he was living with Old Bill.

The two young boys found they had a common bond in that both their fathers were both away fighting the war, each trying to outdo the other with tales of his father's courage and daring. But the lull was short-lived when Freddy caught sight of Stan, one of the older boys, who was approaching at speed.

Without another word Freddy was on his feet and tearing down the road closely, followed by Barney, who was worried the little chap would get lost in this part of London, as he didn't come here very often. Barney only managed to catch up with Freddy when he reached Chancery Lane tube station. Quickly looking around, hardly able to breathe, the two boys could see that the spivs were still on their tail.

'In here!' Barney hissed, pulling on Freddy's arm and protectively holding on to him, weaving through the waiting crowds as he dragged the young boy towards an opening.

'There, there, don't fret, he'll be back,' Olive said, patting Nancy's hand. It was almost an hour later when the men arrived back, sadly shaking their heads. There was no sign of the two boys anywhere. The three men had split up and searched every square inch of the park, in bushes, in prickly shrubs that scratched them to bits, in the air-raid shelter, everywhere they could think of – but there wasn't a single sighting of either of them.

'Mum, I am so sorry that I can't help you but I've got to go now,' Tilly said, lifting her cardboard suitcase bought specially from the market for this very occasion.

'I'll get my coat,' Olive said, turning to her guests. 'I am so sorry I have to do this but...'

'Mum, no,' Tilly said with a hint of panic in her voice. 'You stay here and help out with the search for Freddy and Barney, I've ordered a cab. I prefer it this way, honestly.' She tried her best to stop a sneaky tear from dropping to her cheek as she hurriedly caught her mother in a bear-hug.

'Here,' Olive said quickly, sniffing away a tear herself, 'Agnes left this for you, she said it will keep you...' She couldn't finish the words as her throat caught in a vice-like grip. Tilly nodded, her chin giving a little wobble as her watery smile threatened to overpower her.

Then she said, her voice barely a whisper, 'I know. I'll write as soon as I get there.'

'As soon as you can,' Olive said, her words coming out in a rush. 'Let me know you've arrived safely.' Safely. The word echoed around her head. She had nurtured her daughter from the day she was born and tried to raise her to be the best human being it was possible to be – and she was. Olive had also attempted to hide the fear and the devastation that was now ripping her heart in two, and had busied herself so she didn't have to think about this moment. This agonisingly lonely moment that only a mother would know.

As she followed her only child – who was no longer a child – out to the street to put the luggage in the taxi, her heart felt as if it was trying to burst out of her throat. Any moment now Tilly would be gone. Off to another way of life. Meeting different people. Experiencing new things that she, Olive, had never had a chance to do. But she didn't begrudge Tilly her new life. How could she? She too would have done exactly the same thing if she'd had the chance.

But that didn't mean she wouldn't miss and worry about her until she was safely back home again and it didn't mean she would rest until she saw her darling daughter once more. In her mind she silently scolded the leaders of this great country for wanting her daughter's services. Although it was little consolation, she reminded herself with some pride that they only took the best.'

''Bye Mum,' Tilly said, her eyes brimming with tears. 'I'll let you know how I get on.'

'You better had, my girl.' Olive gave Tilly a gentle admonishment, which seemed to lighten the heavy mood as the neighbours all stood around. Olive so wished they would go away and leave her and Tilly alone for a few moments, but it was not to be.

'You take care of yourself now, Tilly,' said Mrs Windle, 'and may the good lord watch over you and keep you safe.' Tilly nodded and gently withdrew the hand that Mrs Windle was tightly gripping.

'Go on now, love.' Olive took a deep breath, and although she didn't want to see her go, she couldn't bear to witness her daughter's agony

146

much longer, knowing how much Tilly hated goodbyes. 'Before you miss your train.' She was still waving as the taxi pulled around the corner out of sight.

'Agnes, I want you to go down to the deep shelter, there has been a report that something is amiss.'

'What's amiss?' Agnes could feel the panic rise to her throat. It was very dark in the deep-level shelter below the underground that had been built after the bombings had forced the government to re-think their plans and construct a system of deeper shelters linked to existing tube stations.

They had been built at public expense on the understanding the railway could take them over after the war. Although they were places of safety for the public there were no actual stations, as the diameter of the tunnels was too small for trains. Agnes knew each shelter had two decks, fully equipped with bunks and medical posts, kitchens and toilets and each installation could accommodate over eight thousand people; she also knew that, having been only partly finished, none was put to use as yet and it was very lonely down there.

Being scared of her own shadow, Agnes was not too keen to go on her own. However, she knew that if she refused to carry out her duty this could be seen as an act of cowardice and she would have to suffer the consequences; she had no choice. So, firmly gripping her torch, she headed for the circular concrete pillbox that would lead her down to the subterranean tunnel below.

Agnes put her foot on the first rung of the steep-looking spiral staircase that would take her to the shelter whilst in her mouth, now sand-paper dry, she held her torch until she reached the first of the two layers of the dark tunnel.

Taking the torch from her mouth she switched it on and even the tiny click of the switch seemed to echo around the curve of the walls. Agnes stopped for a moment, not sure what she should be listening for. Surely she should have a male porter with her now, she thought nervously. What if there was a German spy waiting to catch her from behind! Her thoughts ran amok and she knew she would have to calm down otherwise her rising hysteria threatened to overwhelm her.

Taking a deep breath, Agnes put her back against the wall, taking no chances, and she slid crab-like along, her torch giving off a weak circular glow until she reached an opening off the main access tunnel.

Suddenly there was a noise and she stopped, hardly daring to breathe. What was it? she wondered. Peering into the feeble light she searched for whatever it was that had made the sound. For she had definitely heard something. Taking low, shallow breaths of dusty air Agnes edged forward, her fear now replaced by something she hadn't felt for a long time: that steely determination she had found from somewhere when one of her little charges had been in danger at the orphanage. She had risen above her dread so they couldn't see her fear. That same feeling was beginning to fill her now; she had to get to the bottom of this. If she could save only one of her countrymen's lives this day it would be worth the fear and the... There it was again!

She heard a low half-moan that chilled her to the bone. It couldn't be an animal. How would one get down here anyway? A little voice inside her head told her a curious cat might find its way in and, being able to see in the dark, would have no bother getting itself into a sticky situation. But what if it was feral? she argued with herself. It could scratch her eyes out and she wouldn't be able to see her way back.

'Is anybody there?' Her quavering voice was growing deceptively stronger; if she was going to do this thing she was going to do it properly, she had to think of her country now, she had to think of the safety of her fellow man. 'Come on, I know you're in here! Show your face before I set the dogs on you. I have a gun and I'm not afraid to use it, so out you come!' She knew she sounded absurd, armed only with a torch, but she just shouted the first thing that came into her head.

A small noise from the far end of the passageway alerted her to whoever it was hiding there and she shone her torch only to see what looked like a small bundle of rags. On closer inspection, Agnes could see it was a small boy and if she wasn't mistaken she had seen him somewhere before.

'Freddy? Freddy, is that you?' Agnes could not believe her eyes, as the little boy, no older than nine or ten, crawled from beneath the building materials left by the workmen and suddenly her heart went out to the sobbing child who, by the looks of it, had been so scared he had wet himself.

'I want my daddy... I want my mummy...' he sobbed over and over again. Hurrying to his side Agnes held him as he sobbed on her shoulder.

149

She wasn't surprised that tears ran down her own face too.

'How did you get down here?' she cried, holding him at arm's length, making sure he wasn't hurt. 'Don't you know it's dangerous to come down here on your own, especially if nobody knows where you are.'

'But ... Barney said...' he sobbed '...he said he had to see the older boys... They were chasing us ... he said he would come back ... for me...'

'When was this?' Agnes asked, sure she had seen the two boys playing near Olive's salad patch earlier.

'I don't know,' the young lad cried as she put her arm around him and hugged him close before calming him and leading him back through the long tunnel towards the spiral staircase and freedom.

'All right, we'll soon get you home,' Agnes said in soothing tones, 'and that Barney will find it hard to sit down when his father gets his hands on him, I'm sure.'

Darkness wrapped itself around the houses in Article Row as the inhabitants grew more frantic. It would be nigh on impossible to find a child in the blackout, they said, causing even more distress to Nancy, who had sat at Olive's hearth all afternoon chewing her nails and wailing like a banshee, although, Olive noted, she didn't seem upset enough to get up and do anything about it.

'When that Barney comes in here he will feel the back of my hand,' she said, her words laced with venom, 'and I hope that you will thrash him until he cannot sit down, Sergeant.'

'I will certainly give him a good talking to when I find out what has happened but I don't hold with thrashing some sense into a boy of his age.'

'Spare the rod and spoil the child, that's what I say,' Nancy spat, 'and we've seen plenty of proof of that with feral children all over the place.'

'Oh, I don't think so, Mrs Black,' said Mrs Windle, the vicar's wife. 'We have some lovely children at Sunday school, they are a credit to their mothers.'

'Be that as it may, Mrs Windle, but I don't think that Barney boy can be redeemed – he isn't the redeeming type.'

'And what is the redeeming type, Nancy?' asked Olive. 'Would that be the type who run off in the night and bring home a premature baby six months later…?'

'I do not know to what you are alluding, Olive, but it sounds quite malicious to me!'

Everybody knew that Nancy's daughter had run away some years earlier, only to come back with a *premature* babe in arms and a new husband in tow.

'Malicious is as malicious does, Nancy,' Olive said, but she was interrupted by a rumpus outside. She hoped that Barney and Freddy had been safely found. If nothing else their return would allow her to have her kitchen back.

'They're here!' cried Agnes, bringing the two boys up the long narrow hallway towards the kitchen, Barney looking dishevelled and sporting a swollen eye that was quickly turning from red to purple whilst Freddy was lagging behind holding Agnes's hand.

After a garbled explanation in which Barney said they had been chased by bigger boys Nancy Black lashed out at him, catching him a walloping thump on the side of his head.

'That's from me,' she spat, causing foaming saliva to spray all over the boy, 'because I know he won't chastise you!' She pointed to Archie. 'And look at the state of you!' she continued, ignoring Agnes who tried to explain that the two boys had been waylaid by bullies twice their size. 'This is what I thought would happen if my Freddy got mixed up with the likes of him.' She pointed to Barney.

'Hang on a minute...' Olive was just about to remonstrate with her neighbour but she was gently stopped by Archie who shook his head.

'It's enough that they are home safe and sound,' Archie said, ruffling Barney's hair. 'C'mon, son, let's get that eye looked at, shall we.'

'Well!' Nancy was affronted. 'It's no supper for this one tonight, I'll show him that he can't just run off and do as he pleases – like some I could mention.'

There was not a hint of gratitude to Agnes or Barney for rescuing the little boy from the bigger bullies. Nor did Nancy show any relief that he had been found safe when she said angrily, 'Now get next door and straight up those stairs to bed. As if I haven't got enough on my plate as it is!'

Everybody assembled in Olive's kitchen looked at each other, no doubt wondering what Nancy had to put up with that was so different to any other beleaguered Londoner just now. Agnes, although not expecting any word of thanks for bringing Freddy back in one piece, had expected his frantic grandmother to show the boy a little compassion and give him a reassuring cuddle.

'That woman would turn the milk of human nature sour, I'm sure,' Olive said, shaking her head in disbelief as she watched Nancy take her young grandson's hand and drag him out of the house.

ELEVEN

Double-checking she had her travel warrant and her identification card, Tilly made her way to Waterloo station where the platform was packed with men dressed in khaki, and the distinctive blues of the air force and navy. She looked around the station, her mouth drying as her stomach did somersaults. She had never travelled alone before and wondered what she had let herself in for.

She'd heard the obnoxious sobriquets, like 'officer's groundsheets', that had been attached to the ATS; she knew they weren't true and had been spread by malicious tongues at the beginning of the war, but she was also aware the ATS had proved themselves invaluable in the three years since, and even though she was proud to be 'doing her bit', she was still anxious at the prospect. This was a new life for her now and she imagined Agnes had felt much the same when she left the orphanage; how she wished she had

153

been there to say goodbye to her good friend and confidante before she left home. She was going to miss their nightly chats about everything: the war, the rationing, their sweethearts. Oh what had she done?

Tilly shuffled on the platform. Apart from the rare week away when she was younger, she had never strayed far from Article Row and her job as Almoner's assistant at Bart's hospital, so as well as being a huge adventure, her enrolment into the Territorials made her feel anxious. What if she wasn't up to the training? What if she didn't like it? Too bad, she thought, it's too late to do anything about it now.

Her thoughts were cut short when the train pulled in five minutes later and, clutching her suitcase and a piece of paper giving her the address of the camp she was to report to, she jostled with the servicemen to try to find somewhere to sit. Coughing in the pall of cigarette smoke that permeated every available space, Tilly moved slowly along the corridor, looking into each carriage and beginning to lose hope that she would ever find an empty one. She didn't want to sit in a carriage full of servicemen, overhearing their stories of war told in the colourful language of men who had somehow forgotten how to behave in the presence of a lady; her mother would have been appalled if she knew Tilly was within earshot of such expletives. But as she sidled towards the back of the train she realised she might not have a choice.

'Here y'are, darlin', there's a seat free in 'ere!' called a soldier, pointing to his knee. Smiling politely, Tilly declined his invitation, feeling very

154

apprehensive indeed, especially as they all laughed when she scurried down the corridor. Just as she was beginning to think she would have to stand for the duration of the journey she encountered a carriage right at the end of the train containing women only; obviously the servicemen were used to this kind of travelling and had made a beeline for the best carriages. Tilly noticed that there was enough space for one more passenger and she was determined it was going to be her.

Already tired from the scramble to find a seat Tilly threw her case onto the luggage rack above the heads of girls of her own age sitting reading and smoking, and who came in all shapes and sizes. One looked dowdy, as if she'd never seen the inside of a bathroom before; another was loud, telling the others what she was going to do when she got her first pay packet – spend it on going dancing and meeting servicemen, no doubt, thought Tilly critically; and a girl near the window, who moved over to let Tilly in, was in tears as the train began to pull out.

Tilly looked out of the window and watched as the train passed through anonymous stations, all signs removed for the duration of the war. She envied the flying birds in passing fields as she watched them swoop and soar in the still-blue sky and realised that she too felt free at last. It was a heady sensation that made her slip down in her seat a little before closing her eyes and wallowing in this new and strange excitement. She loved her mother dearly and would never do anything to upset or disgrace her. But there was no denying there came a time in a girl's life when she had to learn to stand on her own two feet and not rely on her mother. And now was just the right time for her, especially with Drew so far away.

She couldn't imagine what the future would hold, only that she would have to live it without him. However, this was a new chapter in her life – and his – so they would have to make the best of it. She didn't have time to ponder on his lack of communication any further as the train stopped and moments later another girl around the same age as herself trundled into the compartment and, in the midst of chaotic chatter, positioned herself in between Tilly and the whimpering girl sitting next to her who had no choice but to shift herself up, whilst the girls on the other end were squashed.

'Don't mind me!' the girl on the end said raising her eyes from the book she was reading.

'Sorry, love, you don't mind, do you?' said the new girl, who had leaned over to put her suitcase onto the luggage rack just as the train lurched and ended up on Tilly's knee.

'Careful,' Tilly said, slightly peeved at having her quiet reverie disturbed by a crowd of baying hyenas who had no thought for others. The girl excused herself and sat next to Tilly, wriggling into the small space. The manicured blonde, who reminded Tilly of Dulcie going by the rolling eyes under heavily mascaraed lashes, took her cigarettes from her bag with a disgruntled sigh. However she did offer them around and most of the girls took one, but much to Tilly's relief the girl sitting next to her said no. However, Tilly soon realised that her hair, freshly washed that morning with the last of her precious shampoo, would soon smell no better than an ashtray.

'So, where you off to then?' asked the new arrival.

Tilly was just about to tell her that loose lips sink ships when another girl piped up, 'We're all off to the ATS training camp.'

'Should you be telling me that?' Tilly asked, surprised at their candour. 'I could be anyone, you know.'

'Well, "Anyone", I'm Janet. Where you off to then?' the girl sitting next to her asked and Tilly started laughing, thinking Janet was a fast worker and no mistake.

'I'm Tilly, and I suppose I'm going to the same place as you.'

Suddenly the day took an even brighter turn as the girls all got to know each other. By the time they reached their destination it was as if they had been friends with each other for years. Tilly knew her mother would be pleased she had made some pals so soon. And shortly afterwards the train chugged into the station on a cloud of white smoke and a high-pitched, mournful whistle.

All the girls stood up and after grabbing their suitcases and bags from the overhead luggage rack slowly shuffled out of the carriage with Tilly trailing behind them, wondering what was ahead of her. She soon found out when as if out of nowhere came a strident female voice: 'Come on now, get a move on, we've got no time for slouches!'

'Bloomin' heck!' said Janet as she stepped off the train in front of Tilly. 'She's got a gob on 'er that would wake the dead. An' I thought me

157

mam could shout.' Everybody laughed, but not for long as a heavy-set female dashed along the platform to the rear of the breathless gaggle of women who had just clambered off the train.

'I am Drill Sergeant Bison and from now on I will be your replacement mother or your worst nightmare – it's completely up to you.'

'Sounds promising,' said Janet, with her Liverpool accent who sounded so like Sally, and gave Tilly a friendly dig in the arm with her elbow. 'She looks like a barrel of laughs, I don't think.'

'We weren't told about the likes of her in the recruitment office.' Tilly felt her spirits sink.

'The only advice I was given, and that was by me mam, was not to sit down on strange lavatory seats.'

'Why is that?' asked Tilly, beginning to think she had had a rather sheltered upbringing. Janet was staring at her open-mouthed, her eyebrows pleated in confusion.

'You know...?' Janet said, rolling her eyes in a southerly direction. 'You *know*!'

'I don't know.' Tilly was just as confused, especially when she saw Janet shrug her shoulders before trying to put what she meant into words without sounding crude.

'You know ... down there...' She nodded pointedly to the space below Tilly's stomach. 'There ... you can catch things off lavvy seats ... things like,' she lowered her voice to a whisper, 'VD.'

'I've never heard of it,' Tilly said innocently.

But she was sure that was about to change when Janet said, 'Oh wait till I tell yer ... living

158

near the Mersey docks you find out about things like that at a very early age.' She gave a knowing raise of her eyebrows as she dipped her chin, all the time keeping her eyes peeled for nosey-pokes who might be listening.

'Right, move along now,' called the drill sergeant. 'Lef-righ, lef-righ! No slacking at the back.' Without another thought Tilly found herself falling in with the drill sergeant's instructions to move her feet left then right, then left then right and giggling on a hop, skip and a jump as she did so.

'This could be fun,' she whispered to Janet as they fell into step beside each other. But their amusement was short-lived when they saw the huge khaki army truck waiting outside the little country station to take them to the training camp.

'How are we expected to get into that?' cried the blonde girl who looked like Dulcie and was called Pru. 'I've got my new stockings on and I don't want them laddered.'

'Well, if you did you could climb up it and get into the truck,' laughed Janet.

'Until then, you can do the same as everybody else – hitch up your skirt, take the hand that's offered to you and climb in,' said the now fierce-looking sergeant. Pru gave a little sniff before disappearing behind the truck to remove her stockings.

'I ain't laddering these for no one,' she said. 'There are limits to how much a girl is expected to do for king and country.' Tilly could only marvel at her impudence as the sergeant gave her a look that would curdle milk.

'Oh we've got a comedian in our midst,' said

159

the menacing drill sergeant. 'I like comedians, I do.' But it seemed to have no effect on Pru whatsoever as she slipped out of her sling-back shoes, flung them on the flat-back, and, after hitching her skirt and taking the hands of two male soldiers who were already on the truck, she clambered aboard like she was born to it.

'I bag the sack to sit on,' said Pru, giving the drill sergeant a defiant grin. Tilly, wishing she had Pru's gall, clambered on without a murmur and settled herself down before the rickety vehicle rolled and bounced along the country roads and she had to hang on to the sides for dear life.

They had been travelling a long time when someone started singing 'We're Going to Hang Out the Washing on the Siegfried Line', as dusk was drawing in, mainly, Tilly suspected, to allay the fear of the low-flying bats in the trees that lined the narrow lanes. When they reached the wide gates of the army camp, greeted by two women in army uniform who checked their credentials in minute detail, they all breathed a sigh of relief to be on terra firma again in one piece.

'I wish they'd hurry up, I'm starving,' said Janet, who waited at the back with Tilly and didn't make a fuss. 'I haven't eaten a thing since my breakfast this morning. I feel as if I've been travelling forever, Liverpool seems like another country and I'm aching all over.'

'That's nothing to the way you'll be feeling tomorrow night, Scouse,' said the drill sergeant with obvious glee, 'you've got to get through tonight first.'

Janet looked at Tilly and they both grimaced,

each wondering what tomorrow would bring. They had missed the evening meal by three hours and after climbing out of the lorry into the blackness of the open countryside, Tilly found herself standing on what felt like a rough cinder road and by the light of the moon could just about make out two lines of single-storey wooden huts, which they were informed would be their billets for the duration of their training.

'You, you, you and you over there,' barked the drill sergeant, pointing to Tilly, Janet, Veronica and Pru. 'Introduce yourselves to number one hut and you will be given further instructions.'

The four girls dragged their suitcases, which by now seemed considerably heavier, and did as they were told. Once inside they saw the thirty iron bunks that lined the walls of the hut. Tilly grimaced at the four thin unmade iron beds.

There was a chill in the place and the round black stove in the corner didn't seem to be throwing out much heat, Tilly noticed as her eyes scanned the long room where girls in various stages of undress were making beds, playing cards or lying on their bunks reading, or writing letters. All of them looked up when Tilly and the other three came inside.

'Say hello to these four girls,' said Drill Sergeant Bison, looking menacingly down the rows of beds.

'*Hello to these four girls*,' chorused the inhabitants of the hut, making Tilly smile.

'Right, I'll leave you to it. You are now confined to barracks for one week. You will have your vaccinations at o-nine-hundred hours, pick a bunk, settle down and be ready for roll call at o-six-

161

hundred tomorrow morning.'

'No one said anything about vaccinations,' said Tilly, her heart sinking; she hated needles.

'I'm being woken up at six a.m.?' Pru exclaimed, her eyes widening in disbelief.

'No,' the drill sergeant smiled, 'you are being woken at o-five-hundred. By o-six-hundred I expect you to have made your bed, stand at the end of it in readiness for kit muster and be available for roll call, then if everything is to my satisfaction you will go for breakfast, and by the looks of you slovenly lot it most certainly will not be, and in that case you will forgo breakfast altogether.' Tilly noted the gleam of anticipated spats to come in the sergeant's eyes.

'I'm just in the little room at the back if you should have nightmares, girls. Lights out in ten minutes – good night.' With that Drill Sergeant Bison left the room and the four girls looked at each other in dismay.

'I'll never wake up at five o'clock. That's the middle of the night,' Pru said, shoving a pillow into a white cotton case after choosing the bed near the door.

'You will the second time,' a voice from the back of the hut piped up. 'Oh, and I'd advise you to go to the toilet before you get into bed because if you disturb anybody you'll soon know about it.'

'Where are the toilets?' Tilly asked and was disappointed to find they were outside, across the road near the field that contained a rather unfriendly-looking bull.

'I'm not going by myself,' Pru said. 'I've never come across anything bigger than a dog in my life and I ain't arguing with that chap.'

'Come on,' said Veronica, the girl who'd been crying on the train but who seemed to have brightened considerably, and due to the fact that she'd hardly spoken since they all met, nobody realised was from Scotland. 'I'm used to bulls, I'll take ye.'

'Oh, well,' said Tilly, 'no point in us going in twos, let's all go together.'

'I'd take that red scarf off if I were you,' said a girl further down the hut. Tilly hastily shoved the scarf into her coat pocket in the midst of girlish laughter. She wasn't so sure she liked her new-found freedom any more and longed to be tucked up in her own bed sharing confidences with Agnes, especially when she saw the thin mattress and realised why all the girls had referred to it as a 'biscuit'.

Tilly groaned; she had never had to make her own bed before, but then, what could be so hard about it? And she had never been as free as a bird before either. Somehow, she thought, this may just be fun!

'If my mother could see me now,' said Tilly, after being shown how to make a bed army style, whilst unfolding the rough grey blankets that had crisp starched sheets sandwiched between them, a pillow on top of the thin rolled mattress completing the little pile, 'she'd be making this bed for me.'

'If my mother could see this she'd be down the pawnshop hocking the lot,' Janet laughed, making all the other girls smile. Tilly liked Janet; there was no side to her, what you saw was what you got from what she could tell. After making her bed

163

and putting the rest of her belongings away she was settling down to write a letter to her mother about the events of the day when suddenly the lights went out. A collective moan echoed around the room and Tilly was left with her thoughts before drifting into an uncomfortable sleep.

In the cold grey light of dawn before the birds had even woken up, Drill Sergeant Bison flung open the barrack-room door, took a deep breath and emitted a thundering sound that seemed hardly feasible coming from a woman. Tilly wanted to tell her to keep the noise down but knew she would never be so bold.

Within moments every girl was out of her bed and jumping to attention on the frozen linoleum as Sergeant Bison marched up and down the narrow room barking orders that Tilly was sure she would never remember as she hopped from one icy foot to the other.

'Slippers!' Drill Sergeant Bison turned immediately to Tilly. 'Keep still!'

Tilly almost fell backwards onto the bed as the words hit her full in the face. Slippers? she thought, silently shocked. Who did she think she was calling slippers?

'You!' Bison growled in a most unladylike fashion as if reading Tilly's mind. After spending a fitful night on a hard thin mattress Tilly realised that the army didn't look as enticing as it once did. And it was nothing like the glamorous posters.

She couldn't wait to have some breakfast and write to her mother who, she knew, would be eagerly awaiting an update on how she was faring.

However, Tilly was in for a shock when she discovered that they were confined to barracks for a week and prohibited from writing home for the foreseeable future. She then found that breakfast would not be consumed until every inch of the wooden hut they were now to call home was cleaned from top to bottom.

'What, all of it?' asked Janet, with a look of disbelief.

'Every single inch,' said the corporal, Tannaway, who had come into the hut to relieve Drill Sergeant Bison and looked surprisingly fresh and bright as if she had been up all night getting ready for this inspection. 'I want the beds made to specific requirements, every surface cleaned until it gleams, the linoleum polished until you can see your face in it, every cupboard, every bedstead, dust-free and spotless in every area.' She paused. 'Any questions?'

'Does this have to be done *every* week?' Tilly asked. She wasn't used to heavy cleaning, preferring to leave it up to her mum who was much better at it than she would ever be.

'Every *day*! If that's not too much trouble of course, Slippers.' The corporal's words were laced with a heavy inflection of sarcasm and Tilly knew that she didn't want to get on the wrong side of this woman who looked as if she could eat you for breakfast and still look for another morsel.

'I didn't think she could hear me,' Tilly said to nobody in particular, flipping her blanket the way she had seen her mother do it, deciding to keep her head down.

'I can hear the grass grow, Slippers,' said the

165

corporal with obvious pride in her achievement.

'Blimey!' Tilly whispered. 'Good job I didn't say anything wrong.' She soon realised that the drill sergeant had been a mild-mannered pussy-cat compared to Corporal Tannaway and set about doing the best she could in the time she was given.

At breakfast, they all sat at long benches to eat their meal, which was comprised of porridge, fish or eggs and toast, much to the surprised delight of many new recruits who had never seen so much food since the beginning of the war. Later they were lined up outside the medical hut to wait their turn to be inoculated against smallpox, tetanus and cholera, little realising that they might be spending the next few days fighting a fever whilst under Drill Sergeant Bison's beady-eyed observation.

Then it was on to the supply hut where, being a wing of the army, they were provided with everything khaki, from elasticated bloomers and lisle stockings to big heavy greatcoats, issued by a corporal, whose trained eye was not skilled in the weights and measures department, judging by the enormous uniform offered to a pint-sized girl from Birmingham who was lost in a sea of material, and quite reluctant to part with her new clothing even though she was told that she could swap with someone who had a uniform more her size.

'You forgot your "hussif", Soldier,' called the drill sergeant to Tilly. 'Don't you intend to do any mending or have you already got somebody to do your chores for you?'

'*Hussif?*' Tilly looked puzzled, realising that she

would have to try to stay on the right side of Drill Sergeant Bison who looked as if she took no prisoners, before going back to the long desk where the supplies were given out and being handed a white cotton wallet containing needles, thread, spare buttons and other necessities.

'You might think of it as a "housewife",' said the sergeant sweetly, handing Tilly two shoe brushes, a brass strip for cleaning her buttons and finally, balancing on top of the whole lot, a military respirator.

'Guard them with your life, they are the essentials, you will not be supplied with any more, lose them and you die,' Bison said without looking up and then shouted without preamble: 'Next!'

There was a scattering of laughing girls all gauging their sizes when she got back to the barracks, swapping skirts and jackets as the ones they had been given weren't the right fit, and in the commotion Tilly finally managed to accrue a whole uniform that was as near to her size as possible.

'If I roll the top over it will be the right length.'

'Just put a belt around the skirt and nobody will notice.'

'Three square meals a day and I'll soon fill this jacket...'

For the very first time in her life Agnes had a room all of her own and she wasn't sure she liked it. Even in the orphanage she had shared with the other children or, later, with the servants who were employed to care for the officers in control of the establishment.

Pulling the bedclothes up under her chin,

Agnes's thoughts turned to Ted, and she let her imagination roam to the future day when they would be man and wife. She wondered what it would be like being married to Ted, and then she pondered – and where the idea came from she could not imagine – whether his mother would ever allow him to wed whilst she had breath in her body to stop him.

Agnes suddenly pulled the bedclothes over her head as if hiding from the thought she had the audacity to conjure up, like she did when she was a child and had voiced the longing to have a family and a home of her own and been laughed at for it.

Living here with Olive and the other girls was the closest she had ever come to having a real 'family' to call her own, although since Tilly left for training in the ATS Agnes felt as if she had lost a sister.

Tears stung the back of her eyes now as she recalled the nights she and Tilly would lie awake and discuss what they would do when this awful war was over. Tilly would confirm her dearest wish to marry Drew and go and live in America, and she in turn would tell Tilly of her longing to live in a house in the countryside with geese and chickens being chased by laughing children.

It was a daft idea, she knew, but it was that dream which had kept her going all these years – and it didn't look as if it would ever come to fruition, as Ted worked on the railway and there was no chance of having a house in the country-side when you had to drive trains around the underground stations, now was there? Nor a mother who would never contemplate leaving London, she supposed.

Sally was late home, as an unexploded bomb had been found near the hospital and they couldn't leave until it was made safe, so she decided to make herself useful instead. If nothing else it would take her mind off worrying about George, whom she was missing dearly.

Closing the front door with her heel she took off her navy-blue nurse's cloak and noticed a letter addressed to her on the highly polished hall table. It was from Callum.

He was in the South Atlantic fighting through blizzards as well as the blasted enemy. Sally shuddered. She could only imagine how difficult blizzards in the Atlantic must be. He was polite, as usual, asking how everybody was and letting her know that he missed little Alice and to tell his little niece he would bring her something nice when he got home. Whenever that might be.

A small pang of ... what? Pity? Regret? Sally couldn't make up her mind; but she had come to terms with her father's relationship with Callum's sister, her one-time best friend when they were both trainee nurses, and had reconciled herself to the knowledge she had treated Callum very badly when he brought little Alice to her last December.

Sally could not imagine life without her little half-sister now and with that realisation she knew she had to make amends with Callum too. A former teacher, he had initially stolen her heart when they first met and he even told her, on that Boxing Day back at her mother's house, he shouldn't have kissed her like that, calling himself the worst kind of cad because he didn't then have anything to offer her. But that was then.

Things had changed now. She had changed and she had George. No doubt Callum had changed too. She should never have treated him the way she did, she thought, as her eyes skimmed the page of Callum's perfect copperplate handwriting. They had both lost so much, it was about time they became friends again.

Little Alice needed a stable, united family and it was Sally's aim to put that right today. She decided to write to Callum before she went to bed.

As her eyelids grew heavy Agnes's thoughts drifted to the journey home that evening. She missed Ted walking her home from Chancery Lane for two reasons. The first was because that was virtually the only time they had to themselves now, as his mother didn't like him leaving her and his sisters alone in case there was an air raid, and the other was because, silly fool that she was, Agnes thought she was being followed by a man in a gabardine mackintosh and a wide-brimmed hat.

Every time she turned around he stopped and looked in a shop window or turned off down an alleyway, only to emerge from a turning a little further on. A few times she told herself not to be so silly. For what reason would anybody want to follow an underground railway worker? Then, hurrying home, her mind conjured up all sorts of horrors as he drew closer. Agnes had been so scared she went into a shop just to ask what time it was until he had disappeared out of view.

Maybe she was imagining it? He might have been going home from work in the same direction and never even noticed her. But she still couldn't shake the fear from her mind. She wouldn't tell Ted though; he'd think she was being silly.

'Speak up, love, I can't hear you very well.' Tilly felt a lump in her throat as she strained to hear Olive's voice over the crackling telephone wires. Her mother had arranged to use the phone in the Simpsons' house, where Drew and George used to lodge before Drew... She tried not to think of him now, knowing it wouldn't take much to bring her to tears after such gruelling weeks of training. Having never been away from home before, the sound of Olive suddenly made her realise how things were quickly changing.

'Are there any letters for me?' Tilly asked, eager to know if Drew had written yet; it would be lovely if her mother could forward them on to her. It would make this basic training so much easier to bear if she had Drew's letters to look forward to at the end of an exhausting day, or to have them next to her heart when she was on night duty guarding the camp whilst the others slept.

'No, love,' her mother said, 'but never mind, you'll have a lot to keep your mind occupied, I'm sure.' Although her mother's voice was welcome, the advice irritated Tilly and she only just stopped herself from telling her that she and the twenty-nine other girls, in all shapes and sizes and from all walks of life, who were accommodated in the single-storey barracks were becoming quite adept at Drill: marching back and forth across the yard

171

to the loud instructions of a drill sergeant who would put Nancy Black to shame. Indeed it seemed to be the only thing they did all day apart from clean their uniform and barracks.

'I said,' Tilly shouted down the Bakelite receiver, swallowing her disappointment, 'we got here safely and the girls are all wonderful!' She turned to a long line of girls waiting for the telephone who whooped and clapped behind her. She laughed suddenly, the lump in her throat forgotten, waving them away. This was the first chance any of them had of ringing home, if they had a telephone at home, that is. Some of the girls didn't even have a front door any more.

'Come on, hurry up, Anyone,' called a voice from along the line, reminding Tilly of the nickname she had been given on the train, 'we've all got mothers to reassure, you know!'

'I'll have to go, Mum, I'll write to you tonight and let you know how things are.' Tilly only just caught her mother's fading goodbye before the pips could be heard. Putting the Bakelite receiver back on its cradle, she turned, gave a small curtsey, laughing.

TWELVE

'Young Barney's been a good pal to little Freddy whilst he's been staying with Nancy,' Olive told Dulcie who was sitting quietly at the kitchen table drinking a much-needed cup of tea after her shift

172

at the munitions factory. 'Apparently, Barney had heard Agnes telling Nancy about the subterranean shelters below the underground and when they were chased by the bigger boys, Barney hid Freddy in there for safekeeping before taking a terrible beating from the scoundrels... Dulcie, are you all right?'

'I'm just tired, that's all.' Dulcie gave a weak smile and took another sip of her tea. She certainly couldn't tell Olive the true reason.

'You're looking a bit peaky, I must say. Maybe you should go and see Dr Shaw.'

'Oh, don't fuss, Olive,' Dulcie said impatiently. All she wanted to do was take her cup of tea upstairs, crawl into bed and fall into a deep carefree sleep. 'I'm sorry, I didn't mean to sound so rude, I've had a difficult night and I am so tired and longing for my bed.'

'Go on, you go up, I'll make sure you are not disturbed.'

'I wish I could,' said Dulcie, rubbing her eyes with the pad of her hand, and grimacing when she realised she had smudged her heavily mascaraed eyes, 'but I promised I would meet my mother in the Lyons tea rooms at eleven.' Dulcie was dreading the meeting. She had written to her mother a week ago telling her that she needed to see her and explained that she couldn't visit the house, asking her to meet her in Peter Jones in the King's Road before they went on to have something to eat at Lyons Corner House, which had been fixed up after the bombings.

'I'm sure she would understand if you couldn't make it,' Olive offered sympathetically.

'As she's not on the telephone there's no way of getting a message to her at this late notice,' sighed Dulcie. 'I'll just go and have a wash and get changed out of these working clothes.' She scowled at her navy-blue bib and braces.

Olive nodded. Dulcie, irrepressible girl that she usually was, seemed to have an aura of defeat about her lately, and she wondered if it had anything to do with her American friend who had been killed a while ago or was it something more than that. Had he left her with something to remember him by? Olive wondered. Dulcie was a girl who enjoyed herself. She knew what was what. She was nobody's fool; surely she wouldn't be so foolish as to get herself...? No, Olive thought, Dulcie wouldn't fall for that kind of caper and she had no intention of asking. It didn't do to pry and if Dulcie wanted her to know what was on her mind she would tell her soon enough.

But for now she would say nothing and wait until the poor girl wanted to tell her. After all, it must be something quite serious if she needed to see her own mother, who by all accounts had never had much time for her.

'I'm fine, honestly,' Dulcie said, suddenly bringing Olive out of her deep thoughts. 'I haven't seen Mum for a few weeks and I thought I'd be off work, so I promised her a day out in town. I'm off tonight, so I can catch up on my beauty sleep tomorrow.' Her face brightened but Olive could tell there was still something wrong. Maybe she was worrying about her brother, Rick, Olive thought and, satisfying herself that was the problem, she said no more.

'What d'you wanna come all this way for, we could be bombed as we drink our tea,' Dulcie's mother moaned whilst they waited for the waitress, in her black dress and white apron, to come and take their order.

'There haven't been any air raids for ages, Mum,' Dulcie said impatiently, wanting to get straight to the point before her courage failed her.

'Have you seen anything of your sister lately?' her mother asked, giving a little sniff of disgust. 'She ain't even been to see me or your father since ... well, I suppose she's been busy on the stage – it must be hard for her to get away when she's got so little time between shows.'

'I don't know where she is, I'm sure.' Dulcie bridled, realising that even though she had asked her mother here for a pleasant day out her mother still had to bring Edith into it. Dulcie hardly dared think about the trouble that little minx had caused.

'Mum, can I tell you something?' If she didn't say it now... 'I'm pregnant.' The words were blurted out in a sudden rush and her mother's face turned a pale shade of grey and for the first time in her life Dulcie watched as she crumbled.

'I don't know what to do.' Dulcie could feel the unshed tears stinging her eyes, dry through lack of sleep. 'Mum, you have to help me.'

'Oh, I can help you, all right.' Her mother seemed very angry now. 'I knew something like this would happen and if the truth be known I thought it would be Edith who would bring this news to me – I thought you had more sense.' She

175

was quiet for a moment and Dulcie looked out of the window, over the rooftops of London as far as her eyes could see, and she wished that she hadn't had to bring this news to her mother.

'Leave it with me,' her mother said with a weary sigh. 'I'll have a word with someone I know and we can have it all sorted by the weekend and say no more about it. Have you got any money?'

'Of course I've got money, how much do you want?'

'Not me, girl, for the...' Her mother flicked her head to one side instead of saying the word and Dulcie's eyebrows pleated together.

'What?'

'You know, Dulcie, you're not stupid, you've been around ... and look at the result!'

'You mean?' The light went on in Dulcie's head; her mother was actually talking of introducing her to someone who would take her baby away.

'Get rid of it,' her mother said as Dulcie gave a short, almost inaudible gasp and her heart hammered against her ribs. That was the first time she had allowed herself to silently say the word 'baby' and as she did, something inside her changed. But what choice did she have? Her disgrace would be there for all to see if she didn't 'get rid of it', as her mother so succinctly put it.

'I'll get word to you tonight,' said Mrs Simmonds. 'Give me your landlady's address and I'll make sure to get hold of you when I've been to see...' She left the rest of the sentence unspoken and they finished their tea and rock bun in comparative silence.

Later that afternoon Dulcie had a message

from her mother to tell her to be at Aber Street in Stepney at eight o'clock that night. Aber Street was very close to where her family lived before her parents moved at the start of the war, and as Dulcie hadn't been near the East End since then she wasn't looking forward to going there now.

'This time tomorrow all your troubles will be over, gel,' Dulcie heard her mother say before staring at the receiver and replacing it in the black Bakelite cradle. She had heard the stories of back-street abortionists, some of them none too clean and none of them qualified if the truth be known, and her stomach churned.

What if something went wrong? What if she died? What choice did she have? Olive would throw her out for sure and it would prove her right that Dulcie was no better than she ought to be. No, she was being unfair, Olive had never treated her any differently to the other girls who lodged in her comfortable, ordered house. But Dulcie knew she would have nowhere to go. Her mother wouldn't accept her back, that was certain, on account of her father being so strict.

No, Dulcie thought with a heavy sigh, she had no say in the matter. Oh, Lord, what had she let herself in for? She hurried upstairs, flung herself on her bed and sobbed. Thankfully she was left alone to do so.

About two hours later, after a cool bath and carefully applying what little make-up she had left, Dulcie dressed in a pale blue sweetheart-necked dress with puffed sleeves and threw a white cardigan across her shoulders; the day had been particularly warm so she didn't want to wear her heavy coat.

Her mother had told her she would need to bring enough money to pay for the 'procedure' and before she went to the envelope she kept behind the mirror Dulcie took one last look at her reflection. The only change in her figure was a fuller if tender enlargement in the bust department, she thought, but apart from that nothing; her condition was not obvious.

Her eyes were a little sunken and even through her expert make-up she looked pale, she noticed, putting it down to the lack of sleep and worry, as she pinched her cheeks to give them a bit of added colour, not to mention that wretched morning sickness that seemed to last all day – she wouldn't be sorry to see the back of that!

After counting the money she put a roll of ten-bob notes in her handbag. She had worked long hours and risked her life for many weeks to save that amount, and now it was to be used to get rid of her shameful secret. Dulcie's throat tightened but she willed herself not to cry. She had never imagined that she would stoop to this … this terrible thing. Bad girls 'got rid' of their babies. Not the likes of her, she thought. Fighting back the tears Dulcie hurried down the stairs and out of the front door without a word to anybody.

Dulcie tried to block out the memories of 'fixers' her mother knew who 'helped women out', women who were in the family way again and couldn't afford more kids, or whose husband had been serving overseas for the last twelve months and no matter how much they regretted their actions with either knitting needles or hot baths and gin, the cuckoo had to be removed from the nest.

The bus was crowded with women in head-scarves, the air stuffy with the mixed smells of over-ripe body odour combined with a vague waft of carbolic soap, which vied with the rhythmic lurch and sway of the vehicle to make Dulcie's stomach heave. How could she have been so stupid as to go into a public house with a stranger and allow herself to be plied with alcohol?

Because you are vain, that's why! an admonishing voice inside her head scolded as she stared out of the grimy, dust-covered window. The bus was nearing the East End now and Dulcie was horri-fied to see the devastation Hitler's bombs had caused. Almost everything she had known was damaged or destroyed.

The gaping, rubble-strewn spaces where houses once stood looked as desolate as she felt, rows of shops – gone! In their grimy place children scrambled over mounds of masonry that had, at one time, been someone's residence or place of work.

A beautiful golden ray of light caught a shard of discarded glass, producing a dazzling flash that seemed inappropriate in this godforsaken place and Dulcie vowed that any child of hers would never know such degradation. *Any child of hers except this one*, she thought sadly.

Dulcie knew what she was about to do was illegal and was punishable by a prison sentence as no decent doctor worth his salt or reputation would perform an abortion and no hospital would either. But what was she to do? If she had money, lots and lots of money, she could pay a clandestine visit to a doctor who made his fortune out of that sort of thing, but she didn't have lots of money, she was just an ordinary girl working in a munitions factory who'd got herself into a bit of trouble.

If the bus hadn't been so full or if she was back in her own room at Olive's house, Dulcie knew she would have scoffed aloud at the last thought that had popped into her head. *A bit of trouble?* More like a whole heap of it!

Poor women didn't stand a chance once the kids came along, Dulcie could see the evidence all around her as the bus trundled down the Mile End Road. They were doomed if they didn't look out for themselves. Especially when money was tight and some of the men were tighter. And no matter how much pride Stepney housewives took in their homes and no matter how much elbow grease they used to keep their little dwellings clean and well maintained it would never be enough, not for her anyway, and she wanted no part of it. She wanted a nice house with a garden, somewhere for her kids, out of harm's way.

She wanted her children to see trees and flowers and fields and grow strong and healthy – have a good education. All these things her child deserved along with the nurturing love that only a mother could give. All the attention that she never had...

Unconsciously, Dulcie placed a protective hand on the gentle swell of her abdomen as the clippie rang the bell to let the female driver know people wanted to get off at the next stop. And it was only when she arrived at her destination that the first stirrings of doubt began to creep into her head.

'You got the money?' Dulcie's mother asked without preamble; no 'hello' or 'how are you feeling'. In fact it took her mother all her time to even look in her direction and Dulcie, her humiliation obvious, felt that like a bad smell, the woman would have preferred to waft her own daughter away, and have nothing more to do with her.

'Two guineas. You got that, Dulcie?' her mother continued, looking ahead, her back ramrod straight, her proud head held high as they walked down the back streets where teams of children were playing war games amongst the bomb-scarred ruins.

'Of course I've got it,' Dulcie answered, a little out of breath but catching up as her mother knocked on a dilapidated door at the far end of the side road near the turning. Her insides were jumping around like jelly on a plate. Moments later the door was opened by a little woman in a grubby-looking wrapover pinafore that barely hid drab clothing, her hair covered from her frizzy fringe to the nape of her neck in a thick black hairnet, who looked up only momentarily.

'I take it you're Dulcie?' she asked, holding the front door open just wide enough to allow them into the darkened passageway.

'No need for introductions,' her mother said stiffly and Dulcie felt all courage leave her as they were ushered into a front room; the closed curtains only partly concealed the shabby interior, and the stench of overflowing drains and miasma of flying insects did nothing to allay Dulcie's fears.

'*Oh, God, help me,*' Dulcie thought and fleetingly, as the sombre lament of a ship's horn sounded in the nearby dockyard, an old phrase she remembered seeing on a soot-covered Victorian workhouse popped into her head: '*abandon hope all ye who enter...*'

Dulcie looked with pleading eyes at her mother, begging her not to make her do this thing. But her mother, rejecting her silent plea, only nodded in the direction of the woman's open hand, and Dulcie unfurled her tightly clenched fingers and placed the money into the grimy palm.

As the woman opened the little cupboard that housed the gas meter Dulcie was horrified to see her reach inside the dust-covered interior to retrieve an array of vicious-looking paraphernalia: a chipped white enamel bowl containing a length of rubber tubing and a grubby-looking jug as well as evil-looking crochet hooks and knitting needles that filled Dulcie with the fear of God-only-knows.

'Drop yer drawers, dearie, you can leave your stockings on, it's all the same to me,' said the woman whose face was almost unrecognisable in the dimness of the room, quite unabashed. 'Just get yourself on the table, lie down, it'll be over as soon as you like.'

A kettle boiled on the inflamed coals of a black-lead range, adding to the already insufferable clamminess of the little room that housed only a large wooden table and a sideboard littered with dirty clothing.

'*Please forgive me, Lord... I know not what I do.*'

The imploring voice inside Dulcie's head sounded very much like her own, but it couldn't be, she realised, because why would she ask forgiveness for something she could stop at any moment?

She looked at her mother pulling at the collar of her woollen coat and the knot of her scarf, and wondered irrationally what had possibly possessed her to dress in such a way for the occasion. Anything to distract herself from the awful, terrible thing she was about to do. The gossamer-fine hairs on her arms stood on end and a cold chill ran through her even in the heat of the room as the sound of laughter, from children who had been brought back from evacuation now that things had calmed down a bit, carried on the stifling air. It was at that moment that Dulcie knew she couldn't go through with destroying her baby. What had she been thinking? This *thing* she was about to do was wrong.

It didn't matter that hundreds, maybe thousands of women went through it every day; she knew nobody was going to take this precious gift from her. Having her baby removed wasn't like getting rid of an unsightly pimple, she realised – this tiny, helpless creation inside her was a living human being, part of her and part of a man who had been as lonely and as lost as she had been.

Would she ever be able to live with herself again if she went through with getting rid of her little indiscretion for the sake of her mother's good name? Dulcie asked herself. But she didn't want or even need her mother's approval, she was over twenty-one, she didn't depend on her family for money – they wouldn't give her any if she did – and, looking now at the determined set of her mother's thin lips, she knew she couldn't give two hoots any more about the shame she would bring upon her family. What did they care, after all?

People were dying on a daily basis, the world had turned upside down; men were dropping in their thousands. This child had a right to carry on his father's bloodline even if he would never have a paternal link!

Dulcie's stomach heaved its disapproval and before she could disgrace herself there in the front room of a bomb-damaged East End terraced house, she bolted from the room, slamming the front door behind her, and didn't stop until she reached the bus stop at the top of the road, quickly followed by her mother.

'You stupid little cow!' Mrs Simmonds said through clenched teeth. 'Don't you realise what you've done?'

'Oh, I'm ever so sorry, did I embarrass you, Mum? Did I run out without paying enough?' Dulcie rummaged in her bag and took out some more notes and pushed the money into her mother's hand. 'Here, give 'er this, I wouldn't want anybody short-changed.'

'It's not like that, Dulcie,' her mother said. 'Think of what you're doing, think of the life you're going to 'ave now, scrimping and scraping. Living 'and to mouth like...'

'Like who, Mum?' Dulcie asked, knowing her mother had always tried to put a brave face on things, making out her husband's wage was enough to support the family, to the point where

she would pass her weekly bill money to a neighbour to keep the tally men from knocking on their
door of a Friday night. Anything to prevent her
father finding out she couldn't manage on the
pittance he tipped up.

'...Like all the other poor mares what have no
choice, Dulcie! You're a good-lookin' gel, you
ought to know the way things turn out if you
don't play the game, and you're not stupid.'

'Well, that's a first.' Dulcie's eyes were wide but
her voice dripped sarcasm. 'My mother giving
me praise after all these years.'

'Look.' Her mother's long-suffering sigh proved
to Dulcie that she was nothing but an irritation
to her family. 'You gotta do what you gotta do
and that's an end to it.'

'But it isn't an end to it, is it, Mum?' Dulcie
needed to make her mother understand, and with
hands splayed across her abdomen she urged her
mother to see her view for a change. 'Getting rid
of the life in here might only take moments, but it
will stay with me for the rest of my life – there
won't be a day goes by that I won't wonder what
it would have been, or who it would have looked
like. I could be carrying the next Prime Minister,
who knows?'

'Dulcie, you always was a stupid bitch,' her
mother said in exasperated tones, 'but that's what
goes with 'avin' your head stuck in the clouds all
your life. You didn't 'ave a clue what was going on
around you, always wanting better, always wanting
more, but you can't 'ave no more.' Dulcie watched
as her mother spread her arms wide, looking
around as if showing her the place for the first

time. 'This is it,' said Mrs Simmonds. 'It don't get no better than this.' She paused as if waiting for her words to sink in and when Dulcie made no move to agree or disagree she continued in a more persuasive tone, 'I hoped that one day you'd see sense... Look at your sister...'

Dulcie's heart sank. 'I wondered how long it would take before we got around to talking about Edith.' She knew her mother would always favour her sister. ''Bye, Mum, take care,' she said as a bus drew up to the stop and with the single-mindedness that had taken her through her life so far, she vowed that even if she was ridiculed or shamed and called every awful name under the sun, she would live her life her way and she would never speak to her mother again.

With tears coursing freely down her cheeks Dulcie hopped onto the trolley bus. She knew there was only one person she could talk to now.

THIRTEEN

Tilly could feel her face burning in the unseasonably warm weather at the end of her basic training, and she had to keep very still, eyes front, shoes polished, uniform pressed to within an inch of its weave. She stood on the parade ground and stared at a brick in the cookhouse wall, knowing that if she took her eyes from it she would fall over. Spine straight, shoulders back. Her rifle, which she wasn't allowed to fire, was getting heavier by the second.

Initially Tilly had endured rather than enjoyed her basic training under the strident timbre of Drill Sergeant Bison, who had promised to be her best friend or her worst enemy and more often than not had proved to be the latter. Up before dawn and down before dusk, Tilly had peeled a mountain of potatoes every day. She had also learned to strip down the engine of a lorry and put it back together again, drive, march, more times than she could recall, in expert unison with the rest of the company around the parade ground, and salute – she had to salute everybody, it seemed. The lack of privacy, which at first had horrified her, became a way of life and she, like Janet who came from a large family, could strip off at the drop of a hat without batting an eyelid.

Drill Sergeant Bison struck terror into Tilly's heart – the eleventh commandment should have stated that 'thou shalt not be late on parade'. Unfortunately Tilly nearly always was, and found getting up in the morning not the easiest of achievements. Once when she was late she was made to march around the parade ground at seven a.m. the next morning until the rest of the company joined her at eight a.m.

Another reason for strife was the matter of her bed. Each morning she had to strip it, fold the sheets and blankets separately before stacking them up on top of the biscuit mattress. One morning Tilly overslept and didn't have time to do it – it was either that or be late on parade, she thought, so she left the bed. Unfortunately, Tilly only realised there was a CO's inspection that day when she got back to the hut and was sent for, severely reprimanded and confined to camp for seven days. In the beginning she wanted to go home to her mother, vowing that the army life didn't give her the freedom she craved and it wasn't as glamorous as the posters made out.

But now her training was over Tilly was surprised that she felt so forlorn. She had made good friends here and after today, she knew, they would be scattered in various places around the British Isles or even overseas.

She could feel herself beginning to sway slightly. Trying to stay upright during the long speeches, her mind wandered once more over the last few weeks. She had learned to drive and repair engines, she discovered her favourite transport was a motorbike and sidecar, and she dreamed of becoming a dispatch rider delivering important documents all over the country, anything to keep her mind from dwelling on her past relationship with Drew Coleman and his sudden and obviously permanent departure back to America.

Tilly could feel a trickle of moisture running from beneath her cap and down the side of her face but she daren't move to wipe it away. Her naturally curly hair began to spring out of the Kirby grip and plaster itself to her sticky forehead, and she was sure that if she didn't move her legs soon they would buckle; one girl near her had already passed out on the parade ground long before she 'passed out' of basic training. Surely it couldn't be much longer?

And then it came, the long awaited order to 'Dissssmissss!!!!'

Tilly, Janet, Veronica and Pru relaxed with huge sighs along with every other ATS girl before throwing their immaculately brushed caps into the air. Now, their proud passing-out ceremony was over and their hard weeks of training had come to an end.

'I can't wait to rest me poor plates,' Pru said, rubbing her feet after all the hugs and back-slapping. She bent to pick up her discarded cap and flicked the dust from the rim. 'I'm really looking forward to a good sit-down at the concert.'

They were being entertained in the dining hall, which had been temporarily transformed into a makeshift theatre by 'D' company, performing a farewell concert for all the new recruits who were being posted elsewhere. Then afterwards there was a 'let-your-hair-down' dance, after a short respite to turn the mess hall into a dance hall.

'I hope we can stay together,' Tilly said to Janet, Veronica and Pru, who had become good friends since they all started their basic training together. Tilly had joined the army wet behind the ears and not knowing 'drill from drinking water' – or so the sergeant had told her that first day which now seemed so long ago.

'I heard some of us are being transferred to Plymouth,' Veronica said, her gentle Scottish lilt barely audible. All the girls looked at each other and grimaced.

'I wanted to be posted to London,' said Tilly, much to the amusement of the others.

'So you could go home for tea,' Pru laughed. She'd joined only when she was forced to. Janet, being a straight-talking Scouser, challenged Pru, and the atmosphere turned somewhat frosty for a moment until Pru said, 'Obviously, I was only joking. I would not have missed this for the world.' Her eyes were glassy with unshed tears. 'I do hope we can stay together wherever they send us.'

'What, all of us?' said Janet with uncrushable Liverpool humour. 'Hitler would be quaking in his jack-boots.' The others laughed and the teary moment passed as they linked their arms and made their way to the mess hall for the concert, where, much to their delight, Veronica was expected to sing.

'Are you nervous?' Tilly asked as they deposited her at the stage door, commonly known as the back door where army provisions were usually delivered.

'Nervous?' Veronica asked in her soft Highland burr. 'Quaking in *my* boots, more like,' she said paraphrasing Janet, who gave her a huge sisterly hug.

'You'll be fine,' the others cried in unison. 'Break a leg, give 'em what for!' Veronica managed a sickly smile before disappearing inside the hall.

Walking around to the front the rest of them voiced their opinion that Veronica might be too shy to sing her debut tonight. However, later, much to their delight and pride, bringing the farewell concert to a close, Veronica wowed the audience with a heartfelt, poignant rendition of 'The White Cliffs of Dover', the song made famous by the Forces' sweetheart, Vera Lynn.

There wasn't a dry eye in the concert hall when she finished to thunderous applause and a standing ovation. And later, Veronica was being positively pursued by some very handsome and brave soldiers who had already seen action and who were brought over from the military hospital. The others noticed with proud delight that their friend, the quiet, gentle, Scottish lassie, was being sought in the popular 'Paul Jones' dance by American soldiers too, who had been brought to the camp for the passing-out parade.

'They always say it is the quiet ones you have to watch,' Janet laughed and the others all nodded in agreement.

'But it's far too warm for me in here,' Tilly said, tugging at her collar. 'I think I'll go outside and get a breath of fresh air.'

'Good thinking,' said a typically cockney male voice behind her. 'You go outside and I'll order you a drink.' Tilly spun around, indignant that the soldier should presume she would accept hydration from just anybody, and then she saw who it was.

'Rick!' Tilly's mouth refused to close when she saw Dulcie's brother standing there and was soon caught in his strong embrace, which lifted her off her feet, although when he let go of her Tilly noticed that in his left hand, he was holding a white stick.

'Rick? You ... you're...?'

'Blind? Well yes, almost,' Rick said whilst Tilly caught her breath. 'Although I do have a little sight, but not enough to keep me in the army now,' he continued in his familiar matter-of-fact tone, so like his sister's. Tilly recalled having a soft spot for him when Dulcie first moved into Article Row all those years ago before she met and fell in love with

191

Drew. If she was honest, Tilly realised, she'd had more than a soft spot for Rick at first, she was positively besotted by him. And now he had tragically lost almost all the use of his eyes.

'How long have you been...? What happened, can you say? How bad is it? Does your family know? Oh, I'm so sorry, I didn't mean to pry, it was just the...'

'Shock? I know,' said Rick, whose handsome smile still had the power to make her tummy do somersaults even now, she was surprised to discover. 'But not to worry, the doc says I might be as right as ninepence when the scarring at the back of my eyes heals completely.'

'Oh, it sounds painful,' Tilly cried, distressed seeing someone as chirpy and as vital as Rick usually was brought to this.

'I can't complain, it brought me home and you wanna see the nurses at the hospital, angels they are, all of 'em.'

'Trust you to eye up the pretty nurses,' Tilly laughed, immediately covering her mouth with the palm of her hand to stop any more stupid comments from popping out. It was only when Rick laughed that she felt at ease with the situation. That was one of the things she used to love about Rick, his obvious sense of humour and the ease with which he made people feel comfortable.

'They released me from the prisoner-of-war camp. I think I was a bit of a burden to the enemy,' he smiled, 'although they were quite decent to me, so I can't complain.'

'Do your parents know?' Tilly asked, remembering that they had moved out of the East End a while ago.

'Mum and Dad have been told, but I wrote asking them not to visit, it'd be too distressing for them. I don't fancy being stuck out in the countryside where they've moved to either, so I'll have to sort something out.'

'What about Dulcie? Does she know?'

'No. I ain't told her yet, I thought I'd surprise her with a visit and we could paint the town red, go around the West End, see a show,' he laughed softly, then was quiet for a while before adding thoughtfully, 'I'll be fine, you'll see.'

'I'm sure Dulcie would take your injury in her stride the way she does with every other catastrophe that befalls her,' Tilly said, her brain doing little calculations. 'You could stay at Mum's... I don't know where you'd sleep, though, unless Agnes bunks up with Dulcie and you have the room she and I used to share.' Her mind was working overtime now, unable to bear the thought of him struggling alone.

'Or there is the Simmonds' house a few doors down. Drew's room is still empty, so Mum said...' She refused to dwell on Drew right now. 'It's close enough for Dulcie to pop in, and you'd be well looked after by my mum, or Agnes or Sally, she's a nurse, she'll be on hand if you need anything!' Tilly's tongue was going ten to the dozen now – it was all so easy.

'Whoa!' Rick said, putting up his hand. 'This is going too fast for my liking. I only just seen you again since the beginning of the war and already you've got me a room and all these eager females to look after me.' He laughed. 'Did the army train you to organise people's lives or does it come natural?'

'Oh, Rick, I'm sorry,' Tilly said quickly. 'I'm always doing that lately; some call it helping and others call it meddling. I didn't intend to meddle, honestly!'

'It's okay,' Rick said, placing a bronzed hand on Tilly's arm. She realised that she had over-whelmed him quite a bit and silently promised herself not to interfere; he would have his own plans, surely? But there was something else she could do for him.

'I was just thinking,' Tilly said more carefully, not wanting to upset him at all, 'I've got a forty-eight-hour pass soon – I could escort you home.'

'Isn't that supposed to be my line?' Rick asked before his easy laughter was overtaken by a parox-ysm of obviously painful coughing.

'They won't discharge you from hospital with a cough like that,' Tilly said, alarmed, guessing that he must have been given permission to come to the passing-out parade by the nearby military hospital and that he'd be under strict instructions to return by ten o'clock.

'I'll be fine, legacy of good old English chim-neys,' Rick gasped. 'Now, where's that drink?'

'Can you drink whilst on medication?' Tilly asked.

'Only lemonade for me, worse luck,' Rick told her.

Tilly knew they'd been having a bad time of it when in June, General Erwin Rommel captured the port city of Tobruk in North Africa along with twenty-five thousand troops, which was where Rick must have picked up his injuries, not only to his eyes but to his lungs as well by the sound of it. Suddenly she felt the cheer go out of the day; here she was enjoying concert parties and dancing, when her fellow soldiers, sailors, airmen and -women were being injured in this way. She took a deep breath and forced herself to smile again.

'Dulcie will be so pleased to see you.'

It was only when Dulcie looked through the porthole window into David's ward that she realised she had been a little rash in coming to the hospital. He was recovering from the pneumonia he had contracted just before he was due to go home, which had delayed his discharge by nearly two months. Although she'd often been to see him during that time she'd never told him about that time she got drunk and ended up in the air-raid shelter, nor about her 'delicate condition', as Olive would have called it. David would be so disappointed with her, she was sure.

Dulcie could see him sitting at the side of his bed in the easy chair reading a book. Then, as if he sensed that she was there, he lifted his head and looked directly at her. His obvious surprise at seeing her standing outside the ward brought her to her senses. She shouldn't be here! What could she possibly say to explain her sudden visit? It wasn't even visiting time.

He waved to her through the closed door and before she had time to turn and run from the hospital he was urging her to enter the ward. However, recalling the sergeant major of a matron,

Dulcie didn't want to get David into trouble.

But moments later, clearly pleased – if his huge smile was anything to go by – David beckoned her onto the ward with a nod of his head. He was getting stronger every day and he was certainly becoming more independent, but not yet able to manoeuvre the wheelchair with only one arm, so she had no choice but to go in.

David was full of obvious concern after she quietly tiptoed across the ward and automatically took the handles of the wheelchair. 'Dulcie, what's the matter, you look awful.'

'Thanks,' she said, her voice so shaky she could hardly get the words out.

'I'm sorry, I didn't mean...'

'No, it's me, I'm the one who should be sorry,' she said in a rush. 'I've come here upset, and now I've upset you too.'

'Let's go down to the garden, it's awfully warm on the ward,' David said kindly, which was almost too much for her, but she managed to hold back the tears. After all, she'd had years of practice. Expertly she guided the wheelchair down the corridor before coming to rest by the rose bushes, now bare of their flowers. Putting on David's brake she sat on a bench, inhaling the tranquil fragrance of freshly cut grass; this was as far removed from the worldwide atrocities as it was possible to get, she thought.

'I didn't mean to trouble you,' Dulcie said in a low voice, which was most unlike her.

'No you haven't, you could never trouble me, unless you're going to tell me we won't be seeing each other again.' David gently took her hand

and she folded her fingers around his, her eyes never lifting from the perfectly manicured lawn made smaller by the vegetable patch.

'You might not think that when you hear what I've got to say.'

It didn't take Dulcie long to blurt out her sorry tale about Wilder and her sister at the train station back in July, plainly going somewhere given that Edith was carrying a suitcase; how, in her haste to get away, her shoe had snapped, and a nice kind American airman offered to help her ... and then one thing led to another... By this time Dulcie was in tears and her words were coming out in huge sobs.

'I cheapened myself,' she cried, knowing if she didn't tell David everything now she never would. She had been smitten and drunk, she confessed, and the act was over almost before it had begun.

When she finished her story there was a flat silence between the two of them that had never existed before. It was obvious David was trying to digest the enormity of what she'd said. And the only thing that stopped her from getting up and running away from him now was that David still had hold of her hand. He'd never let go all the while she was speaking. Sobbing once more, she tried to explain what happened next, even telling David about her mother taking her to a back-street abortionist; she hadn't meant to mention that bit, but then realised that if David was going to hate her and send her away forever he might as well do it knowing all the facts. Dulcie held nothing back – nothing.

'And where is he now, this over-eager GI?'

David's face was pale and there was a hurt expression in his eyes she had never seen before. Any minute now he was going to tell her he was so disgusted with her he would prefer it if she left and never came back – and she couldn't blame him.

'He was killed on his way back from his first flying mission. I was shocked when I received the news. One of his buddies came to the house with a letter he had written and was too shy to post.' Dulcie took a deep breath as the tears coursed down her cheeks but couldn't resist adding, 'Apparently he never stopped talking about me. Before he went on his only sortie he told his friend to contact me if the worst should happen.' Dulcie tried to calm herself. 'I can't imagine why, we only met the once.'

'And look what that once has left you with,' David said, not unkindly, and Dulcie felt the gentle grip of his fingers tighten around hers. When she looked up into his caring, sympathetic eyes David smiled, and she was so glad she had shared her secret with him, the only other person beside her mother who knew she was having a baby.

The relief made her a little lightheaded now. It was obvious David wasn't judging her. He hadn't told her to get out of his sight and never to come back again. He hadn't called her horrible, shameful names, as her mother had, when she told him she was having another man's child – and he could have done, some men would have done. But not David, kind, understanding David.

'Dulcie, I'm going to say something now.' He hesitated for just a moment and Dulcie's heart leapt to her throat. Maybe David was going to come out with those things after all?

'I don't want you to say a word – just hear me out, will you do that?' He gave her a little smile when she nodded like a child eager to please.

'I'm not much of a catch any more as it goes, and I'm certainly not looking for sympathy, but ... and you must think about it before you answer...' He was quiet for the longest time and then he said, 'Dulcie, will you marry me?'

Dulcie stared at him, hardly able to believe what David had just asked her to do. For a split second she recoiled at the thought, and immediately felt shame. He was her friend and she had flinched for the merest fraction of time, but even that was long enough to see the veil of regret reflected in David's eyes.

'Oh, David, I am so sorry.' Dulcie didn't know what to think, or how to behave, as she was quite overwhelmed by his proposal. They were quiet for a moment, each lost in their own thoughts.

'Please, don't mention it, I should never have asked you, let's forget I said anything.'

'But you are being so kind, David, I don't deserve it,' Dulcie said, wrapping her fingers more readily around his now. 'Your question took me by surprise – it was the last thing I expected.' In her heart Dulcie knew she loved him as a friend – but was that enough, she wondered.

'I'm doing you no favours here, Dulcie,' David said, his voice low, hardly above a whisper. 'If the truth be told, I'm being very selfish indeed. You see, I will never be able to father a child of my own given my injuries,' he was going to make one last effort to change her mind now, 'and the child, he could possibly be my child no matter how he is conceived, he is the innocent party in all of this... Don't you see, I could make you very happy given a chance, Dulcie, if only you would let me.'

Dulcie's tears ran afresh down her cheeks. He was her best friend, he had listened to her deluded ramblings without so much as a word of reproach and, if the truth be known, she had felt so sorry for him. But was kindness and pity the basis for a solid, successful marriage? Her thoughts were all over the place, and a little voice inside her head was telling her that it would be an easy way out of her predicament.

'Don't answer now, think about it, and give yourself time for the shock to subside...'

'I'm worried that you will look at the child in years to come and you would resent me.'

'I've always wanted children,' David said as the ghost of a smile crossed his handsome face and, as if seeing him for the first time, Dulcie noticed a vulnerability she hadn't recognised before. 'I can't see that happening, can you?'

'I don't know what to say.' Dulcie knew David was offering her an escape route. 'But I don't know if I could give you what you want: a loving, stable marriage.'

'I will take anything you want to give, Dulcie, no matter how small. I have loved you from the moment I set eyes on you.'

'You have?' Dulcie could hardly believe what David was saying. 'Maybe you are just being kind and offering a way out but...'

'No, Dulcie, I'm not, if anything I'm the one

being selfish. You can have any man you desire.'

'I can't, and please don't mention desire, that is a very dangerous emotion.' She tried to laugh but this was no laughing matter, she knew, especially when she saw the earnest expression in David's beautiful eyes.

'It is a lot to ask given my injuries but I assure you I'm not looking for a full-time nurse, I have plenty of money to pay for one of those.'

'I don't mind helping you–' David held up his hand to still her words but she carried on regardless '–not just because of your injuries or the care you would need. I would do that in a heartbeat, and nobody is more shocked by that than I am, so that proves you are a really good friend to me, David. No, it's...' She hesitated '...because I'm not worthy of you.' There, she'd admitted it. Dulcie wasn't usually the kind of girl who looked far below the surface. She either wanted something or she didn't. 'I don't go in for soul-searching most of the time. I'm quite straightforward really. See it. Want it. Get it. That's me.'

'Dulcie, you are the least straightforward girl I have ever met,' David laughed. 'I have never come across another woman who has so many layers. One has to dig very far down to get to the real you. In fact I think it is a lifetime's work...'

Dulcie refrained from one of her usual barbs when David added quickly, 'But I love what I see so far.' The smile on his face made her want to smile too.

'Don't say anything, at least not tonight.' David watched her closely. 'I know I could make you the happiest woman in the world given half the chance, I have loved you for such a long time I can't recall the time when I didn't.'

'I'm not sure, David,' Dulcie answered. 'It would be so easy to say yes and take everything you are offering to me, but would I be worthy of your love? Would I be able to live up to the image you have of me – have you created a fantasy of a perfect woman? I don't think I am that woman. Especially not the one you deserve, my love.'

Dulcie realised what she had just said and it felt like the most natural thing in the world to call David her love. They looked at each other, really looked into each other's eyes and saw the love that lay beneath. The realisation, no, the acknowledgment of their love, had been a long time coming but they now knew they didn't need words to convey the deep affection they both shared.

'You need time; I understand that, Dulcie, it is a lot to take in.'

'No, I know exactly what I want, David. I have known it for a long time but I have never dared believe I was worthy of your affection, let alone the offer of marriage...'

'We're not starry-eyed kids, Dulcie, we both know there will be a lot of give and take on both sides, but we can get through it... Can't we?'

With tears of happiness in her eyes Dulcie gently caressed his fingers, not looking at him now when she said in a low voice, 'We can only try, David. I will make mistakes and you will make mistakes, I'm sure of that, so we might as well make mistakes together.'

'And who said romance was dead, my darling Dulcie.' There was a catch in David's voice, and when she looked up Dulcie could see that he too had tears in his eyes and as she gently wiped them away he took her hand and he kissed it, before pulling her towards him and tenderly kissing her cares away.

Moments later he said in a low, loving, happy whisper: 'I'll make arrangements for a special licence; we can be married by the end of the month.'

'Oh, darling, that would be wonderful...'

FOURTEEN

'Married!'

Olive, Sally and Agnes chorused in unison, hardly able to believe what Dulcie had just told them. They had just finished their tea of rissoles, boiled potatoes and veg from the garden when she made her announcement.

'Well, you are a dark horse,' Sally said, secretly aghast, whilst jumping up to throw her arms around her friend and encouraging Olive and Agnes to do likewise. In moments they were all laughing and crying and asking all sorts of questions. When? Where? Why so quick? This last was asked by Sally, and Dulcie laughed, even though she didn't answer.

Sally had always seen Dulcie and David's relationship as one of mutual support and friendship rather than a romantic one, and she still felt that way. She knew Dulcie would always be there for him when he needed her and she would try never to hurt him, and that they respected each other. However, they would have to take each day as it came, whatever happened, and she wondered if Dulcie knew what she was letting herself in for marrying a man with so many injuries. After all, Sally thought, not unkindly, Dulcie hadn't been the kind of girl one would have expected to be the nursing type.

Although, if she was to sum up their relationship she would say they were probably more suited than a lot of married couples she had come across lately and after the war was over, how many marriages would prove to be rock solid? She'd heard tell that there were many soldiers who had been away since the beginning of the war coming home on leave to brand-new babies, especially now the Yanks were over here.

'David is being discharged from hospital on Monday,' Dulcie said, interrupting Sally's thoughts, 'and we will be married by special licence on Friday.' Her eyes were shining brightly now as she went on to tell them that David had made the necessary arrangements for the civil ceremony from his hospital bed. Dulcie didn't know how and she didn't ask, but once she said yes to his proposal everything moved at breakneck speed. 'He has a little flat above his chambers and intends to go back to his barrister work not far from here, and after the honeymoon I will move in there with him, of course.'

'A honeymoon as well, how romantic,' Agnes sighed. She couldn't imagine having a honeymoon. She couldn't imagine having a wedding either, on account of a large chunk of Ted's wages going to support his mother and two sisters, but she didn't like to dwell.

'Oh, this house will be so quiet without you, Dulcie.' Olive scraped back her chair and she took her lodger in her motherly arms and hugged her, realising how fond she had grown of this chippy young woman who, beneath the hair and make-up, was as vulnerable as the rest of them if the truth be known. Then, as if a thought had just struck her, Olive took a pencil and paper from the polished bureau in the front room and began to make a list.

'I'll have to see what I can get from the grocer for the wedding breakfast table.'

'Don't worry, I'll go down to the local food office in the Town Hall, David told me they issue permits for occasions like this, although there is a limit as to how many people you can invite, which rules out my mother and certainly my sister,' Dulcie said determinedly.

'I know I can borrow cardboard icing from the baker to go over the cake – I'm afraid it will only be one tier though, Dulcie...' Dulcie laughed, watching her landlady's mind obviously working overtime. 'How many people will you be inviting?'

Dulcie was thrilled that Olive was thoughtful enough to put on a spread for her wedding. 'It's going to be a very low-key but dignified ceremony, just me and David – obviously – and then,' she turned to Olive, 'I thought you and the girls would like to come,' she added almost shyly.

'Just you try and stop us!' they all cried.

'It's only going to be a very quiet ceremony in

the register office in Marylebone Road. We don't want a fuss.'

'That's not like you, Dulcie,' Agnes chuckled and then lowered her eyes when Olive gave her a little shake of her head.

Olive, meanwhile, was keeping her suspicions to herself, knowing that only time would tell why this particular wedding would be so quiet and so hurried. 'David will want a quiet wedding after being cooped up in hospital for so long, don't you agree, Agnes?'

'Of course he will, how silly of me.' Agnes gave a nervous laugh.

'No, it's not that,' Dulcie said, giving Agnes a warm smile. 'I only want the people around me who matter. David's been married before and he doesn't want a lot of fuss and that suits me fine too.'

'Oh, Dulcie,' Olive exclaimed, 'are you sure you want to go from here and not your mother's house?' Olive had noticed a marked change in Dulcie since that day Tilly had left for her ATS training. Maybe it was because she had more time to observe more closely the other girls who lived here in Article Row, or maybe it was because she needed something to take her fretful mind off her daughter.

Olive wasn't sure, but whatever the reason, she had noticed a definite calm about Dulcie of late, a serenity Olive herself had only experienced when pregnant with Tilly. For the time being, she would keep her suspicions to herself. But one thing she did know, there hadn't been a wedding in this house since her own and no matter what, it was a call for celebration. Dulcie seemed happy enough, she thought; and that was all that mattered.

'No I'm perfectly happy to go from here, Olive; it's all I've ever wanted.' Dulcie didn't tell anybody that she and her mother were not on speaking terms any more.

'And,' Olive said, her face brightening even more, 'Dulcie isn't the only one who has a surprise.' She laughed out loud when the girls clamoured for her good news. 'Tilly will be home on Friday – won't it be wonderful if she arrives in time for the wedding?'

The whoops of delight were deafening as Olive produced a half-full bottle of sherry from the sideboard that had been left over from the previous Christmas. But their cries of happiness were cut short when a knock on the door heralded the arrival of Nancy Black, who wanted to know what all the noise and fuss was about.

'That is quick,' she said when she was told of Dulcie's forthcoming nuptials. 'Is there a reason for that?'

'Yes,' said Dulcie, suddenly feeling wicked. 'David and I want to make mad passionate love.' She knew Nancy would be scandalised, and realised that David would be thrilled if he'd known. As shrieks of delight sent Nancy scurrying back to her own house without the celebratory sherry she had been offered, Dulcie said with an emphatic nod to the newly slammed front door, 'So stick that in your pipe and smoke it, Mrs Black.'

'Oh Dulcie you are a one,' Olive laughed, giving her another hug. 'You'll never change.'

'Oh, I don't know about that.' Dulcie smiled,

quieter now.

'Come in and let me have a good look at you,' Olive declared holding out her arms as Dulcie entered the front room. 'Oh yes, that colour suits you a treat – you look beautiful, David is a very lucky man,' she continued, admiring Dulcie's smart new dove-grey edge-to-edge coat.

'That must have set you back a lot of coupons,' Sally said, examining the square-shouldered coat that looked stunning on Dulcie, and even though it had to conform to the rules of utility clothing, she wore it like a film star. Carrying the chic, classic style to perfection Dulcie had teamed it with a matching dove-grey hat, its upturned brim sitting at an angle on the side of her head, allowing her glamorous blonde hair to sweep up over the crown of her head and form soft curls that framed her forehead above expertly pencilled eyebrows and thick mascaraed lashes.

Audrey Windle came into the front room where everybody was gathered, her lips forming a breathless 'O' as she handed Dulcie a small posy of marvellously fragrant freesia surrounded by the delicate white flowers she said were called Queen Anne's lace and which were still growing in the vicarage garden, filling the room with their wonderful perfume.

Sally's eyes widened as she proclaimed that there was never a more glamorous bride this side of the silver screen. Dulcie, taking the posy and inhaling deeply before turning to the mirror to check her make-up for the third time in ten minutes, nodded in agreement.

Her pregnancy was not yet in evidence and as well as the bridal bouquet, Dulcie knew the cleverly chosen swinging fullness of the coat would hide any expansion her condition had caused, although she didn't have time to dwell when Mrs Windle brought in her wedding present of lovely scented soap she had saved since before the war started, along with a colander containing a bag of sugar, a quarter pound of tea, a tin opener and a bread knife; things that would be more useful than a china dog or a crystal vase, she said with a little embarrassed laugh, and Dulcie hugged her. Scented soap, she hadn't had that for months!

'Oh, this is the best present I've ever had,' she cried, smelling the delicate aroma.

'The car's here.' Sally's face was a picture when she slipped the freshly starched lace curtain to one side and stared past a group of onlookers that lined the curb, gazing in awe at the vision that was David's polished dark maroon Bentley.

'Oh, Dulcie, look at that!' Sally exclaimed. 'Look at what David has sent you.'

As much as Dulcie tried to act nonchalant at the sight of such a magnificent vehicle she couldn't stop the little shriek of glee escaping. She was absolutely thrilled David had not only kept the gleaming Bentley, suspecting he would never again drive it himself, but sent it to pick them up for the register office.

'My word,' she breathed, 'we'll all fit in that!'

'And a good thing too, otherwise we will be late,' Olive said, looking nervously at the clock once more. She had hoped that Tilly would be home in time for the ceremony, but the trains were running so erratically at the moment there was no saying what time she would arrive. 'I suppose we'd better be making tracks otherwise David will think you're not coming.'

'I'm asserting my prerogative,' Dulcie laughed, although secretly she really didn't want to keep David waiting – and she couldn't wait to slip into that luxurious car, even if it was only going to be used for today. She assumed it would be garaged after the ceremony, due to petrol shortages, at least until after the war.

'Oh, it must be lovely to be able to drive such a car,' Dulcie breathed.

'I could always teach you,' Olive said. Her time as a WVS driver had given her the confidence to handle anything. 'There's no point in letting a good car like that go to waste, or worse, be sold off when David will need it now, more than ever.'

'Oh, Olive, you are a dear, thank you so much. I can't wait to tell David.'

Olive could tell that Dulcie was nervous by the way she kept fixing her bouquet of flowers, making sure the freesia was at the front to give off its perfume to best effect, and she had almost licked the lipstick from her lips. Olive made a little gesture to let her know it needed freshening; anything to make Dulcie's day perfect.

Olive cast a practised eye over the pristine table, resplendent with sparkling crystal brought out of the display cabinet especially for the occasion, and the silver cutlery gleamed after she had given it an extra polish. And, even though Nancy Black and Mrs Windle had been left in charge of the buffet arrangements and seemed quite capable, Olive still checked that everything was just so. Dulcie, she was pleased to see, made a lovely bride and the room was now filled with milling guests enjoying a small alcoholic welcome to the day's proceedings. The gentle hubbub of conversation as they waited for the given sign from the driver did not mask the turn of a key in the front door. Olive went to see who it could be.

'Tilly! Oh, my darling girl, you got here just in time,' Olive cried as Dulcie, Sally and Agnes hurried into the hallway and exclaimed in unison, causing everybody else to hurtle from the front room. Tears and laughter filled the house when the girls all clung to each other, back together at last.

'Never mind me, look who else is here,' Tilly announced, stepping aside. Dulcie's mouth opened, closed then opened again but no words came. Sally, Agnes and Archie, who was giving Dulcie's hand in marriage, were all wide-eyed but it was Olive who broke the spell and ushered Rick and his white stick into the house before Dulcie rushed over and threw her arms around her brother's neck.

'Rick, oh, my lor'!' Dulcie cried. 'What have you gone and done?'

'I brought him home to see you,' Tilly said proudly, having escorted Rick, his luggage and her luggage all the way across London. 'And what's this?' she asked, looking around the assembled throng all dressed to the nines. But nobody answered; they were too busy marvelling at Rick's arrival.

'Oh, let me look at you.' Dulcie brought her brother back into the front room and stood him near the table.

'Something smells good – that must be our Dulcie. What is it, au de boiled ham?' Rick laughed, to everybody's relief, particularly Tilly's, as she'd thought it might be a bit awkward, especially since he hadn't told his sister he was back in London let alone injured.

'The last time I saw you,' Dulcie said as tears streamed down her face, smudging her impeccably applied makeup, but she didn't care, 'you were on the pictures.'

'Was I?' Rick chuckled, his arm still around Dulcie's shoulder as if holding on for reassurance. It must be daunting for him, thought Olive, who had seen men coming home injured from the last war and it was no laughing matter, but Rick seemed to be making the best of it right now.

'I can't believe you're home, especially today,' cried Dulcie. Her beloved brother was alive. And he was standing here in front of her. And he was in one piece! After what they'd heard and seen on the Pathé newsreel she had spent many a sleepless night worrying and praying he would return safely, having imaginary conversations with him, planning what she would say-and what she would do, and now all of that went right out of her head as she threw her arms around him once again, hugging him tightly to her. 'You were strolling in the desert making a show of yourself and laughing to the camera – I saw you as plain as I'm seeing you now!'

For a moment her wedding was not uppermost in her mind, all she knew was that her brother was home and he was safe and he was... As she stepped back to get a better look at Rick she noticed the white stick for the first time. Surely not, she thought as more tears blurred her vision.

'Don't let the stick bother you,' Rick said in the amiable tones she remembered so well. 'It might only be temporary and I can see some things, shadows and such, so that's a good sign, isn't it, Dulcie?' There was a long pause and then Rick, as if sensing the discomfort of the assembled company, said in a low voice, 'C'mon, Dulcie, don't cry...'

'I can't help it, I thought it was the happiest day of my life and you have made it complete.'

'It's your big day?' Rick sounded incredulous, and then he burst out laughing. 'Well, we have some celebrating to do, gel, and where is everybody? Mum, Dad, Edith?'

'They're not coming,' Dulcie said quietly. 'I'll tell you all about it later, but just to let you know, I'm ever so glad you're here.'

'Well, what are we waiting for? Wilder will be waiting...'

'Wilder?' Dulcie echoed, suddenly coming to her senses. 'I'm not marrying Wilder...'

'No?' Rick and Tilly chorused. 'Who are you marrying then?'

'David, of course, don't tell me you didn't get my letters?'

Olive laughed and cried all at once, holding Tilly at arm's length and marvelling at how grown-up she looked in her smart ATS uniform. All the girls were asking and answering questions at the same time. Tilly was as overwhelmed as Rick and was holding onto her cap that was sliding down the back of her head as she tried to catch her breath.

'You're getting married?' Tilly's eyes were wide in amazement.

'I can't leave her alone for five minutes and she's gone and got herself hitched,' Rick chuckled. 'That David is a lucky chap to get you, Dulce.' The silence in the room was palpable and Rick looked bemused.

'What did I say?' He might not be able to see their facial expressions but there was nothing wrong with his ears and the audible gasp that swept the room was plain enough until Tilly spoke up.

'You are like the big sister I never had and now you're getting married.' Her words broke the weighty silence even as a lump unexpectedly formed in her throat almost preventing her from telling Dulcie that she was the best 'sister' in the world. 'Not forgetting Sally and Agnes, of course,' she laughed as tears of joyful surprise filled her eyes, trying to push the thought of Drew and their wedding that was never going to happen now to the back of her mind. She had imagined that she would be the next bride in number 13.

'Who is giving you away?' Tilly eventually managed to say, her words coming out in a great rush as Dulcie's father was nowhere to be seen.

'Rick will do the honours, I'm sure,' said Archie, conscious it was only right her brother should have the duty now; he smiled and gave Dulcie a proud nod of approval.

'I'm having nothing to do with that family of mine ever again,' said Dulcie to her brother, 'except you of course.'

Tilly looked at her beloved mum without saying a word, knowing that it must have been a last resort for Dulcie to exclude her own mother from her wedding. Then Dulcie turned to Olive, took her hand and held it.

'You have all been more like a family to me and cared for me more than my own did – they couldn't wait to get rid of me except Rick, and my sister is the last person I would want at my wedding. No,' Dulcie continued determinedly, 'I only want the people around me who...' She left the rest of the statement hanging in the air as the car horn sounded outside.

'It looks like it's time to go,' Dulcie said in a whisper, smiling up at her brother.

'Maybe you would like to redo your make-up before you go, Dulcie?' Olive suggested, handing Dulcie her make-up bag. 'Right,' she went on as Archie came forward, resplendent in his number one dress uniform in honour of the day and offered her his arm and to cover her obvious flurry of embarrassment she said quickly, 'let's be on our way. Tilly, drop your bag upstairs and off we go.'

'I won't be two ticks,' Tilly said, hurrying up the stairs to put her kit bag away, then, from the top step she called, 'Shall I put my stuff in my old room or shall I use Dulcie's room for the weekend?'

'No!' cried Agnes with barely disguised alarm. 'Put it in our room! I want to hear all about the ATS.' She was very red-faced when everybody laughed.

215

David, magnificent in air-force blue, his shoes highly polished, his fighter pilot cap on his knee, sat in the wheelchair waiting for Dulcie's sweeping entrance into the foyer of the register office. When he caught sight of her his face beamed with happiness, especially as she approached him smiling.

'You look stunning, my darling,' he whispered, his eyes gleaming with love as she bent to kiss him. 'Please excuse me for not getting up.'

'David,' she said excitedly, 'this is my brother, Rick, he's home until his eyes get better.' It hadn't occurred to her that Rick's eyes might never be as good as they once were.

'We can compare war wounds later,' David laughed, not taking his eyes from his beautiful bride. He had never felt as proud in all his life as he did now.

Dulcie looked anxious, Olive noted as she watched them both; the girl's usual brash exterior seemed to have deserted her and in its place the vulnerability she always kept so well hidden had now surfaced as she moved closer to her future husband, gently placing her hand on his good arm secured around her waist. His best man, an RAF pal, was at the back of the wheelchair ready to push David inside the register office when they were summoned.

Smiling up at his bride-to-be, David said, 'I don't think I have ever seen a more beautiful woman on her wedding day and I am the happiest, luckiest man alive.'

Once inside, the small gathering settled into their seats, anticipating the lovely ceremony, when the registrar told their guests that David and Dul-

216

cie had requested they exchange their own vows and not the traditional ones. There was a gasp of stunned attentiveness when David, with the initial help of his best man and two walking sticks, managed to stand unaided to make his vows. Dulcie's eyes, shining like diamonds, could not hide her thrill of delight.

David had been practising standing on his new legs for months, and when Dulcie agreed to marry him it spurred him on to surprise her on their wedding day, he told the small gathering, and ensure he stood up to marry the woman he had loved for so long.

'I had to be able to look into your beautiful eyes when you become my wife,' he whispered to Dulcie, 'and I asked the boffins to make them a few inches taller – I quite fancy being a six-footer.' He gave a gentle laugh, never once taking his eyes from his adored bride.

Olive and the girls sat teary-eyed as Rick gave Dulcie's hand to her brave young barrister with the big future ahead of him, and the lump in their throats grew ever larger when Dulcie, in an unfamiliar gentle voice that was just above a whisper, made her vows.

'I, Dulcie, take you, David, to be my lawfully wedded husband, my lifelong friend, my faithful confidant and my love, from this day forward. In the presence of our friends, I offer you my sincere promise to be your faithful partner in sickness and in health, in good times and in bad, and in joy as well as sorrow. I promise to love you, support you, to honour and respect you, to laugh with you and cry with you, and to cherish you for as long as we both shall live.'

As their vows were exchanged a single happy teardrop trailed down Dulcie's face and landed on the gold band David had just slipped onto the third finger of her left hand. And she knew he meant every word when he lifted her hand and kissed it, sealing their love forever.

As David settled once more into his wheelchair, the register office door opened. Everybody, including Dulcie whose eyes were full of starry delight, turned towards the creaking noise of the door hinges, but her new-found happiness was short-lived and the ecstatic smile froze on her face when she saw her sister, Edith, standing in the open doorway, her eyes swollen and red-rimmed. Immediately Dulcie knew there was something very wrong and her guilty thoughts flew to her mother or her father whom she had deliberately ignored on her wedding day.

'I'm sorry to interrupt the happy occasion.' Edith looked directly at Dulcie with a glint of something resembling revulsion and, with her ruby lips turned into a sneer, she said, 'It may not be of any consequence to you now but I felt that you should know. Wilder is dead!'

'Well, of all the spiteful cats,' Sally fumed when they got back to Olive's house, watching the stunned bride and groom make the best of a bad job and cut their single-tiered wedding cake that Olive had managed to find enough fruit for, their hearts no longer in the celebrations. 'She could have waited until after the ceremony was over before she blurted such news.'

'Considering it happened a week ago,' said Tilly. 'Edith had plenty of time to tell Dulcie before today. But it was a heck of a shock to discover Wilder had flown so many dangerous missions, then to be killed after being run over by a ruddy great bus in the blackout.'

'Drunk as a lord apparently,' said Sally, amazed at Tilly's salty language and how much she had matured since she joined the ATS.

'Edith came here looking for Dulcie and it was Nancy who told her where she was,' said Agnes, offering a plate of ham sandwiches to the girls who were huddled in the front room catching up on all the gossip.

'That was a bit mean of Nancy, considering she knew Dulcie didn't want her family at the wedding,' said Sally, 'especially Edith, after what she did with Wilder.'

'I know, it seems that malice against Dulcie is irresistible to some people,' Tilly said as their next-door neighbour brought in a tray of bone china cups and saucers – all matching – which Nancy had lent to Olive for the occasion and watched like a hawk in case anybody was giddy enough to break one.

'I bet she enjoyed every minute of informing Edith that today was her sister's wedding day,' Tilly went on, giving Nancy's retreating back a withering glance.

'Let's try and keep our chins up for Dulcie's sake, hey, girls?' Olive suggested, overhearing the girls' conversation as she passed around a plate of salmon paste sandwiches – her rations, unfortunately, hadn't run to real salmon but nevertheless

Dulcie had told her earlier that she was thrilled with Olive's efforts.

'These are scant reward for Olive's motherly endeavours, I know,' Dulcie said later, handing her landlady a huge bouquet of flowers, 'acquired' from who knew where as they were so scarce. 'I just want to say that even after my sister's untimely entrance, Olive has made today one of the best days of my life.' Olive blushed and gave a little self-deprecating shrug making everybody shout 'hear, hear' and give her a colossal round of applause.

'Get away with you,' Olive protested, hurrying to collect glasses and interrupt the small gathering of men over by the fireside catching up on Rick and David's wartime adventures and quaffing fine brandy, which had been generously supplied by the groom from his pre-war stock. Olive offered Archie a sandwich and noticed that, although he was joining in the conversations, he seemed a little distracted.

'Thank you,' he said, taking a sandwich and breaking away from the company. His eyes seemed full of neighbourly concern as he said in a low voice, 'Olive, you should sit for a while, you have been on your feet looking after everybody's needs since we got back from the register office.'

Olive felt the heat snake up her neck and face at his considerate words and dismissively flapped her hands. 'I can't invite people to my home and expect them to look after themselves, now can I?'

'You enjoy looking after others so much, from what I have seen,' Archie said, smiling now to alleviate the significance of his observation and after a few moments he relaxed. 'May I ask you something, Olive?'

'Of course you can, you can ask me anything, Archie,' Olive replied. However the question he asked her wasn't the one she expected.

'I know you are very busy and I know I've just told you to slow down for your own good but, oh, I'm making a right pig's ear of this, aren't I?' Archie seemed to be searching for the right words. 'It's Mrs Dawson ... even though she's a lot better since she came home from hospital, she's still not her old self, if you see what I mean...'

'You want me to keep my eye on her?'

'No, not at all,' Archie said quickly, then his shoulders slumped and he gave a sheepish grin. 'I feel a right hypocrite now.'

'It's no bother, you know,' Olive assured him. 'I pass your house every day, so it won't be any hardship to knock and ask Mrs Dawson if she needs anything, now will it?'

'Are you sure?' Archie sighed. 'It would be a great weight off my mind. You see, I thought having young Barney around would take her mind off the bombings and being on her own when I was out, and it did for a while but it's coming up to our son's birthday and she always goes a bit quiet around now...'

'I'll certainly see what I can do,' said Olive, concern showing plainly on her face. Being a mother she could empathise with what Mrs Dawson was going through, knowing she would be devastated if anything should ever happen to Tilly.

'It's Barney I'm thinking about the most, she worries the life out of him, poor lad, and he's taken to roaming the streets again whilst I'm out working or fire-watching, so I have the added worry of...' Olive put her hand on Archie's arm in a gesture of reassurance, just as Nancy brought in a fresh plate of sandwiches. Olive removed her hand from Archie's arm as if it were on fire.

'I'm sure you worry that he may fall in with the wrong crowd again.' Olive nodded, knowing it would be so easy for the lad to pick up where he left off with the tearaways he used to hang around with. 'But don't give it another thought, I'll keep my eye on him.' Olive would do anything for Archie if he asked her – just the same as she would do anything for any of her neighbours if they asked her, she thought briskly.

Looking around the room, she noticed that everybody was deep in conversation and seemed to be relaxed and enjoying themselves, when a thought struck her. She wasn't doing anything wrong, how could she possibly in full view of a room full of family and friends? So why did she feel the need to bow to Nancy's disapproval? 'And whilst we're on the subject of Barney,' she said, feeling braver now, 'if he has nowhere to go he can always come in here. He could watch baby Alice whilst I'm doing my chores and Sally's at work. That's only if he wants to,' she added quickly. 'It'll save him walking the streets now the weather is on the turn.'

'Oh, Olive, you are the best.' Archie, in a moment of unrestrained happiness, took Olive's hand and kissed it. Olive was immensely relieved that Nancy had returned to the kitchen and nobody else saw him, but it did give her a feeling of elation for the rest of the day.

'Come on, you lot,' called Sally over the low conversational hubbub, 'let's have a sing-song. We know Dulcie has had some sad news and we are all sorry for that, but it's her wedding day and we mustn't let it overshadow her new status as Mrs James-Thompson – if that's okay with you, Dulcie?'

Dulcie gave a little shake of her head when, a little later, putting the past to the back of her mind for the sake of her new husband, Sergeant Dawson gave a rousing rendition of a song by Noel Coward entitled, 'Could You Please Oblige Us With a Bren Gun', much to general amusement and everybody joined in.

A lot of water had flowed under the bridge since the early days of war, thought Dulcie as she hummed the chorus. Her sister whom they had initially given up for dead had come back only to run off with her man and, Dulcie realised now, she had nothing to reproach herself for. The enthusiastic applause brought her out of her reverie and seeing David's happy expression she realised that it was his day too, she must make him as happy as possible and, in the sweet voice that hardly anybody had heard before she sang 'Bye Bye Blackbird', much to the astonishment of her friends. And as her perfect, soaring notes reached the chorus Dulcie gave David a little wink of her eye knowing they were going to make the best of things.

'We'll have the best marriage, Dulcie,' David said as applause and shouts for more rang in her ears. 'Just you wait and see, I am going to make you the happiest woman in England, if not the world.' Dulcie gazed tenderly at her new husband, and, seeing him in a new light as if for the first time, her heart sang with love for him.

By the end of the revelries there were tears and laughter, old memories resurfaced and new ones were made. Tilly, Sally and Agnes hugged Dulcie so much that David had to beg someone to part them so he and his new wife could leave and begin their married life together.

Dulcie was still singing, thrilled to be whisked away to the Dorchester for her wedding night with her wonderful new husband. And, tucked up in his arms in the back of his Bentley, she radiated blissful happiness.

Olive lay awake in her huge double bed and smiled remembering the girls, all four of them, singing together at the end of the afternoon's joyful celebrations. She had seen a different Dulcie today, the real Dulcie, perhaps.

However, she wasn't so sure she was happy about her daughter, Tilly, who, in a very merry state, had insisted on dragging a reluctant Sally to a local dance. Agnes, possibly secretly relieved, had received a telegram summoning her to report to Chancery Lane underground. Olive knew her daughter's new-found independence did not go unnoticed by the other girls either; Sally had remarked on Tilly's new, outgoing personality and Olive had to agree that it wouldn't do to be a wilting wallflower in the army. Although Olive was glad Tilly was seeing a different way of life and becoming more assertive, she was still her mother who worried and nothing would change that.

However, Olive thought as the full moon, a bomber's moon they called it, shone its silvery beam through her window, she was glad the day went well and she hoped that Dulcie would be as happy with David as she had been with her husband all those years ago.

Olive realised that the dry sherries she had quaffed earlier had given her courage to lie with the blackout curtains wide open so she could enjoy the silent silver sky. She wondered what Archie was doing now, knowing he was on duty, and fervently prayed that there would be no air raid tonight. Her mind wandered over the day and it lingered on the memory of Archie's kiss on her hand, suspecting it had been a moment of madness that had made him do it in front of a room full of people but she was ever so glad of it, knowing Nancy could not make a big boo-ha over it and invent all kinds of snide possibilities.

Then, inexplicably, her mind went to Agnes, who had come for a quiet heart-to-heart chat before the girls went out. Her fiancé, Ted, couldn't make the wedding; he'd had to work his evening shift as a train driver on the underground. But Olive couldn't see why he couldn't have come for a few hours to the daytime reception like Archie did.

She worried about Agnes a little more than about the others, except Tilly of course, as Agnes seemed such a fragile little thing, never disagreeing with anybody and keeping herself to herself unless she and Olive were alone, then she would open up and tell her that all she wanted was a family to call her own. After the little nip of sherry that had been thrust upon her, she'd confided in Olive that she didn't think Ted's mother liked her very much.

'Well, she doesn't recognise a good girl when she sees one then,' Olive had told her. 'She doesn't deserve a lovely future daughter-in-law like you, Agnes.' This maternal outburst had caused Agnes's cheeks to colour bright pink as she quickly refuted the heartfelt compliment.

'Ted wouldn't approve of me going dancing without him anyway,' Agnes said, causing a little grimace of agony to blight her pretty eyes as she read the telegram.

'Well, maybe he should take you, instead of pandering to that ungrateful mother of his.' Olive had stopped suddenly, realising she had said too much, and blamed it on the sherry. Then, she'd added more contritely, 'I won't tell him if you don't, let it be our secret.' This made Agnes smile, and Olive could see the girl didn't have much choice about going to work whilst the others put on a coat of lipstick, and went dancing. But it was the other thing that Agnes said that bothered Olive more. The girl said she thought somebody was following her when she had to come home on her own.

A rare fuddle of alcohol was causing Olive to drift into a lovely sleep when she suddenly heard it. The noise was low at first, barely audible ... then, growing louder by the second, the banshee wail of the air-raid warning began in earnest.

'Oh please, Lord, let my girls come home safely,' was her last thought before sleep finally claimed her.

FIFTEEN

David, with the help of his driver waiting with his wheelchair, was first out of the car when they pulled up outside the Dorchester, the luxurious Mayfair hotel renowned for the politicians, foreign journalists and even Royalty who frequented it, as he wanted to see the look of surprise on the beautiful face of his new wife.

'But, David, I thought...' What Dulcie thought was left unsaid as he held out his hand and she took it, easing her way out of the car with grace, the way she had seen Queen Elizabeth do it on the Pathé newsreels at the pictures. Looking up at the elegant façade, which thanks to its reinforced concrete structure was said to be the safest in London, Dulcie could not stop the sharp intake of breath or the jaw-dropping look of surprise when she realised that this was where she would have dinner on her wedding night.

'Are we having dinner here?' she asked as little darts of excitement ricocheted inside her.

'No, darling, we are staying here until we leave for our honeymoon tomorrow.' David's face was a mixture of pride and adoration. 'Nothing is too good for my wife.' He gave a gentle laugh as Dulcie, forgetting her inflated air of sophistication, gave a little dance and squealed her delight.

'The Dorchester,' she breathed after raining kisses on David's cheeks and lips. 'If my mother could see me now,' she said in a low voice, 'this would knock Edith into a cocked hat!' Then, a sharp zing of panic overwhelmed her momentarily when she realised that she hadn't a thing to wear for dinner at the Dorchester and she had been in the same clothes all day.

'I hope you don't mind,' David said after signing 'Group-Captain and Mrs James-Thompson' with a flourish in the hotel register, which gave Dulcie an added thrill, as they were escorted to one of the opulent lifts to be taken to their room. 'I have taken the liberty of having something brought over for you to change into for dinner.' His eyes twinkled and Dulcie wondered how he had managed to get her best imitation-silk dress out of her wardrobe without her noticing; she was sure it was there this morning.

But the sight that met her when they were escorted into the luxurious accommodation almost took her breath away. It wasn't a room, it was a whole suite of them! And there draped over the lavish double bed was a vision in pewter silk, a dress the likes of which she had only seen on movie stars at the pictures or read about in *Vogue* that she had so avidly digested before... She stopped herself from thinking any further back. That was then, this is now, Dulcie thought.

'Oh, David, pinch me!' she squealed again as she hurried over to the bed whilst David was tipping the bell boy. 'How did you know my size? How did you know this is my all time favourite colour?'

'I'm so glad you like it, darling,' David smiled. 'I took the liberty of asking Olive to covertly pump you for information and to find out your size – I couldn't very well go into Harrods and say "my wife is about this size and this tall", now could I?'

'Harrods?' Dulcie could hardly believe her ears as she slipped the expensive dress from the bed and held it up against her in one smooth, effortless sweep before standing in front of the full-length mirror, and tilting her head to one side she said almost shyly, 'But won't it show my…'

'No, darling, the lady who sold it to me assured me the cut of the dress would show your figure off to its full advantage and,' he gave her a wicked smile, 'if anybody should suspect that Mrs James-Thompson is expecting a happy event, who am I to disillusion them?'

'Oh, David, you are so good to me.' Dulcie felt the happy sting of tears, and as he held out his hand once more for her to come and sit beside him on the opulent sofa she could think of no other person in the whole world who was as good to her.

'Shall we have a pre-dinner champagne celebration all of our own?' His eyes were dancing with delight, she could see.

'Oh, David, do you think we should?' Dulcie asked, feeling elated.

'Well, I hardly think we shouldn't,' David laughed, pulling her towards him.

'I do love you; you know that, don't you, David, and not just because … because…' *he had saved her from the shame of carrying an illegitimate child*; she would never put that into words though because she did love David, she always had. And she was going to make him the best wife she possibly could.

'I am the luckiest man in the world,' David said.

'Oh, David, I feel exactly the same,' Dulcie said as her new husband took her in his arms and kissed her cares away. Then they heard the first whining keen of the air-raid siren.

'We made it to the shelter just in time,' Tilly told Olive a short while later after the 'all clear' had sounded. Olive had spent the time waiting for their return in the Morrison shelter erected in the front room that served as an occasional table with a tablecloth thrown over it when it wasn't otherwise in use.

'It was a quick one tonight,' Sally said as Olive poured cocoa into four cups, 'but if you don't mind, girls, I'll take my drink to bed with me, I'm so tired I don't think I'll see the bottom of the cup.' The murmurs of 'goodnight, sleep tight' followed Sally to the staircase and, reaching her bedroom door, she closed it quietly behind her knowing that despite what she had just said, she would barely get a wink of sleep tonight.

She hadn't been getting as many letters from George as she had hoped and yet ironically she had been getting letters from Callum almost every day, so much so that she began to feel quite embarrassed at the amount of wonderful compliments he was paying her.

Sally, for some strange reason that she couldn't fathom, hadn't thought to mention that she and George were courting; well, she hadn't seen the need at first, reasoning that it had nothing to do with Callum. However, he seemed to have got it into his head that she wanted to be more than just a friend. But that would be impossible; she had her George to think about now. Tomorrow she would have to write to tell Callum what the situation was.

'Oh, why did you do this to me, George?' she cried.

If he truly loved her as George said he did, Sally reasoned as salty tears rolled down her cheeks and wet her pillow, he wouldn't have put her through this pain knowing he could easily have avoided joining the Royal Navy. He should have stayed home to care for the wounded that were already here.

It seemed, she thought as the agonising feeling of loss was already ripping her apart, that she was destined to lose everybody she ever loved. What chance did her baby sister, Alice, have if Sally couldn't hold on to the people she loved? Sobbing quietly now, Sally knew how Tilly felt when Drew went back to America. However, she didn't have a clue how she was going to tell Callum that she was not available for courtship no matter how much he hinted that it would be wonderful if they could get together again.

'David, that man keeps staring at me,' Dulcie said after their main course of roast beef and all the trimmings was brought to their table, looking delicious and more than Dulcie had seen for the past three years. Olive was an excellent manager, the best, but even she couldn't produce a spread like this. And she was determined to enjoy it all the more after the delay when the air-raid siren had sounded.

'He has taste, my darling,' David replied, taking her hand and gently kissing it. 'He is probably wondering why a battered old airman like me is dining with such an exquisite woman.'

'I'll give you "battered old airman",' Dulcie said in mock horror. 'I don't have anything to do with battered, or old, and I am proud to tell anybody that you are my husband.'

'Oh, Dulcie, I'm glad you're on my side because you would make a formidable enemy,' David laughed in a carefree manner that belied the surreptitious glance at the man Dulcie had pointed out.

'I know him ... well, I know *of* him,' David said in low tones. 'He was at one of mother's little soirees before the war. He's in the newspaper business – American – knows a lot of people.'

'Isn't that...?' Dulcie's attention had already wandered as she gazed, wide-eyed, at a couple of faces she had only ever seen in films and David smiled; he was going to enjoy married life with Dulcie, she was such a tonic.

'Dulcie, darling, put your beautiful lips together, you will catch a fly,' David grinned, his eyes full of amusement as her throaty laugh echoed around the opulent restaurant.

'I don't know that a common fly could afford the Dorchester, David,' she remarked.

'Oh, Dulcie, I do love you,' David said. 'I am going to make you the happiest woman in the whole world.'

'You already have, my darling,' Dulcie said, admiring the glint of her new wedding ring as it glimmered in the light from the sparkling chandeliers.

David was in the middle of explaining the history of the Dorchester as they finished their delicious meal with wonderful, mouth-watering chocolate floating islands Dulcie had never seen before.

'Did you know,' David said in conspiratorial tones, 'that a lot of the aristocrats have closed up their huge houses and will now live here for the duration of the war?' Dulcie was amazed that people could actually afford to leave their homes and live in a top-class five-star hotel, not just for one night, but for months, possibly years.

'Most of the servants have left their posts because they can earn more money working in the munitions factories,' he said to Dulcie, who was listening intently. 'You cannot get a decent skivvy for love nor money, these days.' He laughed out loud at Dulcie's astonished expression. 'I'm only pulling your leg,' he continued, 'but it is the truth, the rich and famous do actually live here.'

'I thought I was seeing things when that actress … what's her name?' Dulcie lightly pinched her lower lip and her perfectly arched brows creased in concentration. 'She was in that film … what's it called…? The one about…'

'It doesn't matter, Dulcie,' David smiled. 'I know who you mean.' He didn't have a clue who she was talking about, but surmised they didn't have time to go through the whole of the British as well as American acting nobility before she finally got the right name.

'Do you think I will know anybody?'

'Keep this under your hat, but I have it on good authority that Mr Churchill has been here for talks and also Queen Elizabeth and the princesses have dined here. However, that is top secret so mum's the word.' David gave a knowledgeable nod of his head, enjoying his new wife's wide-eyed wonderment.

Dulcie looked around in case any of them decided to show up at dinner. She wasn't interested in stuffy old politicians but film stars and especially royalty were a different matter altogether. 'Tell me, David, which film stars...?' This was the best day of her life. She could hardly finish her meal, she was so busy watching every glamorous patron and covetously admiring their furs and jewels. The music was playing and the whole day had been wonderfully romantic, she knew, but this was the icing on the cake. This is what she had always dreamed of in her little back room in Stepney. Her, a girl from the East End, living it up with the posh people. Who'd've thought it?

She was listening to the wonderful music when Geraldo, with his band members behind him, asked the audience for requests of their favourite tune and Dulcie realised that now was the ideal time for the song composed by Ted Heath, 'That Lovely Weekend', which was sung so beautifully by Dorothy Carless, and had become an immediate wartime hit. It would round off their wedding day perfectly, she thought as she excused herself as if to go to the powder room, but instead she made a discreet request to one of the band members.

She hadn't told David of her little surprise and his face was a picture when Geraldo himself announced the tune for 'the newly-weds Group Captain and Mrs James-Thompson'. Dulcie had never been so proud in all her life as the whole room stood and gave them a terrific round of applause. She couldn't wait to tell the girls back in Article Row; they would be green with envy, she was sure.

At a nearby table watching the airman and his dazzling companion beaming with obvious pleasure as the room erupted in applause, an American man hooked his index finger at the waiter and beckoned him over.

'Tell me,' he said, 'is this the young lady's wedding day?'

The waiter nodded discreetly. 'Group-Captain and Mrs James-Thomson are staying here in the honeymoon suite, sir.'

'The honeymoon suite, you say? Then bring out your finest champagne and take it to them with my compliments... Vintage ... Bollinger ... Krug ... can you do that?'

'Certainly, sir,' the waiter said patiently.

'Good man,' said the five-star general before stopping the waiter once more. 'But hey, it's from a well-wisher – no names, right?'

'Very good, sir,' said the straight-backed, immaculately uniformed attendant who moved with such silent grace he seemed to glide in the direction of the wine cellar.

David was in deep conversation with his new wife when the waiter came to their table and told them that a gentleman across the room had sent over a bottle of champagne in honour of their wedding day. David, noticing that Dulcie was positively glowing with happiness, looked over to where the American was sitting and nodded his thanks to the Supreme Commander of the Allied Forces in Europe.

'See what happens when you go announcing our wedding day to the band?' David smiled.

The Commander gave a nod and a little smile and accepted David's thanks with a dismissive wave of his hand before disappearing up the magnificent stairs.

'Oh, David, this is the most wonderful day of my life,' Dulcie breathed, realising there was a lot that she had to learn about how the other half lived. Where she came from most people had never even seen a bottle of expensive champagne let alone drunk some. People were too busy keeping body and soul together – and most of the women in Stepney didn't even touch alcohol, unless you counted the odd gill of cream stout on a special occasion.

SIXTEEN

For the third time that week, Agnes had to walk home from her work at the underground station alone as Ted had been moved over to Bethnal Green to stand in for a train driver who had lost his roof in the previous night's bombing. The air raids were not as frequent as they had been during the Blitz but they were still an ever-present threat.

Hurrying through the blackout trying to pick her way through the dark streets towards Holborn and home, Agnes tried to take her mind off pitch-black nooks and crannies by going over Dulcie's wedding day last week and dreaming of what her life would be like when she and Ted became man and wife.

His mother still didn't talk to her on the rare occasion she went to Ted's home, a cramped little flat in the Guinness Trust buildings which Ted's mum kept all neat and tidy, even when Agnes complimented Mrs Jackson on how clean her stairs were; because she was always washing them down with boiling water and Lysol disinfectant they always smelled lovely and clean, but Mrs Jackson didn't seem interested in anything that Agnes had to say and merely nodded to let her know she had heard her.

Trying to ignore the darkness and stop her nerves jangling at every little noise that, no matter how innocent, still had the power to terrify her, Agnes imagined herself doing all those wifely things when she and Ted got married. She had been watching Olive closely when she cooked the meals and was learning a lot from her landlady, who showed her how she worked out her coupons and points to make sure they all had an equal share.

A small, though obvious, noise alerted Agnes to the possibility that someone was following her. Don't be silly, she thought quickly, it'll be someone going home the same way, that's all. She forced herself to think this otherwise the scream that was lying in wait at the back of her throat would leap forth and wake the whole neighbour-hood.

Not far to go until she was home safe and sound, Agnes thought as she rounded the corner at the top of Article Row. As far as she could tell the row was deserted as there were no sounds of people coming or going, just the light tread of another pair of feet behind her. Agnes began to quicken her step and if she wasn't mistaken, the footfall behind her speeded up too. She only had a couple of houses to go and she would be home. The footsteps were coming closer. They were right behind her. Instinctively she began to move faster, and faster, until she was almost at a trot. And as she reached Olive's gate she put her hand on the latch, every nerve in her body screaming, every sinew taut; the latch was stiff in the early winter smog and Agnes put all her weight on it to prise it down. Just as she managed to get it free a hand shot out and touched her arm and Agnes could contain the scream no longer.

'Leave me alone! I'll call a policeman!' she yelled as the door to number 13 suddenly opened.

'Agnes, are you all right?' Olive, her concern obvious, came hurrying down the pathway towards her and to Agnes's relief whoever it was fled from the pathway and hurried down the street. 'Do you want me to get Sergeant Dawson?' Olive asked, but Agnes shook her head, too badly shaken to speak.

'Come on, love,' said Olive, 'let's get you inside.'

After a cup of cocoa and a good talk with Olive and Tilly, Agnes felt a lot better and much more relieved. 'I probably scared myself,' she admitted, wrapping her hands around her cup, grateful for the hot, soothing drink. 'I was dreaming about married life with Ted, not a care in the world.' She blushed as she realised she had just told them about her innermost thoughts. Smiling shyly she continued, 'I didn't hear anything at first and then I thought I heard someone fall off the kerb, well, stumble more than fall, and that's when I became aware that there was someone behind me and even then, although I was alert, I didn't think they would get so close as to touch me.'

'You must have been terrified,' Tilly said, her eyes wide. 'I'll teach you some self-defence lessons tomorrow that we learned in camp.'

'I think I worked myself up into hysterics,' Agnes said, safe in the knowledge she was amongst good friends now. 'Whoever it was might only have wanted a light for their cigarette.'

'But you can't be too careful in the blackout,' Tilly offered and they all agreed.

Staring with unseeing eyes out of the window on her way back to camp, Tilly didn't register the green fields or skeletal trees speeding past. It didn't look as if Drew wanted anything more to do with her now he was back home with his own family; she had expected at least one letter when she got home but was sadly mistaken. Maybe he could be a completely different person when he was with his own kind, but she doubted it. He was far too caring and always thought of others before himself. Or at least she thought he did. She found it hard to doubt the loving words he had spoken to her before he left when he gave her

239

that one last kiss ... to build a dream on, he had said. And she had been building dreams ever since. Especially in the middle of a dark lonely night back at camp surrounded by twenty-nine other girls with their own stories to tell.

There were many different personalities in the world, she realised after being with women from every walk of life during her training. From debutantes to the deprived, everyone was the same in uniform, but would they be the same girls in civvies?

As dusk darkened the autumnal sky, the guard reminded the passengers to pull down their blackout blinds if they wanted to read by the train's dim side lights. Tilly settled herself for the rest of her journey back to camp and she recalled the first stirrings of delight at seeing Rick again.

Grateful for the dim light she closed her eyes and her fingers automatically sought Drew's ring that was now on the leather string around her neck along with her 'dog tags' giving her name, rank, and blood group. Her thoughts returned to the joy of Dulcie's wedding day – especially when Rick surprised his sister by appearing in time to give her away. Poor Rick, thought Tilly, it was such a shame his eyesight had been damaged by a bomb blast. She sincerely hoped that he would make a full recovery, before suddenly realising the elation she thought would always elude her without Drew seemed not to be so intense now. Yet she still loved him with all her heart and she knew deep down that he would come back to her one day and until then she would wait for him.

Olive, being the stoic, no-nonsense type of woman the country could depend on in time of crisis, had already volunteered to do fire-watching duty. She did so before it became compulsory for her to do a minimum forty-eight hours a month, regardless of the strain she was already under, looking after Sally's baby sister and the rest of the family, as well as her WVS duties. And as she walked through the chilly blackout she thanked her lucky stars that she wasn't employed in premises where she would be liable for compulsory duty, as there weren't enough hours in the day.

Branches of the Women's Home Defence Corps were springing up in many districts as the dark nights drew in, and Mrs Windle, the vicar's wife, asked Olive if she would accompany her on visits to various outlying districts to teach women how to handle rifles and hand grenades as she didn't like to travel alone in the dark. She told Olive that Mr Churchill insisted they would never have to – nor be encouraged to – use them in self-defence, which made Olive wonder why they had to learn to use them in the first place? However, she had been happy to be of assistance making tea and sewing fishing nets whilst the others learned how to safely pull a trigger.

'In one unit alone there are over a hundred women of all ages, who want to defend their homes and family,' Mrs Windle told the women gathered in their local church hall, her face alight with enthusiasm. Olive hadn't been so sure about the self-defence lessons at first; she didn't like the idea of pulling a gun on somebody, no matter who they were. She wouldn't want it on her conscience for the rest of her life and reasoned that she was only here to accompany Mrs Windle through the blacked-out streets.

'We don't want to fight! Of course we don't,' said the vicar's wife, who had blossomed in wartime from a rather mousey flower-arranger into a plain-speaking woman who got things done, 'but if it comes down to it we must protect ourselves and our homes, especially when the Ministry of Home Security reminds us that invasion conditions differ widely from blitz conditions – meaning that military labour will not be available for civil purposes.'

'I suppose you're right,' said Olive as the audience murmured their agreement, especially when Mrs Windle pointed out strong women should not be cowed by threats and rumours.

'I don't like answering my front door when it goes dark,' Nancy Black called out from the front of the audience, 'and that can be any time from four o'clock these days. It makes me feel like a prisoner in my own home.'

'I can't see any self-respecting marauder having a go at you, Nancy,' a voice at the back answered, much to the amusement of everybody – except Nancy, who shrugged her shoulders and pursed her skinny lips.

'You'll be laughing on the other side of your face if the Germans get past Wapping,' said Nancy, taking no part in the jocular interlude ... as was usual, Olive noticed.

'Now, ladies, we are all on the same side here, so let us all get on with it.' Mrs Windle seemed so eager to make them understand how important this exercise was. Olive knew that women were getting worried about safety during the blackout and worried not only for themselves but their homes, too. Rumours abounded of midnight raids on poor defenceless women who had no men to protect them and as most of their children were in another part of the country it seemed only right that they should defend themselves.

The last rumour about midnight raids had come straight from Barney who, although he had become a model child of late under the guidance of Archie Dawson, still had a very vivid imagination, and scared the life out of less-robust women who spent many a long night alone when their husbands were on air-raid precaution duties.

'If anybody should come barging into my home when my husband is away I will have no compunction about shooting them.' Nancy had been only too ready to sign up to the Women's Home Defence Corps, Olive observed, recalling that her next-door neighbour felt it her duty to know how to pull the pin on a hand grenade and blow the blighters to smithereens, in her own enthusiastic words.

Exhausted, Olive felt she needed at least another eight hours in the day just to fit in a decent sleep. She hurried home to Article Row, as myriad thoughts filled her head. Since Agnes's scare a few weeks back, she knew Ted had had a word with his foreman and requested his shifts were put back to Chancery Lane. The poor girl was a nervous wreck by the time this could be arranged.

Olive was so deep in thought after leaving the church hall that she jumped when she was approached by a man in a heavy woollen overcoat and a trilby hat who looked very official with his black leather briefcase.

'Excuse me, I ... I wonder if I ... I could trouble you?' he asked from under the rim of his hat. He didn't look suspicious, thought Olive, in fact he looked a little nervous if anything, and if she wasn't mistaken she thought he had a bit of a stammer.

'Yes?' she said, taking a little step back and trying to remember the rudimentary warnings of the self-defence class; one could never be too careful, that had been their first lesson. 'How may I help you?'

'I am looking for a girl called Agnes.'

'There are plenty of girls called Agnes, is there a specific one?' she asked, giving nothing away. The man went on to tell her that he was searching for a girl who was brought up in the orphanage and so Olive knew he was talking about her Agnes, as she had come to think of her, who had no family of her own to look out for her. But she wasn't going to tell this stranger anything at all. The man, who had introduced himself as Sidney Wilson, told Olive he was a solicitor's clerk, which immediately sent her warning signals.

'I'm sorry I can't help you,' Olive said efficiently. As she made to walk away he put his hand on her arm and then, after profusely apologising, told her that he had some good news to give the girl.

'Pull the other one,' thought Olive, still refusing to give him the information he was seeking, and silently vowed to warn Agnes to beware as soon as she came home from work, as she moved quickly away from him. Now that Dulcie was married,

Tilly was away in the ATS and Sally was doing a lot of shifts at the hospital, there was only her and Agnes to protect little Alice from alien intruders who might be lurking and she had no intentions of making their jobs any easier. Solicitor's clerk or no solicitor's clerk.

Olive knew it would be a long time before Agnes left Article Row, as she had to wait for Ted's sisters to grow up and take care of his oppressive mother. She gave a shaky, awkward laugh as she walked down the street; she wouldn't have dared think that way of another woman before the war started, but if you thought every day might be your last it only made good sense to let your thoughts run riot sometimes.

SEVENTEEN

'In the North African campaign,' Dulcie said over the breakfast table as she read the news to David, avidly listening to his beautiful wife who blossomed and became more exquisite every day, 'the British eighth army under Generals Alexander and Montgomery routed the Axis forces in the victorious Battle of Egypt fought at El-Alamein, in a major defeat of the Germans in the field...' She looked over the top of the paper, her eyes gleaming. 'Did you hear that, David? A major defeat of the Germans. Rick will be thrilled; his injuries will not have been in vain, now.'

'I never thought for one moment they were, my

darling, but you're right, it is good news indeed. This seems to be a turning point, don't you think?' David said, scraping a thin sliver of marmalade on his toast and marvelling at how his wife could find such treasures now that rationing was so tight.

'It does indeed, David.' Dulcie, thrilled her husband felt her contribution to their morning conversation was so valuable, mimicked his style of reply as she covered his other round of toast in thick lime marmalade, which she just happened to have been offered by a young acquaintance she used to know back in Stepney, who had heard she was now a happily married woman and could acquire a bit of this and a bit of that – at a price of course, he'd said, insinuating to Dulcie that money was no object to her any more, the cheeky blighter!

However, she had agreed on the spot knowing that if she didn't buy the marmalade, there was a long line of others who would and, as she always said, if you've got the readies what's the use of hoarding them, it was always raining somewhere.

'And how are you feeling this morning?' David asked; his voice full of concern, as Dulcie hadn't had the best of times with morning sickness every morning and then having to lie down until the nausea subsided, so he had engaged one of the best Harley Street consultants to take care of her.

'I'm feeling much better this week,' she said, not chancing the marmalade but instead munching on a dry arrowroot biscuit that her specialist, Oliver Springwell, had advised.

David had sought the advice of the private clinic as soon as they came back from their few days in the Cotswolds after their wedding and had wasted no time in taking her to see the Harley Street obstetrician.

'Mr Springwell says I am in rude health and so is our baby,' Dulcie informed David, who beamed at the news. She always made a point of including David in every aspect of her pregnancy, just as she would have done if the child had really been his, and every day he told her how glad he was that she had agreed to be his wife.

'I can't wait until we are a complete family, Dulcie,' David said on a sigh. 'It will be the proudest day of my life when we take our son...'

'Or daughter,' Dulcie interrupted him and he smiled, taking hold of her hand across the table.

'Or daughter, to the park together.'

Dulcie smiled. Initially she wondered if David would have married her if he hadn't been so badly injured and hadn't had to have his legs amputated below the knees. She knew they got on like a house on fire. However, as her pregnancy progressed, David was still powerless to consummate their marriage and gave no indication the situation bothered him, much to her relief. Dulcie knew their relationship was as good as it had ever been – better, in fact. If in the future things changed, so be it. David still treated her like the best friend he'd ever had.

Her world was now ordered and polite. The exclusive dinner parties they hosted for David's colleagues and clients were the talk of London society, although that doubting niggle she had always been susceptible to occasionally put doubts into Dulcie's mind.

She knew that some of David's peers couldn't

hide their contempt of her, especially when David was not around; then, they would simply turn their backs and talk amongst themselves, like the night they were invited for dinner to the home of Hubert Henderson-Smythe, a colleague of David's.

David, after excusing himself, was taking longer than usual to return, and Dulcie became worried; however she had nobody to ask to check on him as the hosts excused themselves in their turn and disappeared to other rooms, leaving her alone. When David eventually returned he was furious, knowing she had felt uneasy at going to the home of someone so distinguished. If he apologised to her once David apologised a hundred times for putting her through it and vowed never to do it again.

Dulcie suspected the Henderson-Smythes thought her common and uneducated, so much so that her empty little head wouldn't even register the fact she had been ignored. But it wasn't herself she was upset for, it was David; did they think that he was so shallow that all he wanted was a good-looking woman on his arm? Well, thought Dulcie, if that's what they believed then they were wrong. And she would prove it.

Since then she had thrown herself into bettering herself, pouring over etiquette books and learning how to cook meals that Her Majesty Queen Elizabeth could serve at a dinner party. She vowed never to be found wanting and would make sure her husband was the envy of the Inns of Courts. David warned that he would bring back Mrs Jessup when Dulcie gave birth as she couldn't possibly manage with a house and a baby. What,

Dulcie wondered, did all those poor mares in Stepney do without a live-in maid and a nanny? She would show him that she could cope with a house and a little baby. What was there to know?

In the meantime she had become almost obsessed with improving herself and David recognised this, to the point he told her it didn't matter. People were dying all over the world, he'd said, what difference did it make knowing which knife and fork to use? Well, she thought, it might not mean anything to David, he was used to living a lifestyle that most of the people she knew could only dream of, but for herself, she had to be better than the best. Dulcie had to be the perfect wife for David. She owed him that much at least.

Even now she cringed when she remembered how gauche she had been that night at the Henderson-Smythes', wearing a dress that was too low-cut, showing off her even more generous curves, her blonde hair too light. David gave her nothing but compliments, telling her anything she did was fine by him, and he was so angry at their hosts' appalling behaviour he feigned a headache and they left early. And ever since, bit by bit, she changed into the woman he deserved and not the one who looked like a gangster's moll. Surprised, David told her she didn't have to change to keep him happy, but deep down inside it was what Dulcie had always wanted.

'Oy! What you got there?' demanded Olive, carrying a bowl covered with a clean tea towel and gingerly making her way down the very frosty Article Row. Barney, with a hessian sack slung over his shoulder, had tried to sneak past her whilst she was on her way to number 50 to give Mr Whittaker the suet pudding she had made that afternoon. Having spent most of the morning queuing in the teeming rain for the shin of beef that went into the pudding and chancing pneumonia, Olive was in no mood for this young tyke's excuses.

'I didn't see you there, Aunt Olive.'

Barney always called her 'Aunt Olive' these days, she noticed, and Sergeant Dawson's wife was called 'Aunty'; he didn't use her Christian name, just 'Aunty'.

'You can't miss me in this moonlight, I take up half the pavement,' Olive said dryly. She was looking forward to her cocoa tonight, and her bed was beckoning. However, she was surprised that Barney was out so late.

Archie told her that since his wife came home from hospital she liked Barney to be indoors before it grew dark; Mrs Dawson didn't like to be alone in case the bombs came over again.

'Is Aunty in, do you know?' Barney, from what she could tell in the silvery beam of the moon, looked a little perplexed and even a bit worried if she was any judge.

'As far as I know, she is, Barney. Why, what's the matter?' Olive knew it was very rare for Mrs Dawson to show her face outside the house since the treatment for her nerves had involved a prolonged hospital stay and she was still getting used to being home again.

'Oh, nothing,' Barney said, moving off, looking sheepish in the frosty gloom.

'Come here where I can see you,' Olive demanded. He wasn't getting away with it that easily, she thought, her hands on her hips. He was becoming a bit of a handful again lately, and if someone didn't get a grip on him soon he'd go astray.

Mrs Dawson was still bad with her nerves and, from what Olive could gather from Nancy, didn't seem to be paying the boy much attention apart from wanting company whilst Sergeant Dawson was on fire duty or at the police station. Olive had told Nancy that it wasn't true. Mrs Dawson loved the lad like her own and Sergeant Dawson had to work all the shifts God sent, as there was a shortage of younger policemen since so many had been called up, as she knew full well. Nancy had just sniffed and gone about her business.

'What have you got there? And don't say "nothing"!'

'Nothing,' said Barney automatically. Olive raised an eyebrow and gave him a hard stare whilst the lad hung his head, gazing at his scuffed leather shoes; no galoshes for this kid any more, she noticed.

'Come on, tell me what it is, you haven't got anything in there you shouldn't, have you?' Olive glared at the sack, which was moving, she was sure. She watched as the boy placed it on the pavement and proceeded to undo the string that secured the top of it. Olive was right, the sack did move. She stepped back a pace, not taking her eyes off it.

'What's in there?' she asked suspiciously; you never could tell what this boy was up to any more.

'Chicks,' said Barney proudly as he took the

string from around the sack.

'Chicks?' echoed Olive, leaning forward slightly to catch a glimpse.

'You know, baby chickens!' Barney looked at her and shrugged his shoulders.

'Yes, Barney, I do know, thank you.' Olive rolled her eyes.

'Shall I show you?' His voice was breathless with excitement.

'I think you'd better had.' Olive peered inside the deep, dark recess of the sack. Inside there were six yellow fluffy balls of cheeping baby birds.

'Where did you get them from, my lad? And I want none of your stories!'

'I got them off some woman for helping her off the boat down by the Thames. She 'ad loads in a crate,' said Barney proudly.

'A proper little entrepreneur, I must say.' Olive was sure that Sergeant Dawson was going to be very interested in Barney's story. She wished there was something she could do, knowing that Archie had enough on his plate without having to sort this out as well.

'I don't know what one o' them is, Aunt Olive, but it sounds good.' Barney nodded and grinned.

'There'll be skin and hair flying when your dad finds out you've been playing on the wharves.'

'I'll tell him I found them,' Barney said with the uncomplicated air of a twelve-year-old.

'That's right, Barney, you find sacks of chicks lying around all over the place, we're surrounded by farms, don't you know,' Olive said dryly, re-tying the string around the sack.

'Then I'll tell him the truth. That I earned them.'

'Then he'll knock your block off,' said Olive, mildly amused at his audacity.

'But I'll tell him that he can have the eggs an' I won't do it no more.'

Olive wasn't too sure about that. Most people around these parts hadn't seen a fresh egg for months, and although the thought of a nice soft-boiled egg and slice of toast was mouth-wateringly good she knew Sergeant Dawson, being a very fair upholder of the law, would want to return the baby chicks to their rightful owners. However, Barney being in possession of such prized contraband worried Olive greatly right now and she feared he might be running with that crowd of rough boys again. Something would have to be done and soon.

'They'll be on someone's plate, come Christmas, you mark my words.'

'Ahh, don't say that, Aunt Olive.' Barney looked heartbroken at the thought, but Olive knew that unscrupulous persons would find a way of making money from this. First they'd sell the eggs, then sell or eat the chickens.

'You'd better take them into my house,' Olive decided, looking up and down the row, 'otherwise somebody might take them from you.' Not that anybody would have dreamed of doing such a thing before the war, not in this district anyway, but a lot had changed since then and there were some people who didn't like to go without their little luxuries, and a succulent, golden roast chicken was a prize to behold.

'See, you understand, don't you, Aunt Olive,' Barney said with a satisfied nod as he picked up the sack.

'It's not me you've got to worry about.' Olive looked at the wriggling sack. 'Your dad'll make you take them back.'

'I'll tell him that they're orphans!' Barney beamed at the suggestion as if it would make everything all right.

'Tell him what you please, but he won't have it, and if I know anything, after a long day trawling the streets of London and then doing another four hours' fire-watching, he'll be in no mood for chicks.'

'Where is he now?' Barney asked nonchalantly.

'Gone to buy a hat,' Olive said dryly. Barney shrugged and moved towards her house.

'Will you cook us somethin' to eat, Aunt Olive? I'm starving,' he called over his shoulder.

'Just put that sack in the Anderson shelter and then stay with Sally until I get back. I've got to go and see Mr Whittaker and make sure he's had his supper.' Olive tried to sound stern; he was becoming a bit of a handful of late, was Barney, and she didn't know what had got into him.

Sally had just put baby Alice's nightdress on and was combing her curls when the child suddenly looked up and, throwing her chubby little arms around Sally's neck, gave her a huge hug. Sally, delighted, wondered how she could ever have wanted nothing to do with this beautiful little girl, who had been through so much in her young life. Already she had lost her mother and father and had to get used to a new home in a new city with people she had never seen before; it must

254

have been terrifying for her.

But all that was behind her now, Sally vowed, and she would never let the child feel unloved or insecure ever again, especially when she had such a loving 'family' here in Article Row. And when George came home, whenever that might be, he too would lavish every ounce of love he could muster onto this wonderful child.

Looking at her now, all clean and shiny and smelling of talcum powder that Dulcie had managed to get from who knew where, Sally hugged Alice with all the love her heart could hold. But their rare moment of privacy was soon shattered when Barney came into the front room carrying a hessian sack that was making a heck of a racket.

'What have you got there, Barney?' Sally asked, putting Alice onto the rug in front of the guarded fire as Barney brought the sack over to her.

'Mrs Robbins told me to bring these in here and put them in the Anderson,' Barney said, opening the sack and showing her the contents. Sally's mouth fell open as baby Alice shot out a podgy hand to try and grab a tweeting chick, her eyes bright with delighted wonder.

'Don't let her get hold of them, Barney, she'll squeeze the living daylights out of them!' Quickly Barney dived across the rug in front of the fire and tried to snare the speeding escaped chick that had just run beneath the table under the window.

'Where did Olive find a sack of chicks?' Sally asked, amazed at the swift, bright yellow movements of such a tiny bird.

'I found them,' Barney said, his words low. 'I got them for helping a woman who...'

255

'The truth, Barney.' Sally brooked no argument as she was not in the mood for his stories.

'I was asked to keep them safe for someone,' Barney said, looking very contrite as he placed the chick in the sack and shuffled from one foot to the other, his face under the grime of the day growing quite red and not due to the fire in the grate.

'Who asked you to look after them – and why?' Sally was feeling quite suspicious as Barney had been a good boy lately, especially since that time he had protected Nancy Black's grandson, when everyone at number 13 considered him a little hero. But now it looked like he was up to his old tricks again.

'You know what Sergeant Dawson said last time, don't you, Barney?' Sally said in a stern voice. She liked the boy and thought he'd had a rough time of it, but what kid hadn't in these uncertain times? He also had to understand that there was a certain standard of behaviour that was expected of him and he must stick to it. He couldn't carry on behaving like a delinquent and get away with it.

Just then, much to Sally's wide-eyed surprise, Barney burst into tears. That's when Sally realised that Barney probably didn't understand what he was getting himself into.

'I told them I didn't want nuffink to do with their dodges, but they said I'd be in fer it if I didn't do as they said,' Barney managed after a few moments, when he was able to pull himself together enough to speak coherently again.

'Who said this, Barney?' Sally was suddenly fearful of the mess the child had become involved with. 'Tell me the truth, Barney, and we can sort it out.' She gently eased the information from him bit by bit. He admitted he had been waylaid on his way home from school by the dockside boys he had been friendly with before the war, the ones who gave him the shiner near Chancery Lane.

'They said that if I didn't look after their booty, I was going to get another good hiding.'

'Oh, did they now?' Sally said, determined to get every last drop of information from him. And just as the last piece of the jigsaw was completed Olive returned home with Agnes following behind her. It wasn't long before the front room was a hive of chatter.

During the animated exchange there was a knock on the front door and Olive, who was still wearing the WVS coat she'd put on to go to Mr Whittaker's, was undoing her buttons with one hand and turning out the hall light before answering the front door with the other. She was surprised to see Archie, tapping the rim of his fire-watcher's tin hat, and looking very worried indeed.

'Come in, come in, he's here,' Olive smiled, ever glad to see his reassuring presence, but her words didn't seem to make him any more relaxed and then to her horror she discovered why.

'Olive, I know you've been popping in to see my wife and run errands for her when she is unwell, but is Mrs Dawson here now?'

Fixing the blackout curtain into place, she switched on the light, and noticed Archie looked like he'd just seen a bad accident as she ushered him into the hallway.

'No. I haven't seen her at all today, but Barney's

here.' Olive's brow creased in bewilderment as Archie moved forward, passing her in haste as he headed to the front room where everyone was gathered.

'I tried to get in earlier after school,' Barney explained, as he edged closer to the fire after coming in from the Anderson shelter at the bottom of the garden, 'but the door was locked and I couldn't get any answer.' Olive noticed that he didn't mention the chicks.

'This is not right!' Archie said, passing Olive at speed. Quickly she followed him as he flung open the front door and tore up the street towards number 1. No wonder Barney had gone to his old haunts if he couldn't get into his own home, Olive thought, and her heart skipped a beat when she realised that he could still be walking the cold dark streets now if she hadn't met up with him earlier that evening.

In moments Archie had disappeared into the dense blanket of fog. Olive knew there had been talk of Mrs Dawson going to live in the countryside for the duration of the war. Or rather, Nancy Black had told her that, as her nerves were very fragile, Mrs Dawson and Barney would be better off out of the bomb-damaged capital. But Archie wouldn't hear of it according to Nancy; instead he'd said he wasn't eager to fill the mouths of some of Article Row's residents. Archie's disparaging remark was most surely aimed at Nancy, Olive knew, as her next-door neighbour had only recently been heard to say how relaxed Archie had seemed when his wife was in hospital and not at all worried at her slow progress.

'I tried to get inside the house but my key won't work.' Archie's usual calm features were pale. 'I think she's locked herself in because of all the bombings and the disruption, either that or the front-door frame may be in need of attention, but it seemed fine this morning.' He sounded really worried now. 'I thought she may have wandered down to your house for a little assistance... She wouldn't have left the lad to roam the streets... She dotes on him...'

It only took two hefty kicks of Archie's boot to separate the front door from its frame. It hit the wall with such a thud that the occasional table which had been wedged behind it splintered under the force.

Archie swiftly disappeared to the back of the house and into the kitchen where Mrs Dawson would usually be making his supper at this time of night, whilst Olive stood at the front door not wanting to intrude. She hadn't seen Mrs Dawson for a little while; she had popped in a few times, but now she realised she should have done more. She should have invited Mrs Dawson into her own house for a cup of tea and a chat, made friends with her and kept her spirits up. After all, it couldn't be easy losing your own child; maybe she would have liked to talk to another mother?

A small shiver of dread ran down Olive's back and guilty thoughts filled her head. If she hadn't been so busy with other things she knew she could have made more of an effort to help out poor Mrs Dawson. However, her self-admonishment was cut short when Archie came rushing back down the long hallway from the kitchen.

'Go for help!' he called as he lifted his forearm to his face and headed towards the kitchen. As he did so Olive caught a whiff of the overpowering gas smell and, taking her handkerchief from her sleeve, she covered her nose and mouth.

'Oh my word!' she exclaimed, knocked almost sideways by the pungent odour. Fearing that Archie, too, would be overcome by the noxious vapours she hurried into the front room and quickly threw open the windows. Then frantically she hurried back into the hallway and informed Archie that his wife wasn't in there either.

'There must be a leak?' she said as Archie began to open all the other windows and doors to let the damp air come in to blow away the poisonous miasma. A few moments later she heard an anguished cry and a scramble of footsteps, 'Olive, quickly, go and get Sally!'

Olive's heart was beating so fast she could feel it in her throat as she made her way down the street and back to her own house, all the while praying – even though she didn't know what she was praying for.

'It was too late for Mrs Dawson by the time I got to her,' Sally said later as they huddled around Olive's hearth, and although there was a cheery fire in the grate everybody felt suddenly cold. 'The noxious gas fumes had already done their work. I reckon she'd been dead for some hours judging by the degree of rigor mortis.'

The chicks were forgotten for the time being. As was the letter addressed to Agnes. It had been sitting on the hall table all day, with the sender's address on the back of the envelope, Carlton, Mending and Carlton, Solicitors, visible for all to see.

Olive couldn't rid herself of the gnawing guilt that prompted her to question if there was more she could have or *should* have done for Mrs Dawson.

'But, Olive, there was nothing else you could have done,' Sally said as she gave baby Alice her breakfast before dropping the little girl off at the child-minder and going on to work at the hospital. 'How were you to know number 1 had a gas leak?'

That was the story Archie had begged her to offer if she was asked how Mrs Dawson died. Everybody was in bed by the time he got back from the hospital and, as Olive had arranged for a new lock to replace the one that had been broken when he'd had to kick in the front door, he could not use his old key. She'd left a note and he called round, looking shattered, in the early hours of the morning.

'I am so sorry to disturb you, Olive,' Archie had said when she ushered him into the now-freezing kitchen. Lighting the gas on top of the stove to get a modicum of heat in the place, she pulled her woollen dressing gown securely under her chin.

'Don't give it another thought,' Olive had said, handing him a hot cup of sweetened tea as Archie sat at the kitchen table and told her everything. He confessed to Olive how his wife had saved the sleeping tablets she had been given in hospital and fooled everybody into thinking she was well again, then, to make sure she did a thorough job and there would be no chance of revival she'd turned on the gas tap and put her head in the oven, never to wake again. Tears were rolling down both their faces when Archie finished speaking, and for a long time they said nothing.

Eventually, his tea stone-cold, Archie scraped back his chair and got up from the table saying in a low, almost angry voice, 'How could she do it, Olive? How could she put the boy through this again? Not a thought for anybody else…'

'Oh, Archie.' Olive's voice was a mixture of pain and pity. 'The poor woman must have been desperate. The war has taken its toll on everybody.' Nobody was immune to the misery, the shortages, the rationing or the fractured families.

'Nothing will be the same after this,' Archie said, seemingly a broken man as he walked down the hallway towards the front door.

'What will you do now?' Olive asked. 'You need to get some sleep.' Her heart went out to him for the utter misery he was suffering now. If there was anything she could do…

'I have to sort things out, there is a lot to see to and questions will need to be answered.'

'Don't worry about the boy. I'll look after Barney for as long as you need me to.' Olive's voice was hushed, so as not to wake anybody as she followed him down the hallway.

'I'd be grateful if you let people know,' Archie said, looking in the direction of Nancy's house, 'that Mrs Dawson's death was an accident. A tragic accident.'

'Of course, and whilst you are busy making the necessary arrangements I will make sure you are not inconvenienced. If there is anything you need just let me know.'

'I don't know what I'd do without you, Olive,' Archie said as he opened the door.

'Don't give it another thought,' Olive said, patting his hand and feeling so utterly wretched for him. 'If we can't pull together at a time like this what can we do?'

'I'll be at the station...' Archie said before replacing his helmet and, head bent against the cold wind, he disappeared up the street.

EIGHTEEN

A lot had happened over the last few months, Agnes thought. Tilly had joined up and Dulcie had moved into a swanky flat above David's chambers, and the house was usually a quieter place for that, she thought as her hand shot out and silenced the ringing alarm so as not to wake anybody else up at such an early hour.

There was no more frantic rushing around to get ready for dances, nor demands for hot water to bathe in on Saturday nights. Agnes smiled at the thought as she clambered out of bed and, shivering in the December chill, reached under her pillow for her woollen dressing gown, recalling the time when Olive, Sally and herself had been invited to go and see Dulcie's new home after they all attended Mrs Dawson's funeral.

They had been speechless when Dulcie gave

them a guided tour of the flat, and their jaws dropped at the expensive high-class furniture that graced the spacious rooms. No utility here, as the 'standard emergency furniture' was commonly known, thought Agnes. Not for Dulcie the plain, simple plywood tables, chairs and cabinets that had been brought in as the furniture situation had been made worse when the government had cut the already small timber quota.

Dulcie obviously didn't have to worry about the Board of Trade's decision that a young bride should choose from the new utility range of household goods they decreed were needed to fully furnish the new home. No, thought Agnes with a sigh, Dulcie's home was plush and expensively furnished and a long way from anything she and Ted would ever be able to afford, and although she wasn't jealous of Dulcie's triumph, it would be nice to think that she and Ted might have a nice home one day, even if it wasn't up to her friend's standard.

Agnes had to admit that Dulcie had been kindliness itself, the perfect hostess. Wincing as she slipped her foot into a freezing slipper she dreamed of the day when she and Ted could entertain visitors in their own home, which would be years away she knew, given that Ted's two sisters were not old enough to go out and support themselves and his mum, like Ted did. But for now she would continue to dream. A family of her own was a long way off so there was no use torturing herself over it; anyway, she had Alice to spoil and care for.

She was glad that Sally had settled down with Alice, and she was happy that the two girls were a proper little family now, especially since George had joined the Royal Navy and Sally was so busy with work at the hospital and looking after Alice she didn't have much time to worry about him, or at least she gave that impression. Furthermore, Agnes thought, wasn't it lovely that Sally and Callum were now friends again.

Agnes pondered on how much her life had changed over the last few years as she straightened the sheets and blankets, a habit she had gained from her time in the orphanage and had never forgotten. Olive always told her to leave the bed-making as she would do it along with the rest of them, but Agnes didn't like to put her out, her landlady had enough to do.

However, she felt that Sally hurried home from work with a new purpose in her life these days. She'd even admitted to her and Olive that she was ever so glad she hadn't put Alice in an orphanage as she'd originally wanted to. Agnes clearly recalled the time when Alice was first brought here last year by Callum, just before her first birthday. Smiling, she realised that she had fallen in love with the child the moment she saw her and, being an orphan herself, she knew exactly how lost and afraid Alice felt.

Creeping along the landing now, Agnes heard a small mewling sound when she neared Olive's bedroom door and, gently pushing it open a fraction, she saw that Alice had kicked her blankets off and was huddled in the corner of the borrowed cot.

Agnes's heart immediately went out to the small girl as memories of the little ones who had been in her care at the orphanage sprang to mind. Tip-toeing to the cot she tucked the woollen blankets around the little body, and watched as Alice relaxed into its warmth.

Letting her thoughts wander as she descended the stairs as quietly as she could, Agnes recalled Callum promising to come back and see baby Alice soon. However that had been nearly a year ago; his ship was somewhere in the Atlantic now and she realised he wouldn't see her any time soon. When he finally did get back on dry land she was sure he would be thrilled at the progress the child had made since she had lived in this house with all her new aunts.

Busying herself, Agnes put the kettle onto the gas stove before going into the sitting room to light the fire ready for the others getting up. The place would not only be a bit warmer, it would mean one less thing for Olive to do, as she would be busy enough with Alice and young Barney to look after.

Agnes knew Olive was thrilled when Tilly wrote and told her the news that she might be moving back to London, but the information had to be kept under everybody's hat. The only cloud was that she would not be moving back home, she would be staying near the sweet-shop – the name Tilly had given Whitehall. Meanwhile she had learned to drive a lorry as well as fix one.

After toasting a slice of bread and covering it with a scrape of margarine and downing a hot cup of weak, sugarless tea Agnes was ready for work. It was still dark outside and she noted that once she would have felt apprehensive about going outdoors at such a time, but not any more; she had got over her feelings of fear when she found Nancy's grandson that Sunday in the subterranean tunnel and realised that she was an adult now. And adults should be afraid of nothing.

As she headed for the front door she heard a voice from the top of the stairs.

'Agnes,' Olive whispered so as not to wake baby Alice, 'in all the mayhem I forgot to tell you, there's a letter for you – it's been there a couple of days, sorry.'

'Righto,' Agnes whispered back, picking up the envelope lying on the three-legged table in the hallway. Turning it over, she read: Carlton, Mending and Carlton, Solicitors. A tingle zinged up the middle of her ribcage as Agnes let the name sink in. What a solicitor would want with her she didn't know. Suddenly afraid, she slipped the letter in her pocket; she would open it later.

Carlton, Mending and Carlton. Agnes silently mouthed the name of the solicitors who had contacted her to ask if she would attend their office in the strictest confidence. The letter went on to say that they had information which would be to her advantage and so would also like to see some form of identification. Agnes knew she only had her identity card and hoped that it would be enough. But why must she keep it a secret and tell nobody?

Watching the wooden escalator bringing people up from the lower line, Agnes's eyes eagerly awaited sight of Ted, who'd said he would meet her here after work, but there was still no sign of him moments after everybody else had gone their own way. She distinctly remembered him asking her to meet him 'up top', as he called Chancery Lane, when they were on the same shift, and she was always there first as she was so eager to see him.

Her thoughts were all over the place as she waited, recalling the time when she thought Ted wanted nothing to do with her. She'd had the audacity to lay in wait – right on this very spot – to catch him before he started his shift, knowing she had to find out once and for all what she had done so wrong that he didn't want to be her friend any more.

Not seeing Ted had made her so miserable she'd brazened it out and asked him what she had done to offend him. But he'd assured her she had done nothing and then went on to explain that him being the sole breadwinner he didn't think it was right she should have to wait until his sisters were grown-up before they could become better acquainted and she had assured him that she was in no hurry.

The canteen, like now, had been busy in the evening with people rushing home from work as others were starting their nightly visit to the underground with their pillows and covers ready for their ritual of sleeping down there in case of more air raids.

There had been just as many uniformed people crowding the city streets then too. Agnes could hardly remember a time when there weren't uniforms of many different nations in London; it seemed as if they had been here forever.

She shivered as she hopped from one foot to the other to keep the circulation moving in her frozen feet, and wished it was still summer. Being born in July she wasn't very fond of the cold weather. Ted told her that his little sister Sonia wasn't fond of the hotter days as her lungs had suffered because of the heavily polluted London air and would be better off in the countryside.

Ted's mother would never allow her daughters to be evacuated to the countryside, out of her sight, Agnes knew. Both his sisters were over the age when their mother could have gone with them, and Mrs Jackson announced she had no intentions of staying in London without her family. Agnes privately thought there were two ways of looking at that situation; one was that Ted's mother was scared of living alone in London, and who wouldn't be? The other was that she could not relinquish control of her family to the care of someone else. Agnes surmised it might be a bit of both.

Looking after her daughters was one of the reasons Mrs Jackson gave for not being able to go out to work. If Mrs Jackson could have worked she would have saved Ted the strain of toiling all the hours God sent to help pay for Sonia's expensive medical treatment as well as trying to keep his home and family in some sort of respectable order. It was a strain on them both, Agnes knew, but the day Ted told her that it was his duty to look after his family was the day Agnes knew she truly loved him. Loved him with every beat of her heart. She just wished he didn't have to work so hard, that was all.

She also wished his mum liked her a bit more, but, thinking about it now, at least she had Ted's love and that was the main thing, she supposed, as she'd never had anyone love her before.

And now she had a letter that told her a solicitor had information that might be to her advantage. It didn't seem credible, her getting a letter from a solicitor, but it gave her a thrill of excitement she'd never felt before and she wished she could tell Ted about it. 'Carlton, Mending and Carlton,' she whispered.

'Are you talking to yourself, Agnes?' Ted's deep melodic voice came from behind her and made her jump a little as she was so deep in thought. Agnes gave a shaky laugh and felt her colour rise to a warm glow as she stuffed the envelope back in her pocket.

'I was just trying to remember the words of a song,' she fibbed. She didn't like keeping things from Ted because she didn't think it was right that a courting couple should have secrets from each other. She wished she could give him the good news now; he would be so happy for her, she was sure. And she told him everything, usually.

But the letter said she had to keep the news under her hat, and what with the official stamp, it might be against the law to tell anybody. She could feel a dark dread descend. However, she must stay calm, because if she let the cat out of the bag then there was no telling what might happen. What if it was secret railway business? What if she'd done something wrong?

Agnes was quiet as they began the walk home; she'd never had any dealings with solicitors and she didn't want any now. If it was important enough, she thought, she would have a word with Olive who might agree to go with her to the solici-

270

tors if she asked, what with her being like the mother she never had, because Agnes was sure she would never have the courage to go alone. And it wasn't that she was deceiving Ted, she was just postponing the news until she knew what was going on. Yes, that's right, until she knew what was going on.

'Isn't it a lovely night,' Agnes said in a whispery, faraway voice, hardly able to see her hand in front of her, oblivious to the thick fog that cloaked them, her face wreathed in a contented smile as she and Ted walked along together. She loved it when they were alone like this, regardless of the weather.

'You don't half say some daft things sometimes, Agnes.' Ted gave a little laugh as he tied his woollen muffler around his neck and put his hand in the trouser pocket of his driver's uniform. With a nod, he invited Agnes to link her arm through his, which she obediently did. She liked linking arms with Ted and snuggling close in London's winter smog, it made her feel safe, and she was so looking forward to tonight. Olive was off out somewhere with Mrs Windle to a WVS meeting, and Sally was on late duty at Bart's hospital, which meant that she and Ted would have the house to themselves whilst baby-sitting little Alice. Agnes sighed happily. She couldn't wait to be tucked up on the sofa listening to a detective story on the wireless and imagining what it would be like when she and Ted were actually married and had their own place.

'What's the matter with you tonight, Agnes? You're like a cat on a hot wall.'

'I'm just happy, that's all,' Agnes replied as they made their way down Chancery Lane.

'I'm glad to hear that because I wanted to tell you something and I hope you don't mind, love,' said Ted, 'but Mum asked me if I'd stay in and look after the girls tonight as she's been invited to a friend's house for a little get-together.'

'Oh,' said Agnes, trying to hide the disappointment in her voice. 'I told Sally we'd stay in and look after little Alice until Olive gets back from Mrs Windle's, don't you remember me telling you yesterday?' It wasn't often they had the place to themselves and how often did they get a chance to be completely on their own in a house? A whole house to themselves was a lovely idea, seeing as it might be difficult to ever have one themselves, what with the bomb-damaged properties now littering London. Agnes knew that finding a place of their own – when they eventually did marry – was going to be all but impossible. Spending a whole evening alone together had put a spring in her step all day. But she didn't say anything.

'I told Mum that very thing last night before she reminded me that she had this evening planned. It had been organised for weeks although I can't say I recall her mentioning it.' He looked a little puzzled and then, seeing her downcast expression, he said, 'I'm sorry, love.'

'It's all right, Ted,' Agnes said, not wanting him to feel guilty at turning her down in favour of his mother, even if it was becoming a regular occurrence. 'There'll be other times, I'm sure.'

It wasn't Ted's fault, Agnes supposed, shrinking into her heavy coat against the damp evening air, he was just taking care of his family, in the same way she expected he would take care of her in the future, which would be lovely – if she could envisage a future, but she mustn't think that way. Being an honourable type of bloke he wouldn't go back on his word and disappoint his mum and she shouldn't expect him to. Agnes realised that Ted's mum didn't go out all that often and enjoy herself, and it might do her the world of good and settle her nerves a bit.

'That's the spirit, gel, I told mum you wouldn't mind,' Ted said, giving her arm a little squeeze with his elbow.

'No, Ted,' Agnes said, trying to push her disappointment away; she really didn't want to spoil what little time they did have together as they walked back to her lodgings. The silence between them was broken only by the sound of Ted's contented whistle. That's when she decided that she might go and see what the solicitor had to say after all.

'I am sorry that the news has come as such a shock to you, my dear,' said Mr Carlton, the senior partner of Carlton, Mending and Carlton, looking directly at Agnes. He was sitting stiffly behind the huge mahogany desk, and telling her in hushed, almost reverential tones more suited to an undertaker, that she had a father and his name was Mr John Weybridge and he lived on a farm in Surrey.

'We have searched far and wide for you, Agnes – may I call you Agnes?' he asked kindly and when Agnes nodded he continued, 'It is my duty to inform you of news regarding your father.' He

273

looked pointedly at her now as her eyes widened. Agnes had never wondered about a father before, expecting that he had not left a forwarding address when he left her mother in the lurch, although she had always wondered who her mother was and why she had left her on the orphanage steps. But she must concentrate; he was still talking.

'...That is why I thought it prudent to invite you into the office. I need to discuss matters in person rather than through a letter.'

Agnes sat quite still, her back straight as a ram-rod, her imploring blue eyes bright with unshed tears and her mouth paper-dry as she gazed in Olive's direction. Olive gave her a reassuring smile and Agnes turned once again to the greying man who seemed swamped behind the huge desk.

'I have a letter here from your father who is not very well and wants to see you before... Well, suffice to say time is of the essence here. Would you like me to read the letter to you or would you prefer to read it privately?'

'Just give me the gist of it,' Agnes said. 'I can keep it, can't I?'

'Of course you can, it is your property, and it gives details of the place where your father lives. He wants you to visit him, if you'd be so kind.'

Visit him? Agnes could hardly believe her ears. Of course she wanted to visit him!

'And my mother?' Agnes asked when Mr Carlton passed her the envelope containing the letter.

'There is no mention of your mother, suffice to say you will be told everything when you visit but, as I said before, time is of the essence.' He went into more detail before finally rising, and

Agnes, feeling dazed, rose too. She shook his hand and as if in some kind of trance she was guided out towards the busy main road by Olive.

'Oh, just one more thing,' said the ageing solicitor, holding the door for them. 'Your father said he will give you your rightful birth certificate when you visit him.'

'I've got a father...' Agnes could not believe what she had just been told as she left the solicitor's stuffy office with Olive. She wanted to shout out from the rooftops that she was not illegitimate, so great was her happiness. Although she knew she would not. It wasn't in her nature to draw attention to herself. She'd learned that most important of lessons at a very early age back at the orphanage.

But she wasn't an orphan! And, best of all, nor was she the tainted offspring of a dirty slut, as Ted's mother was often fond of hinting when Ted was not around to witness her cruel insinuations. She was 'legitimate'; the word bopped and tumbled inside her head like one of those energetic jitterbugs she'd seen the night she went dancing with Tilly and Sally after Dulcie's wedding.

And, not only was she not illegitimate, she also had a father, a living, breathing father! Moreover, she thought excitedly, not only did she have a father – but he wanted to see her. She looked again at the address on the letter given to her by the solicitor. Surrey! Surrey? She'd never been to Surrey in her life. There must be some mistake. How did she end up in a London orphanage if she had a family who lived in Surrey?

275

'Another night in, Agnes?' Olive asked, securing a hatpin through the red band of her bottle-green WVS hat. Secretly she thought that Ted really was the limit, although she wouldn't hurt Agnes for the world by saying so. But she didn't like the way he left her in the lurch and was always at his mother's beck and call.

'Ted's mum is going to see friends this evening,' Agnes said simply, 'and he has to look after his two sisters. But, it's all right, I can still stay in and look after little Alice. I don't mind, truly.' After all, she thought, Ted hadn't asked her if she would like to sit with him and his sisters whilst their mum went out. And staying in would give her a chance to wash her hair and put it in those little tin curlers and have her hair all nice for tomorrow, and she could have a really good think about going to Surrey...

'Did your mum enjoy her night out?' Agnes asked brightly when Ted came to pick her up at the end of Article Row to go to work, as he'd taken to doing since she'd suspected she was being followed. Ted put his head down and hid his face, making Agnes feel apprehensive. She noticed that he looked a little sheepish and her brows puckered in curiosity.

'Mum didn't go to her friend's house in the end, Agnes,' he said in a low voice.

'She didn't go, Ted?'

'I was going to come around to see you but felt it was a bit of an imposition after letting you down.'

'Oh, you should have come around, Ted.' Agnes was so disappointed. 'It would never be an imposition to see you.'

'Oh, that is good of you, Agnes,' he said when she linked her gloved hand through his arm, 'Mum felt ever so guilty at going out enjoying herself with her friend after ruining our night that she couldn't go in the end.'

'But that was silly, Ted, it meant that everybody's night was ruined.'

'I know,' said Ted. 'She also worried that the girls might be upset, what with Sonia not feeling too well, and she would fret if Mum went out.'

'You could have come around to Olive's.' Agnes was sorely disappointed now but as Sonia was not feeling well she didn't want to give Ted anything more to worry about.

'I know,' Ted said in his usual kindly voice, 'but I thought you would have been well settled by then.'

'I suppose so, Ted,' Agnes said with every ounce of patience she could muster, acknowledging he had enough on his plate without her carping on. What was done was done and that was the end of it, she supposed.

They walked in silence for a while and Agnes began to mull over their relationship in her head. She loved Ted dearly, and she wanted to love his family, too, as he so obviously did. Yet was she being selfish wanting him all to herself? She knew Ted had an obligation to his family, because the girls had no dad, and Mrs Jackson had no husband. However, a little voice in her head said there were a lot of women in the same position these days. Some were worse off and didn't have a home or anything, Agnes silently reasoned; they were the ones that should be pitied, weren't they? After all, Mrs Jackson had a very nice flat and a loving family around her; she should count her blessings. That's what they were always told to do at the orphanage and Agnes made sure she counted hers every single day.

'Mum said to tell you she's very sorry,' Ted said, apologising on his mother's behalf as his long strides covered the cracked pavement.

'That's very kind of her to say that, Ted,' said Agnes, feeling a little guilty for thinking such unkind thoughts about Mrs Jackson and secretly admitting that if Ted had come around last night he would probably have run a mile as her face was covered in an oatmeal face-pack that one of the girls in the underground had told her about, her head was covered with tin curlers and her feet were in a bowl of water.

'Mum couldn't help it really,' Ted continued as they walked down Chancery Lane. 'You understand that, don't you, Agnes?'

'Yes, Ted,' Agnes said in a low voice.

'I like your hair like that, Agnes.' Ted smiled and gave her arm a little squeeze.

'Do you really, Ted?' Agnes tapped her bouncing curls and felt a small thrill at the compliment; everything in her world was perfect again.

'And to make up for upsetting our plans, Mum's invited you around for tea on Sunday. What do you say about that?'

Agnes felt her heart sink to the cosy fur-lined boots she'd had since before the war, which came out every winter. Sunday was the day she was supposed to go to meet her father. She couldn't postpone it now after all this time.

'She's saved her coupons specially.' Ted's voice was brimming with pride. 'Shall we say around four o'clock? I'll come and pick you up; make sure nobody's following you.' He ended his remark with a little chuckle. Agnes didn't have the heart to refuse, especially after his mum had saved all her coupons for the tea. But neither did she want to miss her appointment with her father. She had waited all her life for that day.

'Did you hear me, Agnes?' Ted was saying, bringing her out of her reverie with a little start.

'I'm sorry, Ted, what did you say?' Even in the frosty morning air Agnes could feel her temperature rise in her frozen cheeks. 'I was miles away.'

'You can say that again, gel,' he answered. 'I said, for the third time, what time do you finish this evening?'

'Oh,' Agnes said quickly, 'around six, and you?'

'Half past, wait for me in the café to walk you home.'

Agnes nodded without even thinking. The weather was turning so cold now making her huddle down in her coat, and her teeth were actually chattering against each other as they reached the steps leading down to the underground. Ted gave her a quick peck on the cheek before whistling his way down the steps, leaving Agnes with a lot to think about.

The news of Mrs Dawson's death was a shock to all in Article Row but there was one resident who wasn't convinced it was a leaking gas tap that had brought on her demise. Olive had to silence Nancy Black on more than one occasion when she appointed herself chief spokesperson on Archie's private life without full knowledge of the facts.

'Nancy,' Olive said with the patience born of years living next door to the local busybody, 'we don't know that, do we?' This particular occasion was when, in the butchers shop, Nancy had hinted to a woman from Jubilee Avenue that Mrs Dawson had been very depressed at being left alone for long hours whilst her husband was 'on duty' – the last two words had been loaded with such malice that Olive felt obliged to correct her there and then. Sergeant Dawson was grieving over the death of his beloved wife and yet Nancy still couldn't resist airing her poisonous point of view. She would cause a war in an empty house, Olive thought, wondering what Archie could possibly have done to upset Nancy so much that the woman could not bear the sight of him. And even the death of Archie's wife could not thaw the ice around Nancy's heart.

NINETEEN

Dulcie was resting when she heard a furious ringing of the doorbell. She frowned as she hurried down the stairs to the front door, but her irritation turned to anger when she saw who was making all the noise.

'If you think you can come here and cause trouble you can think again,' Dulcie told her sister, Edith, who was standing on the doorstep. But her anger subsided a little when she saw Edith's expression.

'I haven't come to cause trouble, honest, Dulcie. Can I come in?'

'You wouldn't know honest if it jumped up and poked you in the eye,' Dulcie said, still holding a grudge about her sister's wayward behaviour. Although she had to admit she had never seen Edith looking so down before, and something in the woman's sombre tone told Dulcie that this was no ordinary call.

Curiosity and the opportunity to swank a little were the only reasons for allowing Edith into her home, Dulcie told herself as she led the way back up the fully carpeted stairs to the luxurious flat.

Grateful David was at his chambers now, Dulcie was fully aware her husband didn't much care for her sister and who could blame him after the tricks she had played in the past? What kind of daughter would 'forget' to inform her parents that she was alive after being involved in a bomb attack? And then just as importantly, come back home and waltz off with her sister's boyfriend? It was enough to give anyone the pip.

'In here,' Dulcie said sharply, opening the door to the opulent sitting-room. She didn't dare try to second-guess the reason for Edith's visit but was sure it wasn't a social call.

'Oh, you've landed on your feet, I must say,' Edith remarked, her feet sinking into the thick pile carpet as her sweeping gaze took in the lavish furnishings. Dulcie was delighted to see the wind was taken right out of her sister's sails. Inside, her heart was palpitating fit to burst with justified satisfaction at Edith's obvious amazement, whilst on the outside her features remained calm, her head held high.

Dulcie hoped she was giving the resigned impression of a woman who was so familiar with the finer things in life that her surroundings were as natural to her as breathing. After all, she reasoned, one didn't notice the trappings of wealth when one was acquainted with it day in and day out like she was.

'Close your mouth, Edith, you are dribbling.' Dulcie felt her adrenaline rise; this was the day she had secretly longed for; the day when her sister was rendered speechless at her success – for a change. She was so delighted with her lot she momentarily considered inviting her mother... Then just as quickly, decided against it.

'I'm pregnant, Dulcie,' Edith said, shattering her fleeting triumph. 'I don't know what to do.' Dulcie gave her sister an inflexible stare, and much as she wanted to tell Edith to go and cry on someone else's shoulder, she knew she could not. Dulcie could not turn her back on her own kin when they were in trouble; even though she might be the same flesh and blood as Edith, she thought as she looked her sister up and down, she certainly wasn't of the same nature.

'Is it Wilder's baby?' Dulcie asked, not really wanting to hear the answer but knowing she must. She had never given in to the American airman's obvious charms because she wanted to keep him keen, maintain his interest – but her ploy had backfired when he turned to Edith and changed Dulcie's life forever.

She eyed her sister whose head was now bent as she nodded her affirmation. Dulcie was sure she would never offer Edith the same advice their mother had given her. She had no intention of dragging her sister to a backstreet abortionist to 'get rid' of her dirty little secret, as her mother had claimed Dulcie should have done.

'What do you want me to do?' she asked, nodding towards the lovingly polished leather chesterfield sofa that took pride of place in the centre of the expansive room. Unable to look Edith in the face, Dulcie went over to the corner bay and stared out of the tall window. The street was busy below, everything looked so normal – as normal as a bomb-damaged street could look in wartime, she reasoned, watching people hurrying about their business, some looking as if they didn't have a care and others looking as if they had the weight of the world on their shoulders.

Her emotions were all over the place now as her thoughts travelled back to the day when she saw her younger sister, suitcase in hand, preparing for a weekend away with her man. Fleetingly, the feeling of hurt returned.

'I can't keep it, Dulcie. I've been offered the leading role in a Broadway play. America!' There was a pleading note in Edith's voice when she added, 'This could be the bigtime for me – this is the chance I've been waiting for all my life.'

'You said the same thing when you got the lead in the West End, too.' Dulcie forced her dull, disparaging words through tight lips. 'It didn't stop you running out on the bigtime when you went away with Wilder, though, did it?'

'I … I didn't run out on it – I would never do that.' There were tears in Edith's voice but Dulcie hardened her heart; she couldn't let her sister hurt her so badly all over again.

'I saw your name plastered all over the front of the theatre wall.' Dulcie turned quickly to face her sister. 'You can't deny what you did, Edith. Admit it, you wanted Wilder from the moment you set eyes on him.'

'I don't deny I went away with Wilder that weekend.' Edith shook her head, her eyes red-rimmed, and her voice dipped. 'I can't deny it, can I?'

'Well, what are you denying, then?' Dulcie watched her sister squirm and waited for the new revelation that was bound to be somebody else's fault, because had Edith never admitted culpability for anything she had ever done in the past. Dulcie could feel the dormant loathing begin to stir; Edith had selfishly coveted everything she herself ever strived for, and now she had the temerity to beg for her support and, not only that, expected Dulcie to swallow her excuses too.

'I wasn't the lead in the show that day – I had been fired!'

'Fired?' Dulcie couldn't believe what she was hearing. 'But you couldn't have been, your face was on the board outside the theatre.'

'It was taken down the next day. Wilder had come to see me, and I'll admit it, I did all the running, I made a play for him and…' She paused as if unsure, then taking a deep breath she continued, 'He wasn't made of wood, Dulcie, if a woman offers herself, he was always going to take it. I was feeling low and vulnerable I suppose...'

Dulcie found that very hard to believe but she let her sister go on.

'I knew Wilder liked me and he didn't resist when I said I'd like to get out of London, I was upset, vulnerable... I was ... doing you a favour... You could have ended up marrying him and he was always going to deceive you.'

Dulcie was even more flabbergasted now. Up until a moment ago she had firmly believed that you looked out for your own people. It was an unwritten rule in the East End that if you could help someone it was your duty to do so. But Edith was making it very difficult for her to stick to that reasoning now.

'Vulnerable? You?' Dulcie was so angry she could have spat in her sister's eye. However, she decided to play it down, keep calm and go slowly, so Edith could digest every word she said to her sister who was looking more pale by the minute. 'From what I can make out, Edith, you are one ungrateful, conniving cat from hell, and if I had all the money in the world I would give it to you just to see the back of you.' Dulcie could see it plainly now. 'You thought you were doing me a favour by exposing my boyfriend as the lying cheat he most surely was.' Her voice dripped scorn. 'Yet, Edith, you made it quite clear what you wanted from Wilder from the very moment you met him. The single theatre ticket. The come-hither looks when he walked into the room. You couldn't wait to have him all to yourself, could you?' Dulcie was getting into her stride now and enjoying every minute of her sister's discomfort. She had waited a long time for this. 'I knew what Wilder was; he didn't fool me with his generous, handsome G.I. ways. He took what he could when he could from anyone he could, except me, in the hope that the day would not be his last – and then you came along and his luck ran out.' Dulcie could feel her blood pressure rise and she had to sit down.

'But you don't understand, Dulcie, I loved him – I really loved him.' Edith should have been an actress and not a singer, Dulcie realised, because she was giving a fair impression of someone who was heartbroken right now. Not that Dulcie could be fooled for a minute.

'You loved him so much that you want to be rid of his child?' She threw back her head and laughed. 'That sounds about right coming from you, Edith. If you were a man they would call you a cad. But now I come to think about it, there are a lot of similarities between you and Wilder.' If she drank, Dulcie knew she would be reaching for something strongly alcoholic by now. Her heart was pounding and her head was fit to burst.

'You know I can't have an illegitimate child, Dulcie, it would be the end of my career.' Edith sounded so matter-of-fact. So certain that her older sister's help was what she deserved.

Dulcie sat motionless for a long time and there was only the ticking of the ornate mantle clock to break the silence in the room. Eventually, after thinking long and hard about what she was going to do Dulcie sighed; she had to admire her sister's gall. If she was honest, Edith *had* done her a favour. Because, given the opportunity, Dulcie would have married Wilder in a heartbeat if he'd asked her.

She had to admit she had dreamed of Wilder whisking her off to America to live the Hollywood lifestyle, and that was what Edith secretly wanted too... And David? Where did he fit into all of this, she wondered, but the thought was too painful to pursue.

'Have you been in touch with Wilder's family?' Dulcie asked eventually, trying to block out the suspicion that she wouldn't have given David a moment's thought back then, or the fact that she was reaping the rewards of marrying in haste. 'Have you?' she repeated.

'Why on earth would I want to do that?' Edith's eyes opened wide in amazement at her sister's obviously idiotic question.

'They have a right to know,' Dulcie answered and watched as Edith opened her bag, took something out and clicked it shut again.

'Have a look at this,' Edith said, offering Dulcie a dog-eared photograph which showed an old man and woman and a fair-haired boy of about ten. They were standing in front of a run-down shack and were surrounded by dry-looking earth, not a blade of grass in sight.

'They look really poor, but what's it got to do with anything?'

'Take a closer look, Dulcie. The boy is Wilder, the old people are his parents and guess what? They are not that old, it's their circumstances that have made them look like that.'

Dulcie gasped. She'd always been of the impression that Wilder had come from a really rich family and he'd done nothing to dispel the idea.

'One of his buddies back at the camp gave it to me when he brought me the news. Obviously his parents were told first.'

'Oh, my goodness.' Dulcie's hand flew to her mouth to stop her saying what was on her mind when she realised her sister had done her a bigger favour than she'd first assumed.

'So, you won after all. You have all this and I've got nothing,' Edith said in a dull voice, and suddenly Dulcie felt sorry for her sister who had been such a thorn in her side for so many years. They were the same flesh and blood; Dulcie couldn't turn her away now. 'What can I do?' she asked eventually, knowing she couldn't see her sister in such a desperate predicament.

'Can you help me, Dulcie?'

Dulcie knew she would help her sister but Edith wasn't getting away with it that easily. She wanted her to worry a bit more first. Then after a long, hesitant pause, Dulcie thought *There but for the grace of God go I*, and placing her hand on the gentle swell beneath the expensively tailored cut of her loosely smocked jacket she said a silent thank you for the opulent lifestyle David's money now afforded her.

Her own five-and-a-half-month pregnancy was still not that obvious as she carried herself with an elegant, upright deportment that made her expanding girth less noticeable, and that suited her just fine.

'How far along are you?' Dulcie asked as Edith looked up, and for a fleeting moment her expression was defiant.

'Twenty-two weeks... The first time we'd ... you know?'

Dulcie was astounded. Her sister had come here for her help at twenty-two weeks pregnant – they must have both conceived around the same time. 'So, you are due in April ... May?'

'How do you know that so quickly?' Edith asked, but Dulcie shrugged; she was giving nothing away to her sister at this point.

'We were just having a good time.' Edith admitted, looking at her brown peep-toe shoes and fiddling with the clasp on her box bag.

'So it was just the once?' A stab of pain pierced Dulcie's heart. Just the once, my eye, she thought. 'Are you at home with Mum?' Dulcie watched her sister's face crumple in disgust.

'Are you kidding?' Edith said incredulously. 'She'd have me round to the nearest backstreet midwife. "Job done. Ta, dearie. Next please"...' Edith gave a fair imitation of the woman Dulcie had been introduced to the day her mother took her back to Stepney. 'I'm not even going to tell her.'

'Can't say I blame you,' Dulcie said, recalling that hot day, when she was threatened with an act even more abhorrent than the one that created her unborn child, knowing the backstreet midwives were making money hand over fist since the Americans came over. While the cat was away, the mice were having a fine old time, she thought miserably.

'Leave it with me, I'll talk to David. I know you are not one of his favourite people and he's not your biggest fan but he would never turn you away.'

'Do you think he would let me stay until...'

'...Until the baby's born?' Dulcie asked, watching her sister's head droop even more. Edith nodded without looking at her older sister.

'And then what will you do?'

'I could have it adopted ... I don't want to ... to get rid of it.'

'You have left it far too late for that, my girl. But adopted? I see you've given it plenty of thought, Edith.' Dulcie's sardonic tones were lost on her sister; she could tell by the nod of Edith's perfectly curled head. At least she was keeping up appearances, Dulcie thought, and hadn't succumbed to forgetting to wash because she was so miserable, like some did. No, the Simmonds girls knew how to put a brave face on things, Dulcie thought proudly, two sometimes, if need be. But she could hardly believe her own sister could contemplate such a thing as adoption. 'I'll bloody well bring it up myself before I'd see it adopted!' Dulcie declared and was shocked at the speed at which Edith jumped from the sofa.

'Would you, Dulcie?' the relief on her face was plain. 'Would you do that for me?'

'No, Edith,' Dulcie said through gritted teeth. 'I'd do it for the child.'

TWENTY

In the weeks following Mrs Dawson's death Barney was practically living in Olive's house. Archie had no choice but to go straight back to work after the funeral, feeling duty-bound to carry on as normal for the sake of the boy, and even though he had a sister who lived on a farm somewhere, he told Olive his place was here in Article Row. It gave Olive a chance to give the boy some kind of stable home life, if there was such a thing in these uncertain times and Barney, although quiet at first, seemed to be coming around to the idea of living in a house of women.

Olive had hesitated to tell Barney that things would get better, not knowing how he would react, and decided to take one day at a time. Archie told her he wouldn't retreat to his sister's in the countryside because it would be like running away and after all, there was plenty he had to be getting on with at home.

'Well, if you're sure,' Olive had said. Barney seemed quite content to help her with baby Alice and be as useful as he could around the house whilst Archie was on duty at the station or on fire-watch. Even though there hadn't been a raid for ages, due to the Axis forces being busy elsewhere, his duties still had to be attended to.

Barney was proud to be the 'man of the house' as Sally and Agnes called him, making his chest swell and his back straighten. He was always ready to run an errand or watch over Alice whilst Olive got the meals ready. And now he was with Olive he didn't have any need to go near the old place and meet up with the gangs he used to knock around with.

He was so wrapped up in being helpful, thought Olive, that he seemed to have completely got over Mrs Dawson's death. This was until one day she found him sitting on the back step.

She had just given him the boiled, mashed potato skins to feed the growing chicks when she realised she had forgotten to give him the corn. She saw him looking to where he had built a little chicken coop and realised he was gently stroking a chick cradled in his cupped hands. It was quite still and Barney had tears streaming down his cheeks.

'Barney, whatever's the matter?' Olive asked, worried in case he wasn't feeling well and didn't like to say.

'Everythin's dying,' he said simply in a low, strained voice. 'Even my chicks. All the people I care about are dying... I worried that the same thing might happen to you and Agnes and Sally, especially when I came out here and saw this...' He held up the dead chick to show Olive, who thought that it might be a bit cold in the garden to keep chicks so young.

She knew she could not say anything that would stop him grieving for the people he had lost: his mother, his grandmother, Mrs Dawson, and in some ways his father too because he never got in touch with the boy. Everyone who'd brought him stability and love had gone and his life had changed forever. But at least Olive could assure him of one thing – he was not alone any more.

'I know we are not a substitute for the family you have lost,' Olive said, 'but we are always here, and if you need to get something off your chest or just need to talk to someone, you have got all of us eager females with ever-open ears to listen.' Then she paused and seemed to ponder for a moment. 'And if you want to get news to the other end of London in a hurry, there is always Nancy Black next door.'

There was a moment's silence before Barney raised his head and looked at her. Then a smile plumped his cheeks and showed his straight white teeth, and before she knew it he was laughing and it gladdened her heart when he said in a mock-serious voice, wiping his tearstained face with the back of his hand, 'I ain't tellin' her nuffink.'

'I don't blame you,' Olive said in conspiratorial tones, as a thought struck her. They had been so wrapped up in the events of the last few weeks that she'd never got around to asking him. 'Barney, about these chicks, what if we put them in the cellar until the weather is warmer? They should be a good size by then.'

'Would you do that for me, Aunt Olive?' he asked, jumping up and giving her a loving hug, and Olive understood that she and the girls were the nearest thing he'd had to stability for a long time. Then as if realising what he'd done he gave a jerky little shrug and disentangled himself. Within seconds he was off up the street, leaving Olive to shake her head.

What else could she have done? The remaining eight chicks had no home to go to either, so it was her duty to look after them, and, if they rewarded her with an egg or two, now and then, who was she to refuse them?

'Not today, thank you, Nancy,' Olive said, closing the door behind her neighbour who had seen her coming out of the police station, and now wanted to know if there was 'anything she could do to help'. Well, it would be a poor day when she needed anything from Nancy Black, Olive thought, knowing her neighbour only wanted to find out what she was doing in the police station in the first place, and she didn't have time for idle gossip today as she had something she wanted to discuss with Agnes in private. Finding her young lodger in the kitchen, she gave her the good news. 'Archie said he can take us to Surrey in his police car this afternoon.'

Agnes hadn't told anybody except Olive about her father wanting to see her. 'I have to go to meet him in a police car?' she asked hesitantly. Whilst she was not one to look a gift-horse in the mouth Agnes didn't fancy the idea of turning up to meet a parent she had never seen before looking like a common criminal.

'He can drop us off somewhere and we can walk the rest of the way if that would put your mind at rest?' Olive didn't want to voice what she thought of Agnes's father; suffice to say, it didn't look as if he had been in too much of a hurry to find her – twenty years was a long time to mull over the idea of getting to know his offspring.

Olive couldn't understand how people could reject their children. She couldn't even envisage how she would have reacted if Tilly had been younger and had to be evacuated for her own safety; she didn't think she would have let Tilly leave London without her.

But thousands of parents had had to do it. And some of them hadn't seen their children since the beginning of the war over three years ago. Thankfully it wasn't a decision she'd had to make, and thinking of Tilly now she still missed her and worried what she was up to.

'How come Archie can get the petrol to go to Surrey? I heard the government are even rationing official vehicles now,' Agnes said, not wanting to risk him getting into trouble with his superiors.

'He has to take some confidential files to a police station out that way, they can't be posted, and it just so happens that he has to go near Attersham village to get to it.' Attersham was the place where Agnes's father lived. 'That's a stroke of good luck, isn't it?' When Agnes went to see her father, Olive thought, she and Archie would ... they would talk, she would find out if everything was going the way it should with Barney, and his police duties, if there was anything he needed. She was determined that she would be a better neighbour to Archie than she had been to his poor wife. And if Nancy had anything to say about it she could say it to her face.

Agnes took her seat at the table and folded a piece of toast before handing it to little Alice, not saying anything for a while.

'He said he can take us around two o'clock if

295

you like? Otherwise we'll have a bit of a trek to get to such a small village, that's if there's any trains running that far out and it will be treacherous getting there in this awful wet weather.'

'I don't mind if you don't want to come, Olive,' Agnes said, although not unkindly. 'I'm not sure I want to go, either, now.' She always had to fend for herself in the past so it wasn't any hardship now, and she didn't want to put Olive out by dragging her to Attersham in this bad weather. Besides, Agnes had checked and knew the nearest station would be three miles away.

'It's just nerves,' Olive assured her, 'you'll be fine when you get there.'

'I would prefer to go early, get it out of the way, if I'm going at all,' Agnes said, 'and that way, I won't have to disappoint Ted's mum. She's saved all her coupons for a nice tea.' Agnes so wanted to give Ted and his family, especially his mother, all the good news – if indeed she did go, and if she did have good news to impart.

'I'm not sure if Archie can go this morning,' Olive said doubtfully.

'I don't want to be a burden,' Agnes insisted. 'I can manage, honestly.'

'Well,' said Olive, pulling out a chair and sitting opposite Agnes at the table, 'I'm not one to inter-fere as you know, and seeing as you're like a daughter to me now I'm only giving you the same advice I would give Tilly...' She paused for a moment. 'If I can just say, I think you would be sorry if you didn't go and find out what this man, Mr Weybridge, has to say for himself.'

'You could have knocked me down with a puff

of wind when I found out.' Agnes sounded almost distant as if expecting the answer to come to her from the air. 'And why does he suddenly want to see me now, after twenty years? He could have got in touch any time, surely?'

'That's what I thought,' Olive admitted, 'but I didn't like to say. Anyway, it won't do any harm to find out, will it?'

All her life Agnes had wanted to find out who her real family were. She wanted to know that she belonged to somebody. And most of all she wanted to know who that 'somebody' was.

'If you're worried about Ted, I'm sure he will understand if you are a little late.'

'But Mrs Jackson has saved her coupons especially.' Agnes took a deep breath and looked quite despondent, until Olive offered another suggestion.

'Stop worrying, Agnes, I'll ask Archie if he can take us this morning after all, and if he can't he may let you telephone Mr Weybridge from the police station and postpone it until the trains are running better during the week?'

'He doesn't have a telephone,' said Agnes, 'or at least, there isn't a number on the letter.'

'We'll find a solution, don't you worry,' Olive said, brightening as she put on her coat and saw Agnes smile.

A little while later she was back.

'I've had a word with Archie and he said he would drop us off, and then pick us up again about an hour or so later.' She looked thoughtfully at her lodger. 'So that's all worked out for the best, hasn't it.'

'Are you sure you don't mind, Olive?' Agnes asked, feeling as if she was putting everybody out now.

'I don't mind at all, love,' Olive said, beginning to clear the table 'and Barney can look after Alice for a little while, he'll enjoy that. Sally will be in from her night shift soon anyway, so what do you think?' Olive's eyes were bright with enthusiasm and Agnes threw her arms around her landlady's shoulders and gave her a hug.

'Oh, Olive, you are so good to me, I don't know what I'd do without you.'

'Oh, don't take on so.' Olive gave a modest little laugh. 'Everything will be fine.' She only hoped her words sounded more positive than she felt.

TWENTY-ONE

Sally, weary now after a busy night at the hospital, took George's letter from her pocket and, putting her feet up, decided to have a little read before Alice woke from her nap, whilst Barney, always eager to be of help, promised he would only be in the cellar with the chickens if she needed him.

Her eyes raced down the loving words. She was eager to hear how he was faring, yet she didn't want to reach the end of the last page. He said he missed her so much and couldn't wait until they were together again. He asked how Alice was doing and wanted to know if she was looking forward to Christmas. Sally smiled at that; what

298

child didn't look forward to a visit from Father Christmas? George asked if it was snowing yet, and then, on the last line he wrote: *Don't answer that last question, my darling, for I wonder if it will be snowing in Liverpool on the 24th? With all my love, my darling, yours always George xxx P.S. Give Alice a goodnight kiss from me. xx*

'He's coming home for Christmas!' Sally's shrill cry of excitement echoed around the house as she ran to the top of the cellar steps, sending the chickens squawking in all directions and causing Barney to drop the valuable corn he was feeding them with. She and George had worked out a code for when and if he could get some leave without mentioning the name of the ship or even which service he was with. The letter hadn't said so but she knew George's ship was docking at Liverpool! It couldn't be more perfect. She and George were going to be together at Christmas in her home town. She could go and put a wreath on her parents' grave and finally make her peace with her father and Morag who, by their tragic deaths, had given her the gift of Alice.

'Is everything all right, Sally?' Barney called as he came haring up the cellar steps.

'George is coming home for Christmas!' gasped Sally in an excited voice that was barely above a whisper, with happy tears streaming down her face. 'I can't tell you how I know but we will spend Christmas together, probably not here though...' She stopped herself from going further, realising she had already said too much. Then picking up Barney she swung him around the garden, laughing and dancing.

Barney was feeling quite embarrassed now, having never seen the dutiful nursing sister in this mood before. As Sally put him back on his feet he said, 'That's great news, Sally, and guess what?' He paused for dramatic effect. 'Olive's gonna be thrilled as well, because she had word from the doctor who took George's room in the Simpsons' house. He brought a telephone message from Tilly – she's coming home for Christmas!' Looking up at Sally's ecstatic smile he hoped that when he told Olive the good news she didn't pick him up and swing him around too.

Sergeant Dawson was not in the least put out by his timetable being rearranged; in fact he said he would rather go to Surrey early and that way he would be back in time for his dinner. So he, Olive and Agnes left the bustle of London traffic and weaved their way out of the capital onto the Portsmouth road before heading towards the rolling countryside, ancient woodland and picturesque villages of Surrey. Agnes could hardly contain her excitement.

'Won't you come in with me?' she asked Olive when they arrived at the small farmhouse that seemed to be in the middle of nowhere, suddenly very nervous, especially when she saw chickens and geese running about like demented gate-keepers as Sergeant Dawson's car pulled into the muddy yard.

Olive patted Agnes arm, silently indicating that the girl would be fine without her. She herself was only too relieved to get out and stretch her legs.

'I'm grateful for the lift, Archie, but the journey

has left me feeling like a leaf in a blizzard,' she laughed, knowing she had never been so glad to touch mud in all her life. In the distance she could see a young woman on a tractor out in the field and wondered if she was a land girl or if she was resident here.

'I'll wait outside if you don't mind, Agnes, get a bit of fresh air.' She wrinkled her nose and gave a little grin as the air, at the moment, smelled anything but fresh. Then she spied the pig sty just over the yard. 'Yell if you need me, I'll be having a conversation with that porker.'

'Well, don't go smuggling him out under your coat.' Agnes laughed, trying to quell her jangled nerves.

'Oh, bacon on toast...' sighed Olive. What she wouldn't give for a nice pork chop was nobody's business.

'Don't, you'll have me laughing and this is serious,' Agnes protested.

'You're right,' said Olive, giving her a gentle push. 'Go on, find out what all the fuss is about and I'll see you when you come out again.' She was in a funny kind of mood. It must have been all the winding roads on the journey, she presumed as she turned and watched Archie's police car disappear over the hill.

It wasn't long before he was back, inviting Olive into the car out of the brisk west wind.

'Oh, I'm glad to see you, Archie,' Olive said, smiling although her teeth were beginning to chatter. 'It is so cold out there. I'm sure we'll soon have snow.'

'You said that last year and we didn't, and the

year before if I remember correctly,' Archie said with one of his most disarming grins, causing Olive to feel a sudden rush of heat to her freezing cheeks.

'What a good memory you have Sergeant Dawson.' Olive was suddenly aware of their close proximity to one another, and as she watched Archie looking out of the window, his eyes always on duty, she realised how tired he appeared. He had been working all the hours God sent after his wife died and she wondered if he was running from the truth. Olive, taking stock, reckoned that if he kept working as hard as he had been lately he would not have to face up to what had happened. It was all so very, very sad.

'She never did get over losing our boy,' Archie said, reading Olive's thoughts with unerring accuracy. 'In some ways she blamed herself but...'

'Nobody could be to blame, Archie, it was God's will.' Olive fleetingly covered his hand with hers. It was a small gesture, meant to reassure her friend. But Archie turned to her now and he looked at her, really looked at her, his dark eyes so close to hers that she could see the huge pupils searching her face, her eyes, her hair.

'Oh, Olive, I shouldn't feel this way but I do ... I'm glad she is at peace with our son. I haven't been able to grieve because it was what she wanted for so long. If anything I feel angry sometimes that she took the easy way out, leaving me with all the heartache and...'

'Don't torture hourself, Archie, it's not right, you did everything you possibly could and more. You have nothing to blame yourself for.'

Archie touched her shoulder and gave a tight smile. It was a small gesture but it was done with such warmth that it spoke a thousand words and Olive realised that she had spent so long trying to avoid local gossip that she had actually neglected her very true friend. And he was a friend, the best she could ever have.

'They caught them, you know,' Archie said suddenly, confusing Olive momentarily.

'Who caught who, Archie?' Olive's brows puckered.

'Those spivs who were tormenting Barney and young Freddy. We caught them red-handed in number 49, they were using it as a hiding place for all the loot they pinched from bombed-out houses and, would you believe it, even graveyards... The buggers have got no respect for the living or the dead and we got them banged to rights.'

'Oh, well done, Archie!' Olive could not contain her delight and she reached across to the driver's seat and kissed him lightly on the cheek. Then, feeling suddenly embarrassed at her impulsive performance, Olive sank back into her own seat as the uneasy silence that filled the small interior of the car began to close in on her. She had never done anything so spontaneous in all her life before. Quickly, she turned her head and looked out of the side window to hide the obvious tinge of colour her act had brought on and found the scudding clouds immensely interesting.

After a short while she turned and looked straight ahead beyond the windscreen, engrossed in the stark landscape beyond the farmhouse, whilst out of the corner of her eye she could see

Archie was doing exactly the same thing. Neither of them said a word and Olive was only too aware that if they so wished, her light, friendly kiss could have been taken further. Much further.

If Agnes had dreams of a loving father shedding a tear whilst waiting with outstretched arms for her to fall into, then she was sadly mistaken. The door was opened almost immediately and she was greeted, if she could call it that, by a wizened old man who was bent double and had no teeth, reminding Agnes, to her dismay, of a character in a Punch and Judy show she had watched with other children from the orphanage.

'Come in, come in, come in, you're letting all the heat out,' he said in a grumpy voice. Agnes did as she was told and entered the wide expanse of hallway with four bare-wood doors leading off it, which gave way to a dark, narrow staircase running up the middle of the farmhouse to the floor above. The hallway wasn't very bright as the small high windows were quite dingy and by the looks of it, she thought, hadn't seen a chamois leather for many a long year. But she wasn't here to criticise. She was here to meet her father. And looking at this cantankerous old man, she now wished she hadn't bothered.

'So, you are Agnes, I presume,' the old man said in the local accent, which had Agnes straining her ears and wondering if it would be too much of an effort for him to raise his voice a little.

'Yes, I'm Agnes, and you must be Mr Weybridge?' My father, she thought, although she didn't say so when she held out her hand, which he ignored. She hadn't expected him to look so stern and forbidding. If she was honest, Agnes wasn't sure what she had expected.

'Must I now?' the old man said, looking her up and down. 'Well, that's where you're wrong, see.' He dragged his feet to one of the four doors in slow, painful steps and silently beckoned her to follow.

'Mr Weybridge is in 'ere. You'll do well to wait until he speaks to you first. And keep your 'ands to yourself, you never know as what folk 'ave on theirs.' Agnes shuddered; she had a good idea what the old man was talking about, this being a farm.

Agnes was led to the room opposite and her surprise on entering was evident in her low gasp. She hadn't expected to see a gleaming, oxblood leather sofa and matching high-winged leather chairs in the richly furnished room, nor the highly polished sideboard and occasional tables. It was the kind of room a gentleman would use, she thought, not the kind of room a farmer would live in.

'We don't live like animals just because we rear them,' said a low voice from the vicinity of the winged chair near the roaring fire. Agnes turned quickly.

'Thank you, Darnley,' said the man who was sitting near the blazing fire, his thinning white hair damp as if not long combed down with water, his legs hidden beneath a plaid woollen blanket.

The solicitor had subsequently given her more information in a letter about this man whom she presumed was her father. Apparently he had fought on the Somme and had been injured; perhaps that was why he needed the blanket whilst sitting in front of a roaring fire, she reasoned as Darnley shuffled out without saying a word. On closer assessment she realised that Mr Weybridge was much younger than she first assumed. However, her thoughts were curtailed when he gave a low chuckle.

'I keep Darnley on instead of a guard dog,' he said, not rising from the chair, directing Agnes with a wave of his hand to the other chair opposite his own, whilst a portly woman of indeterminate age brought a tray of tea things.

Before any conversation resumed, the woman filled the cups, cut two slices of rich-looking dark fruit cake and headed for the door. Agnes felt her tension mounting as the man sitting opposite took it all in and said nothing until the door was well and truly shut. Then, lifting his cup and saucer with the delicacy of a man holding a new-born kitten, he said in a kindly voice, 'So, you are Agnes?' Although his face had a yellowish hue and his hair was white as snow, Agnes could see that in his youth he must have been a very handsome man. She nodded, unable to speak, as she watched her father hold the bone china cup and saucer so carefully in his amazingly clean hands, and wondered if he had ever held her with so much care. And at once she felt awkward sitting here in the sitting room of a farmhouse she couldn't even remember.

'We called you Angela, your mother and I,' he said, looking at her now with a mixture of curiosity and something else she could not fathom. Angela,

306

Agnes thought, she liked the name. She would have been proud to be known by such a name given the chance. This was indeed a revelation. She didn't know she had even been given a name before being left on the orphanage step.

Her curiosity was reaching fever pitch now, and she longed to ask if he had married her mother, yet no matter how hard she tried Agnes could not bring herself to be so forward. Instead, she hung onto every word this man was now saying, whilst all the time plucking up the courage to ask the questions spinning in her head.

'What I am about to tell you must not be breathed to a soul, do you hear me?'

Agnes nodded, realising he must think she was struck dumb; she had not yet said a word.

'Before I go any further, I will put you out of your misery, as I am sure you are eager to know the truth. I can now tell you that your mother and I were married. But that is between you and me. The hired hands don't need to know – if they did...Well, suffice to say, they don't need to know.'

'Oh, that is such a relief,' thought Agnes, sighing, even whilst she wondered why the hired hands did not need to know. The question almost sprang to her lips but her sense of propriety stopped her. Her silence encouraged Mr Weybridge to continue.

'We could not marry until your mother was long into her pregnancy. You see, my first wife, Sarah, had been ailing for a long time; she was struck down by a seizure of the brain. For fourteen years she had been bed-bound. Your mother, Peg, was her nurse.' He paused. 'My life was very lonely out here before Peg came to nurse Sarah...' He cleared his throat, obviously troubled by the raking up of old memories, and he stared into the fire as if gathering his thoughts whilst Agnes patiently waited for him to resume. A few moments later, composed now, he reached to the table beside his chair and said in a firm, somewhat impatient voice, 'But none of that matters now. This is what you want to see, I am sure.' He held out the certificate Agnes had so longed for all these years. Taking it she read the perfect copperplate handwriting on the official document telling her who her mother and father were.

Agnes could clearly see that the revelation was causing him considerable distress. And even though she was eager to know all she could about her mother, she could not, for some strange reason, bear to see him so upset.

'Not only this ... Mr Weybridge,' she said tentatively, 'you will let me come back another time when we have both had time to...?' Agnes, too, was quite overwhelmed.

He nodded before taking a sip of his tea, and then, replacing the delicate cup onto the matching saucer, he looked at her and smiled before saying contemplatively, 'You are very much like your mother.'

Agnes felt her heart soar as she had noticed immediately on entering the room that the difference between her and Mr Weybridge was stark, she being so slight and delicately fair, whilst his withered body had obviously once been large and strong. His weather-beaten skin was yellowing now but she could see he'd been a handsome man.

308

Agnes sighed, knowing that even though she desperately wanted more information from him, she couldn't press him because he looked so exhausted, and despite the curiosity burning inside her she could not put him through any more strife. It was enough for now that she had the proof of her birth, which clearly showed who she really was.

'I am so glad you were able to come and collect it yourself,' he said when she could not take her eyes from the precious document that showed she was not illegitimate, no matter how close the wedding was to her birth.

'I would have come here sooner ... had I known.' Agnes felt a new, self-assured spirit.

'We had six precious weeks together as man and wife,' her father said in a low, faraway voice as if talking to himself. 'We had a terrible time bringing you into the world, and afterwards...' His voice trailed off briefly before he resumed. 'You took all of Peg's strength, you see, and she never recovered. I couldn't even look at you.' There was a catch in his voice and Agnes assumed he was still grieving. Did he mean that her mother's death was her fault?

'You see, I blamed you for her suffering...' He looked into the blazing fire again and the spitting, crackling flames were illuminated in his eyes as he returned in his mind to another time. 'The last word she spoke was your name, Angela.' He didn't look at Agnes. 'That was the finish of me; I knew I would never be able to bring you up and so handed you to old Bertha and told her never to bring you back again.'

'Is she the woman who brought in the tea?' Agnes looked towards the door.

'No, that's Darnley's wife, she came up from the village afterwards; oh, don't look so stricken, I had my reasons.' His words were growing weak and he finished with a racking cough that caused him to gasp for breath and turned his once-sallow complexion the colour of a ripened plum. Agnes took the cup and saucer from his juddering hands in case he dropped them.

'As you might have guessed,' he sighed when the spasm passed, 'I am dying. I have a disease of the lung...' He paused to get his breath back, and then his mood seemed to brighten a little. 'I don't want to go to your mother and get an ear-bashing for not having provided for you.'

'It is a bit late to realise that now,' Agnes said, her strong sense of right and wrong reasserting itself, 'twenty years too late.' Then, regretting her outburst she realised that he was trying to make amends at least, and he probably felt remorse enough. 'Maybe this was all I ever wanted,' she conceded, raising the birth certificate. Strangely, she wanted him to feel a little of the hurt he had forced upon her by not giving her the upbringing every child deserved. But, looking at him now, weak and infirm, Agnes knew she could not sustain her anger; it wasn't in her nature to be horrid or unkind – even to the man who had given her away all those years ago. 'I know who I am and where I come from now, and so maybe that is enough for me.'

'You don't know what it means to me to hear you say that.' He gave a painful smile. Then he looked at her for a long while and Agnes felt he was trying to make peace when he said, 'Thank you very much for coming to see me. It makes things much easier now.'

Agnes didn't know what he meant nor what to say.

'You will never know how sorry I am that I rejected you.' He lowered his head. 'The shame and the guilt I have carried around for the last twenty years have eaten me alive, and this is my punishment now.' He waved a feeble hand. 'I never should have abandoned you.'

'Did you never feel the need to come and find me before now?' Agnes did not know where she found the courage to ask such a thing as she watched him shake his head.

'I was punished for loving your mother when my first wife was dying,' he said simply.

'You can't be punished for truly loving someone,' Agnes said. 'Her death was not your fault.'

'It is a comfort to hear you say that, Angela.' He paused, almost causing Agnes to correct him, but then she understood for the last twenty years he'd agonised about the child called Angela whom he had given away – a child who was now a grown woman called Agnes and whose forgiveness he desperately sought before his final hour. 'I adored your mother, she was the light of my life and when she died I felt I'd killed her.' He looked up when he heard Agnes gasp.

'I couldn't bear to watch you grow up, possibly resembling her and finding fault with me for not having the skill to save her.' His eyes were glassy now with unshed tears. 'You see, before I married

311

my first wife, whose father owned this farm, I was the village doctor... Can you believe that?' He gave a short, scornful laugh. 'Yet I could do nothing for the women I loved.'

Agnes was shocked to the very core of her being. All her life she had been belittled, treated like an unpaid skivvy, brought up in an orphanage and wanted by nobody and taught never to question or condemn, but she didn't blame him any more for abandoning her; instead she had an overwhelming urge to hug him. It was pure instinct that made her go over and put her arms around him, feeling his tears upon her face. She had to let him know she had forgiven him, believing now it would have been difficult beyond endurance to see her every day and be reminded of the woman he so dearly loved.

'He summoned a woman from the village to take care of me,' Agnes told Olive when she came out of the farmhouse a short while later. 'When he didn't come for me weeks later she took me to the orphanage near her sister's house in London... Times were hard, he said.' Agnes was surprisingly unemotional about the whole experience, Olive thought.

'The woman from the village didn't leave my name when she left me on the orphanage step. She told him where I was only a couple of years ago when he knew he was dying, he got in touch with solicitors to find me and by that time I had moved from the orphanage and come to live with you,' Agnes said, then a little way into her explanation the brittle veneer began to crack and Olive was relieved to see the young woman's natural caring nature come to the fore.

'He's had people looking for me ever since.' Her voice was full of anguish. 'He didn't know where I was or what had become of me. And now he is dying!' The stinging tears at the back of her eyes could be restrained no longer and she sobbed until she thought her heart would break.

'Shh,' was all that Olive could manage as she held Agnes close in the cold, wintry half-light that barely illuminated the farmyard. They were quiet for a while until Olive could summon up the courage to speak without the threat of her own tears. Finally she asked, 'Will you ever go back again?'

'I don't know,' Agnes answered. 'He's not long for this world and I'm not sure I have the courage to get to know him...' There was a sob in her voice as fresh tears flowed down her face.

'I think you know him already,' Olive said softly, 'but, you've got what you came for.'

'Yes,' said Agnes, holding on tightly to her birth certificate without revealing to Olive the name her mother had given her, 'I got what I came for.'

Agnes accepted a clean cotton handkerchief from Olive to dry her eyes as the sound of Archie's motor-car engine could be clearly heard starting up and she realised they had been standing there for quite some time.

'We'd better be going,' she said as bittersweet feelings raged inside her, then turning she took one last look at the farmhouse, thrilled and saddened that she had met her father at last, yet knowing now her parents loved each other just as much as she and Ted.

As she made her way to Archie's car the old man, Darnley, came scurrying out of the farmhouse on bowed, arthritic legs and in his gnarled and weathered hands he was carrying an unfamiliar object. As he drew near she could see he was holding out an enormous, dead goose by its legs, its head dangling in the frosty air.

'He said to give you this,' said the cantankerous old man with a hint of puzzled resignation, 'and he said to make sure to tell you: have a happy Christmas.'

'Wish him all the joys of the season,' said Agnes, grimacing as she took the dead goose, 'and your family too.'

But the old man was already heading in the opposite direction and gave a bah-humbug wave of his hand as he shuffled back to the house without another word.

Agnes hadn't told her father about Ted, nor did she tell Olive that she had her own name, which had been given to her by her mother, whose name was Peg Weybridge. And she was Angela Weybridge, doctor-turned-farmer's daughter. As she watched the fields and meadows pass by through the car window, she wondered if, like a million times before, she was dreaming again? And then, grasping her birth certificate more tightly, she knew for certain that this was a dream. A dream come true.

TWENTY-TWO

'After all I've done for you, Ted Jackson!'

Mrs Jackson bashed and banged the plates in the tiny kitchenette, although she didn't bash and bang them enough to break them, Ted noticed, just enough to make a racket. 'You are so ungrateful,' she continued. 'I've been on my hands and knees scrubbing this flat already and I'm feeling bone weary. What thanks do I get for slaving for you lot? None, that's what thanks I get!'

Ted, hands in pocket, had his back to his mother as he looked out of the little window to the street below where a few children were knocking on doors and singing Christmas carols. Fat lot of good it would do them, he thought sardonically, knowing some of them had come back from evacuation for Christmas as there hadn't been many raids in London over the past few months and many mothers considered that the worst was nearly over now.

'I give you nice nutritional meals after trawling the streets looking for good food to eat when you get in from work, I make sure you have a nice clean bed to come home to of a morning, and this is how you pay me back. Don't you know I have enough to do!'

'Mum, I only asked Agnes to come for tea, I didn't ask her to move in with us,' he said, thinking that if his mother's face turned any redder it would explode.

Ted hadn't seen much of Agnes since her trip to Surrey with Olive last week as they were on different shifts. It had been such a pity that she'd got back too late to come to tea as they had arranged, and because of that he thought it might be nice for her to come instead on Christmas Eve.

'Move in! Move in, you say? How dare you speak like that in this house! Your sainted father would turn in his grave. I have never heard anything so disgusting in all my born days.'

'Then you've never lived,' Ted wanted to say, but of course he didn't. He would never dare! His mother would have burst into a thousand apoplectic smithereens right where she stood. 'Look, Mum, I know you are finding it hard, what with rationing and all that, but everybody is in the same boat and I've given you extra housekeeping money to cover tea and Agnes doesn't eat all that much. It would do the girls the world of good to get to know her a bit better.'

'Why on earth would they want to get to know a ... a foundling, tell me that!'

'Don't you say that again, Ma.' Ted could not hold his tongue and knew how to enrage his mother by calling her something as common as 'Ma', even though he thought it sounded just as endearing as 'Mum'. But, if he was honest with himself, he was almost past caring what she liked and didn't like any more. He was having a right time of it trying to keep up with her likes and dislikes – why couldn't she be as easy-going as his Agnes?

His mind went back to the debacle the other

week, when he could have had a cosy night in with Agnes in front of the fire, relaxing with the wireless on and, best of all, they would have been alone – just the two of them in Mrs Robbins' lovely front room, bright with electric lighting, unlike his own home that was lit by dull gas mantles that gave off hardly any cheer at all. The thought of it made him shake his head, remembering that when it was too late for him to go to see Agnes, his mother refused to go out after all – and it wasn't the first time either. Oh no, she'd stopped him seeing Agnes on a few occasions with one excuse or another of late. As he opened his mouth to tell her she was going too far he was stopped by his mother's look of self-righteous indignation.

'Well,' said Mrs Jackson, blowing out her cheeks and then pursing her lips, 'that a son of mine would dare speak to me in such a manner, at this time of year as well! I cannot believe my only loving son would say such a thing. After all I've done for this family, you go and stick up for a girl who's not fit to...'

'Ma...' Ted's voice held a warning note. 'I've already told you that I will not listen if you carry on talking about Agnes like that.' He watched his mother give an innocent shrug.

'Never a thought for my own deprivation,' Mrs Jackson said, ignoring her son's raised eyebrows. 'I scrimp and save to give my offspring a loving, comfortable home and this is what I get!' She was quiet for a moment knowing Ted's flinty expression meant she had gone too far and she had to change her approach. 'Well, son,' she said with a sigh, 'you know I only want the best for my family.'

317

'Maybe so,' Ted sighed, only too aware he was the one who did all the providing now, whilst his mother stayed at home and polished the heavy, faded furniture that hadn't changed since she married his father. Hands in pockets, he moved from the window.

He was torn between his duty to his family and his great affection for Agnes. He didn't like the way his mother carped on about her being a 'foundling', it wasn't right, especially when Mum hadn't had such a salubrious childhood either. But now they lived in the tiny two-roomed flat owned by the Guinness Trust, his mother thought she was on nodding terms with the king.

'There isn't room for the four of us to sit down together at the table all at the same time, never mind five!' she exclaimed.

Ted wondered if his mother felt embarrassed about inviting Agnes to their small home and realised her haughty demeanour might just be a front. But the way she carried on sometimes, anyone would think she was brought up in the mews of Buckingham Palace instead of being part of one of the poor but decent families down by the East End docks.

Not that he had anything against such families, Ted silently reasoned, he thought they were the salt of the earth. But his mother soon forgot herself when she moved out of there. No, what he didn't like was his mother's hypocrisy, her total lack of tolerance for anything or anyone she considered wasn't 'respectable' when his Agnes was the most decent person he knew.

'Well, don't think I'm going to fall over myself to

be nice to her,' Mrs Jackson continued, causing Ted to close his eyes and shake his head in exasperation. 'She's just out for what she can get from you, that's what I think. I've met her kind before.'

'But, Mum,' Ted sighed, patiently now, 'Agnes isn't like other girls; she's quiet and lovely.'

'She can see you've got a good job and come from a nice home and she wants it.' Mrs Jackson patted the turban covering her steel curlers, which she'd secreted from the salvage man. 'You mark my words, once she's got you she'll bleed you dry, so think about that!'

It seemed to Ted that it didn't matter how much he pleaded, she was determined to make life unbearable if Agnes came to tea.

His mother had her little routines, like putting the small presents she managed to get for his two sisters into their stockings and putting them on the sofa for Christmas morning, not trusting them to refrain from eating the contents if their stockings were left on the end of the bed. She also liked to have the vegetables peeled and put into pans of cold water in readiness, so they could all open their presents together. These were the rituals that made her life bearable, he supposed, but he hadn't supposed that Agnes would not be part of them this year.

'Would you rather I send someone around with a note and tell her not to come today?' Ted asked, knowing that if Agnes did come to visit there would be a strained atmosphere – and quite rightly, Agnes would get upset, then the girls would get upset, and his mother in turn would get upset, suggesting it was all their visitor's fault.

'You do what you think's best, son, it's not for me to say.' Mrs Jackson patted his arm and gave a tortured smile. 'You know that as the man of the house you have the final say...' Then, calling over her shoulder as she hurried to the front room she added more brightly, 'I managed to get a lovely bit of liver from the butcher, would you like me to cook it with that nice gravy you like? And I've made your favourite steamed pudding with some currants I had left over from last week.'

'Lovely, Mum,' Ted said in a dull voice, his appetite suddenly disappearing.

'Not every mother can say she's got such a loving son who looks after his family like you do, Ted,' Mrs Jackson said after he had summoned a lad from down the street and gave him a penny to take the note around to Article Row. 'Your sainted father would be so proud of you.'

'I'm sure.' Sorely disappointed, Ted could have kicked himself for wanting a quiet life.

Yet, on reflection, what else could he do? A quiet life was his biggest wish, what with a war on and such a forceful mother. But he knew she was a woman who was not naturally strong and being left a widow had made her more dependent upon him than he would have liked. Also he knew that some would like to think she was made of the same stuff as the air-raid shelters, but he knew different; inside, his mother was as scared as everybody else.

Agnes read the note, brought by a boy of about twelve whose grey socks were concertinaed around skinny, grubby legs. The note told her Ted was very sorry but his mother was not feeling too well and was not up to having visitors today. Agnes felt deeply disappointed at being called a 'visitor'; she'd thought she was much more than that to Ted's family.

And she now knew she would not be able to share the good news of discovering her father with Ted; their working shifts had been incompatible over the last week and she had been waiting to speak to him all that time. Her eyes ran over the words again, aware that much as she had longed to tell him today, she could not burden Mrs Jackson with the added pressure of having 'visitors' when she clearly wouldn't be feeling up to it.

'Wait there,' Agnes told the young lad who was waiting not only for any answer she might wish to return, but also, by the looks of his open hand, a tip. 'I'll just go and get a pen.'

Writing on the back of the note, to save paper, Agnes told Ted if there was anything she could do to be of help he only had to ask. Then she gave the young lad a threepenny bit, and he went happily on his way.

Olive could be heard humming a Christmas carol in the kitchen when Agnes came in from work, rubbing her hands together to get the feeling back as she went into the cosy, steamed-up room to find her landlady sitting on a chair, a hessian sack at the ready, plucking the large goose that had been hanging in the cold cellar since they came back from the farm. Tiny feathers were fluttering through the air like snow.

'The butcher has prepared the bird, although he

said he didn't have time to remove the feathers,' Olive said, causing Agnes to presume that this meant he had cut its head off and cleaned it out. 'All I have to do is pluck it and cook it,' Olive smiled, looking happier than Agnes had seen her for weeks. 'I love Christmas Eve, don't you, Agnes?'

Agnes nodded before telling Olive about the Christmas tree that she and three other underground workers had decorated for Chancery Lane station. 'It must be ten feet tall,' she said, 'and it took ages to do, but it looked lovely when we'd finished.'

'It's a pity we haven't got a tree this year, they are so scarce I couldn't get hold of one before they'd sold out,' Olive sighed. 'Little Alice is just at that age where she would be thrilled to see the glass baubles.' She was quiet for a moment. 'Never mind,' she said, brightening, 'we could always put them on the tree beside the disused chicken coop.' The chicks were still indoors so they didn't die of cold. 'That would really annoy Nancy,' she laughed.

Agnes laughed too. 'I heard her complaining that the back garden was looking more like a farmyard every day but she doesn't have anything to carp about now.'

'I'm not going to let Nancy ruin our Christmas,' Olive said thoughtfully, 'but one thing's for sure, she won't be too bothered about chickens being next door when the eggs started coming in about three months' time.'

'That soon?' Agnes said with obvious delight.

'Archie said they start laying at about six months

so they are getting the best attention Barney can give them.'

'Is Barney staying the night?' Agnes asked, knowing that when Archie was on night shift the boy usually did so.

'Yes, Archie is on duty,' said Olive. 'I was supposed to be going to the midnight service at Westminster Abbey with the other WVS but I said I'd look after Barney for Sergeant Dawson. It will be nice to see his face in the morning when he wakes up and finds his presents.' Barney had become something of a fixture in Olive's house of late and he had settled into a nice routine with all of them. She reminded herself that she could always go to the midnight carol service another time.

'I remember the lovely Thanksgiving service. It would have been lovely to have it in St Paul's after it survived the Blitz but it was in Westminster Abbey for the American troops stationed here,' she said, tugging at the remaining feathers of the huge goose, whilst Agnes cut the bread. 'People were standing in the aisles and outside too.'

Even now the dramatic observance in the abbey, where English kings and queens had been crowned for centuries, brought a lump of pride to Olive's throat. Although, she thought with a pang of remorse, hadn't she a more heartbreaking reason to feel the force of tears behind her eyes when she attended the ceremony. She remembered Drew, Tilly's sweetheart, and how he would have loved the splendour and the pageantry as more than three thousand American soldiers filled the abbey's pews to sing 'America, the Beautiful' and 'The Star-Spangled Banner'. No doubt he would have been one of the reporters who commented that, for the first time in the church's nine-hundred-year history, a foreign army was invited to take over the grounds.

Olive smiled now when she remembered one reporter who had said there was a 'hedge of khaki' around the tomb of the Unknown Soldier. However, her happy reverie was short-lived when she noticed that Agnes was looking a little distracted.

'Is anything the matter, Agnes?' she asked, concerned, as she finished plucking the bird.

'It's Ted's mum, she's not feeling too good.'

'Oh, that's a shame.' Olive kept her true thoughts of Mrs Jackson's curmudgeonly attitude to herself. 'Will you be going around see Ted later?'

'I won't bother Mrs Jackson tonight,' said Agnes. 'She won't want visitors if she's not feeling too good.'

'I expect you're right, dear,' Olive answered, tying string around the neck of the hessian sack to stop the feathers escaping. Then, offering little Alice a sliver of carrot to chew whilst waiting for her tea, she silently calculated how many more potatoes she would need to peel, knowing there was enough rabbit pie and vegetables to go around all of them, although she had to convince Alice to eat the carrots, which the child really didn't like much.

'You don't see rabbits wearing glasses, do you, Alice?' Olive said cheerfully. Alice shook her head. 'That's because they eat all their carrots.' She watched with joy as the little girl began to nibble on the carrot with greater enthusiasm.

'I haven't got any icing for the Christmas cake

this year,' she said, smiling at the child, 'although I bought one of those plaster covers to go over the one I made, so that will make the table look nice tomorrow.' Olive sighed; rationing had intensified to such an extent that she even had to give up her egg ration to buy corn for the chickens that hadn't even started to lay eggs yet.

Yet she wouldn't grumble, there were others much worse off, she reasoned. Along with everybody else, she knew that this Christmas would be a lean one with everything in short supply; there was nothing that hadn't been affected in the year. But she had been shrewd in her judgement and had been stockpiling what supplies she could for Christmas.

'Shall I set the table?' Agnes asked, automatically taking the cutlery from the drawer.

Olive was momentarily distracted by a knock on the back door and, putting the huge bird on the table, she went to answer it, reminding herself that it must be locked immediately; she didn't want any of those looters Archie had been telling her about coming into her kitchen and stealing such a precious bird.

'A real goose!' Nancy's covetous eyes slowly examined the huge bird whilst Olive fixed the blackout blind and switched the light back on. 'Well, well, well, aren't you the lucky ones. Black market, I suspect?' she went on as her beady eyes missed nothing in the kitchen. Her rigid voice belied her forced smile as she thought of the mock goose sitting on her own table, which consisted of potatoes, a couple of cooking apples, some cheese from her ration, and a little dried sage for taste, all bound together with vegetable stock and a tablespoon of flour. Not a sniff of meat in it!

'Black market?' Olive's eyes widened and, quelling the rising indignation, she said in a low voice, 'It is no such thing – it was a gift!'

'A gift?' Nancy said, lifting an eyebrow. 'My, oh my, you do know some generous people, Olive, I must say.'

Olive refrained from rising to Nancy's bait. It would be so easy to gloat and enjoy her moment of triumph knowing that her neighbour would have crowed from dawn till dusk had she been in possession of such a magnificent bird for Christmas. But it was the time of goodwill to all men and even to Nancy, she told herself.

'It's been so long since we had a decent bit of meat,' Olive said almost apologetically, observing the utter misery in her neighbour's eyes. Reluctantly she realised that her thoughts were less than charitable, and that she wouldn't be able to enjoy the bird if she didn't at least make the offer.

'There is plenty, if you and Mr Black would care to join us, just don't forget to bring your rations and we can pool our resources and all enjoy Christmas together...'

'Why certainly, of course we would love to come for dinner!' Nancy answered before the invitation had hardly left Olive's lips. Agnes, standing behind Nancy, grimaced causing Olive to give a sickly smile and a little shrug.

'Let's say lunch will be at...'

'Oh, we can be here early as you like, right after church I should think, it'll save me lighting the fire and I can save the coal.'

'Well, Agnes has to work at the station until four as the trains are running until then,' Olive said in a halfhearted attempt to dissuade their neighbour from arriving too early, 'so lunch will be a little later than most people would be expecting on Christmas Day.'

'Oh, that won't bother me and Mr Black,' said Nancy, ignoring the hint. 'We're not fussy.'

'I'm going to wrap my Christmas presents later,' Olive said to Agnes, squashing her unseasonal thoughts about Nancy as her neighbour let herself out of the front door to go and give her husband the good news. 'I know it's not very patriotic of me; I should have put the paper into the collections, but I saved it from last year's presents and I found a lovely bit of red silk ribbon in the clothing exchange to tie them.' She had washed, pressed and cut the ribbon lengthways so there was twice as much to use. Giving baby Alice a little hug she said to the child, 'And later, you can have nice red ribbon for your hair to make you even more beautiful.'

'Oh, you will look lovely, Alice!' Agnes exclaimed, then turning to Olive she said, 'I love Christmas, especially now, with you and Alice.'

'So what is worrying you? Come on, I know you have something on your mind,' Olive said.

'I've been so nervous about meeting my father,' Agnes answered, pulling at the skin on the back of her hand, a sure sign she was upset, 'that I hadn't given Christmas as much thought as I should have, and I haven't done anywhere near the amount of shopping I ought and I forgot to buy Ted's mum a present.'

'Oh, is that all,' Olive laughed, relieved. 'Well, as far as we are concerned, I think you've already given us our present this year.' She nodded towards the huge bird now sitting in the white earthenware sink, as it was too big to fit on the pantry shelf or on the wooden draining board. 'I did manage to save a nicely decorated flour bag, if you want to use that to make a gift for her.'

'But all the shops are shut now, and what can I make with a flour bag?' Agnes asked, her brows creasing.

'I've saved the goose feathers, you can make her a cushion.'

'That's lovely, Olive,' Agnes said, her face wreathed in smiles as she prepared little Alice for bed. 'You have some great ideas to make our lives easier.'

'It comes with practice,' Olive laughed, knowing the goose was going in the oven first thing tomorrow morning, and judging by the size of it, she guessed it would take about five hours to cook. The good thing was that it would be ready in time for Agnes arriving home from work – just as it should be.

'But are you sure you want to give up those precious goose feathers?'

'It was your father who supplied the goose, Agnes, it's only fair that you should have the feathers – and I'll cook the potatoes in the fat and serve it with apple sauce.'

'Oh, Olive, don't,' Agnes laughed. 'I won't be able to sleep for thinking about it. And thanks for the feathers, that will make a lovely present for Ted's mum.' There was a knock at the front door as Agnes carried Alice through to the front room to lie on the sofa.

'Tilly!' Agnes's cry brought Olive running into the hall whilst still wiping her hands on her apron, before throwing her arms around her daughter. Barney had told her that Tilly was coming home though she wasn't sure what time, but that didn't matter now as long as they were all together for Christmas. Olive gave a satisfied sigh as the house came alive to the sound of laughing and questions being asked all at the same time.

'Let me have a look at you,' she said after a few moments, holding Tilly at arm's length. 'Oh, you look tired, have you been travelling long? How long are you home for? Where are your bags? Have you got any washing?'

'Mum, slow down,' Tilly laughed and, taking off her soft cap, registered her mother's amazement at her new shorter hairstyle. 'It's called the Liberty Cut, Mum,' she explained, ruffling the semi-shingle of waves and curls.

'It's very short,' said Olive, walking around her daughter and eyeing the new style from every angle, 'but I like it. It suits you, love.'

'All the girls are having it done,' said Tilly. 'It saves on hairpins, and ears are coming back into fashion, don't you know.' They all laughed and, before long, they were sitting at the kitchen table and excitedly catching up on all the latest news. Olive happily realised that her Tilly seemed to have matured into a woman since she joined the army and her arrival home for the holiday made her Christmas complete. Nothing was going to put a damper on the season now.

TWENTY-THREE

The air raids on Britain had reduced substantially, giving people hope for the future and for an uninterrupted Christmas. People began to think that they dared to celebrate after all. And now that everyone was going to be back together, the atmosphere in the Robbins household was one of pure happiness.

'You should have seen Nancy's face when your mum said she was thinking of building a sty and starting a pig club,' Agnes laughed. Baby Alice had been put to bed and they all sat around the kitchen table with cups of hot cocoa and mince pies that Olive had not long brought out of the oven.

Olive, laughing, was now wrapping her gifts in plain brown paper at the table, saying with mock seriousness, 'Don't mock it, my dear, pigs are very popular in parts of London.'

'Some people are buying goats for their milk, too,' said Tilly, who had travelled around the country a great deal since she joined the ATS.

'Nancy would have a seething fit,' Olive pointed out, 'although I do think that goat's milk is an acquired taste.' If she was completely honest, Olive thought as she wrapped a knitted dolly in newspaper, even though she was fed up with the restrictions forced upon them by this war, the sight of little Alice's face when she got up tomorrow to open her presents would more than make up for it.

After all, Christmas was all about children, and the innocence of the season would be all the more special for Alice and Barney being there.

Barney had spent all day making newspaper chains and was now looping them around the ceiling to give Alice an added surprise when she woke up in the morning, although Olive had a sneaking suspicion that he was enjoying himself very much indeed, too.

She had managed to buy, and was now wrapping, a book called *William and the Evacuees* by Richmal Crompton. Barney was so fond of reading now, a pastime he'd hardly ever bothered with before being taken in by Archie and his poor wife, God rest her soul. Olive had also knitted him a sleeveless pullover from a deep burgundy cardigan she never wore any more and, not being able to measure it properly because it was a surprise, hoped it fitted.

'Barney looks as if he's having the time of his life in there,' Tilly observed coming into the kitchen, and settling down to hear all the latest Article Row gossip. After much discussion about the welfare of baby Alice it was agreed she could have a future working in the police force with Archie after Tilly remarked that she had caught the two-year-old rooting around in her haversack in the sideboard.

'She gets into everything now,' Olive smiled. 'We need eyes in the back of our heads to keep up with her. I remember when you were just the same.' She patted Tilly's hand indulgently; so much had happened since then, she thought, recalling how Tilly brightened up everybody's lives with her sunny nature in the same way that Alice was doing now. It never ceased to amaze Olive how a rag doll or a spinning top – whatever they could afford – would be played with endlessly until bedtime. Jim's mum would sit in quiet contemplation or snooze off the huge dinner Olive had cooked... Happy days.

And now her baby girl was serving with the British Army, helping to win the war and another little one was in the house for Christmas. These were the things that meant the most to her at Christmas time, she thought.

'So much happens when I'm not around,' Tilly laughed, glad to be home, even if it was only until the day after Boxing Day. However another knock at the front door stopped their chatter for a moment, just as Sally ran in through the back door on a gust of freezing air. Olive hurriedly went to answer it as Sally passed her, rushing upstairs to pack.

'I hope the trains are still running,' Sally called, not wanting to miss George's arrival at Liverpool docks. She had fully intended to leave for Liverpool this morning but there was an emergency at the hospital and she couldn't get away. Now she knew she was cutting it fine, but if she hurried she might just make it in time. Cramming her night-clothes and a toothbrush into an overnight bag, Sally's heart was hammering against her ribs; she hoped she hadn't missed the last train. That would be too awful for words.

Dashing back down to the warm, homely kitchen, at first she didn't register the solemn faces of her friends. 'I won't forget to give George your best wishes and I know he's going to be thrilled when I tell him about the huge goose you will all be eating tomorrow!' Sally could not contain the anticipation searing through her right now but her new-found joy turned to an overwhelming cloud of dread when she saw Olive standing near the door. In her hand she held a telegram. And as she gave it to Sally her eyes were full of glistening tears.

'He's not coming home after all,' Sally said before her trembling chin prevented further communication. She lowered her bag to the floor and covered her face in her hands. Olive hurried to her side at the same time as Tilly and they all huddled together.

'What's happened? Is it George... Has he...' Nobody could bring themselves to ask the awful question they so desperately wanted to know the answer to and dreaded in equal measure. Sally shook her head, her eyes bright as another tear rolled down her cheek.

'No, nothing like that, thank goodness,' she exclaimed, suddenly aware of the shock she had just given them all. 'He's still alive but the telegram told me not to go swimming today; it's too cold in the pool.'

'He means Liverpool?' asked Tilly, her eyes sad, understanding her friend's distress and putting her arm around Sally's shoulders. 'Better you knew before you travelled all that way there, and then to be disappointed when you got there and found he wasn't docking after all.'

'We were going to put wreaths on the graves,' Sally said in a hesitant voice.

'Oh, I'm so sorry, I didn't think...' Tilly's hands

flew to her lips and she looked extremely embarrassed. Her eyes were downcast now, unable to meet Sally's.

'Please, don't give it another thought.' Sally patted her arm to reassure her friend. 'I will go in the New Year, then at least it gives me a chance to be with Alice for Christmas and perhaps take her back to Liverpool when the weather warms up a bit.' Sally fell quiet for a moment as her decision began to make more sense. 'After all, Dad would want me to be with her.'

'I'm sure he would,' Olive said with great relief; Sally's telegram, although bringing news she didn't want to receive, was, at least, not the worst kind of news.

'George was in such a rush to get the message to me, by the look of it, that he didn't even wish us a Merry Christmas,' Sally laugh-cried, drying her tears. 'Wait till he comes home, I'll have words.'

'I'm sure he'll look forward to that,' Agnes said and before long the chatty atmosphere resumed and they all continued to swap the news they couldn't write in a letter.

'Oh well, we can all have Christmas together, even if there aren't as many of us,' Tilly said. 'It won't be like last year when Drew played Father Christmas – or Santa Claus, as he used to say. Do you remember how he got his mother to send over money she'd collected from all her society friends? And how he bought presents from Harrods for all those children who wouldn't have had anything otherwise?'

'That reminds me.' Olive looked a bit sheepish. 'I wasn't sure what was happening this year and you know the government is always going on about saving this and saving that and sharing what you have got with others...'

'What have you done, Mum?' Tilly's voice held a note of dread, knowing it wasn't beyond her mother's kindhearted intentions to offer to bring the less-fortunate home on Christmas day.

'Well, I did offer to work in the Forces Canteen but they had enough volunteers this year,' Olive laughed. 'Then I got to thinking, it would be a poor "do" if I let poor Barney and Archie have Christmas dinner on their own, when we have that huge goose and we could all muck in together.'

'Oh, that's a lovely idea,' said Tilly, who really liked Sergeant Dawson and had heard good things about how the young lad was faring now from her mother's letters. She suspected that Archie'd probably welcome company this year above any other.

'It wouldn't be much fun for either of them to be on their own this year – or any year, if the truth be known,' said Sally.

'Oh, that is good to know, I've been saving as many of my points and coupons as I could,' Olive confessed, 'even though there is little to be had in the shops in the way of luxuries.'

'Is Dulcie coming tomorrow?' Tilly asked expectantly. 'I haven't seen her since the wedding. I hear her sister is staying, that's a turn-up for the books, I must say.'

'She said she will come over around five-ish, and she's driving David's car.' Olive took a deep breath. 'I taught her and she wasn't a very good pupil. I'd take my chances walking on ice rather than let Dulcie drive me – and those high heels she wears when she's behind the wheel are lethal.' They all laughed, knowing Dulcie was not the most patient learner; especially in the dark.

Olive's only other worry was that there wouldn't be enough food to go around, to say nothing of the sherry situation, which was looking dire this year due to the shortages. So, she realised, nobody would be getting tipsy. She went on to tell the girls what Nancy said about coming in early to save lighting her own fire and saving coal.

'Not a mention of bringing a shovelful in here,' Tilly said. There was silence for a moment and then everybody burst into uncontrollable laughter and it was only when Sally reminded them that Alice had not long gone off to sleep that they managed to quell their hilarity.

'Will Ted be coming around for tea tomorrow, Agnes?' Olive asked. 'I know he can't be here for lunch, but it would be nice to see him sometime on Christmas Day.'

'Thank you for that, Olive,' Agnes said, ever so grateful that Olive treated her like a member of her own family and included her in everything a normal family would have done. 'Since his mum has been a bit poorly of late and the girls can't cope on their own I'm not too sure but I'll let him know you offered.' Agnes knew her Christmas would be spoiled if Ted couldn't come for a visit, but at least she would see him at work tomorrow.

'How is Dulcie feeling?' Tilly asked. 'Is she getting as big as a house yet?' They laughed again although not unkindly, all keenly aware how Dulcie liked to take care of her appearance and look immaculately groomed at all times.

'I've never seen her so happy,' Olive told her daughter. 'Marriage definitely suits her, although she did say that David's mother is coming to visit them tomorrow morning.'

TWENTY-FOUR

Dulcie had never known a Christmas Eve like it; usually she would be dancing the night away at the Café de Paris or some other sought-after dance hall, not standing over her dining table worrying if everything looked good.

For the fifth time, her nerves jangling, she surveyed the large table in the middle of the dining room, resplendent in a fine white cloth, dazzling as the centre light brought out the opulent sparkle of the silver cutlery and crystal glasses, which she had taken out of storage especially for tomorrow's lunch with David's mother. She wanted everything to be perfect for her first visit.

But if she felt like this now, Dulcie thought, she dreaded what she was going to be like tomorrow. She didn't even have Edith to talk over her worries with, as her sister had gone to stay with theatre friends for Christmas. Then again, it might be a good thing she couldn't be there for Christmas lunch. Dulcie knew what Edith was like in the presence of a title, and there was no saying what she would come out with. No, on reflection, it was probably better that Edith wasn't there.

Glad she was finally meeting David's mother,

Dulcie didn't want to let her husband down, knowing he too was anxious. It was at moments like this that she was glad she had never taken to alcohol otherwise she might be tempted to hit the bottle. It was going to take a convincing performance to trick David's mother into believing she was carrying her grandchild, since Lady James-Thompson knew how badly injured he had been. However, given the fact that he had forbidden the doctors to let his mother know the exact details of his injuries, David had told Dulcie not to worry about a thing. But Dulcie did worry. Women, especially mothers, could sense these things.

Olive realised that there would now be quite a gathering for Christmas lunch, what with Sally and Alice, Tilly, Archie, Barney and the Blacks from next door. Happily she went to collect the milk from the step on Christmas morning, glad she had fought her impulse to stay up to guard the goose all night, having dismissed tales of suspect looters who were determined to neither work nor want and broke into the homes of decent folk to steal whatever they could get their hands on. Alice wasn't up yet and Olive decided to have a cup of tea before Archie came to collect Barney and her girls descended for breakfast.

A chill wind made her shiver in the frosty mist as she pulled up the collar of her plaid woollen dressing gown and peered into the quiet street. She loved this hour of the morning when people were still in their beds and the air was still. She sent a silent prayer to heaven for the repose of the souls of her loved ones, and wished baby Jesus a happy birthday before thanking the good lord above they were all still in one piece.

Then as she bent to lift the milk from the step a low rumbling noise caught her attention and Olive craned her neck, looking first left and then right down the street, hoping the Germans weren't going to raid London today. There was no sign of anybody as the heavy thrum of an engine was disappearing into the distance. Then she noticed a square cardboard box just beyond the milk. Olive was nervous about investigating what it contained. One couldn't be too careful these days. What if it was a trap? What if the Germans had left it there?

'Pull yourself together, woman,' a little voice inside her head told her. If there were any signs of Germans around here then Archie would be the first to know – after Nancy, of course. Olive gave a gentle unassuming laugh knowing the woman's curtains were on permanent twitch alert and she would have been here knocking regardless of the time if anything had been going on last night.

Olive relaxed a little when she worked out that Archie would have finished his shift by now, and to her delight she could hear his soft whistling as he ambled down the row after a full night's work. She was even more pleased when Archie, noticing she was standing on the step, quickened his pace.

Giving her a small grin as he reached her gate, he said, 'Been waiting there for me all night, Olive?' He lifted the latch, ambling up the small path.

'Some hope, Archie, it's freezing out here, I wouldn't be surprised...'

'...if we have snow, yes, you keep saying,' he laughed as she stood aside to allow him into the house. Before she even closed her front door she heard Nancy's front door slam – so, if her neighbour had been on the prowl, thought Olive, she would have heard every word.

'Take no notice,' said Archie. 'If she's got nothing better to do than snoop into other people's lives she must be having a really boring time of it.'

Olive felt soothed by his words; he was good to have around, she thought. Her rock of common sense, that was Archie.

'What's that you've got there?' he asked as she brought the box to the table.

'I don't know, I opened the door and there it was.' As Olive began to pull at the box, Archie stopped her by placing his hand over hers. She felt a rush of pleasure course through her, although she tried hard not to show it.

'Here, let me check it, we can't be too careful.' Cautiously Archie lifted the box and listened carefully before giving it a little shake. Something inside shifted with a dull rattle and Olive gave a start of anxiety but the sergeant calmed her nerves with a little shake of his head.

'Shall we take the box outside?' she asked in hushed tones.

'I think there will be no harm leaving it here for further inspection,' he said, laying the box down. Olive noticed that it took up a quarter of the kitchen table as her curiosity got the better of her.

'Are you going to open it, Archie?' she whispered, dying to know what was inside now… Reaching over, her fingernails caught the lid of the box and she began to tug. The air was electric with anticipation and she wondered if she should have waited for Archie to open it after all. But now the lid was almost off, Olive knew that she had to carry on. Holding her breath she released the tightly fitting top. Just as she was about to open it, a noise behind them made them quickly turn. Tilly yawned her way into the kitchen giving Olive and Archie the fright of their life.

'Oh, you scared the living daylights out of me!' Olive exclaimed, guiltily holding on to the lid of the box with one hand and clutching the neck of her dressing gown with the other. Although what good that would have done her if Tilly had turned out to be a foreign marauder she couldn't have said.

'Eggs!' Archie's eyes were wide. 'Hens' eggs?' Considering that rationing allowed everybody only one egg per month, a tray of thirty eggs was a bountiful gift, the likes of which they had not seen since before the war. They could hardly take their eyes off the precious tray. 'Where did they come from?' Archie wondered, his mouth watering fit to drown him at the thought of a soft-boiled breakfast egg.

'I don't know,' said Olive. 'It was as quiet as the grave except for...' She suddenly remembered the heavy tractor-like thrum of an engine as a vehicle, hidden in a cloak of smog, chugged its way down Article Row and out of sight. 'Here's the note that was under the lid, but I didn't like to open it.'

Archie, without compunction, tore open the envelope and read the words written within. 'It says: *Merry Christmas to Agnes and all her family with best wishes, Mr Weybridge.*'

Olive, stunned, looked at Agnes who had just

341

sauntered into the kitchen, tousle-haired and yawning. They greeted her now with huge smiles.

'Anybody would think it was Christmas,' laughed Agnes, amazed.

'Shall we report it?' Olive asked. 'After all it is...'

'Christmas.' Archie stopped her anxious query. 'It is a gift and must be accepted as such – and I am off-duty.'

'We never would have broken the law in peacetime...' Olive wasn't so sure.

'We never would have needed to,' said Archie, watching Olive fetch a large earthenware bowl from the cupboard to put the eggs in.

'Well, what are we waiting for?' Agnes demanded, suddenly animated. 'Let's get the pan on and start breakfast. Olive, you sit there, you've done enough!' And with that she put the pan onto the stove. Counting how many of them wanted a precious freshly boiled egg she lowered one each into the bubbling water whilst they all stood in anticipation of a proper breakfast, watching as the pan simmered.

Sally, coming into the kitchen, gazed with sleepy eyes at the scene in disbelief and exclaimed with pleasure. 'Eggs?'

'A box of them,' said Olive, 'left on the doorstep with a note saying "Happy Christmas".'

'A box of eggs.' Sally was amazed. 'Do you know who left them?'

'We took them into custody,' Archie said with constabulary importance, 'and interrogated them, but they refused to talk so we had to remove them to a place of safety before disposing of the evidence.' Laughing he lifted his egg with his spoon and declared it suitably arrested as he put it into the egg cup, his jocular explanation averting any further questions.

'There was a note saying they needed a good home and I can't think of one better,' Agnes said, not wanting to let on about her new-found father as she was still getting used to the idea herself.

After they had savoured every mouthful, Archie brought out a bottle of cherry brandy and put it with the sherry Olive had won at the WS Christmas party. The brandy, he said, had been given to him as a Christmas present from a grateful Holborn resident whom he'd helped at some time in the past year.

'I think it would be better if the children open their presents now if that's all right with you?' Olive asked, aware that now Barney and Alice had joined them they would get no peace. None of the adults raised the slightest objection.

Barney was awestruck when Archie gave him a fabulous Avro Anson model aeroplane and examined his wonderful gift in minute detail before whooping around the front room dive-bombing the imaginary enemy. Alice sat cuddling the dolly made for her by Olive.

Treasure unmeasured, thought Olive, happily agreeing that the adults' presents would be given out when Dulcie arrived later. Alice, delightedly, also received a rocking cradle, which Archie had spent hours making from scraps of wood, although nobody would have known it was homemade as he had completed it to a professional finish. Olive was surprised when he admitted that he would have loved to have been a carpenter if he hadn't become a policeman whilst Agnes had made little blankets for the cradle and had quilted a curtain remnant, filling it with freshly washed, if somewhat laddered, nylons. Olive gave Agnes a grateful hug before she went off to work in Chancery Lane until four o'clock.

Barney could not wipe the smile from his face as he put the new knitted jersey on over his pyjama jacket and his nose remained for the rest of the morning in William Brown's wartime adventures. Watching them all in contented conversation now, Olive had tears in her eyes.

Dulcie couldn't wait to see the back of her genteel if somewhat opinionated mother-in-law, who thought nothing of criticising her home in the most courteous of ways.

'What taste you have, my dear,' said Lady James-Thompson, 'this furniture quite puts me in mind of a gentleman's club.' Dulcie smiled nobly, secure in the knowledge that it had been chosen by David and his *first* wife.

'One wasn't around when the furniture was purchased,' Dulcie said in her best Selfridges voice. 'I think David made a superb choice, as it will be so serviceable, especially when the baby arrives. Leather is so much easier to clean, don't you think?'

'I wouldn't know,' said David's mother in ice-cold tones, 'having never had to clean it.'

'Let me get you another aperitif, Mother.' David's tone matched his mother's as he reached for a decanter of Dubonnet. 'Dulcie has worked really hard preparing our lunch and it looks delicious.'

'I'm sure,' said Lady James-Thompson, obviously not in the least interested in what was on her plate as she hardly ate any of the delicious chicken Dulcie had managed to persuade the butcher to keep back for her.

Dulcie had almost balked at what the man had charged, noting that her mother would have been able to feed the whole family for a week for the price of it, before being reminded, if indeed she needed to be, by the snooty butcher that there was a war on.

However, far from being intimidated by David's mother and her haughty attitude, Dulcie felt emboldened, especially when she recalled her husband telling her that his paternal grandmother had been a Gaiety Girl. How thrilling, thought Dulcie as she tucked into her chicken and roast potatoes with gusto.

'I see you take eating for two literally, Dulcie?' said Lady Snooty, as Dulcie had secretly named her mother-in-law.

'Oh, I believe in enjoying what the good lord provides,' Dulcie answered.

'Oh, I thought it was my son,' Lady James-Thompson commented.

Giving Lady J-T her most charming smile Dulcie thought that if she had her way she would tell the woman exactly where she could stuff the parson's nose. But she knew his mother, coming as she did from an earldom, valued nothing more in a daughter-in-law than a large fortune, however it had been made; after all, David's first wife, Lydia, was from a family of wealthy mill owners. Still, thought Dulcie, regaining her equilibrium,

David had never been as happy with Lydia as he was with her!

'Well, I must not keep you from your friends any longer. David was telling me you are visiting this evening,' Lady James-Thompson said as she made to rise from the table, not even touching her coffee and mince pie, for which Dulcie had searched the whole of London before having a word with an ex-friend of a friend who could 'find' that kind of thing. It was obvious to Dulcie, who was nobody's fool, that David's mother could not get out quick enough and was only here under sufferance because of the child Dulcie was carrying. No, she was under no illusions about becoming Lady James-Thompson's favourite daughter-in-law just yet.

Deftly manoeuvring himself, David pulled out his mother's chair so she could quickly move unimpeded from the table.

'Well, I have to say, it's been wonderful,' she said, slipping into her mink coat. Yes, thought Dulcie, you *have* to say so, for the sake of appearances; you don't *want* to say it though.

'You will keep in touch, David.' Lady J-T smiled, giving a little wave as she made for the door. 'Let me know when the baby is born.'

'Of course I will, Mother,' David answered, and with pleading eyes he looked at Dulcie, who dropped her napkin on the table and stood up.

'It was lovely to see you, Lady James-Thompson, you must come again,' Dulcie said, delightedly watching her mother-in-law's thinly veiled look of disgust as she leaned towards her and barely touched her daughter-in-law's shoulder, kissing the air to the side of her cheek. Dutifully Dulcie led the woman down the stairs to the waiting chauffeur-driven Bentley almost identical to David's.

Dulcie walked slowly back up to the flat, glad the ordeal was over and consoling herself with the thought that she didn't have to see David's mother again if she didn't want to. He was certainly in no hurry to encourage cosy nights with the family by the looks of things; in fact he had been only a few degrees above frosty over lunch, she thought.

Slipping off her ever-tightening shoes, Dulcie rubbed her aching feet.

'I am so sorry, darling, she has always been an awkward dragon.'

'Don't give it another thought, David, I know how awkward mothers can be – in fact I'm an expert.' Dulcie suddenly brightened. 'Anyway we have Olive's gathering to look forward to. Did you put the presents in the bag?'

'All presents are correct,' David laughed, before offering to go and make them both a welcome cup of tea.

'Oh, you are a love,' Dulcie said tiredly as she curled up in elegant comfort on the sofa. 'After tea I'll wash those dishes before we go to Article Row.'

She hadn't realised she had nodded off until David woke her with a cup of tea brought into the sitting room on the tray that was fixed onto his wheelchair, after giving the housekeeper the rest of the day off. Dulcie still couldn't get used to being waited on hand and foot and her independent personality made it almost impossible to have another woman doing her shopping and cooking;

she liked looking after David herself and didn't think anyone else could take care of her husband as well as she could. However, David said that she must accept help as her pregnancy progressed and reluctantly, she agreed.

'Why didn't you show your mother that you can walk on your new legs, David?' Dulcie asked as they sat relaxing with their tea.

'If she knew I was able to move about under my own steam and "appear normal" as she so disgustingly puts it, she would have me accompany her to every boring function she possibly could.' He paused and thought for a moment and then he shuddered. 'Heaven forfend, Dulcie.' They both laughed and moments later were snuggled together on the sofa. Dulcie sighed contentedly. She had never loved anybody the way she loved David.

'We'd better get ready for Olive's or she'll think we're not coming,' David said dreamily as the effect of the huge lunch and good brandy took its toll.

'Mmm, I know,' Dulcie responded lazily, not wanting to move at all. 'I've been looking forward to going to Olive's all week and now it seems such an effort.'

'She will be offended if we don't go, darling,' David said, giving her a little push to help her up.

'I know.' Moving with cumbersome gait from the sofa, Dulcie padded barefoot to their bedroom and, looking in the mirror, realised that her dalliance with another man was plain for everyone to see now.

Every day she was growing bigger, although she had tried so hard to keep herself as neat as possible. Dulcie knew that if they put a bit of effort into it she and David could have a wonderful life together. She wasn't talking about the money or the title – although she did enjoy the perks it could bring. They had the same views, the same off-the-wall sense of humour and could discuss almost anything. However, she still sometimes wondered had David only married her to save her from shame, as a friend? He certainly hadn't married her to please his mother who clearly thought her dreadfully common.

'Ready, darling?' David asked, popping his head around the bedroom door, and it was that look in his eyes, that open look of adoration, which told her David really loved her and assured her she had nothing at all to worry about if he could possibly do anything about it. She knew the real David, the one who was kind and sensitive and who would walk to the end of the earth on his wooden legs to please her. She was sure they would find their own way one day.

'Two minutes, David,' Dulcie answered, applying a slick of black-market lipstick

TWENTY-FIVE

Tilly was reflecting on the changes the year had brought whilst her mother was doing the things she loved best, busying herself in the kitchen preparing their luncheon feast to come. And it was a feast, of that there was no question. Tilly knew there wouldn't be many families who would be sitting down to eat such a fabulous spread this Christmas and it was all thanks to her mother's resourceful housekeeping.

She could hear her mother humming to the songs being played on the Home Service wireless programme and clearly enjoying the ENSA concert for war workers. Tilly was looking forward to hearing the Empire link-up, which was to be broadcast at two p.m., entitled 'The Fourth Christmas', which would send messages home to loved ones from the troops who were serving abroad.

The house was really Christmassy this year, Tilly thought, as the smell of roast goose wafted through the house, making her mouth water and her tummy rumble even though there were still two hours to go before everybody arrived and they sat down to eat. However, even though it would be so wonderful to have everybody together again there would still be one place empty... What would Drew be doing right now? she wondered.

'It's lovely to have you home again,' Olive said, going over to the sideboard and retrieving the silver cutlery, which was brought out only for Christmas and other special occasions and had been bought for her parents on their wedding day. 'It is just like old times.'

'I was just thinking the same thing myself,' said Tilly. 'Everything looks lovely as usual, Mum. You have done a fantastic job with what little there is to be had these days.' Tilly was trying desperately to shrug off the pall of melancholy that her home visit had resurrected. It was easier to ignore the longing for her soulmate when she was in camp with the other girls; as there was so much else to do and she was kept busy all of the time.

She had sent Drew and his family a Christmas card, of course, there was no point in being stubborn and childlike about their split. After all, they had shared some very intimate moments in their lives and she knew, she just *knew* that Drew had felt exactly the same way about her as she did about him – even if his love didn't last as long, at least the last two years had been spent with the man she would love for the rest of her life.

Janet, her friend back at camp, thought she was raising her hopes too high, given the reputation the American troops had acquired for 'loving and leaving' their girls since they came over here last January, but Tilly knew that Drew wasn't like the rest of them. He was kind and gentle and moral and upstanding... She could go on listing his qualities recalling the night they vowed, in the little village church, to love each other forever, and as Drew placed the ring on her finger she'd felt a special kind of magic that only truly united souls experienced. She gave a long, drawn-out sigh realising the Christmas card she had hoped to receive hadn't arrived. But it didn't stop her heart from aching with love for him.

'I'm going for a little walk before lunch, Mum,' Tilly said, knowing her mother wouldn't allow her to help with the preparations; the kitchen being Olive's domain today and could not be invaded by anybody.

Taking in the once-familiar landmarks that had

now been irrevocably changed by enemy bomb-ings Tilly's heart slumped as she drove her gloved hands deeper into her pockets, her collar pulled up against the freezing early-afternoon mist. She told herself that if she lost her sense of sight she would still know she was home just by the linger-ing smell of chimney smoke and freshly scrubbed doorsteps.

She had been walking nowhere in particular for a long time, enjoying being home once again and sorting out her thoughts. She didn't want to ruin anybody's – especially her mother's – Christmas by being maudlin. Taking a long stroll would hope-fully clear her head. Thoughts of Drew telling her about his father, a tyrant by all accounts, who wanted his son to go into the newspaper empire he had built from scratch, played on her mind. What if his father had forbidden him to come back to England? What if he had joined the Forces and was fighting somewhere right now? That seemed the most obvious answer to Tilly and it hit her so suddenly she stopped right there on the cracked pavement and the audible gasp was loud enough to give a courting couple reason to turn and stare in her direction. Tilly could feel her cheeks burn even in the frosty haze.

What if Drew had been sent overseas? He could be anywhere! He might not even have seen the Christmas card she sent. But she had to be strong and surrender herself to destiny; if she was to see Drew again, as deep in her heart Tilly believed she would, then the stars would lead him to her once more. Drew had a quietly persevering, some would call it an independent soul, and although he'd told her that he would one day have to comply with his father's demands, he'd also told her he would only do it with her by his side.

However, she had to return home now. Agnes would be off-duty soon, after working until four o'clock, and everybody would be arriving. The least she could do was to be there to help her mother. At the corner of Hatton Garden near the old family department store of Gamages, Tilly headed back home.

'We don't want this on, do we?' Olive asked, going over to the wireless as dedications were being read out from servicemen abroad. She didn't want Tilly any more upset than she imagined she must be feeling now, with Drew not being here this year, and remembering how good last year had been.

'Oh, leave it on low, Mum, maybe we can throw the rug back and have a little dance later.'

'That sounds like a lovely idea,' Olive said, relieved that Tilly seemed to have got over her bout of melancholy.

The house was alive with chattering voices and happy smiling faces. Nancy was helping Olive by handing out the Christmas punch, made by Archie before he went home for a few hours' sleep after being on duty the previous night. Barney was flying his Avro Anson from the kitchen to the front room and making the engine noises to go with it, whilst baby Alice was awestruck with wonder.

Everybody listened to the repeat broadcast of the king's speech being relayed on the evening news and nodded in shared agreement when King George the Sixth reminded them that '...recent victories won by the United Nations enabled me this Christmas to speak with confirmed confidence about the future...'

'That's good news,' said Nancy, before being shushed by all those gathered around the wireless, much to her obvious chagrin.

'...and that the forty tremendous months behind us have taught us to work together for victory...'

'Hear, hear!' chorused the listeners.

'...we must see to it that we keep together after the war to build a worthier future...'

The nine people around the table, even little Alice, stood for the National Anthem and then as the final notes tailed off, everybody including Barney, Nancy and her husband, resplendent in their homemade Robin Hood-style party hats, resumed their seats at the table, which now looked as if it too had been blitzed, with empty plates and glasses, and the huge goose carcass lying redundant on the silver platter. Tilly, offered to do the washing up whilst Agnes went to help.

'You must be thrilled,' Tilly said after Agnes had confided to her friend the news of her father.

'You won't mention it to anybody, will you? I haven't told Ted yet,' Agnes said in a low whisper.

'Of course I won't,' Tilly assured her, turning on the gas-powered geyser for hot water. She hadn't really wanted to talk, just to dream of Drew as she washed the mountain of crockery in readiness for the evening get-together when Dulcie and David would be here along with the vicar and Mrs Windle, but that would be selfish of her after Agnes had revealed her most important news. Her mother had always taught her to think of others before herself and she did – usually.

'It is so frustrating when you can't talk of the thing you most want to discuss,' Agnes said, grabbing a clean tea towel, making Tilly feel doubly contrite.

'Don't you want him to know about your family?' Tilly asked.

'Of course I do,' said Agnes, 'but I feel that it would change things.'

'In what way?' Tilly asked, her brow furrowed as she passed Agnes the plate.

'I think he might feel as if I'm getting above myself.'

'By having a family to call your own?' Tilly's brows shot up. She knew Ted's mother wasn't fond of Alice and she also knew the woman craved respectability, but being a farmer's daughter was nothing to be ashamed of, surely?

'I feel such a failure,' confessed Agnes, drying the dishes and putting them in the cupboard so Tilly couldn't see her crestfallen features.

'What do you mean, Agnes, a failure? You have the kindest, most loving heart I have ever come across, you're not a failure.'

'Oh, Tilly, bless you.' Agnes gave a little nod of her head and said a silent prayer of thanks to the heavens for sending her such a friend.

'Oh, there you are, we were going to send Archie out on horseback to come and find you!' Olive was obviously a little glassy-eyed after a lunchtime sherry, and laughed as she ushered Dulcie and David into the front room, where Sally was banging out a rendition of 'Roll Out the Barrel' on the upright piano.

'David's mother came for lunch and we couldn't shove her out of the door,' Dulcie declared over the cacophony of Sally's tuneless voice, feeling right at home again.

'You should have brought her with you, David,' Archie called over the singing.

'What, and ruin a perfectly good party? I don't think so, do you?' The men laughed and Archie handed David a glass of something dark and alcoholic that he claimed was a punch. Spluttering on the first sip, David gasped that its strength was almost lethal as he passed Archie a wicker basket full of bottles.

'Ask no questions, Sergeant,' David laughed, implying black-market acquisitions, although Archie suspected David had raided his own burgeoning drinks cabinet to cheer the party along. As the sound of seasonal good cheer echoed around the room nobody caught the knock at the front door at first and then a few minutes later Barney, making the sound of an aeroplane in full flight, zoomed into the hallway and opened the front door when he heard an impatient ran-tan.

'Did somebody say there was a war on?' asked a deep male voice from the front-room doorway. Everybody turned – and there stood Callum.

'Hello, everybody, I hope you don't mind me popping in like this,' he said, his face bright with happiness. 'I was in the area and I thought I'd come to see my little niece.' Catching sight of Alice his face beamed even more brightly. 'My, how you've grown!' he exclaimed, picking her up and giving her a huge hug.

356

Sally felt something akin to sheer delight sear through her veins, quickly followed by a rush of shame; she shouldn't still feel this way now, surely? George was the one she was engaged to. She shouldn't enjoy Callum's familiar kiss upon her cheek as much as she did, she reprimanded herself as she felt her face suffuse with heat at his touch.

Everyone at once tried to shake Callum's hand and pat him on the back through his navy blue greatcoat. But when he said, 'A very merry Christmas to you', she felt it was meant for her and her alone. Even though he had been writing to her regularly of late she hadn't expected him to turn up here without warning. Of course she realised if he had some leave it was obvious he would want to see little Alice, after all she was the daughter of his only sister.

'When did you dock?' Sally asked, trying to appear unfazed by his sudden appearance, still remembering that dizzy breath-catching-in-her-throat feeling she had had when Morag had first introduced them. Callum had come to walk his sister home from the Liverpool hospital after they had been on nights, and the minute she'd seen her friend's tall, good-looking brother, with his thick dark hair and his warm smile, Sally had been lost.

Callum was kind, considerate and, well, just everything Sally had ever imagined herself finding attractive in a man. Callum, with his worn Harris tweed jacket with leather patches on the elbows, his Tattersall shirts, and the warmth in his piercing blue eyes whenever he looked at her, had stolen Sally's heart completely. And by kissing her as he had done one Boxing Day evening he had shown that he cared about her too, even if he had said afterwards that he hadn't intended it to happen and that, as a poorly paid assistant teacher with a sister to support, 'I'm the worst kind of a cad for kissing you when I know I have nothing to offer you.' Sally remembered him saying it as clearly as if he had just spoken to her now. However she also remembered, as her face flushed hotly, he had paused and looked at her and said huskily, 'At least not at the moment.'

'That's classified, I'm afraid. I can't tell you where I'm going or where I've been,' Callum laughed in response to her question. 'I couldn't get leave and not see Alice. Look, Alice, darling...' He turned his attention back to the little girl in his arms. 'I brought you this.' He handed Alice a rag doll and the child, thrilled, scrambled down and put it in the cradle that Archie had made.

'Twins!' she squealed with glee, causing the assembled party to smile.

Callum and Sally's eyes locked for a second longer than was necessary before Callum said brightly to the assembled guests, 'I haven't come empty-handed!' Taking his kit bag, to the delight of everybody present, he emptied half a dozen oranges onto the table. 'So am I entitled to join the party now?'

'You bet!' cried Barney, who hadn't seen an orange for at least two years.

'I'll take these, thank you,' Olive said, 'and we will all have some later.' She knew that otherwise the oranges would be gone in minutes. However, if she split them evenly then everybody would get some.

'Oh, you are in for a treat, Alice,' Barney said in a low voice to the little girl who had never seen an orange in her life and tried to bounce one on the floor.

Callum sighed, taking in the cosy atmosphere. 'I'm afraid this is only a flying visit, as I only have shore leave for forty-eight hours,' he admitted, 'so I'll need to be back by midnight tomorrow.'

'Will you make it in time?' Sally asked, knowing the trains would be full to bursting with service-men.

'I'll catch the first one and then I'll stand a good chance – but I couldn't be back in England and not come to see...'

'Alice!' Sally quickly cut in, sure that Callum was going to say something he shouldn't. She stood, and moved towards the kitchen. Callum immediately made to follow her.

'Of course not – and she's so pleased with her new doll!' There was a moment of uneasy silence before Sally said quickly, 'So did you come straight here from Liverpool?' Reaching for the lukewarm kettle, she refilled it and put it back on the stove.

'We took the place of another ship as we were desperate to replenish our stores.'

'Is the other ship HMS...'

'Sally, you know I can't tell you any more, I wish I could,' Callum said, giving her hand a little squeeze. She quickly pulled away as if she had touched something hot, standing just as soon as the kettle boiled. She had to stay calm, act natur-ally, and treat Callum like any other friend... Except he wasn't just any other friend. 'I know you can't say much,' she said, suddenly embarrassed

359

for putting Callum in an awkward situation and was a little relieved when she heard Tilly's voice coming to the kitchen.

'I was just telling Dulcie how beautiful her coat is, wasn't I, Dulcie?' Tilly blithely exclaimed whilst Sally, grateful for the interruption, gasped in awe at the mink wallaby coat swinging about Dulcie's neat, if somewhat rounded, figure. Clearly no points were needed for luxury coats like this one.

'I've been sent to get you back into the front room, please,' Dulcie announced, pirouetting as best she could for maximum effect, before leading them through.

'I feel quite envious,' Tilly admitted. Some of the ATS girls had been given such presents after being seen on the arms of American servicemen, who could well afford mole or beaver coney this Christmas, although at seven or eight guineas a pop that would be way out of the price range of most members of the British armed services.

'David bought it for me, isn't it fabulous?' Dulcie gave a little twirl and everybody laughed.

'Well, come on, everybody, let's open our presents,' said Olive when she saw her daughter's wistful expression.

'Oh, Mum, that's lovely,' Tilly breathed as she opened the newspaper parcel to reveal a beautiful cable-stitched cardigan with short puffed sleeves that her mother had knitted.

'With everything so scarce it's about all I could manage this year,' said Olive, knowing that for some there would be a savings card, containing just two red half-crown stamps as there were so many people to buy for this year. But, she realised, the most precious gift that she could give was that of her time, and she had plenty of that to offer.

'Oh, Mum, you have done so well this year, as always.'

'I did have a lot of help,' Olive said and her smile grew even wider when she opened her present from Tilly, a pair of real leather gloves, which she immediately put on. 'They are beautiful, and so soft! I'll wear them for best.'

'Wear them all the time,' Tilly exclaimed and they all cheered when Olive said she would but not whilst making high tea. 'And I'm just going to get it started now.'

Olive looked up to the heavens as she closed the blue and apple-green gingham curtains that were beginning to look a little faded now, after all these years.

'What are you doing out here, alone in the dark?' Archie asked as he entered the kitchen. Then, realising he had interrupted a quiet moment he said, 'I know, it is difficult for all of us at this time of year when we remember the ones who have gone before us. I didn't mean to intrude, and I am so sorry, Olive.'

And as he turned to go, Olive caught Archie's sleeve. He stopped, turning towards her, and for a long moment the silver strands of moonlight shone through the blackout and in through the kitchen window, reflecting on their spellbound faces.

'You didn't intrude, Archie,' Olive whispered as the moment of magic was broken by footsteps coming towards the kitchen. 'Don't ever think you are intruding.' Olive yearned for her hammering heart to ease.

'I thought Ted was going to come and pick you up and take you to his mother's flat for the evening, Alice?' Tilly asked a little later.

'His mum still isn't well, and I think he's a bit embarrassed to tell you the truth.'

'Why do you say that?' Tilly gave her friend a quizzical look.

'He said he knew he couldn't match last year when Drew had all those expensive gifts delivered, so he was under a bit of a black cloud.'

'He's a proud man, Agnes,' Tilly said with a little shake of her head, 'but surely his sisters are old enough now to know the situation the country, let alone Ted, is in?'

Agnes decided to let her friend into a little secret. 'I blame Mrs Jackson,' she whispered. 'It sounds like she wants to keep her family so close to her that she plays on Ted's good nature. And sometimes a man can't see he's being manipulated, especially by his mother.' Agnes immediately covered her mouth with her hand as if to stop even more treacherous words from escaping and the two girls laughed. She was so glad that Tilly was home and they could share a good old natter. They were like sisters now and Agnes felt she could always speak her mind to Tilly.

'You say what you like in here, Agnes.' Tilly laughed. 'Nobody in this family is going to judge you and if you feel that Ted's mother is taking the mick then you must tell him so.'

'Oh, I'm not sure...' Agnes offered, feeling she had already said too much.

'Well, otherwise he'll keep you dangling for years and have the best of both worlds – a loving girl-friend on one hand, and a pandering mother on the other, both fighting for a crumb of attention – and he'll have the freedom to do as he pleases.'

'Oh, Ted's not like that,' Agnes protested, jumping to his defence.

'I've heard the girls talking back at camp, and some of them have been through a fine old time, I can tell you...' Tilly suddenly stopped when she saw tears in Agnes's eyes. 'Oh, Agnes, I didn't mean to upset you, honestly.'

'You haven't upset me,' Agnes said, giving her nose a good blow on one of the two 'new' em-broidered handkerchiefs that Olive had made for her, 'but I do feel as if I play second fiddle to Ted's family ... and I know I shouldn't moan, he's such a lovely man...'

'You moan away, girl,' said Tilly, whose outlook was much broader since she had joined the ATS.

'It's just that ... I've never had anyone to call my own before,' Agnes sniffed. 'I think Ted's mum sees me as a threat.'

'That woman is the limit, and what does Ted have to say about it all?'

It was obvious to Agnes that Tilly wasn't impres-sed by Mrs Jackson, or even Ted, if what she was coming out with now was anything to go by.

'You could be a valuable part of that family if only he would open his eyes to his mother's wily ways.'

'She doesn't want anybody to come between

her and her family,' Agnes explained.

'Well, she's going the right way about it and no mistake! As far as I'm concerned she couldn't get a better daughter-in-law-to-be, that's all I can say.'

'Oh, Tilly, I do wish you didn't have to go back tomorrow.'

'Keep this under your hat,' said Tilly in a low whisper, 'it's not final yet, so don't say anything to Mum, okay?'

Agnes nodded as Tilly turned and checked the door to make sure nobody was coming in. 'I'm being posted somewhere when I go back, and I have no idea where, but it might be abroad.' Her face was alight with excitement and Agnes felt her heart sink.

TWENTY-SIX

''Bye, Agnes!' Tilly was frantically waving, laughing as the train pulled out of the station, wondering when they would ever be together again like that.

'Come back home soon!' Olive called, as the train pulled out of the station on a mournful whistle and a billowing cloud of grey-white smoke. Tilly hung out of the window until she could see her mother and Agnes no more and then she took her seat, surrounded by other service personnel seemingly submerged in wretched contemplation. It would be lovely if she got her posting to London, as she had requested, but she suspected she

364

was going overseas... Her thoughts drifted as her eyelids grew heavy. She'd only had a couple of hours' sleep, after staying up most of the night talking to Agnes. Fancy Agnes having a father, after all this time...

As the train disappeared, Agnes and Olive made their way out of Waterloo station and caught the tram back to Chancery Lane tube station before they said goodbye, and Agnes went to report for duty in the booking office. 'I'll see you later, Agnes,' Olive called. 'Hopefully I'll be able to find somewhere that will sell me a loaf of bread for tea.'

'You'll be lucky, Olive, but don't worry, we can do without for a change.' Agnes gave a little laugh and disappeared into the station, hoping she and Ted would be on the same break later. It being Boxing Day there weren't that many people about.

Strangely, she hadn't missed him nearly as much yesterday as she thought she would, realising she didn't have to mind her Ps and Qs half as much when he wasn't around, then, feeling that wriggling worm of guilt in the pit of her stomach, she scolded herself for having such treacherous thoughts – Ted thought the world of her.

But Agnes was not feeling so brave about her new style now. Briefly patting her hair, she wondered what Ted would think of her new Liberty Cut? Tilly had cut it into the same semi-shingled style as her own, tapered into the back of her neck whilst the top was left long enough to set in large S-shaped finger waves, and she had made a very good job of it too, Agnes thought, glad she'd had it done.

The new style made her feel really grown-up. She also felt smarter and her railway cap was a much better fit. However, when she saw Ted's face at the canteen counter three hours later, it told her he wasn't as impressed as she was.

'I don't hold with women trying to look like men,' Ted said when they took their seat over in the corner, where he couldn't be overheard and looking everywhere but in her direction.

'I thought it was more practical, Ted, I wanted to surprise you.' Agnes felt her spirits fall; they hadn't seen each other properly for two whole days and she thought he'd be pleased.

'There was nothing wrong with your hair before,' Ted protested, giving her new style the briefest of derisory glances.

'But, Ted, it's all the fashion with all the girls in the Forces now; it's called the Liberty Cut.'

'Well, you're not in the Forces, Agnes, and it is certainly that – a right blooming liberty, that's what I say. And I don't care what you say, Agnes, it ain't right.' Ted's face was growing redder as he spoke. 'This war is changing everything. Women in trousers – they'll never be as strong as men no matter what way they have their hair done. I think you've all gone power mad.'

'Oh, Ted, that's not fair.' Agnes, heartbroken that she had upset Ted after not seeing him for Christmas, tried to make amends. 'It'll grow again in no time – I remember when I was a little girl back in the orphanage, a couple came to see if there was a child that they liked the look of...'

'Is this relevant, Agnes?' Ted asked impatiently, looking anywhere but at her.

'No, Ted, I suppose not.' Her voice dissolved to nothing as she started to drink her tea.

On the last day of nineteen forty-two Sally sailed around the ward as if she was floating on a cloud. She had received a much-awaited letter from George, who was a man of few words and no mistake. Nevertheless, Sally enjoyed the thoughtful, often amusing anecdotes of his fellow officers that always brought a wide smile to her lips and a feeling of joyful contentment, not to mention an extra spring in her step. She promised that as soon as she was off-duty she would reply straight away.

Nothing could spoil her day now, she thought, not even when she discovered another batch of patients ready to fill the ward that had been emptied only hours before. Sally didn't worry or panic – nothing was a bother.

Then, casting her usual exacting eyes across the regimental row of freshly made iron beds, Sally gave a nod of approval to the nurses waiting to tender care and attention to the military patients lined up on stretchers outside in the corridor.

'Right, we are ready now, go to it,' Sally said briskly, looking up as Matron came swiftly down the corridor towards her. This was unusual; Matron made a point of never hurrying, as it caused unnecessary anxiety amongst the wounded and staff alike.

'Sister, there is a telephone call for you in my office,' she said very grimly, and Sally felt her heart sink, knowing Matron did not allow personal telephone calls whilst they were on duty.

'I am so sorry,' Sally began, but was silenced by the light touch of Matron's hand on her shoulder and a seemingly understanding, even sympathetic shake of her head that told Sally not to give it another thought, which, to Sally's acutely intelligent observation, did not usually mean good news...'

Hurrying down the corridor towards Matron's office she made a mental note to remind the caller, whoever it might be, that she was not allowed personal calls and inform them that this was her place of work and not a social club.

'No!' It was the only word Sally could utter as shock waves entered her body and knocked the wind right out of her. She wasn't aware of the Bakelite telephone receiver falling from her hands and onto the floor, nor did she register the impact of Matron's desk as the full force of it caught her head when blackness overcame her.

'Sister! Sister, come along now!'

The no-nonsense, if somewhat far-off, voice was coming from Matron, along with the pungent whiff of smelling salts being wafted under her nose, making Sally cough and splutter her way back to consciousness. For a moment she wondered what had happened.

'You fainted.' As Sally opened her eyes, her wavering vision told her that Matron was kneeling beside her and there was real concern in her voice when she said, 'No, you mustn't move too quickly, here, try a little of this.' Sally felt the rim of a glass being put to her lips and she took a small sip of ice-cold water. The coldness seemed to bring her back to her senses when she realised that she wasn't dreaming nor was she in the middle of a horrid nightmare, she really had taken the call.

'George is dead!' Sally turned onto her side, still on the floor, away from Matron, and curled up into a tight ball. And for a moment there was no sound in Matron's immaculately clean office that smelled of a mixture of mansion polish and ether, and she lay there frozen, taking in the news, trying to digest the implications – but she couldn't, this was too big, too overwhelming, as big as the day she had been told her mother had died. The day Morag and Callum had taken her into their arms and cried with her. But there was no Morag any more. Her friend had gone even before Hitler's bombs had claimed her, along with her father. Dragging herself to her knees and crouching into a rocking position, Sally's hands covered her face as a low keening wail emanated from the very depths of her soul.

Dulcie and David decided that Edith, who had been spending the festive season in Bloomsbury with some theatrical friends, would stay permanently in one of the spare bedrooms until the baby was born. Dulcie refused to dwell on that period of their life when she and her sister didn't get on; her life had changed so dramatically since she married David that she didn't want to remember.

They had discussed the exciting prospect of adopting Edith's baby when the time came and Edith seemed thrilled, telling them that she would then be able to pursue her career on the stage, confessing she had never been the maternal type, so the arrangement suited them all.

Dulcie sighed now, knowing she had made the right decision last year when she agreed to marry wonderfully kind, thoughtful, caring David – who had not made Edith feel in the least bit uncomfortable in the three weeks she had been staying, which he very well could have done.

These thoughts were running through her head when Dulcie, who wasn't used to having house-keepers running around after her, had given David's 'daily' another day off and was feeling very proud of her new-found talent for baking when she checked the pristine electric oven, as unlike her mother's clean but ancient hob as was imaginable, and heard the front door open before the sound of footsteps on the stairs told her that her sister was home.

Edith had spent New Year with friends, and as David had had a lift installed before he came out of hospital for his own independence to come and go in his wheelchair Edith was the only person it could be.

Dulcie and David had been invited to a British Forces charity function given by his mother, but she didn't fancy it. She felt uncomfortable with her burgeoning girth, and dismayed that she couldn't wear the fabulous gowns David had bought for her when they were first married. Dulcie was also extremely uncomfortable in the presence of Lady James-Thompson, knowing that she was tolerated only because David's mother obviously believed Dulcie was carrying her son's heir. However, Dulcie knew that his mother wasn't happy with David's choice of second wife after overhearing her tell a friend in the ladies room at a five-star hotel over the New Year that Dulcie was 'as common as muck'. So she was in no hurry to accept invitations of any sort from the old dragon.

Whilst Dulcie knew she could pass herself off as being as good as any of them when her mouth was shut, she wasn't sure her Selfridges vernacular was enough to get by on permanently, and was now undertaking elocution lessons; it was only fair to David, after all, to be the best wife she possibly could be. He was so wonderful, asking nothing from her but giving her all of this and taking in her wayward sister too.

Her thoughts were interrupted by Edith who had just come into the kitchen.

'Did you enjoy your weekend at the Comptons'?' Dulcie asked, taking a pie out of the oven.

'I met the most wonderful producer,' said Edith, 'although it took some clever theatrical tricks to hide this.' She pointed to her rounded stomach. 'But I don't think he noticed.'

'Did you go and see Mum?' asked Dulcie, who hadn't seen their mother since that time when she introduced her to a 'backstreet fixer'. Still, she was concerned that Edith should keep in touch – especially after their mother had thought her younger daughter was dead for all that time.

'I can't visit Mum looking like this, you know she thinks we only have one black sheep in the family.'

'You might at least have the good grace to look embarrassed when you say terrible things like that, Edith,' said Dulcie.

'Mum telephoned me at the Comptons',' Edith

said, ignoring Dulcie's comment as she went to fill the kettle.

Which was more than she did for me, Dulcie thought, then immediately dismissed the idea when Edith said over her shoulder, 'I spoke to Rick as well; he said he is being pampered to distraction by Mum.'

'Is he all right? I haven't seen much of him lately.' Dulcie looked to her sister. 'I'll have to get word to him and...'

'If you let me speak I'll tell you.' Edith sounded impatient as Dulcie let her continue. 'He's going back to the hospital for tests, chest infection or somethin', you know the sort of thing?'

'No, Edith, I don't! How is he now?' Dulcie was suddenly worried. Rick, being her favourite member of the family, would surely have been to see her had he been well, but since he came home half-blinded from the desert he had been hit by one bug after another and was advised to stay away from Dulcie, so Edith had told her – although, Dulcie noticed, he hadn't been advised to stay away from Edith even though he knew they were both pregnant, which was more than their mother did. There was something fishy there, she could tell. Probably Edith wanted all his attention for herself. That was more like it.

'He's been in and out of hospital since he came home from Tobruk,' said Edith, getting two cups from the cupboard. 'He said he'll write soon.'

'Why didn't anybody tell me?' Dulcie exclaimed, knowing Edith was her only source of information unless Rick wrote or visited.

'I just did,' Edith replied, not answering Dulcie's

372

concern. 'Anyway, you have been so wrapped up in your new life that it seemed improper to disturb you with such things.'

'But he's my brother!' Dulcie didn't like the sound of this but she put a brave face on it. 'Of course I'm worried about him.' He had always been there for her. However, she had no intentions of letting Edith see her wearing her heart on her sleeve when she went on, 'Our Rick's made of sturdy stuff; he'll come and see me when he's better, that's for sure.' The doctor had told her not to worry about anything as her blood pressure was like a volcano waiting to erupt and she had to keep herself as calm as possible and put her feet up. But Dulcie was having none of that. East End women were as tough as they came; she'd be all right. But still, this didn't give Edith the right to keep information from her – especially when it concerned their Rick.

'So, where's this "do" tonight, then?' Edith asked, obviously wanting to change the subject.

'The Ritz,' Dulcie answered in a dull voice, recalling the days when such an invitation would lead to hours of pampering and beautifying herself, worrying over what to wear and what bag went with what shoes. How times were changing, she thought with a sigh.

'Oh, I'll be away for a while next week,' Edith said as Dulcie popped the pie back in the immaculate oven. Frowning now, she hoped she had the temperature right.

'Are you visiting friends?' she asked Edith, closing the oven door.

Dulcie was looking forward to her baby growing up together with her sister's child; her twins, as she now thought of them, would want for nothing and she would treat them equally, unlike her own mother who always favoured Edith over her. What more could Edith ask for? But from her sister's expression now, Dulcie could see she had something on her mind.

'You know I said you could adopt this baby?' Edith said, pointing to her swollen stomach. Dulcie nodded, not liking the expression in her sister's eyes but silently listening.

'I think it would be better all round if I just got shot of it – over and done with, no burden to anybody.'

'An abortion?' Dulcie gasped, hardly able to believe Edith could do such a thing after all they had talked about. She had come to think of the child Edith was carrying as her own, and this suggestion was unbearable. 'You don't mean that, Edith?' Dulcie felt the colour drain from her face and grew lightheaded as the room swum before her eyes.

'You can't. You're too far gone.' Dulcie couldn't believe Edith would even consider such a thing. Nice girls didn't! This was too much to take in. She couldn't do this, Dulcie thought as panic shot through her, before a grudging realisation took over and she wondered when she had ever thought of her sister as 'nice'.

'I've been offered a chance to go abroad with ENSA,' Edith said, as if trying to make Dulcie comprehend that this was the most important thing that had ever happened to her.

'But what about the baby?' Dulcie's voice was

barely above a whisper whilst Edith, looking suitably shamefaced, gave a little shrug of her shoulders.

'Doesn't it matter to you that you are destroying a life?' Dulcie so wanted to hurt her sister.

'Don't say it like that, Dulcie, I'm not like those other girls,' Edith beseeched her but Dulcie was having none of it. How could she be so callous?

'The only reason you are not like the *others*, sister dear, is because you think David will give you the money for a discreet, high-class clinic, whilst *those poor mares* have to make do with a backstreet "midwife". But that's where you're wrong – I won't let him give you money.'

'Don't be like this, Dulcie, I thought you of all people would understand.' The crocodile tears that had enabled Edith to wriggle out of so many scrapes in their childhood were there in plain view, but they had little effect on Dulcie, not now.

'What makes you think that I *of all people* would condone what you are doing?' At that moment her own baby decided to give a hefty kick and Dulcie knew she was right to admonish her sister.

'Oh, come on, Dulcie, nobody liked a good time better than you did,' Edith answered. 'You picked the men up and dropped them at will, no party was ever good unless you attended, dressed to the nines and having the time of your life.'

'You can't hold me up as a reflection of your sordid affair, Edith.' A snarl of disgust caught Dulcie's lips and she could hardly look at her sister.

'You weren't snow white either,' Edith countered, but just as quickly she backed down when she noticed Dulcie's flared nostrils, knowing her

375

older sister was in no mood for censure.

'And where are you being sent that is so much more important than the life of this child?' Dulcie managed to respond.

'I don't know, they won't tell us until we're nearly there,' Edith sniffed into her hanky.

'The Far East? The Middle East?'

'Maybe.' Edith's tears suddenly disappeared. 'It's all very exciting.'

'You sicken me, Edith.' Dulcie could hardly believe what she was hearing; her sister's lack of maternal instinct was awe-inspiring in the worst possible way. 'Don't you realise what you are doing?' There was a long silence before she went on, 'And don't think I don't mean it when I say that David will not help you pay for your *procedure*.' She was practically nose to nose with her sister. 'After all, a Harley Street Clinic does not come cheap.'

'I know someone in the theatre who will lend me the money ... satisfied now?'

Dulcie felt that sinking in the pit of her stomach like going over a steep bridge in a fast-moving car, and her heart began to hammer in her chest causing her to take shallow breaths. 'Who?' she asked, knowing nobody in their right mind would give a woman so far into her pregnancy the money to pay for an abortion, and no doctor would risk their reputation performing one. Dulcie's head went back and she looked down her nose at her sister.

'Tell me who it is – now.' She could see Edith's eyes were a mixture of pain and defiance and they seemed to bore through her, but Dulcie, hands on hips, had no intention of letting her sister off the hook this time.

'Well, I'm waiting...' Dulcie watched Edith squirm, then, she noticed a hard glint in her sister's eyes.

'He's a producer, he's very rich, said I could pay him back after my tour.' She backed off slightly, as if unsure of Dulcie's reaction.

'Oh, I bet he did, and what is he taking on account until you are paid?'

'Nothing, that's what.' Edith almost spat the words. 'Mrs High and Mighty, that's you isn't it, Dulcie.' Her face was almost puce with rage.

'Well, I won't allow it. I'll report him to the police, I'll ruin him! And don't think I can't, Edith, because I can and I will and David will see to it.' Dulcie was so desperate she would do anything not to lose one of her 'twins'. Then after a moment, the penny dropping, Dulcie turned to her sister and said in a low, menacing voice, 'You are not going to a specialist though, are you, Edith?'

'What makes you say that?' Edith asked, her face the picture of guilt now.

'Because being so far gone, only a backstreet butcher would attempt to get rid of it at this stage.' Dulcie drew nearer to her sister, her demeanour more menacing. 'Well?'

Dulcie now knew her sister was tormenting her, goading her like she used to do when they were both at home, but Edith wouldn't get away with it this time. She wouldn't get the money she was obviously looking for and Dulcie knew she was in a position to stop her sister doing something so

377

foolish it was almost beyond comprehension.

'Let me tell you something, my girl, if you do anything to harm that child I will have you arrested – have you got that?' The feeling of satisfaction Dulcie experienced then more than made up for all those years of hurt when Edith was the favoured child.

Without another word Edith turned on her heel and slammed out of the flat as Dulcie slumped onto the opulently upholstered sofa. She knew how callous her sister could be but that took the biscuit. Why did everything have to be me, me, me with their Edith?

'George's ship, HMS *Netherton*, was sunk by a U-boat, torpedoed off the Tobruk coast,' Sally explained to Olive a few weeks later when she'd learned a lot more of the details surrounding her fiancé's death. She could bring herself to talk about the devastating news only to Olive, who was after all like a mother to her. 'It was a last-ditch attempt by the Germans to gain superiority. But they were already beaten so why did they have to do this?'

'How awful,' Olive said, as tears stung her eyes. She liked George; he was a good, kind man who was in the process of becoming a great surgeon. 'Did they manage to tell you anything else?' *They* being the naval officers and friends of George who came to see Sally when they'd eventually returned to England.

'Only that George was so brave, saving everybody he could and not giving a thought for his own safety.' Sally could hardly speak for the tight knot in her throat. 'They said he did all he could ... would receive a medal without a doubt,' she managed before the flood barrier broke. She could only turn to Olive and bury her head on the older woman's shoulder to release the pent-up devastation that had been so well controlled for the last few weeks. 'What good is a medal when he isn't here, Olive?' Sally cried, and remained in Olive's protective arms until she felt strong enough to tell her the rest of what she knew.

'There was an explosion aft... George had gone to save another man who was trapped. He knew it was dangerous... He didn't hesitate, they said...'

'That was George, always thinking of others before himself,' said Olive soothingly.

'They tried to drag George up top but the water was coming in fast by then... There was another explosion...' Sally stared into the grate but didn't see the dancing flames, nor did she take in the condolence cards that lined the mantelpiece.

'There's also a letter from Callum,' Olive said gently when Sally was calmer and they were drinking their tea at the table. Sally didn't answer; instead she just stared into her cup as confused thoughts tumbled through her head, making no sense. She didn't want to think of Callum right now. She didn't want to remember the feelings of elation she got when one of his letters dropped on the mat enquiring about her and Alice. George deserved all her attention now. If she didn't give him the loving thoughts he deserved since he went into the navy then surely he deserved the dignity of her attention in death.

'George knew I didn't want him to join up,'

Sally hesitantly told Olive, feeling as if she was betraying his memory talking this way. 'I thought he'd gone off me but didn't like to tell me – as you said, he was so kind he didn't like to hurt people's feelings...'

'I understand what you mean,' Olive said, giving Sally's hand a gentle pat.

'In some ways I find that a comfort.' Sally realised that she couldn't hold it in any longer, she had to tell someone and who better than this woman.

'I have to tell you something, Olive, and please don't be angry with me ... you see, I feel so wretched about writing to Callum. I wish I hadn't – especially now.'

However, to her relief Olive didn't look angry or hostile; instead she took hold of Sally's hand and said, 'You were only letting Callum know how Alice was faring, which is natural.'

'Is it?' Sally asked. She wasn't sure about anything any more.

TWENTY-SEVEN

Olive was hurrying down Article Row, busy as usual. She was amazed at the mildness of the January weather; it was almost as if spring had come early, which was not a bad thing, she mused, given Sally's terrible news. Yet she was amazed at the girl's stoic resilience, recognising that it must be her nurse's training coming to the fore.

She had thrown herself back into her work at Bart's shortly after the sad news of George's tragic death. Olive also realised that the presence of little Alice, being a lively, curious child who didn't take too well to glum faces, meant that Sally had to put her first and not wallow in her own misfortune. So for the child's sake Sally had no choice but to put on a relaxed if not happy face.

After a morning at the church hall sorting the large quantities of clothing known as 'Bundles for Britain', which were sent over by the American Red Cross and distributed from WVS Emergency Clothing Stores for people in desperate need, Olive was looking forward to a rare afternoon off-duty, wondering if she had enough egg powder to make a custard tart for after tea.

The weather was so mild of late that Barney had decided to put the chickens outside during the day to get them used to the great outdoors, he'd said. Olive smiled. He was a tonic to the female population of Article Row; nothing was a trouble to him and he would run as many errands as were requested of him – a credit to Archie's patient and fatherly guidance. Thinking of Archie now brought a little glow of pleasure to Olive's heart; he was so kind and had suffered so much that he deserved a little contentment too.

Opening the front door she noticed an airmail letter on the mat and her spirits sank. Picking up the envelope Olive saw that the letter was from America. However, it wasn't addressed to Tilly as she had first thought, recalling all the heartache and anguish her daughter had suffered – it was her own name scrawled across the envelope.

In the first week of February, as arranged, Olive stepped into the plush London hotel and immediately felt out of place. She was wearing her best coat with the fox-fur collar but beside the minks and ermines that were paraded around the polished marble foyer by diners going into the restaurant, Olive knew her clothes were shabby at best. Looking around, she felt her nerve begin to leave her. This is what prey must feel like when caught in the gaze of its captor, she thought as a sharp-suited concierge came to her aid.

'Can I help you, madam?' he asked, not in the least as imperiously as she had expected in a place like this. In fact he seemed quite friendly and put her at her ease immediately.

'I am looking for a man named Coleman, Mr Andrew Coleman,' said Olive in a voice that she hoped didn't show how nervous she was. The airmail letter she had received had been from Drew's father; he wanted to meet up with her as he had some very important information and wanted her advice. Olive could not think of a single thing about which she could advise a man like Mr Coleman.

'Certainly. Mrs Robbins?' Olive nodded as he put out his hand palm side up to show her the way before proceeding. 'He is expecting you.'

Olive said nothing as she followed the long strides of the man in front of her.

She had vacillated about telling Tilly about the letter and then decided she would wait until she had actually met Drew's father, to see what he had to say for himself. But no matter what he had to say, it would be a poor excuse for the way Drew had treated her daughter, not even replying to her letters and breaking her heart. Olive surmised that, although Drew saw their romance as being over, he obviously still wanted to remain in contact with her daughter. But sending his father to do his dirty work indicated to Olive that he might not have been as honest and courteous as she had once assumed.

'Ahh, Mrs Robbins, I'm Andrew Coleman, please excuse me for not getting up,' said the large man who was actually sitting in a wheelchair. Olive was surprised as Drew had never mentioned this to her; but why would he?

'May I call you Olive?' he asked, taking the huge cigar from his mouth and placing it in a heavy-looking round glass ashtray.

'Mrs Robbins is fine,' Olive said, thinking the imperious American a tad forward for assuming she liked to be called by her Christian name when they had only just met, especially as he had demanded his son go back to America. She watched as, confidently smiling, he pulled his wheelchair closer to the table, making himself comfortable before summoning the drinks waiter.

'Brandy?' he asked, presumptuously, irritating Olive no end.

'I'll have tea, please.' Olive gave a tight smile. She wasn't going to be soft-soaped by this man; she wasn't a young flibbertigibbet who could be easily flattered by Americans rich enough to toss their money about on *booze*, as they called it, nor did she want her judgement clouded by alcohol, which she hardly ever touched anyway.

'As you know, my son Andrew came home when he discovered his mother was sick.'

Olive nodded and waited for him to continue; he seemed to be taking rather a long time of it.

'Sadly,' said Andrew Coleman, looking anywhere but in her direction, 'she died.'

'Oh, I am sorry,' said Olive, shocked at the news. Mr Coleman acknowledged her condolences with a dismissive wave of his hand.

'That isn't what I wanted to see you about,' said the straight-talking American as their tea was brought to the table. He was silent as it was poured and when the waiter left he continued, examining his delicate porcelain cup all the while. 'You're probably wondering why my son hasn't been in touch with Tilly for over six months...'

'Not really,' Olive lied. 'Young people grow apart all the time – especially these days.' She was not going to sit here and listen to this brash American lording it over her and gloating at his son's shortcomings. Her Tilly was as good as any of them!

'You are right, but...' His voice faltered, momentarily surprising Olive. 'Well, it's like this. Almost the day he got home, he was involved in an accident ... so sudden,' he said as if now talking to himself. 'The truck came out of nowhere, rammed right into the side of his car, trapping him.'

'Oh, my word! Is he...?' Olive's hand flew to her lips to stop the flood of questions she was dying to ask.

'It happened the day after his mother's funeral...'

Olive could see that Drew's father was really upset now and her compassionate heart went out

384

to him. He raised his hand just a little as if to assure her he was all right.

'I blame myself,' Andrew Coleman said, wiping his brow with a large white handkerchief. 'I bought him a Chevrolet Sedan in the hope that it would show him what he was missing back home...'

'Oh, no.' The words slipped unintentionally from Olive's lips. She hadn't been able to give Tilly a new coat for Christmas, never mind a massive car.

'His back was broken, his spinal cord trapped between the fractured bones, leaving my son crippled from the neck down and entirely dependent on others for his every need...'

Olive could see the tears welling in his eyes but the painful constriction in her own throat prevented her from voicing her genuine distress. Tilly was going to be devastated when she told her the awful news.

'Andrew told me about a special girl named Tilly who he met here in London and all about her wonderful family.'

'Oh, she is going to be dreadfully upset... She thought ... we thought...' But Olive could not finish telling Mr Coleman that she believed Drew had unceremoniously dropped her daughter and she had advised her to have nothing more to do with him.

'He doesn't want her to know about his accident. He said it would be better for her to think he had run out on her – let her get on with her own life instead of the drudgery of looking after an invalid for the rest of her days.'

There was a long, painfully strained pause and

Olive, without thinking, grabbed hold of his hand as a gesture of compassion, giving Mr Coleman a reassuring nod of her head. Maybe it was for the best if Tilly remained unaware, because she knew her daughter's tender heart would convince her that it was her duty to care for Drew for the rest of his life, no matter how badly disabled he was.

'Have you come all this way just to tell me that Drew has been badly injured and Tilly mustn't find out?' Olive said in her no-nonsense way.

'No,' he said. 'I am over here because he had an operation with a top pioneering surgeon at St Bartholomew's Hospital. It's our only hope of Drew walking again – the operation took place on Christmas Day as an emergency. I won't know if it's worked until the plaster comes off his back in March and then he will have a long period of recuperation...'

'Would you like me to visit him?' Olive asked, hardly able to believe what she was hearing.

'I have to go back to the States for a short while but he has people with him... I'm afraid he doesn't want anyone to see him the way he is now,' Mr Coleman sighed, unable to hide his pain.

'I understand,' Olive said, nodding her head, 'but please don't hesitate to let me know if there is anything I can do...'

'I just wanted you to know he isn't a cavalier love-'em-and-leave-'em type of guy.'

'I know that.' Olive's voice was barely above a whisper as this latest news caught her unaware and took the wind right out of her sails – how could she ever have doubted such a decent human being

386

as Drew?

'But Tilly mustn't know; it would finish him for sure.'

'I will not say anything,' Olive promised and then after a few moments, her head still reeling, she got up to leave. And as she walked from the hotel Olive had a completely different view of Andrew Coleman to the one she had been harbouring and now her heart went out to him.

TWENTY-EIGHT

To stop herself from dwelling on Andrew Coleman's revelation and her obvious feelings of guilt at deceiving her daughter, Olive promised to do a few more hours in the WVS canteen, a meeting point for servicemen on home leave, and prayed that Drew's operation would be a success.

The canteen proved busier than she had thought it would be and she was glad; it kept her occupied with less time to worry or ponder on what might have been as heavy heads and bloodshot eyes seemed to be the order of the day for soldiers on a forty-eight hour pass. Servicemen from all over gathered to share their stories and enjoy the luxury of a bit of bacon on toasted bread courtesy of the community pig, before haring off to catch their trains to who knew where.

All year round the WVS women from the canteen had saved and donated any scraps of food and vegetable peelings to go towards fattening 'their' pig, which was then slaughtered for customers coming into the canteen. It was almost at an end now.

'Oh, would you look at that gale brewing up,' said Audrey Windle, the vicar's wife, looking up from pouring steaming hot tea into earthenware cups to watch people being eddied along on a fierce wind, hanging onto their hats.

'That wind whipped up a bit sharpish and so strong it's making that soldier run,' Mrs Worthington said with a laugh, gazing through the criss-cross tape that would hold the large glass window together if there should be a bomb blast.

'It was a good thing he could run,' thought Olive, although she didn't voice her melancholy thoughts, trying not to force her miserable considerations on others.

'Are you all right, Olive?' Archie asked as he came into the canteen for his morning cup of tea and a catch-up with whoever was in need of a natter, keeping up community spirits.

'Well, to tell the truth,' Olive said quietly, 'I have got something on my mind. You go and sit over there and I'll bring you a cup of tea – I'm just about ready for a break now.'

Without further enquiry Archie went and took his usual seat near the door, knowing it would be far away from Nancy Black's prying ears. Moments later Olive took the seat opposite and in a low voice she told him all about Drew and what had happened.

'Will you tell Tilly?' Archie asked, noting Nancy's poisonous glares aimed at Olive's back.

'I can't,' said Olive, anguish obvious in her tone.

'She will be devastated and Mr Coleman promised that he will not get in touch with her either – it is better that she just forgets Drew now, as she is young enough to find another love.'

'That's as maybe, Olive,' said Archie, his face etched with concern, 'but don't you think that is her choice? I know you are doing this with the best of intentions but...'

'It is for the best, Archie,' Olive cut in. 'She isn't old enough to fight her heart's desire.'

'It's a good thing she is old enough to fight for her country, then,' Archie said, unusually sharp as he stood up and retrieved his waterproof from the stand by the door. 'It would be something to take her mind off matters of the heart.' Archie made his way towards the canteen door but before he left he turned.

'She's a big girl now, Olive, you must sever the apron strings.' And with that he saluted the other WVS women and left Olive wondering if she was doing the right thing after all?

'They looked nice and cosy,' Nancy Black, who had come in for a cup of tea and a bit of a warm to save her own coal rations, said to Audrey. 'It's all right for some hobnobbing with the local constabulary with free cups of tea. Since the shortages there's no chance of getting anything unless you're in the know.'

'Mrs Black, has it never occurred to you to have a little compassion for the plight of others? Olive must be out of her mind worrying about Tilly.' Audrey was in no mood for Nancy's insinuations.

'She's only billeted in Whitehall,' Nancy exclaimed, 'not exactly a hive of danger!'

'That is one of the most dangerous places in England, I should imagine.' But their observations were cut short when Olive returned to the counter.

'Mind how you go with that sugar, Nancy,' Olive said. 'You're shovelling it like sand, don't you know there's a war on?'

'You're telling me,' Nancy said as she quickly scooped another half a teaspoonful into her cup before Olive removed the basin.

'My nephew's in the desert,' said Audrey, taking the coppers from Nancy and putting them into the wooden drawer they used for a makeshift till.

'The desert, you say?' asked the soldier who was next in line. 'A friend of mine was there but he was brought home injured. As a matter of fact I believe his sister lives around here somewhere, and I've got a message for her.' Looking grim, he paused momentarily. 'I promised I would deliver it but I've gone and lost the address.' After glancing around the cosy, steamed-up canteen he said in a low whisper, 'You don't happen to know where Dulcie Simmonds lives, do you?'

'Her name isn't...' But Nancy was quickly cut off by a glare from Olive.

'Why, who wants to know?' One couldn't be too careful these days, she thought.

'I've got a message for her from her brother Rick, who says he's coming out of hospital next Thursday and he'll call in on her.'

'Oh, that is good news.' Olive clattered the large teapot onto the counter and could have jumped for joy, knowing Dulcie had been so worried when her brother was taken into hospital with suspected pneumonia. Since his stint in the desert with the eighth army he hadn't been quite the same and although his sight was slowly improving he'd had no such luck with his chest now winter had set in. 'If we see her, who shall we say is asking?'

'I'm Raphael Androtti,' said the soldier, whose dark good looks were attracting attention from several of the WVS volunteers. 'It would mean a lot to Rick if you could pass on his message.'

Poor Dulcie, thought Olive, she had been so downhearted since her brother had been taken back into hospital, not her old self at all, even though she did make a real effort when she came to visit, which was often.

And with that thought in mind Olive decided she could not wait until Dulcie's next visit which might be tomorrow or maybe even next week, nobody knew; she just dropped in unannounced and always brought something nice, such as a bag of sugar or tinned stuff; things that were practical and always welcome. Obviously Olive asked no questions – well, nobody did any more, it seemed. However, she knew she couldn't wait for Dulcie to call into Article Row. Instead she'd go to Gray's Inn and give the young woman the good news just as soon as she finished in the canteen.

'Oh, David, Rick's coming out of hospital, thank God!' Happy tears streamed down Dulcie's face as David clasped her hand and hugged her to him.

'Who told you this?' David asked.

'Olive called around this afternoon.' Dulcie was thrilled.

'Oh, that is good news, I'm so happy to see you more cheerful, darling.' David gave her a kiss on the cheek. 'That was very thoughtful of Olive.'

'But that's the type of woman she is, my love, always thinking of others. The world would be a better place if we were all like Olive,' Dulcie said as she took off his wool and cashmere Crombie overcoat and removed the silk cashmere scarf she had given him for Christmas. 'She stayed for a cup of tea, it was lovely, and I told her all about Edith's nasty scare at New Year and how she has now settled down to the idea of living with us until the baby is born...' However, she didn't tell David that she knew the man who had delivered the message to Olive.

'Darling, are you all right?' David looked most concerned as he urged her to sit down on the sofa and Dulcie could only nod enthusiastically, hoping he would not fret about her so much.

How could she tell her wonderful husband that Raphael Androtti, one of the most handsome men she had ever met in her life, and who always had a 'thing' for her, was here in Holborn, and he had been trying to find her? David would be disheartened to hear that one of her old flames was back on the scene, even if it was completely innocent, and she couldn't put him through that after all that had happened to him.

'I'm fine,' said Dulcie, feeling anything but fine, knowing she had found it extremely difficult to resist Raphael's charms in the past. Although now she was a respectable married woman she knew that she would have to put those feelings behind her. If that was possible.

TWENTY-NINE

Near the middle of February Agnes was on her way to visit Mr Carlton, her father's lawyer, after she received a letter telling her he had news for her and requesting she attend his office at ten o'clock on Tuesday morning. Sitting in the outer corridor on a straight-backed chair Agnes took in the austere atmosphere. The main office, through the opaque window, was nothing special, just a room, three flights up in an Edwardian villa, crammed with dusty files. When she was called in she could see that behind a huge mahogany desk sat the rotund, bespectacled man who spoke so softly it was difficult to hear his voice.

'Mr Weybridge wanted me to give you this,' said Mr Carlton in respectful tones, passing her an envelope. 'I'm afraid I have some grave news for you. Your father has died peacefully in his sleep. He left specific instructions that I was not to give you this until after the funeral.'

'He didn't even want me at his funeral?' Agnes felt as if she had been struck; she had found her father after twenty years and now she had lost him again – this time forever. She could not read the words of the letter as her tears were blurring her vision and as one dropped onto the envelope Mr Carlton gently enquired if she would like him to read it to her instead.

Struggling to gain control, Agnes could only nod.

Taking the parchment paper from the envelope the solicitor explained to Agnes that everything Mr Weybridge had owned now belonged to her. When he finished reading, the solicitor pulled down his dark-framed spectacles and looking over the rim asked in almost reverential tones, 'Did you understand what I said, Miss Weybridge?'

For a moment Agnes, whose head was bent as she played with the skin on her fingers, didn't realise he was talking to her as he had used her true name – the one she had only heard for the first time a few short weeks ago. With some difficulty she forced herself to respond.

'He has left me the farm.' Agnes felt sick. She was dreaming. She must be. Things like this didn't happen to people like her... Foundlings, abandoned and brought up in an orphanage. 'He's left it to me. His farm. He's left it to me.'

She walked back to Article Row in a kind of daze and if anybody had asked she couldn't have recalled the journey at all. Somehow she managed to get back to the house and find the door key. It was pure instinct that led her into the kitchen and to the enquiring glance of her landlady.

'It's true; I've inherited a farm from Mr Weybridge! But what about Ted, what will he say?' Agnes said as they sat at the table, cradling cups of tea in their hands.

'I'd say you both have to talk about it, Agnes,' said Olive. 'There is a lot to consider and it is right that he has his say.'

'I wish he could have met ... my father.' The term 'my father' was foreign to her but Agnes felt proud saying it aloud. 'But what do we know about farming? I don't know one end of a cow from another.'

'Maybe the old man, Darnley, will stay on and help you both,' Olive said with a hint of sadness, knowing that if Agnes had inherited a farm it was her duty to go and work on it as the land girls had learned to do.

'But that would mean ... leaving here...' Agnes gasped, suddenly realising the enormity of her inheritance. Slowly it began to sink in that she was no longer free to come and go as she pleased in Article Row. She had responsibilities now. Huge responsibilities. And she wasn't sure she was capable of fulfilling them. Quickly she jumped up from the chair she had been sitting on and hugged Olive as she would have done to her own mother.

'I don't want to leave here to live on a farm, Olive.' There was a muffled crack in her voice as she buried her face in Olive's shoulder and fresh tears began to flow.

'We all have to do our bit, my dear,' Olive said as a cold wind whistled around the house. 'It is our duty to king and country whether we like it or not.'

Olive knew things were going to be very different from now on. Despite her words, she knew she would hate to lose the quiet presence of Agnes around the house. Although she was so shy, the girl had become a real companion and Olive was afraid she would miss her dreadfully. Slowly she rose from the table and cleared the cups, turning to the sink so that her young lodger could not see the look of anguish on her face.

Tilly was pleased that she had been posted to London and was billeted with the rest of the girls near Whitehall where she was stationed. She was able to fix the lorries she proficiently drove and was also skilled in clerical work thanks to her time in the Lady Almoner's office at Bart's hospital where she used to work before joining the ATS. Her most frequent duty was that of a messenger, her knowledge of her native city making her invaluable for the task.

One of the advantages of this posting was that she had been able to visit Rick at his new lodgings in the East End where his family used to live, something her mother would never have allowed her to do. She thought it only right that she made the effort to try to cheer him up through his convalescence, since Dulcie could not be exposed to any infection as she was so heavily pregnant, and most of his old friends were now fighting abroad. She had only managed the occasional visit so far, but, she reflected, she must have said something right as he sent a letter to say he would be coming to the West End soon, so would she like to go to a dance or to the pictures? She was glad his eyesight had improved enough for him to get around without his white stick as he had been so self-conscious about it – but he did need to wear spectacles and on the rare occasion when the sun shone he had to wear dark glasses. But there was no doubt that he was returning to his old irrepressible self.

Tilly loved her new-found freedom as well as her new responsibilities and although she loved her mother very much, she did not relish the idea of returning to Article Row and allowing herself to be comfortably tucked under Olive's ever-protective wing again. Tilly knew that her mother would have had a near heart attack if she saw half the things that she now got up to. Grinning, she remembered the story one of the girls who'd been posted to the Home Office had come back with, keen to share it around their billet. Mr Churchill was at first adamant conscripted women should not be involved in armed combat suspecting that they would have a demoralising effect on the nation – but one of the Home Office girls had spoken up and said women were already doing extremely dangerous work and decreed that 'a fit woman could fire a rifle far better than an unhealthy man'. This had been met with a rowdy cheer – for which they were all severely reprimanded.

Removing her leather gauntlets, goggles and steel crash helmet Tilly, now an accomplished dispatch rider who rode a 350cc Triumph motorcycle, would have filled her mother's heart with dread had she been witness to her haring across London with urgent messages.

Not only London, Tilly smiled, having just returned from France after delivering a very important package. She knew these things had to be done in wartime and she loved it. And if she'd plumped for billeting at home in Article Row her mother would have had no choice but to worry about her and tell her constantly that only a mother knows what is right for her offspring.

Reaching for the top button of her jacket, Tilly's fingers automatically sought the place where Drew's Harvard ring still nestled against her heart. Had he ever finished his book? Did he ever think of her still? She consoled herself with the realisation he would always be a treasured friend, and firmly vowed not to think of him as anything more. Those days were over; besides, wartime changed everybody. Perhaps she would let Rick know that she would take up his offer of a night at the pictures. She didn't think he was quite ready for the frenetic jiving in the dance hall just yet even though...

Pushed under her door she found a letter from her mother and, throwing her gauntlets aside, Tilly hurried to open it. Olive said she hoped Tilly would be home for Easter, which was late this year and maybe a lot warmer than past holidays even though the winter had been relatively mild. Mum told her everybody had promised to try and get back to Article Row for the Sunday, which wasn't until the twenty-fifth of April this year, one of the latest on record apparently.

Life was all so exciting right now, Tilly thought, and it would be fantastic if everybody could be together again all catching up and talking over each other in their eagerness to tell of their exploits – just like the old days. She laughed to herself – since when did she start thinking about 'the old days'? She was still only twenty years old, but now she was sounding like Nancy Black!

Looking out of her billet window Tilly could see very little except the occasional glimpse of a silvery flash of moon peeping through skidding clouds whilst she listened to the rain dancing on the pavement below. Maybe it won't be so wet and drizzly by Easter, she thought as she closed the blackout curtains and switched on the low-wattage bulb. She shared this room with Janet, Pru and Veronica and was grateful they were all still together. As she turned she noticed another envelope, this time propped on the occasional table near the easy chair by the fire. Clearly someone wanted her to notice it. Ripping it open, she read that she was to report immediately to the commander's office on her return. For a brief moment she was disappointed that her longed-for evening by the fire was going to be interrupted, but then admonished herself not to be so selfish. She had a job to do.

In no time at all she was presenting herself to Commander Stracken, an imposing although fair and kindly man in his early fifties who reminded Tilly very much of Sergeant Dawson. In front of him was a package, wrapped tightly to protect it from the weather.

'The army are doing something very hush-hush in the East End's Victoria Park,' he said in low, almost church-like tones, 'so you don't need me to tell you that these files are of the utmost importance and urgency. You need to take them over there as fast as you possibly can. Until you hand them over, do not let them out of your sight.'

Tilly smartly saluted, knowing not to ask questions even though she could be an instant target herself. That didn't stop her enjoying speeding through London's streets and roads dispatching important information on a motorcycle. And not only could she ride well, she could fix the machine if it broke down too. The standards of the women of the ATS had to be higher than the men's before they were considered half as good, as she knew only too well. They had proved their worth and showed their professionalism in everything they did. And it was with this thought that Tilly made her way over to the East End of London.

Agnes was slowly getting used to the idea of owning a farm but Ted had not taken the news very well at all, when she'd managed to find a moment to tell him in their increasingly rare private time together.

'I hope you don't think I've got any intentions of becoming a farmer,' he declared in no uncertain terms. 'And I hope that you've got no inclinations that way either! The very idea of it!' Agnes had been extremely disappointed. It would be nice to live in the countryside, she thought, away from the smoke and the traffic of the city and getting some fresh air into their lungs instead of the thick smog they were breathing in now. She had been trying to persuade Ted to move to the countryside and the farm ever since, but he was adamant he was a city man born and bred and he was adamant he was staying put.

'Don't you think you're getting a bit above yourself now, Agnes?' Ted's poor but honest upbringing was to the fore now, his manly spirit refusing to allow him to live off a woman – he had actually said those words – and Agnes soon came to realise that if she wanted to keep Ted she would have to give up any thoughts of living in Surrey.

She would tell him tonight that she had made up her mind and would stay here in London to be near him. Agnes decided she would ask Mr

Carlton, the solicitor, if he would give her some advice on how she would go about selling the farm and hoped to give Ted the good news when they had their tea break. However, she only caught a glimpse of him at lunchtime when he was hurrying across the station.

'I won't be able to walk you home tonight either, Agnes,' said Ted as they briefly passed each other, 'I've offered to take a message to Bethnal Green.'

'Oh, that's fine, Ted,' Agnes said, looking very pleased indeed, 'because I'm swapping shifts and going over there myself this afternoon. I'll be there until nine o'clock tonight. I'll meet you up top at the end of my shift as usual.'

'Righto, Agnes, see you later,' said Ted. 'Got to go now. Sounds as if something urgent's up.'

All was quiet as Tilly rode from one side of the capital to the other on her Triumph motorcycle, and on this particularly drizzly evening no enemy bombers had been spotted. However, she had heard the news before she came on duty about the bombing raid on Berlin two days ago and although the news was optimistic Tilly knew of old that there would be some kind of retaliation and soon. She only hoped and prayed that it wouldn't be tonight – and if so she hoped she was back in Whitehall, because everybody knew the East End, being so close to the docks, usually took a hammering during an air raid.

'I'll pick you up by the Bethnal Green shelter after I've been to see Mum, Edith,' Dulcie said, leaning over the passenger seat of the Bentley, which

David allowed her to use for her own needs, having just dropped Edith off outside Rick's lodgings. She had forgiven her sister for the scare she gave her when she'd threatened to have an abortion, knowing now it had been a cry for help – her sister really was terrified of giving birth to and raising her baby, unlike Dulcie, who couldn't wait. In some ways she had grown to know and love her sister a lot better since they had lived under the same roof without their mother, whom Edith hadn't seen since her pregnancy began to show. 'Tell Rick I'll call over to see him tomorrow and let him know how I get on with Mum.'

Since he was able to get around more, Rick was almost back to his independent self again and had told Dulcie that he had been a burden on their mother long enough – a thinly veiled comment indicating he'd had enough of her fussing; which was a little unfair of him really, Dulcie realised, knowing that whatever her past failings, their mother was only trying to do her best for him.

With that in mind Dulcie had decided it was time to let bygones be bygones, recognising that whatever her mother had done in the past, no matter how misguided, she'd only wanted what was best for her own kids – like any mother would, she supposed.

'Wish me luck,' she said to Edith through the open window of the car, thinking that it was just like the old days and they were all back in the East End – except the last time she was here she wasn't wearing an expensive fur coat and driving a car that cost as much as the house they used to live in.

Dulcie knew her mother was making a rare visit to the East End visiting her Aunt Birdy – who reportedly sang like a nightingale and who Edith took after. She knew this was where her mother's heart lay and if it hadn't been for Hitler she would never have moved to the countryside. Sighing now, Dulcie started the car, which almost glided the short journey to the café where they'd arranged to meet.

Dulcie was secretly thrilled, even though her mother had said she could only manage it that day as she was visiting the East End anyway. But, uncharacteristically, she hadn't risen to the bait. What would be the point when she had so much now: her husband and the impending arrival of her new baby to occupy her time, and the doctor said she had to watch her blood pressure. Above all Dulcie wanted her mother to enjoy her grandchildren and, if she was honest, she wanted to show off a bit too, let her mother see that she had come up in the world. Dulcie Simmonds has made good! She could see it now written in big lights in the West End – well, she could if there wasn't a blackout.

Pulling neatly into a convenient parking space, Dulcie eased her increasing bulk out from behind the wheel of the Bentley and walked the mercifully short distance down Cambridge Heath Road to the café. Opening the door she immediately spotted her mother sitting near the counter, waving like nothing had ever happened.

'Oh, Mum, it's so lovely to see you again!' Dulcie cried, hugging her mother, overcome with emotion. However before they could even find a table, their reunion was cut short as they heard the siren begin to wail.

'Come on, Mum, leave your tea and let's get to the shelter,' Dulcie said, taking her mother's arm. But when they got outside they could see the searchlights arcing across the night sky before an explosion blocked out the sound of rain hitting the ground. Dulcie wondered if Edith and Rick had managed to get to the underground shelter and hoped they would make it in time. Although Edith usually said she didn't want to go down the tube because she couldn't stand the smell of TCP that was used to disinfect the place, Dulcie suspected she'd be one of the first there, giving an impromptu concert party to entertain the crowds.

It was getting on for a quarter past eight when Tilly, cold, wet and fed up, caught sight of the officer who was waiting to receive the classified documents. Hurriedly she handed them over and saluted, before jumping back on her motorbike and heading briskly away from Victoria Park. It felt like no more than a couple of moments later when the air-raid Civil Defence siren sounded, and almost at once she saw an orderly line of people submerge into the Bethnal Green underground shelter. Of all the nights to be caught out here, Tilly thought, and she hoped that if there really was a raid she could get out of the East End in time.

Dulcie kept a firm hold of her mother's arm as the siren continued to sound. It was just hard luck if Edith and her mother met up now, she

404

thought, as there was no getting away from the air raid when it came. And after the bombing of Berlin she was certain the retaliation would be swift and deadly. The East Enders had taken everything the Germans had thrown at them in the Blitz and they had staunchly stood their ground, but now, eighteen months after Hitler tried to bomb London into submission, people were tired of living hand to mouth.

'I could tell there was going to be a raid, Dulcie,' her mother said. 'The wireless in the caff went dead, did you notice? That's a sure sign.' The woman was now hurrying towards the shelter ahead of her daughter, whose bulging girth was slowing her down a little.

'No, Mum, I didn't,' Dulcie said, recalling that she was too busy trying to get her mother out of the café and persuading her to hurry up and leave her cup of tea.

A gigantic search light came on in the vicinity of Victoria Park and Dulcie began to worry; if there was a raid now there was no way she could throw herself on the ground out of harm's way. Her mother, unperturbed by such thoughts, had already dived for cover near the bus stop.

'Mum, come out of there, we'll make the shelter, get up!' Dulcie could feel her heart racing, sure this wouldn't be doing her unborn child any good.

Then they didn't have time to move anywhere as a huge explosion rent the air and Dulcie had no alternative but to get on the floor. As her mother pulled her down, she noticed a young lad of about fifteen being knocked off his bike by the noise of the overhead volley and everything seemed to be in slow motion as people rushed to the underground. She fervently hoped Edith had managed to get down below before the crowd surged forward.

'Now take your time,' called Ted from the bottom of the narrow stairwell, 'everyone will get in safely as long as you don't push...' But he didn't have time to say any more as another volley of overhead explosions could be plainly heard. In seconds the fifteen-by-eleven-feet stairwell was crowded with nervous people trying to get into the shelter. He could have sworn he saw someone trip on the stairs.

'Here,' he exclaimed to those nearest him, 'let me through there, someone's fell!' But it became impossible to move one way or another as the bodies began to descend. Ted felt himself being lifted off his feet by the sheer mass of people and pushed back against the white-tiled wall in the bottom of the stairwell. He tried to break free from the oncoming throng but it was too difficult. He was still trying as blackness overcame him.

'Edith!' Dulcie yelled, but there was no sign of those Titian curls piled high on her sister's head, whilst all the time the stairwell to the underground was disappearing under a sea of bodies. Would Edith have stayed up top, hoping she'd still get a lift home? Or would Rick have come with her and made her take shelter below?

Dulcie stared in disbelief and growing dread at the scene unfolding before her, as the crowd turned into a desperate crush of bodies. In moments some people, obviously stunned, were pulling at arms and legs, anything they could get hold of, to try and get other people out. Old and young were fighting for theirs and their neighbour's lives. If it hadn't been so horrifically tragic Dulcie would have choked up with pure pride at the bravery of the rescuers; ordinary men, women and even children fought desperately to get everybody above ground.

She let out an agonised cry when she saw people piling up on the stairwell knowing whoever was underneath could surely not be saved. Wasn't there anybody here who could help them? Looking around desperately, Dulcie saw her mother was safely tucked away by some railings and so she edged forward to see if there was anything she could do to help those near the opening of the shelter – but she couldn't get close.

'Dulcie! Come away out of there, you'll get crushed!' As Dulcie turned she saw Tilly throw down her motorcycle and run towards her. Never had she been so glad to see her friend, and the two young women briefly hugged. 'What are you doing here?' Dulcie gasped, aware that Tilly was in her uniform, and a very wet uniform it was too.

'Can't say,' replied Tilly, managing a grin even though the horror. 'What about you? Aren't you meant to be taking it easy with your bump?'

'Yes, but I was going to pick up our Edith from the tube and besides, I had this one chance to meet Mum for a cuppa,' said Dulcie, pointing to the railings – but her mother was nowhere to be seen.

'Oh, no.' Dulcie felt as if the air had been sucked

from her lungs. 'She was there. She was over there. I thought she was safe. Tilly, she's gone, she's gone.'

'Don't panic, Dulcie, there's no time,' Tilly said, more calmly than she would have believed possible. 'What's she wearing? Try to remember. What's she wearing?'

'A red headscarf,' said Dulcie. 'It's horrible. Doesn't suit her at all. But you can't miss it.'

How she burst through the crowd she would never know but with an almost superhuman surge of strength Tilly drove herself towards the railings and somehow caught a glimpse of a red scarf. Reaching out, at the absolute limit of her endurance, she grasped the woman's arm and hauled her backwards out of the crowd and out towards the entrance of the shelter.

'I found her!' she cried. 'But did I save her?'

'Tilly, you did it! You did it! Mother! Mum!' shouted Dulcie, trying to fight her way through the crowd, but it was impossible to get anywhere near the spot where her mother was lying on the pavement panting for breath, the forlorn scarf now around her neck. She couldn't get close enough to reach her. There were just too many people in between and she was far too bulky to worm her way through. Dimly she registered the sound of approaching ambulances and fire engines.

Under ground, Edith, having gone below at the first sound of a siren, was growing increasingly worried for the safety of her mother and her sister. Would they have made for the shelter at the tube station? Or would they have found a way to avoid

408

the raid? Slowly it occurred to her that something wasn't right on the platform; there seemed to be an incident back towards the tunnel to one of the stairwells. Then, just as she saw the first trickle of injuries filtering through to the aid station, the first abdominal pain caught her and took her breath away.

'Oh my Gawd,' Edith exclaimed, 'my baby ain't gonna to be born in the bloody underground!' Gripping her side, she couldn't help but observe it was quite ironic really, because that was where the child had been conceived.

'Tilly, Tilly, is that you?' Olive asked, jumping out of the WVS van and hurrying towards her daughter. 'Why are you here? Sorry, shouldn't ask! We've been called out to help at this emergency, even though no bombs have dropped tonight...'

'I can't say anything, Mum. I have to get back to Whitehall, I'm on duty... Dulcie's over there, she's lost Edith... No, I mean Edith should be around here somewhere, Dulcie can't find her... But it might be too late for her mother... Can you...? I'll ring you...' In moments Tilly, shocked to the core at what she had seen, left her mother with tears in her eyes, grabbed her discarded motorcycle and sped down Bethnal Green Road back towards her next assignment.

Agnes felt that her arms would break if she tried to heave another body from the pile that was now beginning to thin out a bit. Babies, young children, old people who were wide-eyed and lifeless... She would never get over it, she was sure.

'You've been a heroine tonight, Agnes, if it hadn't been for your help we would have seen many more casualties,' said one of the regular staff at Bethnal Green tube station.

'I didn't do anything special,' Agnes said in a flat voice; she would never forget this day as long as she lived. 'It's what anyone would have done. What everybody did. But have you seen my Ted? You know, he usually works as a driver out of Chancery Lane.'

'No,' said the man, 'but that doesn't mean anything. You can't really see what's what down here. Look, here comes the stationmaster, let's ask him.'

But the stationmaster wasted no time when he reached them. 'Come with me,' he said to Agnes, who was startled to be picked out in this way. Full of trepidation, she edged past the pile of bodies that still remained.

'Close the door, Agnes, there is something I have to tell you.'

When the stationmaster informed her that Ted had done all he possibly could to stop the rush of people coming down the steps to the air-raid shelter Agnes felt extraordinarily proud, but the feeling was fleeting when she heard the next words.

'I'm sorry, Agnes, there was nothing anybody could do, and Ted was taken to the local mortuary at Whitechapel Hospital half an hour ago...'

Dulcie was amazed as she made her way over to St John's Church across the road from the tube station, which had been commandeered and turned into a makeshift mortuary.

It felt unreal, but she found herself one of a number of people who were walking up and down the rows of tables searching for the faces of their loved ones. And as she approached the last row Dulcie could clearly see her mother lying there, red scarf now neatly tied around her neck, and it was obvious she was dead.

THIRTY

Easter Sunday was late this year and the weather was warm enough for Olive to put the table out in the garden, which was a good thing as there were so many arriving for tea. Tilly was coming over from Whitehall this afternoon, having been given a few hours' leave. It was a good thing that she had some time off from that demanding posting, thought Olive as she finished ironing the dress she had made for Alice out of some pretty yellow material she'd paid coppers for.

Rick, after the tragic accident that killed his mother, was going to stay with his father, who was so quiet hardly anybody remembered he existed. Truly on the mend now, Rick was going to the pictures with Tilly after tea to celebrate standing as godfather to Edith's child, Anthony, born prematurely in the Bethnal Green underground shelter.

It was strange, Olive thought, that Dulcie failed to mention Edith had been married to a producer chap who had gone to the desert to entertain the troops with a group of ENSA entertainers, but that was the war for you, she sighed, strange things happened all over.

Sally was still keeping herself busy working horrendously long shifts at the hospital to take her mind off poor George, although Callum's letters seemed to be a comfort to her of late and little Alice was eager to see her favourite uncle when he came home again. God willing.

Whilst poor Agnes had recently decided that she could no longer set foot inside the ticket office again now that Ted had gone. She had decided that her place was on the farm her father left her and was leaving on Tuesday. She said she had tried to persuade Ted's mother and two sisters to go with her to Surrey but Mrs Jackson was having none of it. She was born a Londoner, she'd said, and she would if need be die a Londoner. Agnes could only sigh, knowing it wasn't her place to take responsibility for Ted's family, but Olive knew she would have liked to help out if she could.

Dulcie was bearing up, as Dulcie always did, consoling herself with the knowledge she and her mother had at least made amends before Mrs Simmonds died. It transpired, after the post mortem, that the woman had suffered a heart attack and felt no pain whatsoever, which was some comfort, Olive supposed.

'And how's my favourite lady on this wonderful sunny Easter Sunday?'

'Oh, Archie, you made me jump – I was miles away.'

'Was I there with you?' Archie's smile twinkled in his eyes.

412

'Oh, don't let Nancy hear you talking like that or she'll have it around the neighbourhood in no time.'

'Let her,' said Archie as he took Olive's hand and gently kissed it, 'life's too short for regrets.'

'Oh, Archie,' was all that Olive could say.

'Oh David...' was all that Dulcie could say when she looked down at her brand-new baby girl. The birth was so sudden, just after Sunday lunch, before they were due to set off for Olive's Easter tea, that they had barely had time to summon the midwife, let alone drive to hospital.

'Our daughter is beautiful, my love.' David had arranged for Dulcie to be taken to a private nursing home after the birth but now their child was here she was having none of it.

'My mum had three of us with no hot water and an outside lavatory and we didn't turn out so bad,' Dulcie said contentedly.

'Dulcie, you will have all the care you could possibly desire after giving birth,' he said.

'I've made the arrangements,' Dulcie said with a sleepy smile as her eyes grew heavy, handing David his daughter whilst the midwife went into the adjoining bathroom. Moments later as the midwife quietly waved goodbye there was a gentle tap on the door and Dulcie was thrilled to see Olive tiptoe into the room.

'I won't stay long today, I just want to have a little peep... But you know where I am if you need me,' Olive sighed as she looked into the crib. 'Well, aren't you a clever girl, Dulcie, and David is such a lucky man.' She hugged Dulcie, thrilled that she now had something magical to hold on to – the gift of motherhood. Then she realised that Dulcie was gently weeping on her shoulder. It was a strange time for the young woman: losing her mother and gaining a daughter only seven weeks later – a little early by Olive's reckoning, but it didn't matter as mother and baby were perfectly fine.

'Oh, Olive, what am I going to do?' Dulcie cried. 'I haven't got a clue.'

'Of course you have, my girl,' said Olive in exactly the no-nonsense tone of voice that Dulcie needed right now. 'You now have the most precious gift, only a mother knows...'

The publishers hope that this book has given you enjoyable reading. Large Print Books are especially designed to be as easy to see and hold as possible. If you wish a complete list of our books please ask at your local library or write directly to:

Magna Large Print Books
Magna House, Long Preston,
Skipton, North Yorkshire.
BD23 4ND

This Large Print Book for the partially sighted, who cannot read normal print, is published under the auspices of

THE ULVERSCROFT FOUNDATION

THE ULVERSCROFT FOUNDATION

... we hope that you have enjoyed this Large Print Book. Please think for a moment about those people who have worse eyesight problems than you ... and are unable to even read or enjoy Large Print, without great difficulty.

You can help them by sending a donation, large or small to:

The Ulverscroft Foundation, 1, The Green, Bradgate Road, Anstey, Leicestershire, LE7 7FU, England.
or request a copy of our brochure for more details.

The Foundation will use all your help to assist those people who are handicapped by various sight problems and need special attention.

Thank you very much for your help.

Contents

A Word from Diners Club

Welcome to the 2015 Diners Club Platter's Wine Guide.

For 35 years Platter's has been the undisputed leading guide to South African wines, and with good reason. Every new edition is filled with information, hints and tips that are invaluable to wine experts and novices alike.

This year the guide contains info on more than 7,000 wines from 961 producers, merchants and brands, to ensure that you are never at a loss for a well-informed choice.

Cheers to another vintage year!

Ebrahim Matthews
Managing Director, Diners Club South Africa